THE MURDER DANCE

THE MURDER DANCE

Sarah Rayne

SEVERN
HOUSE

First world edition published in Great Britain in 2021 and the USA in 2022
by Severn House, an imprint of Canongate Books Ltd,
14 High Street, Edinburgh EH1 1TE.

Trade paperback edition first published in Great Britain and the USA in 2022
by Severn House, an imprint of Canongate Books Ltd.

severnhouse.com

British Library Cataloguing-in-Publication Data
A CIP catalogue record for this title is available from the British Library.

ISBN-13: 978-0-7278-5012-6 (cased)
ISBN-13: 978-1-4483-0637-4 (trade paper)
ISBN-13: 978-1-4483-0636-7 (e-book)

All Severn House titles are printed on acid-free paper.

Typeset by Palimpsest Book Production Ltd.,
Falkirk, Stirlingshire, Scotland.
Printed and bound in Great Britain by
TJ Books, Padstow, Cornwall.

ONE

The first emotion to strike Quentin Rivers when he read the solicitor's letter was shock. Sheer astonishment that he had apparently inherited the old house that had been a vague legend in his family ever since he could remember. The astonishment was tinged with disbelief at first, but when he read the letter a second – and then a third – time, it was clear that there was no mistake. The Tabor, the house that no one in the family seemed ever to have seen, and that most of them said was only a legend. A story out of somebody's imagination, they said – probably somebody a generation or two back had spun a story, wanting to make the family out to be posh and rich. Even if it had existed, it would long since have passed to some unheard-of branch of the family, or crumbled away to nothing, and had a tower block or a shopping centre built on its foundations.

Zillah's grandmother did not say The Tabor had crumbled away or was just someone's imagination, though. She had a way of nodding to herself if The Tabor were ever mentioned, as if she knew a great deal more than the rest of them.

The aunts and uncles – and Quentin's own parents when they were alive – had always maintained that Zillah's grandmother was a bit odd, and you could not believe a quarter of what she said. Still, the stories were good ones, if you had time to listen to them. Oh, and presumably it was all right to let the children spend so much time with the old girl, was it? Young Quentin and Zillah?

Zillah.

Quentin's second emotion at receiving the news of the legacy had been delight and hope, because it was suddenly possible that this astonishing, unexpected inheritance might mean he could realize his dream. For years he had wanted to protect Zillah from the boys – later the men – who admired her, but who would certainly not treat her as she deserved to be treated. Quentin wanted her to himself. What was that line of poetry . . .? Something about, 'The world forgetting, by the world forgot.' He was not a great one for poetry, but he had come across that once, and it had lodged in his mind. That was how he wanted it to be with Zillah. Just the two of them, in their own world.

There had been one or two girls in his life while Zillah was growing up – of course there had. He thought he could say he was by no means bad-looking, and there had been opportunities. The trouble had always been that the image of Zillah came between him and any girl he ever got close to.

Lately, he had even begun to wonder if it was a mixed blessing to live in the same house as Zillah, but it had seemed the ideal solution after both sets of parents had died in the car crash, leaving Quentin with the tall old house and the modest proceeds of two insurance policies, and Zillah with nothing at all, because her parents had been what everyone called thriftless.

That was when Quentin had divided the house into two flats, living on the ground floor himself, with Zillah on the top floor. He liked to think of her up there; it was like living with a will o' the wisp in the attic – one of those elusive, dancing creatures reputed to flit across marshlands, or beckon tauntingly to travellers to follow them to the rainbow's end and the fabled pot of gold. And there he was again, with the poetic imagery. Zillah would laugh if he said any of that to her; she would say the marshlands would suck you down into their squishy depths, and the rainbow's pot of gold would turn out to be a cracked old stew-pot.

She would not laugh about The Tabor, though. Quentin would tell her all about it this evening – it would give him a good excuse for suggesting they had supper together; not that he needed an excuse, but it would sound better. He would cook a pasta dish for her; she liked pasta. And he would tell her about this elderly cousin, Osbert Rivers, whom he had never heard of before, but who had left a will naming Quentin as his sole heir. He would tell her, as well, about the Norfolk village called Reivers where the house stood, and how, if he went to live there, he would be Rivers of Reivers. Would that impress her, or would she laugh and say, for heaven's sake, Quen, are you living in some mouldy medieval world? She was very modern, of course.

It might be a good idea to look up Reivers beforehand to find out what kind of a place it was. He had better find out what the word *Tabor* meant, as well. Appearing to know such things would impress Zillah; she would listen, and nod, her eyes drinking it all in, and she would occasionally smile, and probably tease him about being a fusty old romantic. And her eyes would crinkle at the corners as they always did when she smiled . . .

She had never known about the jealous rage that seized him if he saw a man going up to her flat, or when he heard her skipping down the stairs to meet someone who was taking her out. None of the men meant anything to her, Quentin knew that, and it would all be completely innocent. But it was good that she had never had the smallest suspicion of how he felt. He would not do anything that might upset the comfortable, happy existence they had. He knew how much she liked living here.

Zillah Rivers had wished for years that she could afford to move out of this house and get away from her cousin Quentin's jealousies and possessiveness. Every time she went out of her own flat and every time she returned to it, he was there, peering furtively through a chink in his curtains in the downstairs half of the house. He was like those inquisitive women in old-fashioned films, twitching the lace curtains to see what their neighbours were up to. It was infuriating and it was also very restricting, because if Zillah was going out with someone, she nearly always had to arrange to be collected at the end of the street, where Quentin could not see her. If she brought anyone back for a drink or coffee, they had to tiptoe up the stairs, not speaking, stepping over the creaking floorboard on the half-landing. At times this could be turned into a joke, but if one of these late-night visits progressed to the bedroom – and Zillah did not pretend to be an angel – there was nothing remotely jokey about having to explain that noise must be kept down because there was a jealous cousin downstairs who would listen to every groan and gasp and creak of bedsprings. That would be the surest passion-shriveller for the most virile man in the world, and if Zillah had enough money to move to another flat, she would do so, and neither Quentin nor this dreary suburban street would see her again. She sometimes thought that the only thing keeping her sane was the knowledge that there was something good ahead – something that would mean she could move away and have her own place, and not have to worry about money, or about keeping Quentin sweet so that he would pay all the bills.

The Tabor. It had been promised to her, and it had been something to cling on to. It had meant she need not bother about actually working or trying to have a career, which was what people expected these days. In the meantime, she drifted into helping Quentin with his small market-research set-up. It mostly meant making telephone calls or emailing questionnaires, finding out what people bought from supermarkets or furniture shops, or what shampoo they used. It was pretty boring, really, but it was at least a job of sorts and Quentin paid her a tiny salary. It was very tiny indeed, because he was as mean as a miser, and Zillah could not possibly afford her own place on this pittance. But it would not be for ever; she had kept a tally of the years, and at intervals she had been able to remind herself that Osbert Rivers must be well over 80 . . . That he must be approaching 90 now . . . Turned 90 . . . And when he died, The Tabor would be hers.

But now, tonight, eating the very good pasta that Quentin had cooked (if you had to say something favourable about him, you would have to say he cooked well), it seemed that after all these years of waiting, The Tabor was not going to be hers after all. Osbert had died, but now that his affairs had been sorted out it seemed the stupid old fool had reneged on his word, and had left The Tabor to Quentin. Zillah could have screamed with rage and thrown things around. She did not, of course. But she stared at Quentin across the table and felt a deep slow anger and resentment begin to burn upwards. Quentin had no right to The Tabor. He had no right to be sitting here, with that maddeningly complacent look, telling her about the house as if he knew it intimately. He did not know it all, and he had no right to it whatsoever.

'I daresay the place will be falling to pieces,' he was saying. 'But it turns out that it really is Elizabethan, just as the stories said. The solicitor says there are dates on the Title Deeds – well, on what's left of them, because they're pretty ancient, but the place dates back to at least Elizabethan times.'

Zillah had to fight not to shout at him that she knew The Tabor was Elizabethan, in fact she knew it was even older than that, and she knew far more about it than Quentin. He passed her the solicitor's letter to read, and then told her what was in it anyway.

'And I phoned the solicitor this afternoon – he sounded a dry old stick, but we had a good talk. I always think it's as well to find out as much as possible about these things,' said Quentin, as if, thought Zillah, inheriting an Elizabethan house was an everyday occurrence. But she read the letter, and listened to Quentin, and she managed to sound interested and pleased. But all the while she could feel the old night-mare stirring in the darkest corner of her mind.

Quentin, folding the letter back into its envelope, said, with an air of importance, that he would have to go to Norfolk to see the house.

'It's quite a long journey, but there are documents I've got to sign, and the solicitor doesn't want to put them in the post because some of the documents are very old and quite fragile. His office is only a few miles from Reivers, though – in a market town, I think. It'll be too far to go there and back in the same day, so we could stay for a night or two.'

'"We"?'

'You'll come with me, won't you? I want to see the house, and I want you to be part of it all.'

'Yes,' said Zillah, managing a smile. 'Yes, I would like to come with you. I would like to be part of all this.'

'I thought you would. In fact, before you came in I booked us into a place in the centre of Reivers village – a local pub who do B&B and bar meals. It sounds quite nice and, according to the map, The Tabor's just on the outskirts of the village.'

*   *   *

'We may as well go straight to the pub,' said Quentin, two days later as they drove through the flat, fen country. 'I'd have liked to stop off and take a look at the house – we won't have the keys until tomorrow, but we could see the outside of it. But it's getting a bit late now, and it'll soon be dark.'

'Let's wait until tomorrow,' said Zillah. 'Let's get the keys and see it properly.' In daylight, said her mind, not like this, in this half-light, where you imagine that figures are crouching, watching, waiting to reach out to you . . .

'Yes, all right. The appointment's for 9.15 anyway, so we'll have most of the day to ourselves after that.'

A roadside sign eventually proclaimed that they were about to enter Reivers, and they went around a curve in the road with a straggle of buildings on each side. Ahead of them was a small market square with several shops and a stone cross at the far end.

'That looks like our pub,' said Quentin, slowing down. 'See over there?'

'You were right – it does look nice,' said Zillah, peering out of the car window. It was a low, double-fronted old place; lights glowed warmly in its windows, and there was the impression that there would be oak beams and chintzes inside. Near the door was an A-board advertising accommodation and good food, and quite a number of cars were parked on the forecourt.

Quentin carried the cases into the panelled reception area, and Zillah was glad that he did not comment on the extra suitcase she had brought. She had packed rather more than was necessary for a single night, on the grounds that it was as well to be prepared for anything.

Over their dinner in the small dining area that opened off the bar, Quentin talked about The Tabor.

'It's bound to be a bit run-down,' he said. 'Osbert died a good two months ago, according to the solicitor, so the place will have been standing empty.'

'We haven't talked about what you'll do,' said Zillah, carefully. 'Will you sell it?'

He did not immediately answer, then he said, 'Properties can be renovated.'

'Renovated? How would you afford it? Or did Osbert leave any money?'

'Nothing to speak of. But I'd sell my present house, of course. That would release a fair amount of dosh.'

He had said 'my' house. Not 'our' house.

'And live in The Tabor?' said Zillah. It was good that her voice sounded absolutely normal.

'Not while the major work's being done, obviously. But I could camp out there for a while later – it might be a bit rough and ready, but I'd be able to oversee the renovations. I wouldn't expect you to live like that, of course. You're such a fragile little plant, aren't you?' There was a half-movement, as if he might have been about to reach for her hand across the table, then thought better of it. 'But once our own house is sold and we've moved out, you could stay here,' he said, glancing about him. 'I expect we could get some kind of reduced rate for a long-term stay. I'd semi-live here – I could have my meals here most of the time, so you wouldn't be on your own very much. You could come and see all the work being done. We might even run to a little car for you.'

Zillah wanted to hit him for this smug condescension, but she said, 'But when it's all done? What then? What would you live on? You couldn't stay with your market-research work, could you? Not all the way out here?' Quentin did not have to travel very much, because a good deal of his work was via phone and email from home, but he sometimes had to make brief trips to companies who commissioned more in-depth surveys and reports. Zillah had never let him know that she lived for those brief absences, or that she made the most of having the entire house to herself.

'As a matter of fact,' said Quentin, 'since I got the solicitor's letter, I've been thinking about an idea I've had for a long time. A kind of dream, really. The kind of thing you pretend you might one day do, but you never really believe you will.' He leaned forward, his pale, rather long face serious and intent. 'One of the things the solicitor mentioned was that in the deeds is a reference to the house having been some kind of lodging house, or even a tavern at one time,' he said. 'Sort of sixteenth-century B&B, I think. Did your grandmother have any stories about that? She used to ramble on a good deal about the place, didn't she?'

'I don't remember any stories like that. And she didn't really ramble.'

'Well, the point is that what's been done once, can be done again.'

'You're not going to make it into an hotel?' said Zillah, after a moment.

'I don't think it would be big enough for that. But I'm going to revive the tradition. I'm going to open a restaurant,' said Quentin, and sat back, clearly very pleased with himself and expecting Zillah to be wide-eyed and admiring of such enterprise. 'An upmarket gourmet country-house restaurant,' he said. 'With the right staff and the right publicity, it could be very successful indeed. It'll be following in the footsteps of my ancestors – well, your ancestors as well, of course,' he said, as if in afterthought. 'And I do know about food and cooking.'

This was an exaggeration. Quentin knew enough to concoct a good pasta dish or a plate of tarragon chicken; he also did a mean salmon en croûte, and he baked a really good fudge cake. That was about the extent of it.

Zillah said, carefully, 'Where would you live?'

'I've thought about that, as well. On that ground plan the solicitor sent – you saw it, didn't you? Oh, I thought I'd shown it to you. Well, there seems to be a kind of semi-separate wing on one side of the building. That could make a really comfortable set of rooms for us.'

The courtyard rooms, thought Zillah. That's what they were always called. Over what were once stables. A door opening off a first-floor balcony, and windows . . . The windows all had bars . . .

'It looked quite substantial on the plan,' Quentin said. 'If we could turn it into private apartments – if it's big enough – we could live there, you and I, and I'd be on the premises, managing the restaurant.' He reached across the table again, and this time he did take her hand. 'Don't you think it's a good idea, Zillah?'

Zillah tried to think of something to say, but could not, and after a moment Quentin withdrew his hand. 'You're very quiet,' he said. 'Are your grandmother's stories about The Tabor's past bothering you? Don't let them. We could live there perfectly comfortably. I know some of her stories were a bit eerie, but nobody ever actually believed them.'

'You never really listened to her stories, though, did you?'

'They were all nonsense,' said Quentin, dismissively. 'But I know you listened to them. Some people in the family were a bit worried about you spending so much time with her and being fed all that rubbish. Stories about ancestors and old legends and all the rest of it. They were only tales, Zillah.'

'Everyone thought The Tabor was only a tale, but now it seems it wasn't.'

'Well, that's true. But as for there being anything eerie or macabre . . .' He gave a small laugh at the absurdity of this, then said, 'Have you finished eating? That was quite an acceptable meal, wasn't it?' He said this critically, clearly already taking what he thought was an expert's view of restaurant food. 'Shall we have some coffee in the bar – they serve it in there, I think. And there's a log fire and an inglenook. You'll like that.'

He was speaking to her as if she was a child, but Zillah nodded, and got up from the table.

'Find us a couple of seats, and I'll bring the coffee through,' said Quentin. 'Then I can tell you a bit more about my ideas for the restaurant, and how it can be run and financed.'

Zillah went into the bar, and sat down by the fire. She could hear Quentin talking to the receptionist, or maybe it was the waitress. It was annoying and actually a bit embarrassing that he had to make himself out to be so knowledgeable and important. He would tell her that he was Rivers of Reivers in a minute. He did tell her – Zillah heard him say it, making a joke of it, but loving the sound of it all the same.

Staring into the flames, she managed to tune Quentin out, and thought instead about The Tabor. Nothing eerie or macabre, Quentin had said, and she had wanted to shout at him that he was wrong – The Tabor was full of eeriness and macabre things.

As a child she had listened to her grandmother's stories

about The Tabor, utterly entranced by them. When her grand-mother reached down to take her hand, to the small Zillah it had been as if she was being led into the past, to the time when her grandmother had been a young girl exploring the secrets and the mysteries of a strange old house.

'There were secrets in there,' she would say. 'And once, Zillah, there was a night I never forgot. It was the night the local people performed the Reivers Dance.'

Her eyes were staring straight ahead, and Zillah thought her grandmother had forgotten she was there. Greatly daring, not wanting to break the spell but fascinated, she asked about the Reivers Dance.

'They said that no one had seen it for – oh, for three hundred years,' said the soft old voice. 'Perhaps longer. But most people in Reivers knew about it, because it was handed down within families. People who live in Reivers stay there, you see. They don't often move away, and memories are long. And on that particular night, Zillah, the children of Reivers were kept inside their houses. They were forbidden to venture out, in case they saw . . .' The thin hand tightened its grip. 'It was always called the Reivers Dance for outsiders,' she said, very quietly, 'but the local people whispered that it had always been known by a different name.'

'What name? Grandma, tell me.'

For a moment, something that was no longer dream-filled or reminiscent looked out of the blue eyes. 'The Murder Dance,' she said. 'That was what people called it. And on that night I hid in a corner of the courtyard, and I saw it, Zillah.'

After a moment, Zillah said, 'Why was it called the Murder Dance?'

Her grandmother was still staring back to that long-ago night. Then, very softly, she said, 'Evelyn was part of it that night. There, at the centre of it. And Evelyn is still there, of course – I've always known that. Evelyn is still inside The Tabor.'

Evelyn . . . It was curious how the name lay on the air, leaving a cold trail. Zillah waited, but her grandmother made an impatient gesture with a hand, as if pushing something away. 'Enough about the past, my dear. It doesn't do to look back.'

Zillah shivered now, remembering those words, remembering Evelyn . . . But when Quentin set the coffee down on the low table, she smiled up at him, stretching out her legs to the fire. She had rather good legs, with slim ankles, and it was a pity not to display them. It would also tantalize Quentin, who would tighten his lips and look determinedly away. It always made Zillah laugh to herself to see him struggling like that.

She listened to his idea of creating a small company and what he called a community project to fund part of the renovations to fund his restaurant, and she put on her admiring face, and asked questions at suitable intervals.

'There'll have to be a bank loan of course,' said Quentin. 'The community project idea wouldn't be enough for everything. But I'll be able to get a loan, of course. I shall present a proper business plan – it isn't as if I don't know how these things are done. I've gathered statistics for a number of clients.'

Zillah nodded and listened, and put on the falsest of all her false faces, and smiled and said it all sounded marvellous.

And then Quentin said, 'And, of course, I shall find out as much as I can about The Tabor's past, so that it can be used for publicity.'

The Tabor's past. Zillah felt as if the warm, comfortable old room had tilted and was spinning around her. Its *past* . . .

Whatever it took, Quentin must be stopped from finding out about The Tabor's past.

TWO

The solicitor's office was in a small town six or seven miles from Reivers, and the solicitor was called Mr Codling. Quentin thought he matched his voice on the phone, which people hardly ever did, but Mr Codling was sparse and dry-looking, exactly as his voice had been. He had pale eyes and hair like thin straw. Quentin introduced Zillah, and Mr Codling shook hands with her. She had dressed in quite a formal outfit for the meeting – a very smart grey jacket which Quentin had not seen before, over a black shirt of some silky stuff, although he would have to find a way of tactfully indicating to her that a button of her shirt had become unfastened. She would not want to be embarrassed.

Mr Codling did not waste time over preliminaries. He asked Quentin to sign several documents, which his clerk witnessed, and then he sat back, and said he would be straight about things: he was not inclined to approve of the plans for The Tabor that Mr Rivers had outlined on the phone.

'A restaurant,' he said, frowning slightly.

'A gourmet restaurant. Very upmarket.'

'Yes.' A pause, then, 'I have to say, Mr Rivers, that house in any guise is nothing more than a liability, and my advice to you is to sell it as soon as possible.'

'I shan't do that,' said Quentin, annoyed. 'I'm going to set up a Trust – an investment arrangement. I'll be talking to investment banks and finance companies, but I want to involve local businesses as well, so it will be very much a community thing. And once the place is up and running, and dividends paid—'

'Mr Rivers, a dozen investment banks and a hundred Trusts wouldn't put The Tabor to rights, and it certainly wouldn't end in it being a profitable restaurant. It'd need a millionaire to do that. But I imagine an organization like the National Trust or English Heritage would be interested,' said Mr Codling. 'I could probably make enquiries on your behalf. Developers might be approached, as well, because the house could be demolished and several properties built on the land.'

Zillah leaned forward at this. 'But isn't The Tabor – well, historic?' she said, rather hesitantly. 'Won't there be . . . protection, or orders on it that will mean it can't be demolished?'

This was a very intelligent point, and in fact Quentin had been about to make it himself.

'It might be historic, but it's so run-down it could well have gone beyond the point where it can be reclaimed, Miss Rivers,' said Mr Codling, rather coldly. 'And it isn't protected in the sense I think you mean. I believe there's something called Historic England, and a long-winded process involving the

Secretary of State to get a building listed, but nobody's ever applied to have The Tabor on the list. As far as I'm aware, you could do anything you want to it – including bulldozing it. It's probably a considerable health-and-safety risk by this time, as well. In fact, Mr Rivers, you might find you'll be hearing from one or two local council departments on that count. Now that Osbert Rivers is dead, they'll most likely gather like vultures.'

'Great-Uncle Osbert,' said Quentin, half to himself.

'I think he was more of a third cousin to you,' said Mr Codling. 'Miss Rivers, did you say something?'

'No. Did you know him – Osbert? It would be really nice to hear about him from someone who had met him.'

Quentin thought, as he so often did, that Zillah charmed everyone she met. She was charming old Codling now, leaning forward eagerly as she asked about Osbert. It was a pity the unfastened button caused her blouse to gape a bit at the top.

'I did meet him a couple of times,' said Mr Codling, suddenly intent on shuffling some papers. 'My father knew him better, though. Theirs was an old friendship.'

Zillah said, 'It's nice that you knew him, though, Mr Codling, even just a little. It makes a link to the past. He lived alone, didn't he? Wasn't he ever married?'

'No.'

'Wasn't he lonely?'

'I believe there had been one or two . . . companions at times,' said Mr Codling. 'But of course it would have been long before my association with the family, and I never pried into his private life. He never referred to any lady in particular.'

Quentin thought this was very correct of Mr Codling – you did not want solicitors delving into private family matters. However, Zillah was looking wistful, and clasping her hands together. 'Perhaps he had a tragic love affair.'

'I couldn't say, Miss Rivers.'

'I didn't mean to be inquisitive,' said Zillah, at once. 'It's only that we know so little about our family. You're very knowledgeable, though, Mr Codling – about the family, and about The Tabor itself.' She gave him one of her lovely smiles. It was remarkable how she could warm a room with her smiles, although Codling did not look especially warmed; in fact he looked distinctly disapproving. Probably he was a touch embarrassed, because when Zillah reached down for her handbag, which was on the floor, it was slightly unfortunate that the partly unbuttoned blouse opened a little more, revealing a corner of some black lace.

'There's also the question of your will, Mr Rivers,' he was saying. 'I suppose you already have one in place?'

'Well, no. It never seemed important.'

'Ah. I don't know your present circumstances or financial affairs, of course, but once we've got probate, you'll be very much what the Victorians called "A man of property". I strongly advise you to make a will as soon as possible.

'And now,' he said, reaching into a drawer of his desk, 'I must hand over the keys of The Tabor. I expect you'll be keen to see the place.'

'Oh yes,' said Quentin. 'We're going straight out there now, in fact.'

His hands closed on the massive bunch of keys.

Zillah had thought they would go back to the pub first, but Quentin said they might as well make the most of the day – it was only half past ten, and they would go straight to The Tabor itself.

'Shall we do that? I can't wait to see the place.'

'Yes, let's.' But Zillah had to force herself not to clench her fists. She took deep slow breaths to calm the racing of her heart and the nervous lurching of her stomach.

There was not very much traffic on the main road, and Quentin drove fairly slowly, looking for the turning.

'It's called Drum Lane, according to the sat-nav,' he said. 'It should be just along here.'

'It's there,' said Zillah, pointing to a narrow turning on their right. 'Just by that old beech tree and the white railings.'

'How did you—? Oh, there's a sign low down, isn't there? Almost hidden by the hedge, but I can see it now. Drum Lane. Tabor means drum, did you know that?'

'Oh, does it?'

As he turned into the lane, Zillah thought it was strange

how it had felt so entirely ordinary to drive along the modern highway, with the twenty-first-century markings and signs, but how very different Drum Lane felt. It was narrow and not very well maintained, and there was almost the sense that it lay in some indefinable past. There were quite high hedges fringing the road, and there were hardly any buildings to be seen over them.

'Fen country,' said Quentin. 'Probably too marshy for building on a large scale. I don't think it's much further, though.'

Not much further, said Zillah's mind. Only another few yards. There'll be a break in the hedge on the left—

'I wonder if that's it,' said Quentin, slowing down and peering over the steering wheel. 'That break in the hedge on the left up there. D'you see?'

'Yes. That must be it.'

Quentin swung the car into the opening and in front of them were gates, waist-high, the iron scrollwork a bit battered, but still substantial and still firmly attached to the stone pillars on each side of them. On the left-hand pillar was a weather-beaten oblong with lettering – the letters worn and defaced by time and partly obscured by moss, so that they were only just readable. Zillah did not need to read the sign, though. She knew what it said. This was The Tabor. The apprehension returned, clenching at her stomach.

She got out to open the gates – they swung screechingly back, and Quentin drove through, frowning at the section of badly rutted ground just inside. If he was driving up to the Gates of Heaven, he would still be more concerned about his car's suspension than what might be ahead.

There was a sharp curve around to the left, and the house came into view. It crouched amidst untidy gardens and overgrown shrubs, and even from here it looked as if it was hugging its secrets to itself, and eyeing their approach. The Tabor.

'So that's it,' said Quentin, finally parking on a relatively flat bit of ground, and studying the house critically. 'It's an odd shape, isn't it? Bits jut out here and there, as if people have just stuck pieces on at random over the centuries.'

'I expect they'd have done it before planning permissions and things had to be got.'

'Yes. Oh, and there's the courtyard over there on the right. Through that archway – d'you see it? That's where I thought we might have our own apartment.'

'Yes.'

'Everywhere looks secure,' he said, as they walked towards the studded door at the house's centre. 'I was a bit worried about squatters, but it all looks all right.'

'Yes.' Zillah did not say that it also looked as if The Tabor would need a massive amount of money spending on it just to put it in order, never mind turning it into an upmarket restaurant. But it was still so beautiful. It would not take much to bring it out of its neglected state, and make it look . . .

Make it look how it had looked all those years ago. She pushed the thought away, and turned to Quentin, who was trying the keys, one at a time.

'The locks seem to be resisting, a bit. It doesn't look as if anyone's been out here for weeks. Ah, it's all right, I hadn't been using the right key.'

The key turned, the door swung inwards, and they stepped inside The Tabor.

The scents of age and damp and dust gusted into Zillah's face. Normally she would have shuddered and complained about the smell, but she followed Quentin inside without saying anything.

The door opened onto a big hall – it was not exactly a sunken hall, but three steps led down into it, so that there was the sense of going downwards into a dim old well. When night fell it would be very easy to miss your footing on these steps and fall. But a dusty sunlight came in from two tall latticed windows on one side of the hall, making it possible to see that the walls were partly panelled and partly covered with old-fashioned embossed paper, faded almost to grey in places. High-backed chairs had been pushed against the walls, and on the left was a staircase with an elaborately carved banister.

Quentin went eagerly across to double doors directly facing the main door, and pushed them open, revealing a long room. Zillah stayed where she was, watching him as he peered into corners, frowning and prodding at walls as if he knew all about buildings. After a few moments he came back into the hall and opened a second door a little further along, looked inside, then said in a pleased voice, 'Two very large rooms alongside each other – they take up almost half of the entire ground floor, I should think. Come and see, Zill.'

Zillah walked slowly across the hall. It was ridiculous to imagine that there would be people in that long room – figures from The Tabor's past, grey shadowy figures who would turn their heads to see who was intruding on their solitude . . . Osbert Rivers, standing up and holding out a thin old hand in greeting . . .

Quentin had gone back to tapping at the wall between the two rooms.

'This is the dividing wall,' he said, as if, thought Zillah, it was not glaringly obvious. 'And I should think the two rooms could be knocked into one for the main restaurant. Hold on, while I look at the other room again.' He went out to the hall again, and tapped and knocked from the other side.

'All good,' he said, coming back. 'I don't think that's a very substantial wall at all. I wonder if these rooms used to be one – even whether this was the old tavern. Somebody could have put that wall there later – when the place was made into a private house again, I mean. I'll ask if there are any plans or builders' sketches showing the internal layout.' He stood at the centre of the room, looking about him with a proprietorial air. Rivers of Reivers, thought Zillah. That's how he's seeing himself. Except that he isn't. This house was promised to me. It's mine.

'Gloomy old furniture, isn't it?' Quentin was saying, disparagingly. 'But I expect it can be polished up and it might fetch a few pounds. Oh – and there's the remains of a terrace out there,' he said, going over to one of the long windows. 'Very nice. I'll have it properly paved so that diners can take drinks out there in the summer.' He reached for his phone, and flipped to its camera. 'And there could be music playing just very softly, too – maybe loudspeakers positioned discreetly around.' He took several photos of the overgrown terrace with its cracked paving, then began to get shots of the room itself.

Zillah watched him for a few moments, then went into the

adjoining room. It was smaller, but Quentin was probably right that the two rooms could be knocked through into one large one. She walked round, looking at the paintings, moving slowly. You're pretending it won't be here, said her mind. You're trying to believe it will have gone long ago. You know quite well that it is here, though.

And there, in a dim corner, away from the windows so the light could not touch it and cause it to fade, was the tapestry. She stood very still looking at it. It was exactly as she remembered – exactly as it was in the dreams she sometimes had.

It was not large as tapestries went, and compared to the huge famous ones like the Bruges tapestries or the Bayeux tapestry, it was quite small. Perhaps it was about two feet in width, and about eighteen inches high. The colours were soft and dim, but that would be because they had faded – when this had been created the colours would have been strong and vivid.

It showed a dance – men and women wearing what looked like medieval costumes, leaping into the air, waving and gesturing with their arms, and pointing their feet. Some of the dancers had musical instruments – there was a drum and a violin and something she thought was a lute. And behind the dancers was a house that was certainly meant to be The Tabor.

Zillah stood looking at the tapestry for a long time. If she half closed her eyes she could think they were moving, dancing through the gardens, playing the music, leaping and shouting and laughing.

They were real people, Zillah . . . They lived here . . .

The figures at the centre were not dancing. They were shown as bigger than the rest, and one of them was kneeling down, its head bent, hair falling over the face. Memory looped back across the years, and Zillah could hear again that voice whispering to her – a harsh voice that had made her think of a dry old wind stirring dead leaves.

The tapestry shows an execution, Zillah . . .

The memory of that dreadful whispering voice was as clear as it had ever been, but even without it, it was plain what the tapestry was depicting. Zillah shivered, then went back to the other room where Quentin was still making frowning notes and measuring bits of wall. She said, 'While you're doing that, I'll take a look outside.'

'All right, but don't trip on that uneven ground. Perhaps you'd better wait until I've finished in here, then I can come with you.'

'No, I'll be fine,' said Zillah, going out before he could try to stop her.

She went across the hall and outside. When she looked at the house from here it was remote and almost tranquil, but then she turned her head to the right, and there ahead of her was the stone archway.

Keep clear of the old stone archway that leads into the courtyard . . . That was what she had been told all those years ago. Zillah hesitated, then walked towards the arch. It was quite high up and it was quite wide, as well – three or four people walking alongside one another could go through. Beyond it was a semi-enclosed area, with high walls on three sides. The courtyard rooms, thought Zillah, and something sick and fearful twisted her stomach for a moment. Go on, said her mind. You've got this far, go on and confront the nightmare. She glanced back at the main house, then took a deep breath and went through the arch on the side, and into the semi-enclosed courtyard.

At once the air felt cooler and some of the bright morning was dimmed. That would be because the tall walls were blotting out the sunshine, of course. A rickety staircase went up to a kind of gallery that extended the full length of the main wall, and then along part of the shorter wall at the far end. There was a door halfway along. It would open slowly because it was heavy, and it would not open inwards like other doors, but outwards . . . Beyond it would be a wide inner hall with doors opening off . . .

She had not brought the bunch of keys, but this door did not need a key, because it had been made so that it could open from the outside, but not from the inside . . . She shivered, but she would go on, because she needed to make sure that nothing lingered that might drag the past out into the light.

The steps creaked and sagged, and Zillah tested each tread before actually stepping on it. The staircase seemed relatively sound though, apart from the railing, which was not very secure. She would have to be careful with that on the way down.

It felt strange to be walking along the wide old balcony. In places the floor had rotted away, showing what Zillah thought were steel struts underpinning them. That would not be part of the original structure, of course. There were deep scores and dents in places, as if chairs or tables had stood out here for a long time and left their imprint. Zillah went cautiously along, and as she walked past the first of the windows, she thought a movement came from within. Her heart leapt with panic. Someone in there. Someone creeping through the shadowy rooms . . . Watching and waiting . . .

'Why don't you come inside, so I can see you more clearly . . .'

There was a stab of panic, then Zillah saw that it had only been her own reflection. And the words she had heard had been inside her own head. After a moment she was able to walk towards the door. She would not try it to see if it opened, of course—

But her hand went out to the handle, twisting it, pulling it backwards, contrary to how most door handles had to be turned. It grated slightly, and then Zillah felt the lock spring back. Flecks of rust showered onto the ground, but the door swung slowly outwards. And there it was, exactly as in the nightmare. The wide, inner hall, the doors opening off. The smell of age and dust came at her, and the memories stirred again.

'Evelyn?' Zillah heard her own voice whisper the name, very softly into the waiting silence, and she heard the echoes whisper back at her, very faintly, as if mocking her. But of course there was no one here, and it was already obvious that nothing had been here for a very long time. Even Osbert Rivers would not have been out here for years. Still, she would take a quick look round. To make sure there's no one here? said a small sly voice in her head. Zillah pushed the voice away, and reached in her bag for her phone, flipping on its torch. The small light cut through the dimness, showing up thick cobwebs dripping from the ceilings. In the current of air from the open door, they stirred, and floated towards her, like grey ragged fingers. Like hands reaching for her, only they were not like other people's hands . . .

Beneath the scents of age and dirt was the scent of old timbers that once had been polished with beeswax, and that had soaked up the sunlight of decades. A few pieces of furniture still stood around – a small table, and a carved oak chest under the window. There was a deep hearth facing the window, with alcoves on each side, and drawn up to it was a rocking chair, the upholstery of the seat faded and tattered, but still intact. Zillah had a sudden image of a figure rocking in that chair by the fire, and for a moment so strong was it that she could see the figure turn its head, and she could hear the whispered words . . .

'Why don't you come inside . . . I like to have a visitor . . .'

If she stared at this image any longer she would start to think the shadowy figure was standing up and walking towards her, arms outstretched, exactly like the grey cobwebs had seemed to stretch out earlier . . .

But the rocking chair was covered with dust, and no one could have sat there for a very long time. It moved slightly when she touched it, with a creak that sounded like old bones struggling into life, and Zillah recoiled, and went back out of the rooms, slamming the door hard, and back down the rickety steps, and into the main house again.

THREE

Quentin was waiting for her – had he been listening and watching, wondering where she had been?

Zillah said, 'The gardens are massive, aren't they? Dreadfully overgrown, but they could be made really lovely.'

'I wondered where you were. I've been thinking,' said Quentin, 'that it's only just after eleven – what d'you think about making a start on clearing some of the stuff out while we're here? I don't mean lugging furniture around, but it looks as if there's masses of old papers and things in the cupboards.

We could tip it all into rubbish bags – there's sure to be a recycling centre somewhere. It's got to be done, and any clearance firms coming in will probably charge by the hour, and it all mounts up.'

Zillah thought, resentfully, you've just inherited an Elizabethan mansion, and you're talking airily about borrowing huge sums to turn it into an upmarket restaurant, but you're carping about a few extra pounds for a house clearance firm.

But she said, temperately, 'Yes, we could do that. How about if I make a start and you go back to the pub and put on some jeans and a sweater – you've got your good jacket on, haven't you, and you don't want to get it all cobwebby. You could get my flat shoes from my bedroom as well, if you wouldn't mind. Easier to scoot around than in these heels.'

Please agree, she thought. Leave me here on my own, even for a short while, so I can confront the nightmare. 'And you'll be much quicker than I would,' she said. 'You know what I'm like with directions – I'd be sure to take a wrong turning somewhere.'

He hesitated. 'You don't mind being here on your own?'

'Oh, no. It's a friendly kind of house, somehow. And you'll only be half an hour or so, won't you?'

'All right. I'll pick up some sandwiches for lunch, shall I, then we can work straight through.'

'Good idea. And see if you can get three or four of those big garden waste bags as well. The pub might have some they'd let you have,' said Zillah, as he went out.

She waited until she heard the car start up and go back down the overgrown drive, then glanced towards the stairs. Going up them brought the memories tumbling all over again – here was the smooth-as-silk banister that was like that because so many people had slid their hands along it . . . And now the half-turn of the stair with the narrow latticed window that looked across to the courtyard rooms and the old stone arch . . .

She went unhesitatingly into the large bedroom on the right. It was a big room, dustily dim, but Zillah crossed to the two windows and pulled back the curtains. Sunlight poured in, sending the dust motes dancing, and showing up the faded carpet and the old-fashioned wallpaper. It fell across the massive bed, showing up the faded colours of the old-fashioned bedspread.

The bed belonged to Rosalind Rivers . . . Your ancestor, Zillah . . . the most beautiful Rivers lady ever . . . All the men used to fall in love with her . . . And then, *remember how you lay in that bed, and pretended you were Rosalind?* said the echoes.

Facing the bed was a massive chimney breast, and on each side were cupboards – dull and scuffed with age, but with the figuring of the oak still visible. And what might be in those cupboards . . .? Zillah opened the right-hand one warily, flinching slightly as the smell of old paper and dust came out at her.

Papers and old folders and newspaper cuttings, all of them yellowed and tattered. Probably none of them held anything in the least bit damaging, but it would be as well to get them stacked into a kind of rubbish pile, so that Quentin would not be able to look through them. He had already talked about seeing if there were any odds and ends of the house's past that he could use for publicity.

The left-hand cupboard held piles of folded linen, and Zillah dragged out a couple of thin old sheets, and spread them on the floor. Then she began to sweep the crumbling old papers from the cupboard, tipping them all onto the centre of the sheets. Even seeing them like this reassured her, because they were mostly old catalogues and inventories and receipts. A few newspaper cuttings about local events. Nothing else. It's all right, thought Zillah. There isn't going to be anything in here I need worry about.

But there was.

It was at the very back of the cupboard in an old shoebox that held several letters. Zillah sat on the side of the bed to flip through them. The dates were fifteen or sixteen years ago, but the odd thing was that the top one seemed to have been sent by Osbert Rivers, and from this house. This was strange, because when you sent a letter, it stayed with the recipient; it did not come back to the sender. It took several moments for her to realize that what she was seeing was a carbon copy.

How long had it been since people typed letters on a typewriter, and slotted a sheet of carbon in to make a copy? Zillah was not even sure if you could buy typewriters and carbon paper these days. But sitting in this faded quiet old room, she could suddenly visualize Osbert Rivers in his declining years, impatiently waving away computers and laptops, and hunched over an old-fashioned typewriter, pecking at the keys.

The carbon copy was quite smudged and the print was blurred in places, and Zillah was about to consign the box and its contents to the sheet, when a name on the letter caught her eye.

The letter was addressed to Mr Codling's firm, but the name that leapt out was Elwen.

Elwen.

Zillah stared at it for a moment, then took the blurred letter over to the window where the light was better, and sat in the padded window-seat to read it.

> My dear Codling,
> After our meeting last week I have accepted that it's my responsibility to leave my affairs in a tidy state for when I am gone. Therefore I am yielding to your many persuasions, and I shall finally make a will.
>
> As you know, I made a promise to Elwen all those years ago, and the promise was that I would leave The Tabor to her granddaughter. However, even then I think I knew I would not honour that promise, and now that Elwen is dead, I no longer feel constrained by my word. So I am going to name Quentin Rivers as my heir. I don't know anything about him, and he's very young, but he's the most direct in line after Elwen's girl. I trust you to keep an eye on him when the time comes.
>
> My good old friend, you know the taint in this family. You know how Juliette Rivers – and later, Evelyn – both had it, and you know it's a truly dreadful thing. It cropped up in the family long before Juliette and Evelyn's day, of course – stories still linger of the Murder Dance, and of how and why the courtyard prison was originally created, and why those bars had to be put at the windows.

I don't know the details though, and after all this time I shouldn't think anyone knows them.

I almost managed to convince myself that Elwen's granddaughter did not deliberately commit murder that afternoon. And yet . . .

And yet I have never been able to forget the look on her face when we found her with Evelyn's body. I don't need to describe that look to you – we both saw it on Evelyn's own face all those years ago, and although neither of us remembers Juliette, we both know from people we can trust that she had the same look years earlier. A gloating. Incredibly, even, a look of enjoyment. And along with all of that, a sly awareness of cleverness and a belief that there will be no retribution, no punishment.

I have no idea how much the child knew of what we did to cover up what had happened, and to protect her. I wonder now – I have frequently wondered – if it was the right thing to do, but Elwen was distraught, sobbing and begging me to help her. At the time I felt I had no choice.

We took the child upstairs to lie down – to get her out of the way – but when Elwen eventually took her away from The Tabor, she still had the look, and I swear it was more strongly marked. She looked at me very directly, as if she felt we shared some huge and exciting secret. As if it bound us together.

Elwen died believing that her granddaughter would inherit The Tabor. It's possible the child heard me make that promise, and that she grew up believing it. I have always hoped not, but I can't be sure.

You are the only one still alive who knows the truth, and I know I can trust you completely. I have kept a copy of this letter as a statement of my wishes in case I should die before you have completed the drawing up of my will. But once it's properly drawn up and I have signed it, then I shall destroy my copy of this letter. I would ask you to do the same with the original. I imagine your son will eventually take over the running of the firm – although I am convinced you will live to a ripe and active old age

– but there is no need for him to know any of what happened on that day. About that, also, I know I can trust you.
With warm affection,
Ever your grateful friend,
Osbert Rivers

Zillah remained on the window-seat staring at the thin sheet of paper. Words and phrases seemed to keep leaping off the page.

Elwen . . . The promise I made . . . The taint in this family . . .

But over and above that were the two sentences that stood out, as clear as a curse. *I almost managed to convince myself that Elwen's granddaughter did not deliberately commit murder that afternoon,* Osbert had written. And, *I have never been able to forget the look on her face when we found her with Evelyn's body . . .*

Zillah's first reaction was blazing fury – bitter, hurting anger at Osbert, who not only had deceived her, but who had set down all this for a solicitor to see. Codling's father, would he have been writing to? Yes, certainly. But he was dead, and there was no hint that his successor – the person Zillah and Quentin had seen earlier today – had ever seen this letter.

Beneath the anger was fear, because supposing Quentin had found this – supposing, even, that there were other things that hinted at the truth, and that he found those? She began to tear the letter into strips, and then into shreds, finally putting the fragments onto the sheet with the other old papers. She glanced at her watch and saw that already half an hour had passed, and that Quentin might be back at any moment. No time, then, to go through all the other papers – instead she swept them from the shelves, tipped them all onto the sheet, then folded it up, knotting the corners to form a kind of sack.

Could she feel safe now? But supposing Quentin did find other things? Supposing his delving into The Tabor's past for a publicity campaign brought out other clues? Zillah had no idea what such clues might be, but finding Osbert's letter had set her every instinct alert.

When Quentin first told her he had inherited The Tabor, she had had to beat down anger and resentment, but through it she had thought that if she could hit on a way to get the house away from him, she would use it. That thought came back now, stronger and more definite. The Tabor was Zillah's, and it had always been intended to be hers. But a stupid, probably senile old man, had decided she had brought about a death, and with a sweep of his pen had changed everything. Ruined everything.

But an idea was starting to take shape. Zillah sat on the edge of Rosalind Rivers' bed and looked at this idea – it was dim and blurred and it was like looking into a shadowy room, and only being able to make out the edges of what was in there. The shapes of the idea were there though, and she went on looking at them.

It was only the sound of Quentin's car outside, and the slam of the door and his footsteps on the stairs that jolted her back to her surroundings. And the idea was not one that ought to be looked at for too long. Even blurred and indistinct, it would be better not to give it a moment's consideration. Zillah would certainly not do so. Of course she would not.

Quentin had been slightly surprised that Zillah had been happy to stay in The Tabor by herself this morning. She was such a sensitive little soul that the place's atmosphere could well have been too much for her, but she had seemed to love it and to want to explore it and find out about it. When they had cleared out all the rubbish, if there was time, he would take her over to the courtyard rooms, and they would work out how to make them into really splendid apartments. She would like that.

Driving back along Drum Lane he smiled, thinking how marvellous the future was going to be, thinking how he had loved Zillah ever since he could remember. He had always planned that one day they would be together, although he had never actually made any move to take her to bed. It had never seemed to be quite the right time. She had been too young – they were cousins . . . They were only second cousins, of course, but still.

One day he would make that move, of course, but the time had to be right. That was what he was waiting for. He was not altogether inexperienced – who was in these days? – but there was no need to look back to the rather awkward, sometimes even embarrassing encounters he had had in the past. Admittedly there had not been many, but there had been a few. Not everyone could be the great lover of legends and pub boasts, though, and Quentin was not going to look too closely at those handful of experiences, although he was inclined to think the girls themselves had been to blame for things not being as good as they might have been. They had been too eager, too blatant, and most men would agree that such behaviour could be – well, a bit emasculating. He had not been especially worried, though; he had consoled himself with the conviction that with Zillah it would be different. There would be no shrugs of annoyance and dismissal, no disappointed regaining of clothes so optimistically flung off.

He parked the car and went back into the house, calling out to her.

'Zill? Where are you? I've got everything – some huge garden waste bags, and I got your shoes . . . oh, and I took your jeans from the wardrobe – I thought you'd probably want to put them on for all this clearing-out work.'

'Sounds good. I'm up here,' came her voice. 'I'm getting on really well.'

Quentin ran up the stairs to where Zillah was in a big bedroom, piling old papers into a couple of tied-up sheets. Her hair was a bit dishevelled and there was a smudge of dust on one cheekbone, but she smiled and said it was great that he had been so quick.

'I got these rubbish bags from the pub,' said Quentin, 'and they made up some sandwiches and even put in a flask of coffee. We can have a picnic lunch and work right through the day. Have you found anything exciting? Anything I could use for publicity?'

'No, nothing,' said Zillah, as he poured the coffee into two small cups. As she took the cup from him, Quentin had a sudden strange feeling that although she was smiling at him, there was something behind the smile. As if she was hiding something? As if she was looking at him in a different way? No, he was being stupid.

He said, 'The pub says there's a recycling centre just the other side of Reivers, so we can take everything out there.'

'Good. I've almost finished in here, anyway. How about if I stay with the bedroom stuff while you see what can be thrown out downstairs?'

She smiled again and this time it was the real smile, and Quentin relaxed, because of course he had imagined that strange look earlier. Most likely it had been a trick of the sunlight and the dust that was lying on the air.

For the second evening they had coffee in the bar after they had eaten. Quentin talked about his ideas for The Tabor, and Zillah listened, saying admiringly that it all sounded absolutely marvellous.

As she leaned back in the comfortable chair, the plan that had slid slyly into her mind earlier came fractionally more into focus. As if light was starting to trickle into that shadowy room in her mind.

She smiled at Quentin, and agreed that this was a very comfortable pub – he had been clever to find it for them, so close to The Tabor and everything.

'I love the oak beams, don't you? And that old fireplace. You don't come across an inglenook very often these days, do you? How many people even know what one is?'

She looked about her with contentment. This was a place where plans could be made. A place where you could pretty much redesign your life and your entire future. A place where all kinds of things could happen.

FOUR

'I met her in an inglenook in an old country pub,' said Toby Tallis. 'Firelight and wine and so on – and I'm sorry if I'm sounding like a 1940s love song – although that kind of music isn't your field of research, is it, so probably you don't know what I'm talking about—'

Phineas Fox, who had been making a half-hearted attempt to tidy his study, looked up from sorting through a stack of dog-eared music scores, and said, indignantly, that he knew perfectly well what Toby was talking about. 'An entire world of very lovely romantic music was composed in that era.'

'It was the classic setting,' said Toby. 'A crackling fire and oak beams and whatnot. I'm surprised there wasn't a forty-piece orchestra playing that old Fred Astaire/Ginger Rogers song—'

'"The Way You Look Tonight"?'

'That's the one,' said Toby, pleased at this instant comprehension, and Phin did not say he had sometimes had a wild fantasy of himself seated at a grand piano, wearing a dinner jacket, and playing this very song for Toby's cousin. 'I knew at once that I had met the real love of my life,' went on Toby.

'Again?'

'There's no need for that quizzical look,' said Toby. 'Although I will admit that I may have said something on similar lines in the past. Once or twice. Possibly.'

'About every six months on average.' But Phin was smiling. 'Pass me that box of old newspaper cuttings, will you? Who is this inglenook lady?'

'Her name's Zillah Rivers, and she's like a – a water sprite,' said Toby, reaching for the newspaper cuttings. 'And don't hoot derisively like that, wait till you see her. There's a sort of other-worldly air. She's like one of the girls in those 1890s paintings. Masses of coppery corrugated hair and incredibly thin wrists and ankles. Mind you, that's probably a precursor of osteoporosis.'

'That physiotherapist girlfriend last autumn had some influence on you after all,' observed Phin. 'I'm not going to ask what osteo – whatever you called it – is.'

'Brittle bones.'

'Ah. Clearly you're one of the few remaining romantics of the world,' said Phin.

'Don't knock it. Did I jibe when you fell for Arabella? No, I did not. I provided her with cousinly support and you with neighbourly approval.'

'So you did. Tell me about the brittle-boned water sprite,' said Phin. 'What was she doing in a country pub? Does she live in Norfolk?'

'No. She and her cousin have just inherited a house in the village – at least, the cousin has – and they were staying there to sort things out. It's quite a big house, but it's ancient and a bit run-down, apparently. I haven't seen it yet. But the cousin's intending to do it up, so they'll be staying in Reivers for the time being while he has meetings with builders and surveyors and whatnot.'

'What were you doing in Norfolk, anyway?' said Phin. 'I thought you and Arabella were going to see an elderly great-aunt in Peterborough.'

'We were. We did. And we had a good weekend with her. But on the way home, Arabella thought we could make a bit of a detour into Norwich. She said it wouldn't add more than an hour or so to the journey, and we could have lunch there, and then sit in the cathedral and commune with the spirit of somebody who was a famous nun or philosopher or something.'

'Dame Julian of Norwich,' said Phin, after a moment.

'That's the one. Arabella said it would be soothing and energizing all at the same time. She's in a bit of a mystical phase at the moment, isn't she?'

'Yes.' Phin could easily see Arabella enthusiastically propounding to Toby this plan to commune with spirits in a cathedral. The image reminded him that it was the best part of a week since he had seen her. He did not actually need reminding and a week was not a very long time, but it seemed very long indeed when it was Arabella.

'But we took a wrong turning,' Toby was saying. 'As you know, Arabella's sense of direction isn't always entirely trust-worthy. And we were miles from anywhere when the car started clanking and growling. There wasn't even a glimmer of a garage on the horizon, or any other building, come to that, and the mobile signal was so bad we might as well have tried to phone the international space station. I had to sort of coax the car along and hope it didn't burst into flames before we got back to civilization. That's how we finally reached this place – Reivers, it's called. I think there was a cluster of villages once and they've got joined up over the centuries because of extra roads being built at various times. Reivers is still quite villagey, though. We found a garage, but it turned out that there was something massively wrong with the car, and they couldn't get the part there and then, so we booked in at The Daunsen.'

'The Daunsen? That's an odd name.'

'I know. Arabella's going to see if she can trace its origins. Anyhow, when the garage still hadn't got the part yesterday I had to leave the car there, and get a taxi to the nearest railway station because of being on that rotation in ENT, which isn't really a place I want to be at the moment, well, not at any moment, because it isn't a branch of medicine that especially attracts me, only you have to work your way through all departments if you're ever going to qualify.'

'You came back, leaving Arabella on her own in the middle of nowhere?' demanded Phin, as Toby paused for breath.

'Yes, but I'll explain about that in a minute. And The Daunsen's a perfectly respectable pub, in fact it's very nice. Arabella said she phoned you to tell you what had happened.'

'She tried to, but the mobile signal was so bad that all I got was a series of crackles and a few disembodied phrases. She managed to say she'd try to email though. Is she driving the car back to London when it's fixed, or what?' Phin was not going to admit he had been counting the days until Arabella could return to London.

'Well, actually I'm going back to Reivers this weekend,' said Toby, who was exploring more of the boxes. 'I promised Zillah I would. What are you going to do with these boxes of books? None of them look as if they've been opened for about a hundred years – are you throwing them out, or can they go on the shelves by the window? There's room at one end.'

'I'm not throwing them out,' said Phin. 'I'm always afraid to throw books out, because you never know what you might want. They can go on those shelves, but be careful, because they're the ones your DIY man put up last year, and there's a skew on one side, so the right-hand side has to be weighted down.'

'If,' said Toby, starting to stack the books with due regard to the skew, 'you and Arabella ever get together properly – I mean under the same roof – you'd have to have a house with its own library. She's got nearly as many books as you.'

'I know.'

'But then you could sit in the library in the evenings wearing a velvet smoking jacket like somebody out of a Victorian novel – you've even got an authentic leather chair that would fit in. Is that the one Arabella found in the Portobello Road and had renovated for your birthday?'

'Yes, but she had the wrong castors fitted,' said Phin. 'It propels you across the room without warning. It nearly shot Professor Liripine through the window and down into the street when he was here to work on that peculiar Russian business last year.[1] Tell me about Norfolk.'

'Well, Zillah's cousin – Quentin Rivers – has come up with a scheme for The Tabor – that's the name of the house he's inherited,' said Toby. 'He'll get finance – properly, from banks and people like that – but he wants it to be a sort of community project, as well. Local people and local businesses putting money in. He wants to turn The Tabor into a really swish restaurant. Gourmet level. It'll benefit the area hugely, of course. Anyone can see that. But it's going to take an emperor's ransom to do it, so he's going to invite investments from local people and businessmen. It's often done these days in small places. Investors get a dividend when the profits start rolling in.'

Toby was looking and sounding ingenuously delighted. Phin left the music scores to sort out another day, and sat down to pay more attention.

'How much are they hoping to pay out as a dividend?' he said. 'Because I should think it'll take a great deal of money to get a tumbledown house up to Michelin-star level. As well as a Michelin-level chef to cook the food.'

'Yes, but once it's set up and they've got a few thousand in the kitty to get them going, the whole thing will be ramped up to national level. Then they can apply for lottery money

[1] See *The Devil's Harmony*

and grants and things,' said Toby, waving a vague hand, and
overturning the box of newspaper cuttings in the process.
'Arabella's stayed there to give them some ideas about
publicity. One odd thing, though – she didn't seem to take to
Zillah particularly warmly, which is odd, because Arabella
usually takes to most people. But she's got some terrific ideas
for the project already – you know Arabella. Well, by this time
you probably know her even better than I do, not that I'm
asking questions, you understand, or turning Victorian and
demanding to know what your intentions are. I wouldn't mind
having you in the family, though,' he added, rather wistfully.
'You'd be a cousin-in-law, if there is such a thing.'

Phin avoided this veiled question, and said, 'Is the project
worth a publicity campaign? Because if it's just a small country
restaurant and a small local community . . .?'

'Well, yes, it could be very worth it – oh, and in case you
were wondering, Quentin's offered Arabella a fee if she'll
officially take on the role of publicist. And there are all kinds
of local legends to make use of. Apparently some famous
Shakespearean personage once performed there, and Arabella
thought that could be made use of. If,' said Toby, looking at
Phin from the corners of his eyes, 'the identity of the
Shakespearean personage could be discovered. It wasn't
William himself, of course, but we both thought—'

'That I might be able to discover who it was?'

'It'd be an interesting bit of research,' said Toby, hopefully.
'And the stories are supposed to have a bit of a musical basis,
so it's very much your glass of vino. I even looked up *tabor*
as a starting point, and it was a sort of portable drum that
Elizabethan performers and dancers used. It all points to a
music background for the legend, doesn't it?'

As casually as he could, Phin said, 'These two – Zillah and
her cousin – I suppose they haven't actually started collecting
money from people yet?'

'Well, not exactly, although I think Quentin's talking to
people about it. Making initial approaches.'

Phin looked at him for a moment, then said, 'Has he
approached you? Initially or otherwise?'

'I have said I might be interested,' said Toby, elaborately

casual. 'It'd be a question of transferring some money. You remember I opened that investment account when we did that book together on *Bawdy Ballads Down the Ages*.[2] You said it would be a good thing to put the money into that kind of account, and Arabella said it would, and so did the bank. But there's a thirty-day wait to actually get at any of the dosh, so I had to explain that to Zillah. Well, and to Quentin. They quite understood. Quentin explained to me how it will all work. It's a very good investment, honestly it is.'

The book in question had been a frivolous and light-hearted collaboration between Toby and Phin, mainly inspired by Toby's cheerful habit of singing rugby songs in the shower, the sounds of which were usually audible through the wall between the two flats. Phin, initially slightly startled at Toby's suggestion, had become swept up in his enthusiasm, and had greatly enjoyed the project. His energetic agent had found a publisher for the finished product, which, suitably illustrated, had managed to sell a fair number of copies.

But the possibility of Toby – who had been perennially broke ever since Phin had known him – investing this money in what sounded like a very risky venture caused alarm bells to sound in his mind. But he only said, 'It sounds intriguing. Especially the Shakespearean touch.'

'I hoped you'd think that. You could come down and see the place. Just for a couple of days. Stay at the pub – meet Zillah. And delve into the Shakespearean performer story.'

Phin considered the idea. His various musical researches had not, so far, taken him very deeply into Elizabethan territory, and he did not really want to make the long trek into the wilds of Norfolk, even if it turned out that Will Shakespeare had quarrelled with Kit Marlowe in The Daunsen's jug and bottle, or that Burbage had been a regular quaffer of its ale in the inglenook. But Toby was clearly so delighted at the idea of Phin coming to Reivers with him, that Phin did not have the heart to refuse. There was no reason why he could not drive out to Norfolk, in fact; he did not have any particularly pressing research commissions at present, and it would be

[2] See *Chord of Evil*

nice to spend a couple of days in a country pub with Arabella. There was also the point that he could see at close quarters if the marvellous investment in The Tabor was as marvellous as Toby seemed to think, and to make sure that neither he nor Arabella had got tangled up with a pair of con-artists.

So he said, 'All right. Will you have finished your ENT stint by the weekend?'

'Free as a bird after Saturday.'

'Then how about if I do a bit of preliminary delving into any Shakespearean performers who might have cavorted across Norfolk between now and Friday?' suggested Phin. 'Then I could drive us both out to Norfolk on Sunday morning.'

After Toby had gone back to his own flat, cheerfully calling out to one or two neighbours on the stairs as he did so, Phin checked his emails, seeing with pleasure that an email from Arabella had bounced in while he was talking to Toby.

> Phin dear,
> You forget, don't you, that modern technology isn't absolutely foolproof, and you curse it furiously when something goes wrong. When the phones did grudgingly connect on Tuesday evening, I only really heard snatches of your dulcet tones, so I'm not at all sure if you got the gist of what I said.
>
> However, Toby should be back in London now, so he'll have told everything that's happened, and you'll know I haven't absconded with anyone or been kidnapped or press-ganged or fled the country as a fugitive.
>
> It was just like that wretched car of Toby's to choose the most deserted part of Norfolk to break down. It didn't even give so much as a warning. The engine gave a sort of malevolent chuckle, then there was a truly dreadful series of clankings, as if a couple of gleeful spooks were bashing their chains at the carburettor. (Which gave a whole new meaning to that line from somewhere or other about a ghost in the machine.)
>
> Toby thought something vital had dropped off or

burned out, and that the only course of action was for us to crawl along the road at a funereal pace, and hope the car didn't burst into flames until we found a garage or somewhere with a phone signal. I wanted to get my red hat out of my bag and walk in front, waving it like a flag – like people used to do with red flags when cars were first invented and everyone had to be warned that a motor vehicle was coming. But Toby thought that would be going a bit too far, and in any case there were no people to warn, only a few cows in a turnip field, and I shouldn't think cows would mind about clanking ghosts in engines, would they?

And at last I spotted a turning that I thought would take us to a main road, but anyone can mistake a signpost, although it was a bit of a nuisance that it went down to an expanse of mudflat, and if Toby hadn't slammed on the brakes, we might have ended up being swallowed in the mud like somebody out of *The Hound of the Baskervilles* drowning in Grimpen Mire. It only took twenty minutes to slither the car out, though, so it wasn't so bad, and I even managed to retrieve my shoe. And from there we reached this place called Reivers, and this pub called The Daunsen. Very nice people run it – they helped with getting an internet connection for the laptop, and they were perfectly charming when I tripped over a cable, which apparently put all the computers in the pub out of action, along with the cash machine and the tablets they use in the restaurant for sending the orders for food into the kitchen. But they promised it could be put right, and it was fine by the next morning.

Has Toby told you about the couple staying here – Zillah and Quentin Rivers? He's sure to have done, because he's fallen like a ton of bricks for Zillah. I usually like Toby's girlfriends, but I don't think this one is going to turn out at all well. I suspect Zillah Rivers is one of those kitten-faced adventuresses – all purring voice and soulful eyes, but with *very* acquisitive claws just under the surface. She's most likely a tigress in the sack, too, although as it's Toby who's involved and he's always felt more like my brother than my cousin, I'm not speculating on that aspect.

Quentin Rivers is one of those utterly humourless people, with a long, dour face, like a bloodhound with poached-egg eyes. He watches Zillah a great deal, which I find vaguely creepy. But he's inherited an ancient house called The Tabor – I haven't seen it yet, and it sounds semi-tumbledown, but Quentin wants to untumble it and turn it into a really swish restaurant – like those country-house places run by the top chefs, where you have to allow the entire day to have lunch, because you get about fifteen courses served to you in a procession, like a Tudor banquet or the wilder cavortings of the decadent Roman emperors. Tasting menu it's called, isn't it? Let's try to go to one of those restaurants some day, shall we? I can't think of anything better than getting glammed up and spending about five hours eating. Well, I can, of course, but at the moment you're in London and I'm a couple of hundred miles away. I hope the twain will meet quite soon, though, because I'm missing you very much. I miss seeing your eyes narrow when you're amused, so that they're like slivers of silver, and I miss the way you get so absorbed in your work and your music that you aren't always aware of the rest of the world. If the Four Horsemen of the Apocalypse rode into town on Monday morning, I bet you'd still be at your desk on Tuesday afternoon, listening to somebody's Fifth Symphony and writing a monograph comparing Bach with Handel.

Quentin has asked if I might be able to come up with a few initial ideas for some PR, and, depending on how things go, whether I might be interested in taking on the publicity for the whole project. He's suggested quite a reasonable fee, and I'm rather drawn towards it. I've already got a few ideas, and I can see that his plans might work fairly well, providing he can raise the dosh. Toby promised that when he got back to London he'd explain it all to you, and ask you to come out here for a couple of days to see what you can dig up about this mysterious seventeenth-century performer. What do you think? The local stories are all beautifully mysterious and possibly disreputable and it's exactly the kind of thing you're brilliant at unravelling.

I can book you in at the pub. It's a nice old place, and there's an intriguing sketch in the bar. It isn't dated as far as I can tell, but the point I want to make about it is that in the corner somebody has written these words:

Cwellan Daunsen.

This pub's called The Daunsen, but I don't know what a cwellan is. I do know what *daunsen* is, though, because at school I once had to learn two pages by heart from Chaucer for having accidentally let off a firework during a lecture by a visiting professor of Medieval History. And there was a section in those two pages where Chaucer says something about fair ladies dancing and singing, except that his words, as near as I can remember, were, "What ladies fairest best *dauncen* and synge". So *daunsen* has to be dancing, and if you really needed a music connection to tempt you to come out here, there it is.

And the rather odd thing is that the sketch isn't of The Daunsen, which you'd expect it to be. The staff, when I asked them, say the sketch is The Tabor in what they endearingly call its younger days. I expect that means fifteen or sixteen hundred and something.

Please try to come. Every time something amusing happens, I look round for you, to have that moment of silently sharing of a joke nobody else has picked up. Only you're not there to share anything with.

On a completely different note, my room here is a double. There are views across fenlands and meadows and you can see the sun setting into the North Sea, setting it on fire.

And the bed itself is *very* comfortable . . .

Phin typed a reply to Arabella, saying Toby had indeed related the entire Daunsen and Tabor saga, and that he would be driving the two of them to Reivers and The Daunsen this coming Sunday. They should be there by mid-afternoon, so if there was anything

from Arabella's flat she wanted him to collect would she say,
only please to not send several pages of requirements because
he would never find them all. He added a note to say the
comfortable bed sounded extremely alluring.

After this, he set about searching his bookshelves, finally
running to earth a much-thumbed dictionary that gave the
roots and possible origins of words.

Cwellan Daunsen.

As usual, there were various spellings and any number of
theories as to where most words had come from and in
which language they had first seen the light of day. Geoffrey
Chaucer, of course, had been apt to import all kinds of quirky
fragments of words into the English tongue.

Cwellan appeared to have descended from High German,
with a nod in the direction of Dutch, Danish, and old Norse.

And it seemed that no matter how you spelled it, it translated,
near enough, as murder or murderer. And, as Arabella had said,
daunsen or, more usually, *dauncen*, was dance or dancing.

Which meant that if you did not mind blurring Old English
from around the 1100s into Middle English from around the
Norman Conquest to the 1500s – which Phin was perfectly
happy to do in this context – you found yourself with what
could be a reasonable interpretation of the words on the old
sketch.

Cwellan Daunsen translated, near enough, as The Dancing
Murderer.

FIVE

P hin spent the next two hours in a fruitless search of his
bookshelves for Dancing Murderers. After a while he
almost managed to convince himself that as he had not
really expected to find any, he was not in the smallest bit
disappointed at not doing so.

A diligent trawl of the internet yielded nothing, either – at
least, nothing that fitted into the context Phin wanted. It was

of no help to read about sly, smooth gentlemen (also several ladies) who had tempted their unsuspecting dance partners to foxtrot into marriage and then had polished them off for their money. Nor was there anything to be gleaned by wandering amidst the darker levels of gothic, black metal, or dark-wave punk music – although Phin made a few notes, since it might be interesting to explore these avenues sometime, and you never knew what you might be asked to research.

But no Elizabethan performers who might briefly have visited a Norfolk village and who might have caused that phrase, The Dancing Murderer, to be coined, seemed to be recorded anywhere, and he was just trying to think what other sources he might plunder, when Toby clattered along the hall from his own flat. He had, he said, rather glumly, tried to phone Zillah three times, but had only managed a few brief words, because of the unreliable phone signal. It had been really good to hear her voice, though; Phin would very likely know how he was feeling on account of Arabella being still in Reivers.

Phin, who had never seen Toby in this mournful enamoured state, said, rather helplessly, that it was only a couple of days until the weekend, and they would set off early on Sunday morning.

'And the roads are likely to be fairly clear at that hour.'

'That's true. What I really came to say was that I'll have to get up at crack of dawn tomorrow, because I'm on early duty in ENT and Saturday's always a frantic day. But how about trundling along to the trattoria down the road this evening and having a bite to eat. What with you being on your own as well.'

'Toby, normally I'd say yes, but I want to find out a bit more about Reivers and The Tabor before the weekend, so—'

'How are you getting on with that? Could I help?' said Toby, hopefully, and Phin understood that Toby was trying to fill up the hours until he could be with Zillah. He hoped the lady was worth all this emotion and that she was not simply using Toby to cheer up an enforced stay in a boring place – or, more worryingly, to get at his carefully hoarded bit of money for the restaurant project.

He explained about the sketch of The Tabor which Arabella had found in the pub, and the possible interpretation of *Cwellan Daunsen*.

'I didn't see the sketch,' said Toby, sweeping a pile of books from a chair, and sitting down. 'Although when you're in a bar, you're in a bar, and you aren't looking at the walls, are you? But we can look at it this weekend.'

'I haven't tracked down anyone who was known as the Dancing Murderer yet,' said Phin, 'although I think it's a fair assumption that there's a link to the pub. It's a pity the place hasn't got a website with one of those potted histories, but it hasn't. And the name could have come into being any time during the last – well, four or even five hundred years.'

'Or the Dancing Murderer might not even have been a real person,' said Toby. 'Have you thought about that? It might be a character from a play or a book. Like you might call a pub The Oliver Twist, or The Count Dracula—'

'Toby, you're sitting on my notebook.'

'So I am. Sorry. Or The Lady Chatterley or The Hannibal Lecter. Or—'

Phin said, 'Do you really think people would say to one another, "Let's go along for a meal at The Hannibel Lecter or The Count Dracula"?'

'It'd depend on the food,' said Toby. 'And, speaking of food, if we aren't going out to the trattoria, shall I order in some food? Chinese?'

'That would be good.'

Toby went out to his own flat to find the menu and phone number of his favourite Chinese restaurant, and Phin leaned back from his book-strewn desk for a moment, hoping all over again that the Tabor project was not an elaborate scam – or a wildcat scheme doomed to failure.

But he would suspend judgement until he met Quentin and Zillah Rivers, and for the moment he would concentrate on the contents of a battered tome whose foxed pages chronicled the exploits of 'clowns, jesters, wise fools, and other such entertainers', but none of which seemed to have any relevance to murderers, dancing or otherwise.

Toby reappeared to report that the food would be about twenty minutes, and picked up several of the books.

'You've got half of the sixteenth century spread out here,' he said. 'I suppose you've homed in on that because of the Reivers legend. The unknown Shakespearean person who cavorted around the village. And you're linking it to the sketch.'

'Only tentatively,' said Phin. 'And if there was a Dancing Murderer, he – or she – could have been hailed off to justice and ended up on the gallows.'

'But that would have got into the legend,' objected Toby. 'They'd have written ballads about it. At the very least there'd be places with names like Gallows End, or Hangman's Crossroads, and there aren't – and it's a very small place, so I think I'd have seen them.'

'All right, we'll say if the Dancing Murderer existed, he escaped hanging. But his victims would be remembered. They could even be buried in the churchyard at Reivers, with inscriptions on headstones . . . Has Reivers got a church? Of its own, I mean, rather than one of those shared arrangements between several parishes?'

'Don't know. But we can find out at the weekend.'

'Also,' went on Phin, 'if he was a dancer, what music did he dance to? It might be useful to know that.'

'Like a signature tune?' said Toby, hopefully. 'Like hearing *The Archers* theme tune on the radio and knowing everybody was yomping off to Ambridge?'

'Well, sort of. I wish I knew a bit more about the Elizabethans,' said Phin. 'I know a good many of them wrote lyrical love songs or religious music, of course, but that wouldn't . . . What's that you've picked up?'

'Biographical dictionary of composers,' said Toby, sitting cross-legged on the floor, and turning the pages. 'There's a Tallis in here – he wrote mostly church music, so I shouldn't think he was a relative, should you? Oh, and John Dowland – I've heard of him. He had some good titles, didn't he? But I can't see the Dancing Murderer waving a lute in one hand and a meat cleaver in the other, and singing "The Frog Galliard" or "My Lady Hundson's Puffe" while he lopped off people's

heads or skewered them with a marlinspike, can you, and . . .
Ah, that sounds like our food arriving. I told them to deliver
it here.'

As Toby scrambled out of his chair and went out to the
hall, Phin returned to clowns, jesters and wise fools, hoping
that the name of Reivers would leap up off the page, but not
really surprised when it did not.

'Didn't I order plum sauce with the duck?' said Toby's
voice, worriedly, from the hall. 'Because I thought – oh, no,
that's it, isn't it? And that's the dim sum platter, is it? Excellent.
Yes, beautifully substantial. And the jasmine rice . . . Lovely.
I can manage to carry it all in, I think . . . Damn, I've dropped
the spring rolls. Can you reach that one – it's rolled under the
umbrella stand . . .'

Phin shut out the thought of spring rolls trapped under the
umbrella stand, and concentrated on the editor's notes, with
mentions of a few of the songs that had survived from the
fifteenth century. 'Most of them have their own local connections, of course,' he wrote, 'such as the Abbots Bromley
Horn Dance, which is believed to have its roots in pre-
Christian days.'

'Don't worry about the carpet,' Toby was saying. 'I'll sponge
it later. Black bean sauce doesn't leave a stain anyway, does it?
Oh, does it? Still, it's only in that corner . . .'

'. . . but also there are the darker ballads,' went on the book.
'Such as the grim saga unfolded in "The Cruel Mother". And,
of course, fragments of what seems to have been called in its
own locale, the Murder Dance [see footnote].'

The Murder Dance. Phin's mind sprang to attention, and
he riffled the pages to find the relevant footnote. The author
headed them with a warning to readers not to confuse the
Murder Dance with the *Danse Macabre* or *Dance of Death,*
in which skeletons escort living humans to their graves in a
lively capering. The Murder Dance, he explained, appeared
to fall into a very different category, possibly dealing with
a ritual depiction of a murder, preceded by a folk dance,
although the sources were so tenuous and fragmented that it
had been impossible to establish whether the piece had even
existed at all. His own opinion was that it had not; that it

was nothing more than myth – shreds of gossip that had attached themselves to some of the darker legends in certain parts of Norfolk.

Murder Dance, thought Phin, staring at the page. And a Murder Dance that's tangled into Norfolk's legends. Is this what I've been looking for?

'Shall I get plates and things?' said Toby's voice, re-entering the study, laden with foil containers and two small carrier bags. 'Or do you want to eat straight from the foil?'

'I don't care.'

'Then let's be civilized,' said Toby, and went off to clatter cheerfully around the kitchen. He dropped something on his foot, swore profusely, but eventually returned to the study assuring Phin that nothing had been broken.

'And I've brought forks and spoons, as well,' he said, 'in case you don't want to twirl chopsticks. You'd got a bottle of wine open, as well, so I've brought that, too. It seemed a pity not to drink it, once it was open.' He sat down and began to spoon out the food. 'Have some of this duck first – that restaurant does a really good duck.'

Phin took the plate, still frowning at the book open in front of him. He said, 'I'm coming to the conclusion that if there was an Elizabethan dancer in Reivers at all, he's likely to have been a strolling player.'

'A wandering minstrel,' said Toby, through a mouthful of rice. 'A thing of shreds and patches. I could sing the entire verse for you after I finish eating this, if you like.'

'No, it's all right,' said Phin, who was familiar with Toby's method of rendering the works of Gilbert & Sullivan.

'It was a way of life for them, wasn't it, those strolling performers?' said Toby, investigating the contents of another of the containers. 'And you can almost see their point. Wherever you went, you got a warm welcome and a bed for the night, and you only had to sing for your supper.'

'You also had to sleep in barns and under hedges when no bed was on offer, and tramp the roads during the days,' observed Phin. 'Not to mention falling victim to cut-throats and highwaymen and probably being taken up for transgressing the vagrancy laws.'

'Yes, but you didn't have to worry about rent or electricity, or the gloomy prospect of repaying a socking great student loan.' Toby frowned, and Phin glanced at him, remembering the earlier concerns about Toby's apparent involvement with the Tabor project.

'Still, if Zillah and Quentin's scheme gets properly off the ground, I shan't need to worry about money in the future,' said Toby. 'It could do really well, you know, that restaurant.' He refilled his wine glass. 'Tell me about those performers. I suppose they'd have been a bit like Harlequin and Columbine and that crowd?'

'The entertainment would have been a bit more rustic,' said Phin. 'There'd have been music, though, and – well, song-and-dance routines, for want of a better term. I think they often improvised those. The dances would have plots, and they were often quite bawdy.' He turned several more pages, turned back, reread a section, then sat up very straight.

'What is it?'

'I've been trying to pin something down,' said Phin, staring at the page. 'And I think I have. Norfolk and dancing and a Shakespearean performer— Toby, there was a player in Shakespeare's company called Will Kempe. Not a massive amount's known about him, except that he was a comic – a clown – and some people maintain he was the original model for Falstaff. I'll have to look it up in a bit more detail, but I think Kempe was one of the original group of players along-side Shakespeare himself.' He drank some more of his wine. 'But what Kempe is more commonly remembered for is that after he parted company with the London theatres, he embarked on a kind of dance marathon, with the aim of dancing his way from London to Norfolk in nine days.'

'Nine days? He danced for nine days? Did he survive? Because if he did, he'd be worthy of a mention in *The Lancet*, or whatever the sixteenth-century equivalent was.'

'Of course he didn't dance non-stop for nine days,' said Phin. 'He'd dance into a town, with his musicians tootling and strumming along behind him, and all the people of the town would turn out and cheer him on, and he'd stay there for a night, and move on next day. Altogether, he spent nine days actually on the road. He called it a Nine Days' Dance or the Nine Days' Jig, or something like that.'

'And one of the places he jigged into was Reivers? This sounds promising. If Arabella can't use that to get The Tabor into the Michelin guide, I'll be very surprised. Well, always assuming they can get a decent chef to actually cook the Michelin-level food in the restaurant, of course. You're not identifying Kempe with the killer, are you? I hope you aren't, because anyone who decides to dance his way from London to Norfolk – and who's supposed to have been the original Falstaff, as well—'

'No, I'm not,' said Phin. 'But Kempe's plan was certainly to dance from London to Norfolk, and according to this book there was something they called the Murder Dance actually in Norfolk. That could chime with the title of that sketch, couldn't it? And listen to this – it's what gave me the connection between Kempe and Norfolk – which might mean to Reivers itself.' He turned a page back. 'Shortly after Kempe's death – believed to be around 1603 – a local newssheet called *Tydings*, which covered the general area, published what's more or less an obituary on Kempe. That would be because of Kempe's visit to the county, I should think. He'd have given the area a bit of a boost, probably. There's an extract quoted here – it's certainly been abridged and probably tarted up a bit, and I shouldn't think there's any chance of tracking down the original. But one of the things that *Tydings* seems to have referred to was how, after the famous "Nine Daies Wonder" was achieved, Master Kempe and his troupe found themselves in a small village where they opted to spend a few nights. Apparently Kempe had strained his hip on account of "having danced ten miles between Bury and Thetford in three hours, and having recourse to the surgeon's ministrations".'

'If he'd danced ten miles in three hours, I'm surprised he could still stand up, never mind recoursing to a surgeon. Was the small village Reivers?'

'It doesn't actually say so, but it does say that one of Kempe's company called it the "village of the rioters".'

'So?'

'Reive or reiver is an old English word – or actually old Scottish, I think – for rioter,' said Phin. 'And Arabella said Reivers had been tangled up with the Peasants' Revolt in thirteen hundred and something.'

'Aren't you making a bit of a leap of faith, though? Have some more plum sauce.'

'Kempe and his gang seem to have enjoyed themselves in the village,' said Phin, still reading. 'Apparently on the first night, "Master Kempe made much merrimentes in the local tavern with home-brewed cyder".'

'Elizabethan equivalent of getting rat-arsed,' nodded Toby. 'I like the sound of Kempe.'

'And he agreed to "give the locals his Morrice on the morrow"—'

'You'd have to say he had an eye for a phrase,' said Toby, approvingly. 'Write that down for Arabella's PR stuff.'

'I will. Oh, and Kempe and his gang were "much cheered" by the reception they received,' said Phin. 'There was great carousing, and *Tydings* reported that three people were taken up by the Watch for poaching, some local girls were hustled away for soliciting, and two cut-purses, found to have pilfered several people's pockets, were sentenced to spend the following afternoon in the pillory – "which pronouncement caused great delight among the company, it being generally agreed that there was nothing to beat a good pillory, and shouts being heard to the inn-keeper to put aside some bags of rotting tomatoes and windfall apples".' He glanced at Toby, and grinned. 'Good, isn't it?'

'Very Merrie England. There's nothing like an afternoon spent pelting poor sods in the pillory with rotten fruit.'

'But,' went on Phin, '*Tydings* reported that it was in that village that Kempe is believed to have given his final public performance, even though, "his chronicler tried most earnestly to persuade him against it".'

'I wonder why that was.'

'No idea. But it goes on to say, "Contemporary accounts do indeed suggest Master Kempe never did perform again anywhere. A veil of secrecy seems to have been drawn down over his time there . . . local people only ever spoke of his sojourn there in whispers, but it was said that Master Kempe was a changed man afterwards. He is believed never to have talked of his time in Reivers, and thereafter sank into obscurity, dying some two or possibly three years hence". Then there's a bit about Kempe's earlier career, and his "august and lively years with William Shakespeare and Richard Tarlton", and how he had been one of a core of five actor-shareholders in the company of the Lord Chamberlain's Men, alongside Shakespeare and Burbage.'

He sat back frowning, his eyes still on the page. 'So there was a mystery, and whatever it was, Kempe never referred to it, and local people only spoke of it in whispers.' He sat back. 'I'd like to know a bit more about that,' he said. 'About the whispers and the veil of secrecy.'

'You're sure, are you, that you aren't seeing a mystery where there isn't one?'

'No, I'm not sure at all,' said Phin. 'But I'd like to know a bit more. I'd certainly like to know a bit more about the Murder Dance of Norfolk.'

'I'd like to know more about the companion – the chronicle-writer – who tried most earnestly to stop Kempe giving that last performance,' said Toby. 'Who was it, and why did he – or she – think Kempe shouldn't give a performance in that village?' He frowned, then said, 'D'you want the remains of the duck?'

SIX

Greenberry's diaries, circa 1600

When Will Kempe approached me fourteen days ago in London, I was startled, but rather complimented. He wanted, he explained, a proper account to be kept of a journey he was about to make – a dancing odyssey he was calling it, he said, giving me a crooked, rather endearing grin. He intended to keep a small diary of his own, but he had thought he would also like a more detailed chronicle. It was – I would understand – impossible to know what people were saying when you were capering across a market square or dancing along the streets of a town, not to mention coping with the intricacies of a hobby-horse which had the annoying habit of twisting a leg in the wrong direction due to a loosened joint. The hobby, said Master Kempe, seriously, formed a part of a good many of his dances.

I said, thoughtfully, 'All the small side stories of local people – all the little interplays of the people who will come out to watch you.'

'Yes,' he said, clearly pleased. 'We'll discuss the putting of money in the purse – you're a professional man, Master Greenberry, and should be paid accordingly. But I expect we'll find we can "clap hands and a bargain".'

I supposed that, having worked with the Stratford dramatist, it was to be expected that he would throw in a quote or two from the plays. But we clapped hands, solemnly and firmly, especially since, when it came to the putting of the money in the purse, he was more than generous. This is not something to be lightly regarded; a man must eat and pay his modest reckoning at his lodgings, even if the lodgings are only two rooms in Cheapside. Even so, rent has to be paid each quarter, and Master Kempe's idea of what was suitable by way of a fee was very acceptable.

I have not said that in my own mind I have the writings of Geoffrey Chaucer's *Canterbury Tales* as my model for this task, but I should like to make this into a modern version of Master Chaucer's *Tales*. I could title it *The Travels of Will Kempe – Chronicles of a Dauncer* (the Chaucerian spelling of 'dancer' pleases me), and in it would be the various small tales and incidental adventures of the people we meet along the way.

I have not mentioned this intention to Master Kempe, of course, nor to the two somewhat lugubrious persons who have accompanied us as servant and musician.

*   *   *

And so we embarked on the 'Nine Days', and it has to be said that we have received warm welcomes in all the places we visited. Master Kempe was delighted at the way people turned out to watch him, and how they cheered him.

His own notes are somewhat erratic, and we have already lost most of his account of the performance at Chelmsford, when he tipped over a burning candle and it scorched the entire page and spilled melted tallow over the adjoining ones. It's one of life's ironies, though, that his version will probably be the one to survive the years, while mine will end in being flung on a rubbish heap, or used for kindling.

I expect I shall scratch out that last sentence tomorrow, before Master Kempe can see it. This is not an unusual practice for a writer. Several of my master's theatrical confrères produced very questionable original drafts for some of their stage works. In at least two cases, I know for a fact that the piece that finally reached the stage bore scant resemblance to the original concept. I mention no names in this respect, though.

Earlier today we reached the Norfolk village of Reivers. It had not been planned that we would come here as part of Master Kempe's dancing jaunt – in fact, we had finished the entire jaunt two days earlier. However, it is easy to misunderstand a signpost at a crossroads, especially when the signpost's lettering is so weathered it is almost unreadable in a downpour of rain. I did apologize, and Master Kempe was very nice about it.

And now I'm seated in a room with a window looking down onto a courtyard, and I'm writing this while events are still fresh in my mind – and doing so by the light of a warm fire and several candles in wall sconces.

The Tabor is a strange house – part private residence and part tavern. The courtyard below our rooms, we've been told, is sometimes used for local entertainments. Certainly it would lend itself to that very well.

It seemed to be expected that we would go into the tavern part of the house to join a company of locals. Word of our arrival had spread, and the long oak-beamed room was crowded. There was a roaring fire in the hearth at one end of the room, a friendly welcome, and wooden-topped tables set with platters of food. Tankards of ale and cider were circulating very freely indeed.

It's remarkable how a few tankards of ale start people singing and, once the singing did start, it was lusty and loud. It's a pity that three people had their pockets pilfered, and that a couple of the local girls were taken up by the Watch for lewd approaches to some of the men, but I suppose Reivers is no different from the rest of the world, and these are things that happen everywhere.

At this point, I had better record that nobody made any lewd approaches to me, and if any were made to my master, I didn't see them, although to be fair he was standing on a table for much of the night, so any such proposition would have been quite public. Also, the parish parson, one Humbert Marplot, was among the company, which I thought might have restrained the ladies' behaviour. That is to say, I thought it at the time, but later I changed my opinion, because Parson Marplot, having sunk a goodly quantity of ale, took the centre of the floor to render for the company a ballad detailing the misfortunes of a Norfolk gentleman, who, confronted with a lady of voracious appetite, was quite unable to satisfy her requirements. The parson sang it loudly and with vigour, although it was not at all the kind of song I would have expected from a man of the cloth. However, I thought it as well to write down the verses there and then, since Master Kempe is always eager to add a new ballad to his collection. For that reason I always have writing materials to hand, although I would add that in this instance, even I, who have heard a good many of the more rustic terms in the English language, had to pause several times to think how to spell some of the words in the parson's song.

It was near the end of our convivial evening that my master, likely invigorated by the amount of wine he had drunk, made his announcement. With considerable exuberance, he told them that tomorrow afternoon he would give a special dance for them.

'I see your splendid courtyard,' he said, waving a hand in the vague direction of the window, beyond which the courtyard could just be glimpsed. 'And so I shall give you my Morrice on the Morrow, that's what I shall do.'

This was greeted with cheers, and then someone called out to say that if Master Kempe would indeed give them of one of his jigs – a special performance for the people of Reivers, you might call it – then the people of Reivers, by way of reciprocation (the voice had to make three attempts at the word), then they would put on their own special performance that same evening in return.

At once suggestions were made as to what might be performed, and a heated argument began between two rival factions. However, a determined voice rang out, shouting down the rest. 'Only one dance we can give on such an occasion,' said this voice.

'Ho, Master Grindall, and what might that dance be?'

Master Grindall, unseen by myself until then, strode to the centre of the room and took up a challenging stance.

'Why,' he said, beetling his brows at his listeners, and hooking his thumbs in his belt, 'what else should we give our guests other than our very own piece of history? Tomorrow night, as the sun sets, we'll perform for Master Kempe and his company the famous and ancient Reivers Dance itself.'

An extraordinary silence fell on the room, and people glanced at one another. Then someone – I think it was one of the women – called out, 'How about the old legend? Aren't you worried about that, Jeremiah Grindall?'

'No, I am not,' said Jeremiah Grindall, still standing in the room's centre.

And still no one responded, but after another few moments – Master Kempe and I glanced at one another, half wondering if we should intervene – someone else called out, 'Well, 'course he isn't worried. Catch Jeremiah worried about anything – not in a pig's eye, you wouldn't. Caper across a legend any day, those Grindalls. Nimble Grindalls, that's what they call them.'

There was some laughter, but there was affection in it, and the odd little moment seemed to have passed. There now seemed to be general acceptance that this dance, whatever it was, should be performed, and everyone who could manage it should join in.

'Could we do it, though?' asked a worried voice from a corner. 'For it hasn't been seen for – well, since Evelyn Rivers was put to the sword in that very courtyard.'

There was a vague murmur of acknowledgement of this, but then a sprightly old gentleman banged the table with his fist, and said that o'course they could do it.

'It was writ down since many a long year and more,' he declared. 'And I say it should be performed again, and we'll remember Evelyn Rivers when we do it. That's the way to honour our ancestors,' he said, glaring round the room.

'I say we leave the Reivers Dance where it is,' said the first voice. 'Blood-tainted, that's what it is. Because for why was Evelyn executed that day? For speaking out against the King, that was for why. Richard II it was on the Throne in those days, and him no more than a beardless boy at the time, and ruled by his ministers. Evelyn Rivers should have known better, I say.'

The elderly one was not having this. 'It's part of our history, the Reivers Dance,' he said. 'We don't forget our history in Reivers, and we don't forget Evelyn, neither. I say we perform it.'

'Also,' piped up Master Grindall, 'the Dance is still there in church records, all wrote down, and all parson's got to do is open the records, and there it'll be for us to follow.'

'If,' muttered the doubter from the other corner, 'someone'll read it all out for them as aren't in the way of reading.'

But this gloomy view was drowned by a cheer, and people began to say that of course they ought to revive the Dance, for wasn't this the famous Master Kempe all the way from London? And of course they'd all be able to follow the steps, never mind if it did have to be read out for some of them.

The worried section thought they ought to go along to the church to find the writing that very night, for you couldn't tell how easy it might be to lay hand on the paper, but Parson Marplot said no one need trouble about that; he knew exactly where to put his hand on the Dance, and they would look it out first thing in the morning. There could be a bit of a practice, he said. He was in favour of honouring the past, as his forebears in Reivers church had been. He beamed and pretended not to hear several people muttering that earlier Reivers' parsons had been nothing but ranters, and that there was a story of how one former incumbent had been thrown into the local duckpond for preaching against the taking of strong drink on the Sabbath.

'How times change,' observed someone else, eyeing Parson Marplot's newly replenished tankard of ale.

And now, in my own room, on the comfortable window seat that looks down over that very courtyard, I'm setting it all down while it's still fresh in my mind. I should also set down that I don't like the sound of the Reivers Dance. I don't care how far back its origins are, or even if it was handed down by William the Conqueror when he landed at Hastings, or whether the druids offered it in pagan libation in the deep past – I'm increasingly unhappy about its performance tomorrow.

I wonder whether I can persuade Master Kempe to leave Reivers at first light tomorrow.

*   *   *

Phin had suspected that tracking down information about Will Kempe would be difficult, and it was looking as if he had been right. He had not yet tracked down a copy of Kempe's own account of his nine days' dance from London to Norfolk. Except for the vague mentions of Kempe in the seventeenth-century *Tydings*, and the even vaguer hints of an old Norfolk dancing legend in the turgid work on clowns, jesters and wise fools, all he had unearthed was a waspish exchange between a pair of eighteenth-century academics. One of these gentlemen stated truculently that Will Kempe had been illiterate, while the other said that although Kempe had possessed no classical learning, he had been very far from illiterate – you had only to remember his famous *Nine Daies' Wonder*. This had brought forth a scoffing rejoinder that everyone knew perfectly well that Will Kempe had employed a chronicler on his journey, and that it was the chronicler who had written the *Nine Daies' Wonder*, very likely spicing it up on his own account, since it was believed that he (the chronicler), had been one of the worst womanizers in London, and had rogered his way across

Norfolk and had met some nameless, but probably apt, fate there as a result.

Phin's attention was instantly caught, and he was just wondering whether it would be possible to track down the chronicler, when an email from Arabella announced itself as having arrived. Anything involving Arabella would certainly be more cheerful than carping eighteenth-century scholars, so Phin abandoned Will and the ill-fated chronicler, and read the email.

> Phin, dear,
>
> This wretched phone signal is still refusing to make any real connection – we had a reasonable series of crackles earlier, didn't we, but only about one word in ten was audible – although at least we'll be connecting in a better sense tomorrow. I'm looking forward to you seeing The Daunsen and the ancient sketch of The Tabor, and most of all I'm looking forward to you seeing The Tabor itself. Because this morning I saw it.
>
> I was eating my breakfast, and I'd found a couple of old books on local history in a little antique in the square outside – gorgeous old place, and there's a separate little book section, so you'll have to see that when you get here. I'd got one of the books propped up against the marmalade pot so I could make a few notes about the Peasants' Revolt. There was a really good chapter on how several Reivers' people had been involved, but were squashed by Henry le Despenser who had them summarily executed. It all sounded very public and grisly.
>
> I was just trying to decide whether any of this would fit into a modern-day publicity campaign, when Quentin materialized at the table. He sat down, and asked if I could go out to The Tabor later that day. He added (with a smiling shrug) that he supposed he had to regard himself as Rivers of Reivers. Can you believe he actually said that! It made me think about robber barons, and all the ribald old practices like *droit du seigneur* – or do I mean that other thing – *jus primae noctis*? Anyway, that trad- ition where the lord of the manor had first go at any local

maidens who took his eye, particularly on the night before the girl's wedding. Literally, 'Right of the first night', the licentious old goats. Can you imagine using that one on today's, 'Your place or mine?' generation? Nobody's actually said that the inhabitants of Reivers ever did any of those things, of course, but still.

According to Quentin, a builder and a surveyor were due at the house that morning, and Quentin had the idea that it might be useful for me to be in on some of the renovation plans. I'd suggested to him last evening that we could do some 'before, during and after' illustrations.

'You won't expect too much at this stage, will you?' said Quentin, leaving me to the marmalade pot and the Peasants' Revolt. 'Drive straight in – I'll leave the gates open for you.' From his tone, he might easily have been saying, 'I'll have the drawbridge lowered.'

'It isn't in a very good state of repair,' he added. 'But you'll be able to look beyond that, I know.'

Fortunately, Toby's car was returned this morning, so I was able to drive out there under my own steam. The Tabor is in a very bad state of repair indeed, even to my untutored eye. But the brickwork has that marvellous coppery glow that you only ever see in a genuinely old house, and if it really is fifteenth or sixteenth century, you have to hand it to the Tudors, who might have pillaged and plundered and beheaded regardless, but who knew how to build. I think it must have been a beautiful house in its heyday, with sunshine on lawns and well-mannered children playing in the gardens. But it's clearly a very long time since it had a heyday, or any kind of day at all.

The builder was already there. He turned out to be a chatty soul wearing a colourful jumper, and his van proclaimed him to be George Grindall, and his company master builders to the county since the 1800s.

We set off on the tour, with George Grindall taking measurements and making gleeful notes as he totted up how much everything was going to cost. The surveyor arrived while we were halfway round. He jabbed spiky things into bits of woodwork and muttered about

Coniophora puteana, and how the roof has *Merulius lacrymans*. I politely asked for clarification, and it turns out that one is wet rot and the other is dry rot. I suppose he thought it would sound better in Latin, although I should think it'll be expensive to remedy no matter what language you put it into.

I helped Mr Grindall to prop his stepladder against a wall in the attics, so he could get into the roof space. He was very nice when I got part of the ladder wedged between two joists, causing a section of timber to fall onto his toe. He said it was a thing that could happen to anyone, and it went to show what a shocking state the woodwork was in. The surveyor muttered in Latin again, and Mr Grindall added another row of figures to his scribbled estimate.

Then we tramped around the bedroom floor. They all made notes, and I tried to look serious and scholarly.

'This'll have been old Osbert's room, I daresay,' said Mr Grindall, opening a door on to a large, high-ceilinged room with grubby wall hangings and a rickety-looking four-poster.

It appears that Osbert Rivers is the gentleman who died recently, leaving the house to Quentin. Mr Grindall confided that he had had a great-aunt who used to do a bit of cleaning at the house in her youth. 'A few of the local girls did,' he said. 'They were always very strictly supervised, though. My great-aunt used to tell that Osbert Rivers had been a bit of a lively lad at times. In fact, Miss Tallis, she often said that the four-poster in this room could tell a few tales.' (At this point he gestured to the four-poster.) 'Not meaning any disrespect, of course,' he added, with one eye on the door, where Quentin was holding a glum conversation with the surveyor.

I was about to ask him about Osbert, but Quentin came back into the room, clearly having heard most of the conversation, and obviously ready to quell the over-familiar peasants. Mr Grindall began to talk determinedly about window frames, and Quentin frowned at him, then went away to measure something.

And now I don't know whether to regard The Tabor as a fascinating old country house, and a possible source of robust gossip, or whether to see it as just a crumbling ruin, best left to its own devices.

PS . . . You notice I haven't once mentioned the possibility of it being haunted.

Typing a suitable reply, Phin was not inclined to think very favourably of Quentin Rivers, who seemed to have such astonishing ideas of feudalism, and who invited a female into a rickety old house with rotten timbers and unreliable floors. But he was becoming increasingly intrigued by The Tabor, although when it came to ghosts he was going to reserve judgement.

Driving to Norfolk with Toby on Sunday morning, he tried to think that Reivers would be an ordinary English market town with no more melodrama and murder in its past than any other village.

Toby provided an enthusiastic commentary on their route, telling Phin where Arabella had misread the map and taken them miles out of their way; he had also tried phoning and texting Zillah several times without any success.

'But she'll be very busy,' he said, firmly. 'She and her cousin will have a great many things to do. She'll be waiting for me at the pub, though.'

SEVEN

Zillah had decided she would be conveniently out of the way when Toby reached The Daunsen on Sunday. In a way it was a pity not to allow things to develop, and Toby had certainly been smitten from the outset. But she would need to tread a very delicate path with Quentin for the next week or two, and she did not want to risk doing anything that might antagonize him. Also, Quentin's bedroom at The Daunsen was next to Zillah's, so he would know – and hear – everything she did, and who she did it with.

She would not brush Toby away altogether, of course, mainly because he had offered to invest in Quentin's project, and although no actual amount had been mentioned, Zillah was not going to upset things to the extent of losing out on any funds that might be coming in, because she was starting to see that if she really did put her plan into action, whatever went into Quentin's bank account might end up in her own.

Toby had texted to say he and Phineas Fox would probably reach Reivers shortly after lunch, so Zillah had an early snack at The Daunsen, then went out to explore. There would not be much to see on a Sunday afternoon, but she would rather be out of the way when they arrived.

Reivers was too big to be called a village – it had been added to, and small modern housing estates had grown up around it over the years – but it was nowhere near large enough to qualify as a town. There was an ancient church, but even from the footpath it looked small and damp and as if it would be filled with sad echoes, so she thought she would not bother, and instead came back into the square. She peered in one or two of the shop windows – there was a little antique shop, which was called Savory Antiques and which had a sign over its door saying, 'Proud to be a family-owned business since 1920'. Zillah had been into the shop the previous day; there was a lot of old furniture and things which were probably quite valuable, and the Savorys were two rather frumpy ladies who might be any age between fifty and seventy. They had been delighted when Zillah bought a jade necklace from a display of Victorian jewellery, and explained eagerly that she might not have seen any of it at all if it had not been for Miss Tallis visiting the shop earlier. They did not normally put jewellery on open display, they explained – you could not be too careful these days, could you?

Miss Tallis had been particularly interested in their small stock of books about local history, and while she was looking through them, somehow or other the locked glass-topped case of jewellery had been tipped off its plinth, and everything had tumbled out on to the floor. She had insisted on putting everything back for them, and had crawled into all the little corners, which was very helpful, because their rheumatics made getting down like that a bit awkward for them. But she had fielded some mourning brooches with locks of hair, and a bracelet, and also a necklace that was said to have been worn at the famous Waterloo Ball in 1815, and which it would have been a pity to have lost down the gap in the floorboards. The glass top had been perfectly intact, but Miss Tallis had insisted on going along to the little local stationer's shop to buy them a length of green baize by way of apology, which had certainly not been necessary, and had helped to rearrange the entire display against it. The sisters would not have thought of green baize, which they associated with billiard tables, but when it was all set out, they were extremely pleased, because the baize made a very nice background indeed for the jewellery.

But Savory's was firmly closed this afternoon, and everywhere was shrouded in what Zillah supposed was a Sabbath hush, so there was nothing to do but return to The Daunsen. Annoyingly Toby was in the little bar by the main reception area. He had a newspaper propped up on the table, but Zillah knew he would have been watching for her.

'I've missed you,' he said, jumping up and putting out his hands. 'Didn't you get my calls?'

'Oh, did you try to call? The signal here is dreadful.'

'Never mind, I'm here now,' he said. 'Let's go up to my room – or yours – before dinner. Just so we can have an hour alone to catch up on how our week's been. I'm looking forward to hearing how it's all going with The Tabor and what you've been doing.'

He had made this kind of overture soon after their meeting, but Zillah had declined, and she was going to decline now. Even if she had intended to let this go further, it was far too soon for the bed thing. She was not having Toby or anyone else think she was no better than a tart.

So she smiled and said, 'It's really lovely to see you again, Toby, but at the moment I need to talk to Quentin about something. Would you mind? There's so much to do – I hadn't realized how much there would be. And The Tabor . . .' A slightly bewildered gesture of hands. 'So time-consuming. I'll see you at dinner, though, of course.'

'Good. You've got to meet Phin, too, of course.'

'I'm looking forward to that,' said Zillah, and escaped to her room.

She had packed a really smart dark blue two-piece, which she could wear this evening to meet Phineas Fox. Trying the effect of the jade necklace against it, she remembered how Arabella's voice had changed when she had talked about Phineas that morning. How must it be to feel like that about someone? Zillah could not imagine ever doing so, but she was becoming curious about Phineas Fox, who brought that lift to Arabella's voice. He was something to do with research – music and history, seemingly, and he sounded rather distinguished. He might be quite well-off, though, and if so, it would be a pity that he was linked to Arabella. In the normal way something might have been done about that, but Zillah's mind was too taken up with The Tabor. Because the plan she had glimpsed that first day in the house had pushed its way a little more into the light. She still was not intending to actually put it into action, although . . .

Although the more she thought about it, the more possible it began to seem.

The timing had to be right, though. Old Codling was going to draft a will for Quentin, so if she was going to do anything, it ought to be after the will had been done. Zillah was not going to take huge risks and then find it had all been for nothing. She would wait until the will was drawn up and signed, and then she would think again.

But she found she was already thinking. She was thinking how the house itself might be her ally – exactly as it had been all those years ago when Evelyn . . . No. Shut that thought down.

Still, it had to be remembered that Quentin had no real right to The Tabor, so there would be a kind of poetic justice if the house turned on him. There was a great deal wrong with the place, and tragic things could happen in such a ramshackle building. There were loose gutterings on the edges of the roof that might become dislodged when someone was standing beneath them. There were floorboards that were rotten and that might collapse when trodden on, sending someone tumbling through.

She went on thinking.

Phin and Arabella stood in front of the sketch in The Daunsen's bar.

'*Cwellan Daunsen*,' said Phin, staring at it.

'Yes. It's faded and a bit smudged, but that's certainly The Tabor.'

The sketch was very faded, but its outlines were clear and Phin sat down in front of it.

'It's odd that it's here, not in The Tabor itself, isn't it?'

'I thought that, but then I thought that somebody probably saw the word *Daunsen* and assumed it was something to do with the pub,' said Arabella. 'And commandeered it. What is it? Have you seen something I've missed?'

'I'm not sure.' Phin glanced around and caught the eye of the waitress who was polishing glasses behind the bar. 'Is it all right if I take that old sketch down for a moment? It's an interesting drawing – I'd like to take a closer look.'

'Sure you can take it down. Mind it doesn't bring the wall down with it, though, because it's been there since forever. Call out if you want anything.'

The sketch, carefully lifted from its hook, did not bring the wall down, and Phin set it on a table, turning it towards the window so that the light fell across it.

After a moment, he said, 'If you were going to draw a building – any building – wouldn't you position it centre stage, so to speak? Set it against its surroundings so that it's framed by sky or trees and things?'

'Yes.'

'This isn't centred at all. It's crammed onto one side of the paper. Almost as if—'

He broke off, and Arabella said, 'Almost as if this is only half the sketch.'

'Exactly.'

'I hadn't seen that,' said Arabella. 'I was more interested in the title. But you're right. Could this have been cut off a larger sketch? I know that sounds weird, but if part of the original was damaged, someone could have folded it to hide the damaged part . . . You're looking doubtful.'

'I expect I'm seeing mysteries where mysteries don't exist,' said Phin, 'but you're looking for material for Quentin's PR campaign, and there're all these hints about the Reivers Dance—'

'Which some sources call the Murder Dance.'

'Yes. I wonder how secure this frame is? It's not much more than a sheet of card held in place by a clip at each corner.'

'Can you . . .?' began Arabella, then stopped, because Phin was already twisting the clips back. The card stayed in place, but when he slid a fingernail into the edge it came free, bringing with it the accreted dust and dried glue of years. Shreds of old, dry paper showered down, and with them came a faint scent of age. But inside, hidden from view . . .

'You were right,' said Arabella, in a half-whisper. 'The sketch was folded in half. And whoever drew it did set The Tabor in the centre of the paper – if you flatten it out you see the whole drawing – sky all around, and that clump of trees, and the bit of path winding around the side, just there. Phin, be careful, it's been folded for so long it'll split if you so much as breathe on it.'

'I am being careful. I was hoping there might be a date or a signature, but I can't see one, and I daren't lift the whole thing out of the frame – it's too fragile. I suppose it could be carbon-dated or something – or is it radiocarbon they use now?'

'No idea. It looks like quite good-quality paper, and it's been drawn with a lot of attention to detail,' said Arabella. She leaned forward to see more closely, and a strand of her hair brushed Phin's face, but for once he hardly noticed. 'Phin, why would anyone fold the sketch like this? It isn't damaged or anything. I suppose it wouldn't be something as mundane as this being the only size of frame that could be got at the time?'

'I wouldn't have thought so, although we'd better keep that in mind, because . . . Oh,' said Phin, in a different voice. 'Look at that.'

'What? Where?'

'On the right, near the edge of the whole drawing – the

part that was hidden. Are they outbuildings? Didn't you say something about a courtyard and a kind of extra wing?'

'There is a courtyard,' said Arabella, eagerly. 'At least, there's the remains of one. And it looked as if there was a set of extra rooms – quite substantial, ground and upper floor, sort of enclosing the courtyard on three sides It looked a bit dismal and the lower half was just a blank wall. Maybe old stables that were bricked up.'

'Look at those two windows at the far end.'

Arabella bent over the sketch again. After a moment, she said, 'Bars? At two of the windows? Or is it another crease in the paper . . . No, it is bars, isn't it?' She frowned, then said, 'Phin, there's someone inside those rooms. Someone looking out through the bars.'

'Yes. It even looks as if fingers are curled around the bars.'

Arabella said, in a whisper, 'A prisoner. Someone clutching the bars, staring out – staring down into the courtyard beneath.' She sat back, her eyes still on the sketch. 'That's why it was folded, isn't it? Whoever did it, didn't want to lose the sketch, but wanted to hide the barred rooms and the person shut away in them.'

'It's a reasonable assumption,' said Phin. 'Don't look like that – whatever the truth of all this, it was a very long time ago.' He glanced towards the bar again, then said, quietly, 'See if you can stand between this table and the bar, so I can get a photo of this without the staff realizing. Not that there's any reason why I wouldn't photograph it, but still . . . OK,' he said after a couple of moments. 'I managed two shots, and they might be a bit fuzzy, because the light isn't brilliant, but it ought to be enough for us to study later if it seems useful.'

He folded the sketch carefully back into the frame, then said, 'Let's look at this as a piece of ordinary research. Let's try to uncover a bit more of The Tabor's history. Former owners. Local newspaper articles – or no, newspaper records would more likely be stored in the nearest town, wouldn't they? Norwich, even. It's not very far to go, though – we could do that after the weekend. How about parish registers – records of births and deaths and marriages?'

'There's a village church,' said Arabella. 'It's only just off the square – there's a footpath. Ten minutes' walk at most.'

'That would be a good start. Gravestones with inscriptions – memorial plaques on pews. It ought to be open on a Sunday afternoon.'

As they walked across the square, Phin looking with interest at the shops, noting a bookshop and Savory Antiques, Arabella said, 'Phin, why would someone go to the trouble of drawing that courtyard with the rooms overlooking it and the barred windows and the prisoner – and then fold it over like that?'

'It mightn't have been the artist who did the folding and hiding,' said Phin. 'It might have been whoever did the imprisoning. Two different people.'

'But why not simply destroy the whole sketch?' demanded Arabella. 'Why not tear it into tiny pieces and fling them to the four winds? Or burn it and scatter the ashes on hallowed ground?'

'I don't know. Is this the footpath to the church?'

The footpath was between a small wine shop and Savory Antiques. There were trees fringing it, and at the far end was a rather weather-beaten lychgate with, beyond it, rows of well-tended graves. Several of the memorial stones were slightly askew where the ground would have settled over the years.

As they walked up to the porch, Arabella said, 'With all the build-up about ancient mysteries and prisoners locked in barred rooms and Dancing Murderers, I almost feel as if we should have a background of organ music to play us into the church, don't you? The one that's the classic horror-film introduction would do nicely. You know the one I mean – huge crashing chords accompanying shots of ancient crypts and cobwebby stone pillars and an overgrown graveyard.'

'"Toccata and Fugue in D Minor",' said Phin. 'Usually ascribed to J.S. Bach.' He paused, then said, 'But if I were to walk into a church with you and organ music was playing, I don't think we'd want to have horror-film harmony, would we?'

He felt her start of surprise, and he was in fact aware of his own surprise. Did I mean to say that? thought Phin. And if I did, what was behind it? Before Arabella could react, and before he could explore this any deeper, he said, 'This doesn't look like a horror-film church, does it?'

He had a brief impression that she was searching for the right response, but then she just said, 'It's nice, isn't it? Look at that lovely old bell tower and the spire – and that gorgeous stained-glass window. And the graveyard didn't look in the least overgrown. Quite the reverse. This is more Parson Woodforde and *Diary of a Country Parson* than Dracula rising from the crypt.'

The moment's gone, thought Phin, and then he wondered if there had even been a moment, or, if there had, what the moment had held. They stepped into the shadowy old porch, and he reached for the iron ring handle of the door, prepared for the church to be locked up. But the handle turned easily, and the door creaked open.

'Dim and peaceful and beautiful,' said Arabella, standing just inside the door, and looking round with pleasure. 'Polish and age and something that might even be a whiff of incenses. None of it at all conducive to sinister murderers or Bach fugues.'

The polished pews were quiet and dim, apart from small splashes of colour here and there from several embroidered hassocks. It was a very small church, with no alluring cupboards or even, apparently, a vestry, and Phin, who was enjoying the tranquillity and the sense that centuries of music and prayer had soaked into these walls, thought any records would probably be in the vicar's keeping, under lock and key.

They walked slowly around, but there did not seem to be anything related to the Rivers family.

'But we'll come back and try to talk to the vicar to see if there are any archives we can look through,' said Phin, as they retraced their steps and went back out.

As they walked down the path towards the lychgate, Arabella suddenly said, 'There's a brass plate on that bench over there. D'you see? It's probably just a memorial to some long-dead local person, or a defunct vicar, or something, but—'

'But there could be a useful name or a date on it,' said Phin, as they went across the grass.

The bench was very typical of the kind of benches people often donated to churchyards and cemeteries to commemorate a lost loved one.

'It is a memorial,' said Arabella.

'Yes. It's a bit worn, but it's just about readable. Where's my notebook? Can you make it out and I'll note it down?'

Arabella sat on the end of the bench and leaned across to see the plaque more closely. 'It says, "*In grateful thanks to Walter Rivers who generously made available to the Parish of Reivers a part of his residence, The Tabor, to be used as almshouses for the indigent and needy of Reivers*".'

'Is there a date?' said Phin, writing this down.

'I can't see one . . . Oh, wait, yes, I can, it's in quite small lettering in one corner. June 1921,' said Arabella. She sat back, still looking at the small oblong with its lettering. 'So part of The Tabor was turned into almshouses. That's quite interesting. I should think it would have been the courtyard rooms. They're more or less separate from the house.'

Phin sat next to her, and reached for his phone to take a close-up shot of the brass plate. 'You don't find it a bit odd that Walter Rivers handed over part of his house?' he said.

'Do you?'

'Well, that date – 1921. The Great War swept aside a lot of the class divide, but I should think that in small villages like Reivers it would still have been very much evident. I'm wondering whether Walter would have turned The Tabor into an open house to the – what's that wording? The indigent and the needy?'

'Homeless people,' said Arabella, nodding. 'People who fell on hard times. He might have done. He might have been an out-and-out philanthropist.'

'It would be nice to think so. I'm all for helping people who need it. How closely did you look at the courtyard section while you were there? Was there anything on a wall anywhere?'

'I didn't see anything, although I wasn't looking. I don't think there were any signs saying, "This way for a night's lodging", though.'

Phin said, 'I wonder why this memorial is out here? I wonder why it isn't inside the church? I don't know a great deal about almshouses, but I think they were tied up with the church. You'd expect someone who had made such a massive donation – giving over part of his own house for the poor – to be mentioned in the church itself.'

Arabella stared at him. 'You think there's something peculiar about the almshouses? That they weren't real? That they were – what? – a smokescreen?'

'I can't really see what they could be a smokescreen for, though.'

'There could be masses of things,' said Arabella, promptly. 'How about if Walter was storing smuggled goods – no, Reivers is a bit far from the coast for that, isn't it? Or wait, he might have had a printing press in there and a gang of forgers working for him. Or an illicit still for brewing hooch and flogging to The Daunsen . . . Oh, and here's a lovely one – maybe he was a member of one of those furtive organizations for assassinating kings and heads of states, or getting pretenders on to thrones. Like the Black Hand crowd who assassinated the Archduke in Sarajevo and triggered the Great War, or those earnest little groups drinking to the King over the Water and trying to restore Bonnie Prince Charlie. Or what if he was part of a Black Magic sect like that one in the nineteenth century – the Golden Dawn, was it called? – with Aleister Crowley trying to summon the devil – no, that's a bit off the wall, isn't it?'

Phin said, slowly, 'How about the almshouse set-up being a cover for someone shut away in a barred room?'

'A secret prisoner? That sketch – *Cwellan Daunsen*? Phin, I know I get a bit carried away, but you're straying into *Prisoner of Zenda* territory now. Or *The Man in the Iron Mask*.'

'But,' said Phin, 'in that sketch is a prisoner looking through bars in one of The Tabor's courtyard rooms. And somebody folded the sketch in half so that the prisoner couldn't be seen.'

Arabella stared at him. 'But that sketch shows The Tabor at least two, if not three centuries ago. I'm sure it's much older than 1921.' She shuddered. 'I can't get that image of the prisoner and the bars out of my mind.'

Phin put his arm round her. 'It'll probably turn out to be all perfectly ordinary and innocent,' he said. 'Don't let it give you nightmares.'

'I'll try. But if I wake up screaming, at least you'll be there tonight, won't you?'

'Yes,' he said, very quietly. 'I always will be.'

She looked at him, and he felt the atmosphere change between them. Then she said very quietly, 'I'm glad about that.'

'I'm glad you're glad.'

The moment lengthened, then with an effort, Phin said in a down-to-earth voice, 'I expect there's a perfectly ordinary explanation,' He got up and held out a hand to her, and as they went through the lychgate and along the footpath towards The Daunsen, he suddenly said, 'Let's forget about Dancing Murderers and vengeful executions and dubious almshouses for a while. D'you realize that I've been here for several hours, and we haven't done anything yet about being reunited after a week apart.'

'We haven't, have we?' Arabella's eyes lit up.

'What time is dinner?'

'Any time from seven on. And it's only half past four, now,' said Arabella.

'So it is.' Phin held out his hand, and she took it. 'Is Toby likely to be around for the next couple of hours, do you think?' he said. 'Not that I'm not always pleased to see him, but—'

'I'm always pleased to see him, as well,' said Arabella. 'But just for once, shall we tiptoe past his bedroom so he doesn't hear us? Let's pretend we're in a French farce, and I'm smuggling you into my bedchamber. Or we can be in D.H. Lawrence, and you can be the sexy gamekeeper—'

'Arabella, you don't know how much I've missed your inconsequence,' said Phin, smiling at her.

'Well then, Mellors, come and be consequential upstairs.'

A considerable time later, Arabella said, 'Phin, have you fallen asleep or are you mentally looking for clues between Dancing Murderers and dubious philanthropists?'

Phin had been falling into a comfortable half-sleep, with Arabella's head against his shoulder, but he said, 'Only half-looking.'

'For Walter Rivers or Will Kempe?'

'Will Kempe,' he said, at once. 'And the Murder Dance.'

'I've been thinking about that, too. Could there really be a connection between Kempe and the Dance?'

'I don't know.' Phin sat up and reached for a pillow. 'I'm

trying not to make connections yet,' he said. 'But that material I found before I came here – always supposing it can be trusted – hints that something might have happened while Kempe was in Reivers. Always assuming it was Reivers, because it wasn't actually named. But then he died quite soon afterwards. "In poverty and unregarded".'

'That's sad, isn't it.'

'Yes, it is. He isn't especially revered or even particularly remembered,' said Phin, 'but he'd performed with some of the theatre world's finest in his day. He's supposed to have been Shakespeare's inspiration for Falstaff and he was hailed as the great clown actor of his day.'

'He's got to you, hasn't he? Oh – are you getting up?'

'Yes, although I'd much rather stay here, and maybe have some food sent up,' said Phin. 'But then we'd have to face Toby's knowing eye later.' He reached for his shirt. 'I hope Will Kempe doesn't turn out to be First Murderer,' he said. 'But he's not very well documented, so at the moment all I know about him for sure is that he danced his way from London to Norfolk and that he took nine days to do it.'

EIGHT

Greenberry's diaries, circa 1600

'd like to think that if anyone does read these pages, he or she might want to try forming a small mental image of the author – by which I mean me – scribbling away in an encroaching twilight, in a house on the edge of a Norfolk village. In case that unknown reader might consider likening me to Geoffrey Chaucer, I will explain that although I'm hoping I might emulate in some small way his *Tales*, I bear no resemblance to him physically. Instead, a rather thin-faced man should be pictured – pale, but not certainly sallow, and not a callow youth, although definitely not in the sere and yellow. I'd like it known that I am neither sallow nor callow nor yellow. Add to the image a flop of light brown hair which is slightly longer than the prevailing custom, owing to my ears being set slightly high which I do not care for, even though it has moved more than one lady to use the word 'elvish' about my looks. I do not care for being considered elvish either, which is why I wear my hair quite long. I sometimes look a bit careless.

The Tabor looks a bit careless as well. It's still a beautiful place, though – as lovely and imposing as any we've stayed in during our journey, and we have stayed in some very grand places as well as the more modest ones. The Tabor has been passed down over the generations – like the Reivers Dance – and now it's lived in by a brother and sister. Ralph Rivers, who has darting, watchful eyes. And his sister.

Rosalind Rivers.

I've heard men – occasionally ladies – lyricize about this kind of sudden lightning-strike feeling, but I never believed it existed. Until tonight. Because there was what I can only describe as recognition when I saw Rosalind Rivers – not recognition in the way you might see a friend and put out a hand in greeting, but something deeper. I looked at her, and the thought: *so here you are at last*, formed in my mind, exactly as if I had been waiting at a pre-arranged meeting – and as if she had arrived a little late, but arrived nonetheless. Because there she was. Black cloudy hair like smoke, and a little, sweet face, with guileless eyes, and a mouth that was made for mischief and kisses.

I suppose I sat there staring at her like a yokel, and she turned to look at me, almost as if she had felt my regard. She smiled – a slightly three-cornered smile it was, and absurd as I know this is going to sound, I had the sense of our minds locking. There was a feeling of such absolute *rightness*, that I simply sat there like a moonstruck youth. Eventually I managed to smile back, and the moment moved on.

Having reread those sentences, I see I was right. They do sound absurd.

And yet, and yet . . .

It's the wildest daydream man ever had to wonder if there could be a future for me with Rosalind Rivers. On a single meeting – on the basis of a smile exchanged through a smoke-filled room – I'm reshaping my entire life.

It's an impossibility. Rosalind belongs here – people have a place in the world; not all of them find that place, and a great many of them spend most of their lives searching for it. But some people are born into their rightful places, and I think The Tabor and Reivers is Rosalind's rightful place. Even if she did agree to leave, what sort of life could I possibly offer her? I have hardly any money, no property of my own, and precious little in the way of prospects.

There's also the question of her brother. He's presumably her sole male relative and her protector, and as such he would have to give his consent to her marriage. He might not be wealthy by many people's standards, but he's Rivers of Reivers, owner of The Tabor. He's hardly likely to hand over his sister to a penniless scribe she met yesterday – a man who has spent the last two weeks wandering the hedgerows and byways of England in company with an itinerant player.

Master Kempe is quite dejected about one aspect of our evening. This is very unlike him, but he's gloomily remembering how he blithely offered to provide his own entertainment for the local people.

'Morrice on the Morrow – that's what I said, wasn't it, Greenberry,' he's just said, glumly. 'I said I'd give them a Morrice on the Morrow. My God, man, why didn't you stop me?'

There's no point in telling him that at the time he said it, he was standing on a table, waving a tankard and leading a rousing chorus of 'Cuckolds All Awry'. It would have been nigh on impossible even to make my voice heard above the singing, never mind restrain him from scattering extravagant promises around. Nobody can restrain Will Kempe when he's leading a roomful of people in a song.

'Tell me I didn't say it,' he said, hopefully.

'You did say it, and in those very words. As a phrase, I thought it had a good sound to it,' I said, hopefully.

'As a phrase, I think it has a disastrous sound to it,' said my master. 'I was drunk, you know, Greenberry – well, of course you know, because we were all of us drunk to larger or lesser extent. I expect I still am. I expect you are, too, because I don't suppose you passed up the ale that was circulating so freely, yourself.'

I had passed up most of the ale, and the cider too, as it happened, but I did not say this. After a moment, Master Kempe went to sit on the far window seat, leaning out to look down. Then he turned back, and in a brighter tone, said, 'Greenberry, anything I do tomorrow is going to be overshadowed by this local Dance they're planning. Would you agree?'

'I would.' He has finally seen a graceful way out. I had seen it ages ago, but it was more tactful to let him get to it by himself. I said, thoughtfully, 'I suppose you can't very well suggest that you dance for them the following day, can you?' This principle of making a negative statement – with the aim of getting the opposite in a response to it – is a trick I learned long ago. It nearly always works, and it worked now.

'Why can't I suggest it?' demanded Master Kempe. 'Dammit, Greenberry, I shall suggest it.' He beamed at me. 'This is a very good plan,' he said. 'There'll be much more time for us, as well, because this performance they're giving tomorrow sounds a bit long-winded. They're going to march along the streets to this house—'

'Accompanied by a variety of musical instruments.'

'And it's all timed for the actual Dance to commence at sunset. That will be very effective – dancing figures seen against a setting sun. I don't know but what I mightn't try to achieve that myself some time.'

Now it was the man of the theatre speaking, and he had cheered up and I was relieved. He's now thinking about this sunset figure, which is allowing me a few moments to set down that our small entourage is housed in this set of rooms, which are apparently called the courtyard rooms. I say, 'entourage', but it's actually my master and myself, along with Slye, our drummer, and Bee, who is my master's general servant. They're sharing a room across the passage.

'That courtyard below our windows is a very good setting for a performance of any kind,' Master Kempe said, still leaning out of the window.

'As long as it doesn't rain.'

'It won't rain. There's plenty of room around the sides for folk to gather,' he said, still looking down at the courtyard. 'And also there's that walkway arrangement up here, just outside these rooms. Did you notice that? It's quite a theatrical setting, isn't it, although it's hardly The Globe or The Rose, but then—'

'But then what is?'

'What indeed?' nodded my master. He found his nightcap, and donned it, saying he would be grateful for a good night's sleep in a decent bed.

'For here I am with blisters up to my knees, not to mention a strained hip. You remember about the strained hip, Greenberry?'

'I remember. We were between Bury and Thetford when you began to suffer it,' I said. 'We were lodging with the Widow Everett that night, and she sent for a surgeon.'

'Yes, and the wretched man wanted to wrap my hips in a cabbage leaf, or apply a compound of pigs' marrow boiled up with herbs and the gall of a hare.'

He shuddered, then said, 'But she was a generous and kindly soul, the Widow Everett. Ah well, Greenberry, tomorrow's a new day, and tomorrow we'll watch this Reivers Dance for ourselves. Handed down, father to son, so they said, and for a good two hundred years. And while we watch, we'll have a tankard of that remarkable cider.'

I have no objection to the cider, although I suspect it's better taken in moderate quantities.

I'm writing this in my own bedchamber. Master Kempe tumbled himself into his bed about half an hour ago, complete with nightcap, and I came along to the room allotted to me. The twilight is thickening and the day drowsing and drooping, but in here wax candles are casting a soft glow over these pages as I write. It's warm and comfortable, and there's a faint scent of beeswax and lavender from the Spanish chest under the window.

Slye and Bee are in their own room, at the far end of the passage. They like this house, and Slye, a taborer since he was a boy, is pleased at its name, seeing it as a good omen for Master Kempe's future. He has stacked his drums with jealous care against his bed, and woe will betide anyone who trips over them, which is something Bee is likely to do during the night, probably fumbling for the chamber pot in the dark, especially after the imbibing of all that cider. He has already complained of a symptom that my master, with reasonable delicacy, calls bloating, but which Bee refers to as The Belches. Whatever name it's given, I suspect Slye is in for a disturbed night, but neither is likely to hear me if I steal along the moonlit passage and down to the courtyard below, and from there across to the main house.

Am I going to do that? And if I do, will she have left a door open for me? Perhaps I misread that strange, startling moment earlier on. Even as I write the words, I know I did not, though. I know it at some deep instinctive level – a level I never knew I possessed until now. It means that I know if I steal into the house, she will be waiting.

If my master were privy to my thoughts about Rosalind Rivers, he would probably shake his head, call it folly, and borrow from the lines of his former friend at The Globe, to say, ah, Greenberry, remember that love is merely a madness, and it deserves no better than a dark house—

Madness and a dark house. The words conjure up an image of places such as Bedlam, with poor mad creatures shut away in perpetual darkness.

I could wish I had not lit upon that line. Love is not madness, even if tonight it was born in a dark house.

Later

A soft dawn-light is trickling through the windows of The Tabor as I write this.

My mind is in turmoil, and I'm hoping it may restore a degree of calm if I set down what has happened. I shall need to destroy the pages later, of course – of all my writings, inking out these lines will not be enough. But for now, this is my confessional.

The light that is coming into my room, is lying across the floor in diamond shapes, because almost all of The Tabor's windows are of the kind the Queen has always admired – thin strips of metal that trellis the glass panes. Owing to the Queen's preference, such windows have been fitted in a number of buildings during her reign. They're beautiful, and earlier tonight they caused moonlight to lie like a silken carpet across the floor of a large bedchamber in the main house. There was a moment earlier tonight when I stood at an open door and saw the moonlight, and when I felt as if an enchanted carpet from one of the old Persian tales of love and intrigue and passion had been unfurled for me to tread on.

Because of course I went from my room and crossed the courtyard to the main house. I took no light with me – even the tiniest flame from a candle might have been seen, but I could see my way perfectly easily.

At first I feared I might find my way to the wrong bedchamber, and end up in the bed of some unsuspecting serving maid, my ardour wilting embarrassingly at the horrified realization of my mistake. (I should mention that I have never been at all prone to wilting – for that I thank whichever of the gods has sway over such things – but circumstances alter cases, and a man never knows what may shrivel his fervour.)

I did not enter the wrong room, though. There are any number of sayings about how a lover's arousal will always point unerringly and uncontrollably in the direction of his lady's bedchamber, in the way the iron needle points towards the northern star. Some of the sayings are quite solemn and poetic, while others are outright bawdy. I shall not set any of them down here, though; I shall only write that a deep instinct guided me to the right room.

The door was not locked, and she was sitting on a deep window seat, her head turned towards the door, as if she had been watching for it to open. The diamond-shaped moonlight painted its patterns in her hair.

'I knew you'd come,' she said, softly. 'I wanted to come downstairs to meet you, only I didn't dare. But nor did I want you to get lost and end up in the wrong bedchamber, like a character in a stage comedy.'

And there it was again – that meeting of minds, that way of seeing the same wry amusement in a situation.

I said, 'I found the way. I wasn't sure if I would be welcome, though.'

'Oh, Greenberry,' she said. 'How could you think that?'

'Easily.' I went over to her and took her hands. 'Even now I'm here,' I said, 'I'm not sure what is going to happen next.'

The three-cornered smile came again. 'Isn't that up to you?' she said, demurely. But her eyes went to the bed, where the coverlet was turned back. My arm was around her waist by that time, and we walked towards the bed together. It was as simple and as natural as that.

If I do decide against destroying these pages, and if my unknown reader is hoping for revelations and descriptions in the style of Bocaccio, I shall disappoint. I am only going to say that it was a night filled with the most explosive delight any man could ever wish to experience.

If only we could have remained safely inside in that magical world, Rosalind and I.

It was some time later – it was quite a long time later, in fact – that I came partly out of a sleep that might have been the drowsy mandragora-induced slumber of any number of Will Shakespeare's fictional lovers. At first I had no idea what had waked me; there was only a deep pleasure at the realization of where I was, and that she was here with me – Rosalind, her hair spilling across the pillow like silk, her head warm against my shoulders, a faint sheen on her eyelids.

And then I was aware of some sound close at hand, and I half sat up in the bed, trying to identify what it was. I was not especially concerned, for all houses have their own small sounds and whisperings, and The Tabor was old enough to have a great many.

It came again, and with it a faint concern, because I was able to identify it. The door to Rosalind's bedchamber was thick and heavy, but I had shut it when I came in. Now it was ajar, and light from the galleried landing beyond trickled in and lay across the floor. Outlined in the bar of light was a blurred outline. I watched it, trying to believe it was the shape of something outside the door – a wall hanging, even a statue. But there are no statues in The Tabor, and as I watched, my heart began to beat faster with apprehension. Because the outline had moved. Someone was out there – someone was standing just outside the door, and whoever it was must have eased the door very slightly open. To listen? To peer in and watch? I felt a lurch of what was almost sickness at the thought of someone witnessing what had happened between myself and Rosalind tonight.

Then the light shifted and the blurred shape seemed to step back. A floorboard creaked, and there was a faint, stealthy sound that might have been footsteps going away, or that might only have been old timbers settling slightly. Even so, I slid out of bed, padded to the door, and peered cautiously out. There was nothing there, though, only a faint greyness from the breaking dawn. No one was there. Had there ever been anyone? Perhaps an inquisitive maidservant, wanting to giggle with the other servants later, and tell how their mistress had been made love to by the impudent travelling player? If that was the truth, I hoped I would not lose in the telling. That's outrageous vanity, of course, but we are what we are.

I closed the door, got back into bed, and pulled Rosalind against me one more time. 'Marry me,' I said, afterwards.

Her face lit up with the purest delight imaginable.

'Oh, if I could—'

'You can. You must.' I made an impatient gesture. 'I should be able to make speeches that will burn into your heart and remain there like fire for ever,' I said. 'Only I can't. I could write them, if you like,' I said, hopefully.

She laughed, and reached up to cup my face in her hands, as if she wanted to trap the image and keep it for ever. Then without warning her expression changed. 'I can't marry you. It's impossible. He won't allow it.'

'"He"?'

'My brother. Ralph.' All of the light had gone from her eyes and the delight from her face.

'I'll talk to him. This morning. I'll formally request the honour of your hand. I can do those things properly, you know. I'm not just a travelling player with no manners or—'

'I don't care what you are. I wouldn't care if you were a convicted felon or a pirate or a cut-purse, or anything else,' she said. 'But you mustn't talk to Ralph. Promise you won't.' She was clutching me, her eyes wide and fearful. 'He mustn't know about tonight – not ever . . . Promise you won't.'

But I didn't promise. I only kissed her again, whispered that I would creep back to the courtyard rooms before anyone woke, and made good my exit.

Except it was not a good exit. It was a disastrous exist, because as I went across the shadowy hall, treading in and out of the chequered moonlight purely out of sheer joy, I was suddenly aware that someone was watching me. That strange, almost-extinct sense that sends cold pinpricks across your skin, slammed into my brain, and I whipped round instantly. At first I thought there was nothing, that it had been a trick of the mind. And then the shadows beneath the stairway stirred, and he was walking towards me, the grey dawn-light falling across him, so that his eyes glittered coldly. Ralph Rivers, the man in possession – not just of The Tabor, but also of the person I loved better than anything I had ever known. Incredibly, even after a single night with her, I can write that about her, but so it is.

Ralph Rivers said, 'Master Greenberry. Soft-footing it back to your bed, like a homing tomcat, after treating my sister as if she's the town whore.'

It was not immediately apparent what I could best say to him. But of course he had been the blurred shape that had peered in through the door of Rosalind's bedchamber, and of course I was the villain of the situation. That being so, he had every right to be furious, to throw me from his house, to inflict whatever punishment on me he thought suitable.

But I held on to my temper, and I said, temperately, 'You have every justification for anger. I've behaved appallingly – I've abused your hospitality, but please will you believe me that I haven't abused your sister. Tonight was . . . I want to marry her. Honourably and openly and with your permission and blessing.'

He took a step closer. 'You arrogant little thrust-prick,' he said, in a vicious whisper. 'For that's all you are. A ragtag vagabond – swiving every available female you meet. I saw you for what you were from the start, and now I know I was right.'

'I said, "Then it was you outside her room earlier."'

'Yes.'

'Watching. Prying.'

'I'd seen how you looked at her,' he said. 'Lust, open and shameless, that was what was in your eyes. I suspected you were the one who would take her innocence. I always knew there'd be someone . . . That someone would come here and ruin her.'

'She isn't ruined,' I said, at once. 'What you saw isn't open to misinterpretation, but . . .' I searched for words because knowing he had seen us – witnessed that deep sweet intimacy; heard my avowal of love to her, and hers in return – was sickening. I said, 'Tell me, Master Rivers, how did it make you feel, to see your sister with me? Did you expend your own lust while you watched?' I know this was unforgivable, but the scalding pain was being replaced by fury. I flinched, though, from the sudden blaze of hatred in his face. I don't think I am a coward, but I was alone with a man whose eyes burned with a dreadful violence, and – facts have to be faced – I was the one in the wrong.

'I'm sorry,' I said, after a moment, managing to resist a compulsion to put out my hands in a gesture of defence. 'I shouldn't have said that, and I ask your pardon. We're both upset and . . .' I frowned, then said, 'I meant it about marriage. Won't you agree to it?' I hated the pleading note in my voice. 'I would do my best to make her happy,' I said.

He laughed derisively. 'You to marry into my family?' he said. 'You're mad as well as a fornicator. I'll never let anyone marry her – not even now, after she's been spoiled.'

Spoiled, I thought. That wasn't a spoiling. Yes, but it's how he sees it.

Almost to himself, Ralph said, 'That sin of all the sins . . . I've never been able to bear the thought of anyone ever committing that sin with her . . .'

He stopped, but in that moment I understood. He could not bear to think of anyone making love to Rosalind, because he wanted to make love to her himself. And that's putting it in polite terms. With the sudden understanding came a sick disgust, and yet I was aware of pity for him.

'I'll leave Reivers,' I said, because clearly there was nothing else to say. 'I'll go at first light.' It sounded suitably contrite, and it sounded honourable and as if I was acknowledging my sin. Not for nothing have I moved around the edges of theatrical circles and picked up a few tricks on how to convey a mood or a meaning. I was not contrite in the least, though, and I certainly did not consider I had committed a sin.

Ralph Rivers said, sharply, 'No. You won't leave. Not yet. Not until . . .' His lips twisted into a distorted smile. 'Not until you have witnessed the performance of the Reivers Dance,' he said, softly. 'You'll stay for that, Master Greenberry.'

I stared at him, unsure that I had heard him right. 'In God's name, man, why? What difference will it make? No, I'll go at once. In an hour I'll be away from here.'

'I don't think you will,' he said.

'Are you going to lock me up? You'd have a hard job to do that. I think I'm a good deal stronger than you.'

'I don't need to lock you up,' he said. 'You'll stay here because you won't leave Rosalind in The Tabor.' A pause. Then, very deliberately, 'You won't leave her here with me,' he said.

I stared at him, and realized that he was right. I had no idea at that moment – and I have no idea now, as I write this, whether I'm fearful that he might wreak some kind of revenge on Rosalind, or whether tonight's events might have caused his sick desire to spiral out of his control, so that he—

I can't face that latter prospect. He's quite right to say I can't leave her here. But nor can I feel certain that she'd come away with me. As I write this, with dawn turning the diamond-shaped light to grey, turning my life to grey with it, I'm remembering that Rosalind has never been outside Reivers in her life. I'm also remembering that I have no idea where I could take her, or how we could travel. I have precious little money, and she probably has none at all.

I suppose a lesser man would leave at this point – would fling his few possessions into his bag, and go quietly and unobtrusively. But that would mean leaving Rosalind to whatever madness takes over Ralph Rivers' mind. And I think he might well be mad. That thought frightens me very much.

NINE

The hours of the morning are passing slowly and there's no sign of either Ralph or Rosalind. I have tried to go over to the main house, of course, doing so openly and almost casually, but the doors are locked. Is this usual? Or are they locked to keep me out? Or – this is far more worrying – to keep Rosalind in?

Master Kempe, Slye and Bee have partaken heartily of breakfast that one of the serving girls carried over to us. I choked down half a mug of ale, dispiritedly crumbled some bread, and I'm hoping both will stay with me, because I feel sick and cold. I wonder if this is how a condemned man feels awaiting execution? That's a ridiculous way to think, though, because whatever else he might have in mind, Ralph Rivers is hardly going to execute me. Of course he isn't.

Earlier I walked around the courtyard, making it seem as if I'm looking at the various arrangements for today's performance, but in reality wanting to catch sight of her at a window. But there's no sign. This, also, is deeply worrying.

Master Kempe is planning to write down, as nearly as possible, the steps of the Reivers Dance as it's performed. He's good at drawing detailed sketches of the dancers and of the shapes and patterns of a dance, as well – often with floor plans and numbers allotted to the various performers and their steps. I suspect that if he likes this Reivers Dance, he won't be averse to pilfering one or two of the step sequences for himself, although he'll give credit to Reivers village, for he always does. He's a fair and honest man, Will Kempe.

And now Slye and I are down in the courtyard, and I've found for myself a table with a good view. It's all very clean and tidy – serving girls were plying brooms earlier on, sweeping away leaves and twigs, and then carrying in chairs

and small tables – and there's an atmosphere of pleased expect-
ation. It's clear that people are looking forward to the evening
– I suppose this is a big event in what are presumably rather
placid and predictable lives. At the moment I wish my own
life was placid and predictable.

Master Kempe has just come to sit with me, and Parson
Marplot has joined us. Slye and Bee are at the next table.

The skies are starting to darken. It's very slight, but it's
perceptible. How long until sunset? Will they light candles, or
will the dancers really perform against the dying sun? I have
no idea, and as well as that, I no longer have any sense of
time. In a city you don't take much notice of the hour the sun
sets – you just see that the street lights have been lit, and that
there are candles or rush lights in people's windows. But out
here, with huge skies and flat countryside stretching for miles,
the changing of light is somehow an essential part of life.

The local people are coming into the courtyard in little
groups – threes and fours. They don't seem especially overawed
at entering what must be an important house in Reivers, but
then The Tabor is their tavern, and most of them will be used
to coming here. They're all talking eagerly and helping older
ones to the chairs. But as I sit here, making these notes,
watching everything, something very strange is starting to
occur to me. It's the fact that there are no children present.

In every town and every village we have visited during our
nine days, and at every performance Master Kempe has given,
children have been there. They have crowded excitedly into market
squares, and lined streets, waving and cheering, their parents
clearly delighted to be with them, to be giving them such a treat.

Then why have the children of Reivers not been brought
here today? It's not especially late, and there must surely be
children in the village.

As I finished writing that sentence, I heard, very faintly,
music, and I was aware of a fresh lurch of apprehension, because
that means it's begun. The performers will have assembled in
the centre of Reivers, and they'll have struck up their music,
and be about to begin the procession to The Tabor. The music
is still very distant – it's more as if something's tapping rhyth-
mically on the air – as if fingertips are beating lightly against

a stretched drumskin. There's no reason for me to feel fear, but it's what I am feeling, and my heart is starting to pound.

I keep looking around, hoping to see Rosalind, because I can't believe she won't be here. But she isn't, and that's causing the panic to surge up all over again. Where is she? Has Ralph shut her away somewhere? But just as there's no sign of Rosalind, there's no sign of Ralph, either. Could they both be part of the Dance – marching with the people who are making their procession to this house? Might it be a tradition of the Reivers Dance that a member of the family is part of it? But if so, surely Rosalind would have told me about it last night.

The music is coming nearer, and it's not sounding as I expected it to sound, although I'm not sure what I did expect. There's a menacing quality to it – and a kind of prowling rhythm, and I'm starting to dislike it very much. But everyone is looking eagerly towards the courtyard entrance, and there's the flicker of torchlight now, which means they must be getting nearer.

Unexpectedly the music and the sounds of the dancers' voices aren't coming from the front of the house, but from the side of The Tabor. Master Kempe and I turned our heads in the direction of the music, both of us slightly surprised, and the parson, seeing this, said, 'Are you thinking they'll come along the main highway?'

'Well, yes.'

'Ah, but they won't,' he said. 'They'll come through an old garden gate – a gate set into the wall over yonder.' There was a vague gesture, pointing.

'Why?' said Master Kempe. 'Why not come along the main roadway – it's wide and much better suited.'

Marplot's eyes slid away, and for a moment he looked almost furtive. 'They're following an old tradition,' he said. 'They're keeping to the way the Dance was performed for the very first time. It's where they were brought that first time, the dancers.'

'How long ago was that?' That was Master Kempe, of course, always keen to know about the origins of such things.

'A very long time. More than two hundred years,' he said. 'Ah, now they're here.'

And now they are indeed here. They're streaming into the

courtyard, leaping and prancing, the torches flaring up against the ever-darkening sky, and casting shadows on the walls that surround us. The music is everywhere, and the figures are taking up their positions.

I can see my master eagerly writing notes and sketching one of his layouts showing the positions of the performers. But as I scribble these words – which will very likely be unreadable in the morning – I'm seeing two things that are striking a cold dread within me. One is the sight of Ralph Rivers. He walked out of The Tabor a few moments ago, and he's greeting the performers. Then – I'm not sure how this was done, and there are too many people to see everything – but he seemed to direct them into the courtyard, and to walk with them. It's as if he's clothed himself in the mantle and the authority of lord of the manor. It's an extraordinary thing to see, because last night in the tavern room he was simply a genial host – well, maybe not exactly genial, but hospitable, certainly. It's as if he can don whatever face he wants – and not in the good, wholesome way of a player at The Globe or The Rose. It's in the way of a man disguising his real self. I hate all of his selves, and most of all I hate this one – not because it's reminding everyone that he's The Tabor's owner, but because it's reminding them of his power over the whole of this village – and in particular over Rosalind.

Rosalind. He's got my dear beloved girl at his side. She's wearing a plain gown – white linen, I think – and her hair is unbound and tumbling around her shoulders in the way it did last night, against her pillow . . .

I still can't see clearly, but I think he's got a very firm hold of her, and I have the impression that she's trying to pull away. I don't think I can bear this. But what can I do? Can I suddenly bound across the courtyard and wrench her from his grasp, and then run into the night with her. But where can we run? And to what?

The dancers are in position now – it doesn't take a man of the theatre to see that they're preparing to depict a story, and, of course, my master has seen it.

'Half-Morrice, half-mumming, if I don't mistake,' he's just said, noting it all down. 'And that's a very old tradition indeed. Greenberry, I'm very glad indeed that we didn't miss this.'

Even as I write this, Humbert Marplot is leaning forward, and

I'm writing his words down at furious speed, because it suddenly seems vital to record what's been said, in case of—

I don't know what it's in case of, but Parson Marplot's words have made my stomach churn with sick fear.

'Mother of God,' he's just said. 'Surely they aren't going to—'

'Going to what?'

Marplot is still staring at the main group at the centre, and I broke off to glance at him. 'The positions that Ralph Rivers is making them take up,' he said. 'It looks as if they're going to perform the entire Dance.' He spoke in a whisper, but it was impossible not to hear the sudden horror in his voice.

'Isn't that the point, parson?' This is my master, intent on scribbling his own notes. 'You have a beginning, a middle, and an end. The ancient art of telling a story. This is half-Morrice, half-mumming.'

'You don't understand. This Dance is never performed in its entirety. Never.' Marplot is looking about him, as if fearful of someone listening, but all eyes are on the courtyard's centre, and everyone is laughing and pointing out costumes.

The men are starting to move into formations, but even from here it looks as if the formations are hemming Rosalind in, so that she's at the centre with her brother. He's stepped on to a box or a stool, so he's a good foot above the rest. That surely doesn't matter, though.

Marplot is speaking again, and the horror in his tone is unmistakable. 'They're going to perform the execution scene,' he's saying. 'That's what this circling of the dancers – this linking of hands and gesturing – is leading up to. It's the scene that was created to commemorate the slaying of the Reivers rebels over two hundred years ago. In particular this Dance was composed to mark the death of a long-ago member of the Rivers family—'

'Yes?'

'He was slaughtered by Henry le Despenser's men,' said Marplot. 'They came out here to The Tabor specifically to execute him. But they came slyly, at sunset, creeping in through the old garden door—'

'As these dancers did earlier.'

'Yes. They trapped him in this very courtyard. And then they executed him.'

Even as my master and Marplot are speaking, and even as I'm writing as if my pen is driven by the Furies themselves, I'm managing to watch the dancers. They're closing in on Ralph – or is it Rosalind they're closing in on? Whichever it is, Ralph is controlling them. Their faces are lit by the setting sun mingling with the torch flares, but they're still the ordinary friendly people I met last night. I don't believe – and I won't believe – that they're seeing any sinister intent in any of this.

There isn't any sinister intent in it, of course. But Ralph is still holding Rosalind in that firm grip, and she's starting to turn her head this way and that, as if looking for someone . . . In a moment I will stand up and let her see I'm here. Or would that tip Ralph into some dreadful act of violence?

As if from down a long tunnel, I've just heard Master Kempe ask a question of the parson. 'The execution?' he's said. 'It would have been beheading, of course?'

And with the words I see now what Ralph Rivers is holding in his free hand. An axe, with a viciously sharpened blade that's catching the rays of the setting sun, and glinting crimson. It's only a stage prop, of course – it can't be anything else. But even writing that, I know it isn't. It's real – it's heavy enough to cut through bone and sinew – powerful enough to sever a man's head. Or a woman's. And I know now why no children have been permitted here tonight. Ralph Rivers banned them because he intended the Dance to be performed to its ultimate, terrible finale.

Rosalind is in the most dreadful danger. I can't believe Ralph will do anything to her in full view of everyone – I can't believe those nice, innocent people taking part in the Dance will allow themselves to be part of it—

But someone has made sure that no children would be here, and I can feel that something dreadful is about to happen. And so I must summon every shred of resolve and strength I possess, and run forward across that crimson-bathed square, and get Rosalind away before anyone can stop me.

Somehow I must find the courage. I *must* . . .

TEN

I take up my pen with a heavy heart and with a smothering darkness on my soul – always supposing I believe in the existence of the soul, which is by no means a sure thing for me any longer – but I know I must write what has happened. I owe it to my beloved Greenberry to set it down, fairly and honestly.

Greenberry. How do I begin to describe him for the eyes and the mind of whoever might one day read these pages? How do I explain the effect that meeting him had on me – that moment when he looked at me in The Tabor's tavern room, and I felt as if my very bones had melted, and I knew here was the one for whom I would finally dare oppose my brother?

I could write of Greenberry's unremarkable brown hair – but say that although it was unremarkable as to colour, it felt like silk against my bare shoulders that night. I can write, too, of eyes that seemed to hold more light and life than any man has the right to possess. And of hands that, the moment I felt their touch, traced such a fire across my skin I wanted to die for the sheer joy of it.

Since I have vowed to be honest in these pages, I should also admit that I also wanted to be in bed with him. Until that night I never had been in bed with – or even kissed by – a man, and I wanted to find out what it was like. But I wanted to find out with Greenberry.

When I was twelve, a cousin – the revolting Cedric Rivers – cornered me in the old courtyard once, and lunged at me, pressing a wet, slobbery kiss on my face, but I don't intend to count that.

And Mother, hearing about it afterwards, said Cedric's father had always wanted to get their hands on The Tabor.

'But The Tabor will go to Ralph,' I said. I knew this; men owned property and inherited it. Girls did not.

'Yes, but Cedric and his father might see you as a means of getting a foot in the door,' she said. 'They're probably lining you up for marriage.'

I could not think of anything I would hate worse than being married to my cousin Cedric, with his fish eyes and his loose wet mouth and pudgy hands.

'Oh, Cedric won't get his hands on you,' Mother said cheerfully. 'He won't get The Tabor, either. Don't tell Father about this, though – he'll probably go rampaging off to horsewhip the wretched boy . . . Let's forget him – come and help me with a tapestry I have a mind to work.'

She was very interested in her tapestry. She said tapestries were important, because they showed things in history – battles and important events. Sometimes it took years for them to be completed. Mother thought her own tapestry could be called the Tabor Tapestry when it was finished, and she said there was no knowing but that it might one day take its place with all the beautiful and well-known ones that were in splendid palaces and castles.

Ralph knew about Cedric wanting to marry me – I have no idea how, but he did. He said once, 'You needn't marry anyone, Rosalind. It can be just the two of us. One day The Tabor will be mine—'

'Will it?'

'Of course. It has to go to the next son of the Rivers name. So one day we can be together here. Just the two of us.' Then suddenly, he said, 'Did you let Cedric kiss you? If you did, I'll kill him. Nobody must ever touch you, Rosalind.'

When he said this, the look came into his eyes that had always frightened me. I don't know if anyone else ever saw that look, and I don't know if anyone else ever realized that Ralph can don different faces, wearing whatever will serve him best in any situation. People at masquerades do that – I know about masquerades, because travellers who come here tell about them.

Some of the villagers have always considered it rather shocking for a part of The Tabor to be a tavern. That the squire of the manor, and his lady with him, should open up a large room on the side of the house – where local people go to buy ale and cider, and where travellers could spend an occasional night in the courtyard rooms – was surely not right.

My parents paid no heed to this. My father said cheerfully that needs must when the devil drove, and that if The Tabor was to be kept at all, the time had come when it must work for its living. For himself, he enjoyed the company and the liveliness of the tavern room, he said, and my mother, who would probably have agreed with him if he had proposed an expedition into Satan's own domain and a festive banquet with the Prince of Darkness when they got there, said it was a perfectly respectable means of making a living. She liked supervising the baking of pasties and gingerbread to offer to the folk who came to the tavern room, and overseeing the preparation of meals for the occasional guest.

The vague disapproval never stopped the village people frequenting The Tabor's tavern room. And when my parents died of the Plague, caught during a brief visit to Norwich, the entire village came to their funeral, and the Savory sisters, whose family had lived in Reivers almost as long as my own, wept openly, and had to be comforted by Parson Marplot with plum brandy.

After our parents' deaths, Ralph needed me to help with serving in the tavern, which I rather enjoyed. I liked seeing people and talking to them and getting to know all the villagers. But if I ever fell into conversation with any of the chance travellers who occasionally came to The Tabor, Ralph would always somehow find a way to keep me away. Sometimes, during those years, I made plans for running away, but I never knew where I could run to, or how I would travel, and what I would do for money.

And yet, growing up, I often wondered how the act of love would be with someone you cared about. This was not a feeling I could share with anyone, of course, in case they thought me a wanton. Does what I did with Greenberry that night – within hours of meeting him – make me a wanton? Above all, does it make acceptable my brother's vicious retribution on the night of the Murder Dance?

That's the first time I've called it by that name, but it's what it was on that night, and it's how I shall always think of it. The Murder Dance.

It was not long after my eighteenth birthday that Will Kempe, who was famous for having been on the London stages, came to Reivers. With him came Greenberry. And the moment I saw him, there was no room in my mind or my heart for anything or anyone else. After our night together, I counted the world well lost for love, but now the world for me is certainly lost, and I must live with the consequences.

Because it was that night I spent with Greenberry that twisted Ralph's hatred into outright madness.

The following morning I was scarcely aware of anything that went on around me. I was still more than half lost in a shining dream in which Greenberry and I were together – and in which Ralph would preside benevolently over our marriage, and there would be a happy life ahead for us all. I should have known better. But I do know that somewhere beneath the bemused happiness, I was feeling uneasy about the performance of the Dance.

Everyone in the village knew about the Dance. It had been handed down for more than two hundred years – probably it was remembered because it was the only really noteworthy thing that had ever happened in Reivers. It had been created after Evelyn Rivers had joined the famous Rebellion against Richard II, and had been slaughtered by Henry le Despenser's men in our own courtyard.

'But,' my father always said when discussions about Evelyn and the Reivers Dance became a bit too wild, 'the Dance has never been performed since that day. Let's always remember that, if you please.'

But this evening the Dance was going to be performed – in our own courtyard, where Evelyn had been slaughtered.

Parson Marplot had found the Dance, as he had promised.

'And a cobwebby old bit of paper it was, as well, Mistress Rosalind,' said Master Grindall, who came puffing out to The Tabor to report. 'But the steps and the music were written on it, and now folk are capering around like mad things, and them as understands music are playing it for all they're worth.'

As the afternoon began to slide down into evening, people began coming to The Tabor, walking happily into the courtyard, and seating themselves at the small tables Ralph had caused to be carried out. The serving girls (we had three of them at that time) carried out trays with tankards of ale and cider. I was still in the sculleries, but there's a side door that looks directly across to the courtyard and it had been left open so the talk and the laughter and the sense of anticipation reached me. Everyone was listening for the music to begin, although some people were disputing whether it could be heard all the way from the village square where the procession would start, or whether the dancers and the musicians would have to get as far as the crossroads before it was loud enough to reach The Tabor.

I was thinking that once the dancers came pouring in, I would seize my chance to go across to Greenberry. He had come into the courtyard with Master Kempe, and he was seated at a table with him, and with Parson Marplot. But he kept looking about him, and I thought: he's looking for me, and delight burned up all over again.

But beneath that was a growing sense of unease, because something was wrong. Something here that ought not be here, was it? Or was it the other way about – was there something missing . . .?

Something missing. That was when I realized there was indeed something missing. There were no children here – not a single one. And that was very curious, because there are a good many children in Reivers, and although we don't permit them to come into the tavern rooms, they're always part of village gatherings. They're dressed in their best for all the baptisms and weddings and for all the important church events – Harvest Thanksgiving and Easter Sunday. And there is the nativity play each Christmas that Parson Marplot and the Savory ladies arrange, with the children enacting the parts.

But the children were not present to watch the Reivers Dance – the village's own piece of history. Why not?

It was a shock to suddenly hear Ralph's voice close to me, but I turned to him. 'Ralph, why aren't any of the children here?'

He did not immediately reply, but then, as if having come to a decision, he said, 'I made it clear that none of them were to be brought here tonight.'

'Why? Surely the children would enjoy this – a piece of our own history being performed after so long? They're all taught the story of Evelyn and the Peasants' Revolt.'

Teaching was quite an important part of the village children's lives. The Savory ladies took over a room within the church on two afternoons each week, and taught reading and writing and simple figuring. My mother used to help them – teaching needlework and house crafts to the girls, and I had tried to continue her work. Parson Marplot gave little talks about history. Almost all of the children attended these lessons. We've always been proud of our children in Reivers.

But Ralph said, very softly, 'Rosalind, the children aren't here because the entire Dance is going to be performed today.'

I stared at him, not really understanding. Then I said, 'The scene with the execution? But it's never been performed – not ever. It was written afterwards – after the King's men killed Evelyn. Nobody's ever danced it.'

'Which is a very good reason why we should do so now,' he said, coming closer. 'We can show Master Kempe a little piece of our history. The dancers don't know, of course – they'll dance through the lanes and into the courtyard, just as the dancers did on the day of Evelyn's murder. But . . .' He paused, and then he took my arm tightly, 'But when they reach the zenith,' he said, 'you and I will step forward. We'll play the parts of our ancestors.'

'Of course we won't,' I said, at once. 'In any case, no one even knows the steps, the movements.'

'I know them,' he said. 'And you'll do them with me. Tonight, Rosalind, you're going to be my lady,' he said. 'Just as I promised you, all those years ago.' His grip tightened around my waist, making me wince, then for a nightmare moment he pressed against me, so that I could feel his excitement, hard and thrusting against my thigh. It was a grotesque echo of what had happened with Greenberry last night, but I managed to move back a little, although his hands were still holding my wrists as tightly as if they were gyves.

I struggled, but he held me, and began to force me towards the courtyard. It was like a nightmare. And the music was getting closer, and people were standing up to catch a first glimpse of the dancers, cheering and shouting. But a dreadful madness was blazing in Ralph's eyes, and there was fear inside the music. That's a strange thing to say about music, but I could hear it and I could feel it. This was music that had been written more than two hundred years ago – it had been played to herald the brutal slaughter of Evelyn. I began to shiver uncontrollably, because I was beginning to feel that Evelyn was close to me – that Evelyn's voice was telling me to run away as far as I could, because something was about to happen, and it was something appalling and terrible . . .

You know what they did to me, Evelyn was saying. *You know and your brother knows, because it's one of the secrets handed down within the family . . . But no one else knows – so no one else will guess what Ralph is going to do . . .*

The old gate that we always called the garden gate was opening – it has a loud creak, like dry old bones scraping against each other, and it's unmistakable. It would have been unmistakable on that long-ago night when the King's men came, but the sound would have been hidden by the music and the revelry. Everyone would have been watching the dancers, and all the Rivers family would have been with them, pleased to be all gathered together like this, happy to be providing hospitality. None of them would have heard the soldiers' approach.

Here came our own villagers now, laughing and leaping gleefully in the air, whirling around as they did so, the two fiddlers playing enthusiastically and the boy who carried the small drum – the tabor itself – with them. He was tapping against the tabor's surface in thrumming time with the fiddlers. The music was pounding on the air, the drumbeat going faster and faster.

We were at the centre of the dancers now, and Ralph was still holding me firmly against him. It was then that I saw at his feet a large box – an oak chest, that must have been carried out here earlier. Ralph stepped up on to the box, which was deep and wide, causing him to tower over everyone. He was placing himself in a position of authority, of course. Rivers of Reivers. It had never mattered to me, but it had always mattered to him.

Over the heads of the dancers I could see Greenberry, his brows drawn into a frown, and I thought – he knows there's something wrong, that something's going to happen, but he doesn't know what it is. But a voice in my mind was whispering that I knew what was going to happen, I knew what was ahead . . .

The dancers were prancing around, although several times they appeared to get the steps wrong, bumping into one another, and then capering off in a different direction. Normally I would have found this endearing, and the watchers seemed to find it so, for Master Grindall called out to his son who was with them that another hour's practice would not have come amiss, which raised much laughter.

Ralph was leading the cheers, calling out that this was what had been done in the past.

'This is the Search,' he shouted. 'That's what Evelyn's descendants wrote, to show how the executioners sought out the rebel of our family. It's almost as if they're playing a children's game, isn't it?'

His voice was cheerful and encouraging, but I could hear the false note – the *wrong* note, and I saw that some of the watchers were aware of it as well, because they were frowning and murmuring to one another. As for Greenberry . . .

Even in that crowded moment I saw that he had been scribbling something down, and I had the thought that it would always be his way to do that. But he laid down his pen and stood up, as if he were about to come running towards me.

Ralph shouted, 'Light the torches! Let's have the scene as it was meant to be! Torch flares and a dying sun mingling. And the music reaching its zenith.'

For the first time I saw that tied bundles of sticks had been wedged in the old iron sconces on the walls – relicts of The Tabor's early years – and Master Grindall's son and one of the other young men were going all around the walls, reaching up with glowing tapers. Light began to flare up, bathing the courtyard in crimson and orange.

There was a wildness in Ralph's voice now, and I thought: he's lost control. He kept that other Ralph banked down all these years, but tonight it's taken him over – and he doesn't realize it.

The music was gathering speed, like someone running too fast down a steep hill, or like a child's spinning top being whipped to a blurred frenzy. The dancers circled, and Ralph's voice rose above the music again.

'The execution scene,' he cried out. 'As it was all those years ago – the sinner given justice. Rosalind and I will play that scene for you.'

He was still holding me so tightly I could not break free. The dancers faltered, uncertain what was expected of them, because this had not been planned. There was a sense of puzzlement in the courtyard – perhaps some of the people were thinking that Master Rivers had had a drop more of his own ale than was good for him, but I could see others looking worried.

And then the balance of Ralph's grip on me changed, and he leapt off the oak chest, and with the toe of his boot kicked open its lid. As it fell back, I saw with horror what lay inside, and I saw Ralph's hand go down to grasp it. As he raised it above his head, it glinted, the finely honed steel edge catching the light of the torches and the sunset.

The dancers – also the onlookers – were coming closer, as if trying to understand. One of them – I think it was Master Grindall – cried out, 'The slaughter of Evelyn Rivers . . . Master Ralph, surely to God, you aren't going to . . . Let his memory rest—'

'Something could go wrong!' called another voice, and I recognized it as Parson Marplot.

That's the moment that's stayed with me. Those words calling out that something could go wrong, and the sudden understanding that it was what Ralph intended. He intended something to go wrong. It would appear to be acting – mumming, it's often called – but it would happen.

Parson Marplot was on his feet now. 'Master Ralph, stop this now,' he shouted. 'Because you've got it wrong. You've got the history wrong. You can't enact Evelyn's death – because Evelyn wasn't beheaded that day.'

Bewildered faces turned to him, and then, still holding me
against him, Ralph said, 'I know he wasn't,' and his face
contorted with sudden jealous fury.

Reverend Marplot took a step closer, and Ralph pulled me
closer to him. Marplot said, 'I've read the old accounts in the
church, and the sentence was quite a different one.' He paused,
then said, 'The sentence was for, "The traitorous rebel's hands
to be cut and severed completely, since those were the instruments of death that wielded sword against the King, our
beloved Richard Plantagenet, Second of his Name".'

The words lay thickly and terribly on the air. *The traitorous
rebel's hands to be cut and severed completely . . .*

It was then that I felt Ralph's muscles tighten, and he cried
out, 'That was the punishment then, and it will be the punishment now.'

His voice soared into wildness, and I knew he had lost
whatever rags of sanity he might still have had. His muscles
tightened and I felt him raise his arm with the glinting axe.

And then he stopped, as if something had caught and held
him. I struggled again, and tried to scream, but the scream
never came. In another minute he would bring the axe
smashing down on me, because it was the punishment,
because I had lain with a man, because he could not bear to
know it . . .

Greenberry was bounding across the courtyard, straight
towards Ralph. I felt a bolt of emotion go through Ralph, as
if lightning had speared him, and in that moment I understood
properly. I was not the one Ralph intended to kill. I was the
bait. It was Greenberry he wanted, because Greenberry had
dared to come to my bed – he had been the one who had taken
what Ralph had always wanted.

As Greenberry reached the platform, Ralph pushed me from
him. I half fell against the oak chest, and from a distance I
could hear people screaming and chairs being overturned as
the men rushed forward.

Ralph was holding the axe above his head, and as Greenberry
reached up to stop him, the blade whistled through the air
with a vicious whine. It caught the red glow from the dying
sun and the flares of the burning torches, and it came down

on Greenberry's outstretched hands. He gave a terrible cry and slumped to the ground.

The courtyard was filling up with screaming, and blood was gushing on to the old stones, whose surface had once been stained with the blood of Evelyn Rivers – Evelyn, whose 'traitorous rebel's hands' were cut and severed . . .

But this time the blood was the blood of my beloved Greenberry.

ELEVEN

Quentin was looking forward to meeting Phineas Fox. He dared say Fox would be very interested in everything Quentin could tell him about The Tabor, and impressed with the prospect of researching into such an old family.

Toby Tallis certainly seemed interested, although Quentin was a bit inclined to question Toby's motives, because he had seen how Toby looked at Zillah. Zillah would not have recognized that look, but Quentin recognized it, and he was not going to have any goings-on between Toby and Zillah. Even so, the situation would have to be handled with some delicacy, because Toby's interest had extended to him offering to make a small investment in The Tabor restaurant. 'Modest,' he had called it, but it did not matter how modest it was, because Quentin was not going to refuse any investment at this stage.

Toby's cousin, Arabella, was quite a different prospect. It had transpired that she often worked in the world of PR, so of course Quentin had talked to her about publicity for The Tabor. He had explained all his plans to her, because he had known she would be interested.

Arabella had been impressed – Quentin had seen that from the way her eyes suddenly lit up – and he was going to talk to her in more detail this evening, and to this Phineas Fox, as well.

Immediately after breakfast, though, he was meeting George Grindall at The Tabor. Grindall had said he could spare an hour or two this morning, if Mr Rivers had no objection to a

Sunday meeting? Very good, then they would say eleven
o'clock.

Each time he saw The Tabor, Quentin felt all over again the
emotion he had felt on his first sight of the house. It was,
quite simply, pride and ownership. The house would have to
earn its keep, but even before seeing it he had conceived the
idea of having a country-house restaurant. He had worked on
a couple of restaurant marketing commissions recently, so he
had picked up all kinds of useful information. All you needed
was the right staff and some good publicity. People made such
a fuss about these things, quoting depressing stories about
businesses that had gone bankrupt. Quentin was not going to
pay any attention to such gloom-mongers.

This time, though, in company with George Grindall, he
found himself seeing how much work was going to be needed
on the place. The roof for instance . . . Anyone with half an
eye could see that the roof wandered up and down several
different levels and supported a few erratic chimneys on its way.

'But the upper floors look sound,' he said to Grindall. 'No
damp patches on any of the ceilings.'

'That's as maybe. Did you say you were getting a full
structural survey done?' asked Mr Grindall. 'You'll need one
for planners and building regulations and permissions. There'll
have to be soil samples and checks on the foundations, and
you don't know what that might show up.'

He made glum notes, and passed to the question of dry rot.
Once you had dry rot in a building, you had a lot of trouble,
he said, and Quentin tried not to think the man was mentally
rubbing his hands and totting up a potential bill.

As they walked around the side of the house, Grindall
pointed to the stone archway and the courtyard rooms beyond.
'Have you thought what you'll do with those?' he said. 'It's
a strange arrangement. Old stables, I suppose, and at some
time somebody bricked them up, but these days they're neither
fish, nor fowl, nor good red herring, to my mind.'

'I'd like to make them into private apartments for myself and
my cousin,' said Quentin. 'I'll get you to take a look some time.'

Grindall stood for a moment, looking across at the courtyard
beyond the stone arch, and for a really odd moment Quentin

had the impression that he wrapped his jacket more tightly around him, as if suddenly cold. But he only said, 'Looks as if those stairs will need replacing. But let me know when you want me to take a proper look,' and took himself off.

Quentin drove back to The Daunsen, pleased with the morning's work. He was pleased, too, to think that he was going to see Mr Codling tomorrow. Codling had promised that the draft of a will would be ready then, and if Quentin could go along to the offices to go through it, it would be ready for him to sign in a couple of days.

Quentin was looking forward to telling Zillah about the will and that he had named her as his sole heir. He would explain that it would mean she would be financially secure if anything were to happen to him. Not that it would, of course.

When it came to it, Zillah did not think Phineas Fox was anything special. He was rather quiet and she even thought he was a bit dull. You would certainly say he was reserved. Zillah would admit that he had a nice smile, but she found his eyes disconcerting. They were a kind of steely grey, rimmed with black, and she had the impression that he looked at her as if he did not want to get too close to her, which was very unusual, because men generally wanted to get very close. In other circumstances, she would have rather enjoyed dissolving that remote politeness, but she had so much on her plate at the moment that it was not to be thought of. He was perfectly polite though. He shook her hand and said it was good to meet her, but after that he seemed more interested in discussing The Tabor.

Arabella talked about the research into Reivers' and The Tabor's history for the publicity.

'Phin's found some references to a local dance – it sounds quite intriguing, and we wondered if you knew anything about it.'

Phineas Fox said, 'It's referred to as the Reivers Dance in most of the sources, but one or two call it the Murder Dance.'

Zillah felt as if something had punched into her stomach, but it was only momentary, because she had been prepared for this. It had been inevitable that the Dance would be mentioned at some stage, and there was no need to feel in the least bit worried.

'Your family has had links to this village for a very long
time, hasn't it, Quentin?' Phin was saying. 'Were any stories
about the Reivers Dance passed down?'

Quentin said, slowly, 'I don't recall hearing any. Zillah, you
didn't, did you?'

'No. My grandmother used to talk about The Tabor occasionally, but I don't remember anything about a local dance.'

'That's a shame. It sounded intriguing,' said Phineas. 'It
would be interesting to find out when it was last performed.'

'And it might be something you could use for your PR
campaign, Quentin,' said Arabella, eagerly.

'It'd certainly grab people's attention,' put in Toby. 'We
could revive it for the restaurant's opening. Actually perform
it, I mean. Are there likely to be any words to it? A few rousing
verses would liven things up, and if there aren't we can write
our own. Phin and I did a book a couple of years ago about
bawdy ballads down the ages – did I tell you about that, Zillah?
It was pretty good as well, although I says it as shouldn't – I
must let you have a copy. So I should think I could dash off
a few suitable lyrics. Phin certainly could, because for all he
likes to put out that scholarly image, at times he can be
extremely—'

'Toby,' said Phin, repressively, 'shut up. We haven't found
the Dance and, even if we do find it, Quentin might not want
to have it capered all over The Tabor.'

'If I'm honest, I don't really care for the idea,' said Quentin.
'Not for a gourmet restaurant. Probably it was just some local
cavorting around on the village green, anyway. I shouldn't
think it's been seen for centuries.'

Zillah thought, but it's there. It existed – it's shown on
that tapestry in the house. Hadn't Quentin seen it? But
clearly he had not, so she said, off-handedly, 'Even if it
did exist, it sounds as if it was too far back to interest
anyone now.'

'Yes, it does,' said Quentin. 'I much prefer your idea of
local newspapers and maybe even local TV, Arabella.'

'Good. And I thought we could take videos of the restoration at various stages. We might even get the workmen in
on that – Mr Grindall would be marvellous. And local people

too – maybe The Daunsen people – oh, and the Savory ladies from the antique shop. And we ought to do a "Before and After" display – I'd like to get some photos of the house as it is now – is that all right? Phin collected my camera from the flat – it's not professional level, but it's not bad. I'm particularly thinking of that stone archway and the old courtyard. They give such a brilliant sense of the house's age.'

'Feel free to go out there whenever you want,' said Quentin, sounding pleased. 'Let me know if you want a key at any stage.'

'We found out a bit about that part of the house earlier this afternoon,' said Phin. 'And there might almost be a bit of a mystery attached to it.'

This time Zillah felt as if something had squeezed a cold hand around her heart, but after a moment, she managed to say, 'A mystery about the courtyard?'

'About the rooms overlooking it,' said Phin. 'Do either of you know anything about a Walter Rivers? He hails from the early 1900s.'

'Never heard of him,' said Quentin. 'It was Osbert Rivers I inherited from. Who was Walter?'

'I don't know where he fits in, but there's a nice old bench in the churchyard with his name on it. Apparently it was put there as a memorial to him, because he handed over part of The Tabor to be used for the poor.'

'Handed over part of—?'

'For almshouses,' said Phin.

Quentin stared at him. 'I've never heard that,' he said.

'Nor have I,' said Zillah. This did not sound quite as worrying, but she listened carefully to what Phineas was saying.

'The inscription on the churchyard seat says Walter made over the courtyard rooms for the homeless,' he said. 'Hold on, I took a photo.' He reached for his phone, and opened the camera. 'It doesn't say which part of the house, but Arabella thought the courtyard rooms were the likeliest place for almshouses.'

'I should think they'd be the only part,' said Quentin, studying the image. 'I haven't been in those rooms yet – so much else to see to, you know – but I think they were the original stable block, although the stable part's all bricked up now. It's quite near to the house – you only have to go through the stone arch – but it is separate. I'm hoping to turn it into a private apartment for Zillah and myself,' he said, passing the phone back to Phin. 'So those rooms were once almshouses,' he said, thoughtfully. 'That's a very old system, isn't it – almshouses?'

'It more or less faded out when things like National Assistance and the Welfare State got going early in the twentieth century,' said Phin. 'I think it's quite an ancient concept, though. Maybe even as far back as the medieval era.'

'What do you mean about a mystery?' said Quentin.

Phin said, 'In 1921, in a place like this, the class divide would still be very much observed. Walter Rivers would have been more or less regarded as the lord of the manor, for want of a better term, and I find it a bit odd that he had almshouses inside his own property.'

'Yes, I do see what you mean,' said Quentin, frowning.

'I haven't seen The Tabor at all yet,' put in Toby, who had been listening with interest, 'but wouldn't it be a bit too remote? Some of the people who would have been housed would've been elderly – frail. Widows left without a farthing to their name. How would they have managed for ordinary daily life – getting provisions and food and things? They'd have had to tramp down into the village – or would Walter have trundled them down there himself?'

'Depends how far his philanthropy took him,' said Phin. 'But it's a good point, Toby. It would have been far more straightforward for Walter to just build conventional almshouses in the village. Purpose-built, as they say nowadays.'

'There'll be church records, though, won't there?' said Toby. 'You could burrow into all kinds of ancient scrolls and documents and whatnot and find out some more He's very good at that kind of thing,' he said to Zillah.

'Yes, I'm sure.' Zillah said it lightly and politely, but she was considering whether this sudden appearance of the unknown Walter Rivers and almshouses was likely to pose a threat. It was not likely, though. None of this could have anything to do with her – or with Evelyn. Evelyn. Even hearing the name in her head brought back the past.

They all seemed to have accepted that it was unlikely that the Murder Dance had been performed for hundreds of years. Zillah knew that was not so. She knew the Dance had been performed almost in living memory.

She knew because her grandmother had seen the Murder Dance for herself as a young girl. She had hidden in The Tabor's courtyard and she had watched the Dance, and she had never forgotten what had happened that night.

During school holidays, Zillah often stayed with her grand-mother, and they sometimes went out together. There were shopping trips and cinema expeditions. Very often Quentin came with them.

'He comes even when he's not invited,' Zillah's grand-mother remarked. 'And he gets in the way, sometimes. Don't let him try to take you over when you're both older, will you? I suspect he might try, and I won't always be here to look after you.'

Sometimes they went farther afield than cinemas and shops; Zillah's grandmother said it was important for Zillah to see at least a little of the world beyond their house and outside the family circle. Zillah had thought that by family circle, her grandmother meant away from Quentin, but neither of them said this.

The farther-afield outings were always really good, and for most of them they managed to avoid Quentin, which was even better. Zillah's grandmother had her own little car, which she still drove on short journeys, despite most of the family telling her she should have stopped driving long ago.

But, shortly after Zillah's eighth birthday, her grandmother suddenly said they were going to Norfolk later in the week – to the village that had almost the same name as their own. Reivers. When Zillah looked up, startled, wondering if this might be a late birthday present, grandmother said, 'And when we get there, Zillah, we're going to The Tabor.'

The Tabor. With those two words Zillah felt the most tremendous excitement welling up. The Tabor – the mysterious house that no one in the family had ever seemed to believe was real. But now it seemed it was real, and that Zillah was going to see it.

'It's just going to be the two of us,' said her grandmother, and she looked at Zillah very directly. 'No one else. You understand me?'

'Yes.' Zillah knew that this meant no one else in the family must know about the visit to The Tabor. It had to be a secret, and secrets were always exciting, and Zillah would certainly not tell anyone about it. She would very specially not tell Quentin, who would instantly think he should go with them which would spoil the whole thing.

There were crowds of questions she wanted to ask, but grandmother did not always like questions, so after a moment Zillah said, carefully, 'Who lives at The Tabor?'

'A cousin,' said her grandmother. 'His name is Osbert Rivers, but you'd better call him Mr Rivers, unless he tells you different.'

'Just him?' said Zillah. 'Hasn't he got, um, a wife or anything?'

'No. No, it's just him now,' said her grandmother, sounding a bit sad. 'And he'll be a very old gentleman by this time. And I'm glad you're polite enough not to say, "Is he as old as you, Gran?".'

They smiled at one another, and Zillah thought it was pretty great to have this kind of understanding with your grandmother. People at school seemed to think grandmothers – grandfathers, too – were dreary and dull and always talking about the past. Zillah's grandmother did talk about the past, but it was a really interesting past, and Zillah could have listened to the stories about it for ever, even when her grandmother's mind wandered into the dark bits. Even when she talked about Evelyn.

Once, Zillah had dared to ask who Evelyn was, but her grandmother only said, 'It was a long time ago. And it was all hushed up, because they didn't dare let anyone find out the truth. They couldn't risk it.' A pause, then she leaned forward, and her voice dropped to a soft whisper. 'But Evelyn is still there, you know. Somewhere inside The Tabor. Still there.'

She rocked to and fro in her chair, smiling. 'I could tell the family stories about Evelyn,' she said. 'I could tell them stories that would harrow up their souls.'

Zillah had no idea what harrow meant, but it sounded pretty grim, and she did not want it being done to her soul. Getting ready to travel to The Tabor, she hoped there was not likely to be any harrowing involved.

They went to Reivers in a train. 'But I've arranged for us to hire a car when we get there,' said Zillah's grandmother. 'So we'll be able to drive wherever we want.'

'To The Tabor.'

'Yes.'

'Do you know the way?' Grown-ups usually knew the way to places, but Zillah thought it would be as well to make sure.

'Oh, yes,' said her grandmother, almost to herself. 'Yes, I know the way.'

They were going to stay in an hotel for the night, which would be another adventure, because Zillah, at that age, had never stayed in an hotel. She enjoyed the journey; they had seats by themselves, and her grandmother talked a bit more about The Tabor.

'We're going there because I think one day it will be yours,' she said. 'I'm going to make sure of it. Now that your parents have gone . . .' There was a break in the soft old voice, and Zillah waited. Then her grandmother said, 'Now that they've gone, The Tabor must come to you. So tomorrow we're going to make sure it does.' A strange expression flickered on her face, and Zillah felt a brief jab of fear, because for a moment it had almost felt as if her grandmother was worried about what might be ahead. This was ridiculous, because she was never worried about anything.

Zillah said, 'What about Quentin? Mightn't The Tabor one day be his?' Quentin was older and he did important things at school that he told everyone about, and when he left school he was going to have a splendid career and make a lot of money.

They had really nice bedrooms in the hotel, next to one another with a bathroom between the two rooms. Zillah was allowed to have dinner in the restaurant that night, and it would all have been extremely exciting if it had not been for the feeling that her grandmother was still worried about going to The Tabor. But she had wanted to come here, and she had wanted Zillah to come, as well. It would be all right.

The next morning, immediately after breakfast, they got into the hire car, and spent ten minutes making sure where switches were for things like lights and indicators, and then they set off.

They drove out of the town where they had stayed, and Zillah's grandmother seemed to be concentrating on the driving. Zillah knew people did that, so she looked quietly out of the windows, not speaking. The countryside was flat and not very interesting, though. There were deep ditches gouged out of the countryside, which were very ugly.

Her grandmother seemed to know the way very well. Once or twice she said things like, 'That's where there's a famous old church,' or 'Along that road on the right there's the site of a long-ago battle. We might go back that way if there's time, then if you learn about it at school, you'll be able to say you've been there.'

But after about fifteen minutes, she said, 'We're almost there, Zillah,' and there was a note in her voice Zillah had never heard before. 'There's a turning just up ahead.'

'Where?' said Zillah, peering through the windows.

'There should be white railings, and a beech tree – although after so long, the beech tree might not . . . No, there it is. And there's the turning. Drum Lane.'

Drum Lane made you think of rat-a-tat music and men in uniforms marching past palaces, with flags waving and people shouting. But Drum Lane was an ordinary country lane, winding between trees and high hedges so that you could not see what was on the other side. The feeling of nervousness in the car was getting worse, so it was important to remember that this was an adventure and they were going to see a house that might one day belong to Zillah.

In front of them, set back into the hedge, were wide gates, made up of scrolly patterns and curly bits of iron. On one side was a sign in big letters that said *The Tabor.*

Zillah had to hop out to open the gates, and then close them when Gran had driven through. The gates creaked loudly, as if they were not opened very often and did not really like letting people through. But they swung inwards, although when Zillah closed them there was a grateful sighing sound.

Beyond the gates was a long drive, cracked and bumpy, so that the car bounced up and down. Zillah was about to ask whether they should stop and walk the rest of the way – although she had no idea how far that might be – when they came round the last bit of the drive, and there, crouching in a small dip in the ground, was the house.

TWELVE

It was like a house that somebody had drawn, doing it against the skies and the trees, but then adding extra pieces afterwards, because bits stuck out at peculiar angles. But the windows caught the morning sunlight, and the bricks of all the walls were a deep soft red, and it was the most beautiful house Zillah had ever seen.

Gran stopped the car, and sat for quite a long time, staring at the house, not speaking. At last, Zillah said, 'Does he – Mr Rivers – does he know we're coming?'

'Yes. I wrote to him, and he said we would be very welcome today. He also said I would probably find The Tabor somewhat different.' Her eyes went over the house. 'But it isn't so very different, although it could do with a bit of attention here and there. The gardens are overgrown, too. Tanglewood, that's what they are.'

She got out of the car, walked up to the massive oak door at the house's centre, and pulled on a kind of twisty iron rope. A bell jangled somewhere inside the house, and then the door opened.

There were shadows beyond the door, but they were somehow good shadows, and they joined themselves up into the figure of a man; thin, a bit bent and a bit grey-looking, so that there might be times when you would not be able to see him against the shadows.

As he stood looking at them, as Zillah's eyes got used to the dimness, he seemed to come more clearly into focus – like when you had a fuzzy picture on a TV and then it cleared. But there was still the impression that old shadows had somehow got together to make up a person.

Osbert Rivers said, 'Well. My family, converging on the ancestral home.'

His voice was not at all fuzzy. Zillah thought it was rather a nice voice.

'Hardly the whole family, Osbert,' said Gran. 'Only myself and Zillah.'

Osbert Rivers said, 'Zillah.' It was not quite a greeting, but it was as if he was recognizing her.

Zillah said, firmly, 'Hello, Mr Rivers.'

He smiled and his entire face changed and the shadows seemed to step back. He said, 'Someone's taught her a modicum of good manners.'

'Of course.'

'Since you're here, I suppose you'd better come in.'

'I suppose we had, Osbert. You're on your own now, aren't you?'

'I am.'

'I heard. I'm sorry.' And then, with an impatient movement, as if she was pushing something away, her grandmother said, 'You've let this place go downhill a bit, haven't you?'

'No money,' he said, shortly. 'And you know why that is. You know what I inherited. But come inside.' He led them across a hall that was somehow lower than the rest of the house, as if it might have sunk over the years. There was a stairway on the left, and there were scents of oldness and echoes and memories.

He took them to a long, large room, which was quite untidy, but with a nice untidiness of books strewn around and cushions that had fallen on to the floor and not been picked up. There was a huge fireplace and the walls were covered with dark wallpaper, but here and there were paintings of people with old-fashioned hairstyles and clothes. At one end were windows that looked as if they were actually doors, so that you could walk straight out into the gardens. Osbert Rivers waved them to sit down, and took a chair with a warm crimson velvet cover, facing them across the massive hearth.

'Zillah, you might like that little chair there. But wander around if you want. It's an interesting old house. You might find all kinds of things.'

Zillah began to walk round slowly, careful not to touch anything in case it might dislodge a pile of books or fragile-looking china, but wanting to look at the paintings hanging on the walls. The ladies were very dressed-up, with hair that must have taken hours to do, and the men either had thumbs in their waistcoat pockets or a book in their hands. They looked a bit pompous. Were any of them her own family? If they were great-grandmothers and great-grandfathers and things, she could boast about it to Quentin. She stood on tiptoe to see the paintings more closely.

'If you're looking for ancestors, Zillah,' said her grand-mother's voice suddenly, 'you won't find many on those walls. Walter bought most of them as a job lot from a market trader in Norwich. He did it for his wife – she was a Rivers as much as he was; two cousins marrying, in fact – and she liked to stress the Rivers lineage, God help her. When she realized there weren't any ancestors' portraits, she got Walter to buy a few likely looking ones in to impress people.'

'I never knew her,' said Osbert. 'In fact, I hardly knew Walter.'

'And yet despite that,' said Zillah's grandmother, in a voice Zillah had never heard her use, 'Walter left The Tabor to you.'

'You thought you should have had it, didn't you?' he said.

'I was promised it.'

'In return for your silence?'

'Yes. But Walter reneged on his promise and it went to you.' Gran made an angry gesture, then said, 'I've long since got over it, but now I want The Tabor for Zillah. She's the direct heir, you know. And I'm a good ten years ahead of you in age, Osbert, so you'll certainly outlive me.'

'But there's Evelyn,' he said. 'That's the barrier. I can't do anything about this house while Evelyn is still here. And if I die first—'

'I do understand,' said Gran.

And then they both suddenly seemed to remember that Zillah was there, and began to talk about how once there had been a terrace just outside this room, and how people used to have meals out there.

Zillah pretended not to have heard what had been said. But as she went through a sort of folded-back door, where another room opened off this one, her mind was tumbling. Gran was getting this house for her. Did that mean that after Osbert Rivers died, Zillah would own it? She thought that was how things worked. When somebody died, if they had a house it was given to a son or daughter to live in. It had to be written down, but Zillah knew about it because a really old aunt in the family had died last year, and Gran had explained about things being inherited. It was all very straightforward, she said.

But inheriting The Tabor would not be straightforward, because somebody – Evelyn – was in the way. A barrier.

The adjoining room was smaller, and there were some more paintings. Zillah walked round, not really seeing them, still thinking about The Tabor. Would it really be hers one day? Osbert Rivers was pretty old, so it might happen quite soon. But there was someone called Evelyn who was in the way . . .

She put out a hand to touch the nearest wall, liking the idea that it would one day belong to her, and that was when she saw the strange picture.

It was embroidered, not painted, which was not something Zillah could remember seeing before, but she thought people had once made pictures by sewing onto pieces of cloth. This was quite a large piece of cloth – it looked like a kind of canvas – and it was about the size of her school exercise book opened and flattened out. The picture had been made from silk threads and cottons and what looked like thin wool; the colours were faded, but you could see that once they must have been really bright.

The picture showed people in old-fashioned costumes dancing. Behind them was a house that was certainly meant to be The Tabor. It was really easy to imagine it coming to life – those people dancing and playing their music.

But when she looked more closely at the figures at the centre, she suddenly felt frightened. One of the figures was kneeling down, and the wrists were tied together and they were being held up over the figure's head. It would hurt to have your hands tied like that and be forced to hold them over your head. But the worst thing of all was the man standing over the tied-up figure. He was looking down at the tied-up person, and he was holding up an axe. Once Zillah had looked at this man, she could not look away, because it was clear that he was about to bring the blade down on the kneeling figure.

She could hear Gran and Osbert still talking – were they still talking about Zillah being given this house one day? Evelyn was being mentioned again – something about a tragedy, but there having been no other way to deal with it.

She gave the embroidered picture a last look, then went back into the main room, careful to seem ordinary and to smile.

They looked round, and Osbert Rivers said, 'Zillah, your grandmother thinks you might like to look round the gardens while she and I talk. Then we'll have a cup of tea.'

They wanted her completely out of the way. So that they could talk about her having this house?

'You can go through these long windows and be outside at once. I know they look like long windows, but really they're doors.' Osbert got up and opened one of the windows for her. 'Shall we say we'll have our cup of tea at four o'clock? Can you tell the time – oh, yes, you've got a watch. Make sure to stay in the main part of the grounds, won't you?'

'Yes, do what Mr Rivers says, Zillah. Those gardens don't look as if they've had much attention for years. There were potholes in the drive, and goodness knows what there might be on the sides of the house and around the back. You could trip over and sprain an ankle. I suppose gardeners cost money, do they, Osbert?'

'Yes,' he said, and smiled. 'We'll be having toasted teacakes with our cup of tea, Zillah, and they need to be eaten while they're still warm. Oh, and keep clear of the old stone archway that leads into the courtyard. That's very important.'

'It was never very safe, that arch, was it, Osbert?' said Gran. She glanced at him, and once again Zillah had the sense of something shared between them.

'No, and it still isn't,' he said. 'Don't go through that old stone archway, Zillah.'

Don't go through the old archway . . .

Zillah thought the words might be out of one of the old fairy stories. She did not read fairy stories now, because she was too old for them, but once she had done. In a lot of them, the person at the centre – it was usually a girl – was told not to go to a particular place. Not to open a door, not to walk through a dark old forest . . .

Not to go through an old archway that led into a courtyard . . .?

But Zillah wanted to know everything about this house, because one day it would be hers, and if she went through the archway no one would see her. Also, this would be one more thing to tell Quentin, who would be annoyed not to have been here. That certainly made it worth ignoring what Mr Rivers and grandmother had said.

It was important to walk carefully across the ground, because they had been right about the holes and ruts. And she was wearing her best shoes, which it would be a pity to spoil.

It was very quiet in the gardens. The sun was warm and there was a buzz of bees, and a scent of grass and of wild-flowers that had grown up by themselves, and of herby things that were in clumps here and there. Zillah did not know the names of the herbs or the wildflowers, but she liked the scent from them and she liked the sound of the bees. She wondered whether to pretend that these were the gardens that had grown up around Sleeping Beauty – the princess in the story who had slept in her bedroom for a hundred years, while briar hedges and thorny plants had grown up everywhere around her castle . . .

No, she would not pretend that, because it was actually quite a frightening story, with the princess shut away from the world, helpless and remote in her woodland prison, and all the bad people you got in fairy stories wanting to get at her. Crones and witches and things. Zillah was not sure what a crone was, but everyone knew what witches were. Not that there were such things, of course, and even if there had been once, there would not be any around today.

Here was the arch. It was high over her head, and it joined up two walls, so that it made a kind of giant doorway to go through. She went forward, and once beyond the arch she shivered, because everywhere seemed to suddenly have gone cold. That would be because of the high walls that shut out some of the sunlight, though. Zillah looked up at the walls, which had windows quite high up. There were no windows down here and no doors, but there was a stairway that went all the way up from the ground and there was a door. At the top of the stairs was a kind of narrow path, fixed to the wall. It went all the way along the building, and Zillah thought it was what was called a balcony. It would be pretty good to go up those steps and look down on everything from up there.

The stairs creaked a lot, but the wood was probably old, and the creaking was like when really old people said their bones were creaking. They were a bit wobbly as well, and Zillah had to hold tightly to the railing and make sure to walk in the centre of the steps. If you looked through them you could see all the way down to the ground. Once at the top, it was not so very high up, though, and now she could see the windows – she counted that there were five – and also the door. There did not seem to be curtains at any of the windows, so it did not look as if anyone lived up here. She would just peep through one of the windows to see what was in there; it would be something else to tell Quentin to make him jealous.

The balcony creaked and sagged as well, but Zillah walked along it to the row of windows. There was a kind of criss-cross on all of them – thin black strips making tiny diamond shapes on the glass. She put up a hand to trace the diamond shapes; the black stuff was hard and sharp, like metal. Zillah had never heard of people putting strips of metal across windows like this.

And then her heart jumped, because she thought there had been a movement in the glass – like when you went past a mirror, or when you saw your ghost-reflection in a window. Or when someone stepped up to a window and stared back at you from the other side . . .

But there was no one on the other side of the window – she could see the room more clearly now, although parts were in shadow. But even with the shadows, it was a really interesting room. There was old furniture – desks and a table and deep chairs, all properly set out as if somebody lived in there, not just piled up as if they had been bundled out of the way.

And there were shelves on each side of a fireplace, with rows of books. Zillah suddenly had a picture in her mind of a fire burning in that hearth, with someone sitting by it in the rocking chair. If anybody did live in this room, it would be someone who liked to sit and rock by the fire, and reach down a book from the shelf and sit reading it by the firelight. That was what people used to do in the olden days, when they did not have TV or radio or anything.

The door was only a few steps along; Zillah looked at it, then went towards it. It would be locked – or would it? Supposing she pushed it open, just a little way, so that she could go inside and see that room with the books and the hearth? Nobody would know. And it would be one more thing to tell Quentin. He would be annoyed at missing being taken to The Tabor, and he would be double-extra-annoyed about missing seeing secret rooms. This was such a good thought, that she took a deep breath and went up to the door. It had a twisty kind of handle, which was not like a door handle she had ever seen, and at first she thought it was not going to turn – that it was either locked after all, or stuck because it was old. But then she tried it the other way – like turning it backwards – and there was a peculiar click, as if something had been released. The door sprang open, but oddly it did not spring in like most doors, but out. Zillah pulled it a bit wider. Her hand shook a bit, she was not sure if it was with nervousness or excitement, but she was not going to turn back now, so she pulled the door wider, and stepped inside.

Beyond it was a big hall. There were no windows, but

enough light came in through the half-open door for Zillah to see that there were several inner doors. They were all shut, but this was so much like an ordinary house with rooms opening off a hall that she began to feel braver.

The floorboards creaked as she walked across them, and for a moment it seemed that a second lot of floorboards creaked from one of the rooms as well. This was a bit scary, but it was most likely the floorboards out here settling back into place after having been walked across. Gran's own house was quite old, and if you went up the stairs they creaked exactly like this, so that you found yourself looking back over your shoulder to make sure there was no one creeping up behind you.

But nobody would be creeping after Zillah in here, because nobody would be living out here all alone. The room with the rocking chair was on the right of the window, so she would look in there first. The door had the same strange handle, and Zillah had to twist it backwards again. But again came the click, and Zillah opened the door and stepped inside.

And now she could see the fireplace and the chair drawn up to the hearth. It was partly in the shadows, but she could see the edges of it, and it really was a rocking chair.

But although Zillah was standing quite still just inside the door, the creaking was going on. There it came again – a slow, steady sound, almost like a rhythm. She looked about her, and then fear started to wrap round her, because she knew what the sound was.

It was the rocking chair. It was moving, rocking back and forth, doing so quite slowly, but quite definitely. And it was doing so because someone was sitting in it. Zillah gasped, and began to back away towards the door, but as she did so the creaking stopped, and it was as if the shadows suddenly got up and took on the shape of a figure.

A voice from inside these shadows said, 'Who are you?'

This should have been quite an ordinary question, especially as Zillah had walked into these rooms without knocking or anything. But it was actually frightening. She was trying to think how to answer, and whether it would be very rude to simply run outside, when the voice said, 'Why don't you come in properly, so I can see you more clearly?'

At this, Zillah felt even more frightened, and she was turning back to the door, when the voice said, 'Do come inside – come over to the fireplace. I'd like to have a visitor . . . I have very few visitors . . . They don't want me to get out, you know. They've put a lock on the door that I can't open from the inside. Tell me your name.'

Zillah still wanted to run outside, but she also wanted to know who this person was, and the question about her name was perfectly ordinary. And it would only take a minute – less than a minute – to step back into the hall and be safely outside. She glanced back into the hall. Yes, the door was still open, so she could run out at any minute. Also, this was a person who liked to have visitors and hardly ever had any, which was pretty sad, so she said, 'I'm Zillah Rivers. I'm here with my grandmother.'

'Your grandmother?' There was a sudden movement from the shadow figure, as if it had sat up very straight. 'Elwen? Is your grandmother Elwen?'

'Um, yes. She brought me to meet Mr Rivers.'

'You've been in the house?' Again, there was the impression that the figure was sitting bolt upright.

'Yes.'

'Did you look round it?'

'Well, a bit.'

'Did you see the tapestry?'

'I don't know what—'

'A picture – done in embroidery. Stitching. He's got it hanging on one of the walls – I know he has. It's the Dance,' said the voice, and there was such urgency in the tone, that Zillah flinched.

But she said, 'I didn't know it was called a tapestry. It's a picture in silk and wool. It's on the wall in a frame.'

There was a pause, then, 'Did you understand it?'

'There were people dancing and playing music. And someone was tied up, and – there was a man – holding up an axe—'

'Ah.' The sound was that of a dry old wind stirring dead

leaves. 'The axe. The tapestry shows an execution, Zillah. Do you know what that word means?'

'I think so.'

'And do you know who it is in that picture, Zillah?'

The figure was standing up and starting to come towards her, and Zillah took a few more steps back. But she said, 'The picture was history, wasn't it? Old-fashioned clothes and things. Not real people.'

'But they were real people,' said the voice. 'They lived here. I know all about that Dance, Zillah, and a very long time ago – before you were born – I got people to perform it. Nobody had seen it for hundreds of years, but I found the steps and the music in the church, and I arranged it all.' There was a note of pride, as if this had been a very clever thing to have done. 'I took part in it, Zillah. I was at the centre – like the figures in the tapestry.'

It was as if the strange shadowy room with the hearth and the bookshelves that had looked so safe and comfortable was distorting, like when somebody broke their arm and it all went out of shape. It was as if something was twisting this whole room out of shape.

Zillah heard herself say, 'Were you the person tied up?'

'Oh, no,' said the voice, at once. 'I wasn't the victim. I was the one with the axe. I was the executioner.'

The figure came closer, the arms raised, and Zillah felt sick horror wash over her, because the arms were outstretched, and the hands, *the hands* . . .

She began to back away, trying not to look at the hands that were reaching out, but as she did so the figure came towards her.

In a terrified whisper, Zillah said, 'I don't understand any of this. I don't even know who you are—?'

The figure came towards her. The frightening voice said, 'I'm Evelyn, Zillah.'

Evelyn. The room seemed to tip completely upside-down, and the words spoken by Osbert and Zillah's grandmother came roaring into Zillah's head.

'*I can't do anything while Evelyn is still here*,' Osbert had said. And Gran had said, almost to herself, '*Evelyn is the barrier of course . . .*' And then, '*It can't go on for ever, Osbert.*'

In that moment Zillah had understood that it was the person called Evelyn who stood between her and The Tabor. She understood it now, and something very strange was starting to unfold inside her mind. It was as if something that had been huddled in a dark corner was opening.

She ran from the room, the thing in her mind still unfolding, and went through the door that was always locked – the door Evelyn could not open from inside. Because of those hands, thought Zillah, shuddering.

But her mind was filling up with light, and although her heart was pounding so furiously, she thought it might explode, her mind was racing, and images were pouring in. The Tabor. If Evelyn was not in the way, once Osbert was dead, The Tabor would be Zillah's. She stood very still on the balcony. She could see through the window into the room with the rocking chair and the bookshelves. She could see Evelyn moving slowly across the room, coming towards the open door.

They don't want me to get out . . . They've put a lock on the door that I can't open from the inside . . .

The dreadful hands were pushing the door even wider, and Zillah pressed back against the wall, keeping to the side of the door, where Evelyn would not see her.

There was a moment when she thought nothing was going to happen, and then slowly – cautiously – the thin figure appeared in the doorway. For the first time light fell across the figure, and Evelyn flinched slightly, as if direct daylight was something unknown, something to shy away from. There were a few more uncertain steps, then hands reached out to grasp the railings. But they were hands that could not really grasp anything, and that would not be able to clutch at the railings . . . And even then, the railings were really shaky. The figure standing there was shaky, too – as if walking out here and facing daylight was something that had been forgotten about.

As the figure turned its head to look round, Zillah ran

forward, and with every ounce of strength she possessed, she pushed Evelyn as hard as she could.

Evelyn fell back against the railings, arms flung out as if desperately trying to grasp on to something to prevent a fall. But the railings were already splintering, and a section of them broke away. The splintered wood fell from the balcony, and there was a dreadful cry of pain and terror. Evelyn fell with the splintered railings – down, down, all the way on to the cobbled courtyard below.

There was a really dreadful sound – a kind of wet crunch, and for several moments Zillah could not move. Then she took a shaky step forward, and looked down. Evelyn was lying on the ground, the head a mess of blood and bone.

And then Zillah lifted her eyes and looked towards the stone archway and saw that standing beneath it were her grandmother and Osbert.

THIRTEEN

Zillah was huddled up in a chair in the long room. A thick rug was wrapped round her, and her hands were cupped around a mug of hot milk, laced with honey. Gran had made her swallow half a paracetamol tablet, and Osbert Rivers had gone all round the room turning up dials on heaters, saying any kind of shock left you feeling icily cold.

Zillah did not say she did not feel cold in the least. She pretended to shiver and she managed to cry a bit as well. But the remarkable thing – the thing she knew she was going to remember for a very long time and probably her entire life – was how marvellous it had been to do what she had just done. To push Evelyn all the way over those railings and watch what happened. Evelyn had deserved it – 'I was the executioner', those had been the exact words. And Evelyn had been in the way of Zillah having this beautiful house. Osbert had said it earlier, and Gran had said Evelyn was the barrier.

Gran and Osbert were telling her she was not in any trouble, and she was not to be in the least frightened, because nobody was angry with her.

'What happened was an accident,' Gran said. 'We'll deal with everything, and we'll make sure you're all right.'

'We'll look after you,' said Osbert. His voice was a bit wobbly, and he had poured himself something from a bottle on the side of his chair and gulped it down in one go.

Gran said, 'Did . . . did Evelyn talk to you, at all, Zillah?'

'Oh, no. I just wanted to see what was in those rooms. I know I shouldn't have gone there. I'm very sorry indeed.' It would be a good idea to cry again; Zillah managed to do so.

Gran and Osbert went over to the far side of the room, and talked quietly for a few moments. It was annoying not to be able to hear what they were saying, but when they came back, Osbert said, 'Zillah, one day, when you're old enough to understand, your grandmother will tell you about Evelyn. For now I'll just say that Evelyn's story was a very sad one. It goes back a very long way – your grandmother was a young girl at the time, and I was even younger. I think I was about the age you are now, Zillah. We were both here for the first time.' He glanced at Gran.

'It was while we were here that Evelyn had be locked away in those rooms,' she said. 'And no one who was there that night will ever have forgotten it.' Her eyes had taken on the odd look that always made Zillah think she was staring into a long-ago time that no one else could see or knew about. She waited, and after a moment Gran said, 'It was the night that something called the Reivers Dance was revived, Zillah. It was the first time it had been performed for – how long had it been, Osbert?'

'Almost three hundred and fifty years,' he said. 'It's a massively long time, isn't it, Zillah? No one had seen the Dance in all that time – no one had ever danced it. No one had dared,' he said, softly. 'You were eighteen at the time, weren't you, Elwen?'

'Yes.'

'There was an old document in the church,' said Osbert, to Zillah. 'Someone had made notes about the Dance a very long time ago, and those notes had been copied. Evelyn found the document and got people to learn the steps and the music, so it could be performed again.'

'Osbert and I had been invited to stay here by Walter,' said Gran, as if eager to explain. 'We were told it was a great privilege – hardly anyone was ever asked here, you see.'

'Some people even insisted The Tabor was nothing more than a myth,' put in Osbert.

'It was never that,' said Gran. And then, in a sharper voice, 'Osbert – what are we going to do about what's happened today? We can't risk calling a doctor, can we? Or the police?'

Zillah looked up at this, but Osbert was already saying, 'No, of course we can't. Evelyn's death was an accident – Zillah didn't intend . . . But Evelyn's supposed to have died many years ago, and if there were enquiries now – an inquest . . . The whole thing would come out. Everything that happened all those years ago would come out.'

'Would it matter after so long . . . Yes, of course it would,' she said, before he could speak. 'Apart from everything else, there's the damage it would do to Zillah. I've got to protect her above everything else.'

This sounded very good indeed. Zillah had known that nothing would happen to her, but it was nice to hear it said.

'Also,' said Osbert, 'there are the people who lied and covered up the truth and helped with the deception on that night. Some of them are still here in Reivers, and they need to be considered, as well.'

'You and I were among those people, Osbert. You were only a child, but—'

'I was old enough to understand,' said Osbert. 'I was Zillah's age.' There was suddenly a bad moment when he looked very directly at Zillah, but then he came back to his chair and reached for Gran's hand. 'Don't look like that,' he said, very gently. 'This family's covered up more than one strange event over the years. We'll think of a way to do so again.' He frowned. 'If I had been ten years younger I could have dealt with this myself, and no one would have needed to know. But I couldn't do it now, and you certainly couldn't.'

'If only Trigg—'

'Yes, Trigg would have thought of a way,' said Osbert.

'I always wished I had known him better,' said Gran. 'It's curious, but during that week I was here – I had a strong sense of connection between us. Only a feeling, but—'

'One of those might-have-been things?'

'Yes. Osbert, he's been dead for two years now, hasn't he? How have you coped with Evelyn?'

'As a matter of fact, I've had help from a surprising source,' said Osbert. 'Do you remember the ladies in the antique shop in the village?'

'I think so. An odd name they had.'

'Savory,' said Osbert. 'Two of them were here that night. They're both dead now, of course, but over the years I got to know them well. And then some nieces inherited the shop, and I got to know them, as well.'

'Ah. And the nieces inherited the truth about Evelyn?'

'Yes. And I think they could be trusted now,' he said. 'And there's one other person who could be trusted – someone who could help in a practical way.'

'Who—?'

'D'you remember that local builder who was there that night?'

'Grindall,' said Zillah's grandmother, after a moment.

'Yes, Giff Grindall. He died years ago, of course, but the firm's still going. In fact it's flourishing – I shouldn't think there's a building contract within fifty miles that isn't handled by Grindall's. Old Giff's son's been running things for years, although he's getting on as well, of course. He must be almost seventy. But he's a spry old boy, and he's training up his own son to take over in a few years.'

'It was Giff Grindall who created those courtyard rooms, wasn't it?' said Zillah's grandmother, thoughtfully. 'You were too young to take much notice of the practicalities, but I remember how Trigg designed the mechanism for the doors, and how Mr Grindall made it. He fitted all the doors in those rooms. Is it his son you've got in mind now?'

'Yes. He helped that night. He couldn't have been more than about sixteen, but he knew what had happened all right.'

'Can we risk it?'

'I don't think we've got a choice,' said Osbert.

As he reached for the phone, Gran said in a sudden, urgent voice, 'Osbert—'

'Yes?'

'Before Grindall gets here, there's something one of us must do.'

Osbert said, in a voice so quiet Zillah knew she had not been meant to hear it. But she did hear it. Osbert said, in that quiet, secret voice, 'The hands. We must cover up the hands.'

It seemed that Mr Grindall was at his builder's yard, and could come out to The Tabor within the next half-hour. Before he arrived, though, Zillah was taken to lie down in a bedroom, which Gran said would be the best thing for her after such a terrible experience. Zillah knew quite well that she was being got out of the way so that she would not hear what was said to Mr Grindall, which was annoying, because she wanted to know what was happening.

The bedroom was at the top of a creaky staircase leading off the big hall. The stairs were quite steep, but there was a banister to hold on to; it was glossy and smooth, and it felt like silk.

'That's because it's extremely old,' said Gran. 'It's because so many people have gone up and down these stairs, sliding their hands along this banister as they went. I'm glad to see Osbert's kept a bit of polish going around the place, though. I suppose a cleaner comes in – I must ask him about that. I can't see him flicking dusters or trundling a vacuum cleaner around.'

Zillah could not see it, either, but she was more interested in the bedroom Gran had taken her to, which was the biggest bedroom she had ever seen. The windows looked down over the gardens, towards a wall at the very end, and a garden gate.

The bed in the room was the hugest bed Zillah had ever seen; Gran said it had belonged to an ancestor called Rosalind Rivers.

'Your ancestor and mine – and Osbert's, as well. They say Rosalind was the most beautiful Rivers lady ever, and all the men used to fall in love with her the minute they saw her. And now you're going to lie down in her bed.'

This was quite a good story. Zillah liked knowing she was in Rosalind Rivers' bed, and she pretended for a while that she was Rosalind, and that men were all falling in love with her.

There was a faint hum of voices downstairs – Gran and Mr Rivers, and a rumbly voice which must be Mr Grindall. Was there anyone else with them? Osbert Rivers had talked about some people in an antique shop somewhere.

Zillah was suddenly very curious about these people who could be trusted, so much so that she stopped thinking about Rosalind Rivers, and started wondering who else might be downstairs and what they were saying. Moving cautiously so that no one would hear her, she got out of bed and went to the door. She did not put her shoes on, because it would be quieter to tiptoe along in her socks. The landing was a big one, with lots of doors opening off it, but Zillah was not going to look in any of the rooms; she was just going to creep a little way down the stairs. Listening to other people talking like this was not something you were supposed to do, but they would be talking about Evelyn and she might find out a bit more. Also, they would probably be talking about Zillah herself.

But as she reached the twisty bit of the stairs, the rumbly-voiced man was leaving. Zillah could still hear him, but he was standing just outside the door, so she could not see him.

But he was saying that no one would find out. 'You can trust me for that, Mr Rivers,' he said. 'I'll fetch a few things from the yard, and I'll be straight back. Everything'll be done by teatime.' A pause, and then, 'After that, it's my advice that you seal up those rooms and all the bad memories with them, and you let Evelyn Rivers and all those grisly tales about the Murder Dance be forgotten once and for all.'

Forgotten once and for all. That was what should have happened, thought Zillah, sitting in the inglenook at The Daunsen, only half-listening to Phineas Fox and Arabella talking to Quentin.

Toby had gone to the bar to collect more drinks, and Zillah forced her mind back to what was being said. It seemed that

Phineas and Arabella were driving into Norwich the following day to look at local archives and back issues of old local newspapers.

'There's a big library with what sounds like a really good section for Norfolk's history,' said Arabella. 'Maps and documents and hopefully old photographs and newspapers. Phin will probably want to camp out there for the next fortnight.'

Phin smiled at her, and quite suddenly it was as if a light had come on. For a really startling moment, Zillah wondered if this was how he might look when he was in bed with someone. Alight and alive and filled with energy.

But he had turned back to Quentin. 'I know you don't want the Dance to be part of the PR,' he said, 'but you wouldn't mind if I looked into it a bit more deeply, would you?'

'Oh, no. My family doesn't own it,' said Quentin, with what Zillah recognized as his Rivers of Reivers manner. 'And I'd be interested in anything you can find out,' he said, and almost as an afterthought, added, 'It's Zillah's family too, of course.'

'What's really attracting me,' said Phin, 'is that it seems to be such a strong memory. It doesn't sound as if the Dance has been performed for a very long time – maybe several centuries – but it's still remembered. So you'd expect it to have been revived for centenary things and the millennium and whatnot. Villages often do that – there are plenty of them in this country – probably in a lot of other countries, too. Old dances and processions and things preserved and trotted out every so often. Why hasn't that happened with the Reivers Dance?'

Arabella said, 'The memory might have survived because of the rumour that one of Shakespeare's men performed in it. Will Kempe,' she said, looking at Quentin and Zillah, and Zillah saw Quentin nod solemnly, as if he knew all about Will Kempe.

He said, 'I didn't realize it was as old as that. But will you find anything from so far back?'

'You might,' said Toby, coming back with the drinks. 'Phin, d'you remember when we were writing *Bawdy Ballads*? We found pamphlets and leaflets about what MPs were up to or the latest murder, and who had been carted off to Newgate for debt.'

Zillah put on her interested face, and said it was all really
fascinating, and she thought it was great that they were taking
so much trouble over Quentin's restaurant idea.

'Particularly since you must have masses of commitments
in London.'

'Not too many at the moment,' said Phineas. 'This is actually a welcome diversion.'

'And if Arabella does take on the publicity for the restaurant,
I shall expect to pay a proper fee, of course,' said Quentin.

'Oh, yes, I know that,' said Zillah, and thought Quentin had
said that in the tone of one correcting an ignorant child who
has forgotten its manners.

It was annoying that on the way to bed Toby tried to separate
her from the others. But Zillah adroitly fell into step with
Quentin, and, as it turned out, it was a very good thing she
did, because it seemed that he had been out to Codling's office
that very afternoon.

'Come into my room for a moment and I'll tell you,' he
said, opening the door.

Zillah perched on the dressing-table stool, and Quentin said,
in his serious voice, 'Zill, I want to tell you something very
important. I've made a will and it's all drafted out, and it'll
be ready for me to sign tomorrow or the day after. It's got
to be . . . I think the word Codling used was endorsed.'

Zillah's heart had begun to race, but she said in an ordinary
voice, 'I didn't know you were going to make a will.'

'Of course I'd make a will, after inheriting The Tabor,' he
said, and his hand came out as if to touch her hair, and then
fell back, as if he had thought better of it. He said, 'I wanted
you to know that if anything bad should happen to me, you'll
be well provided for.'

'I don't understand . . . Oh,' said Zillah, clasping her hands
together. 'You don't mean that you're going to leave The
Tabor to me?'

'Who else would I leave it to?'

He was smiling in that stupid slushy way, but for once it
did not matter because he had done what she had hoped – he
was leaving her The Tabor; the house that should have been
hers anyway, that had been promised to her . . . Evelyn had

stood in the way once, but she had dealt with Evelyn. Now Quentin stood in the way. The shadow-plan nudged at her again.

She murmured something about being grateful, adding that of course Quentin would live until he was a hundred anyway, then went along to her own room. Lying in bed, she was aware of a scudding excitement. It was the feeling she had had that day when Evelyn fell over the ramshackle balcony. How could she have forgotten how it had felt? But she had not forgotten, of course, not really.

And in two days, three at the most, Quentin would have signed a will, bequeathing everything to Zillah. Including The Tabor.

With the thought came the memory of how she had stood at the side of the door into the courtyard rooms, and how, when Evelyn came timidly out into the light, Zillah had bounded forward and pushed. The railings had given way so easily.

As she finally drifted into sleep, she was smiling.

Quentin, undressing for bed, thought the evening had gone well. He thought he was handling things exactly in the right way, and he was pleased at how enthusiastic Arabella was about tracing the Rivers family – arranging with Phineas Fox to go out to the big Norwich library. As for Phineas, Quentin would admit to a slight unease, because Fox was not like anyone he had ever met. It was something to do with the way he listened to what people said, with such complete absorption. Still, he seemed interested in The Tabor's history, and Quentin was not going to turn down any help.

As he got into bed, he dwelled with pleasure on Zillah's reaction when he had told her about intending to leave her The Tabor. Her little face had lit up, and she had been delighted and utterly taken by surprise.

He lay awake for a while, thinking about that separate building at The Tabor. He would get Grindall to draw up some plans for turning it into private living quarters for himself and Zillah. How big were the rooms? They would want a sitting room, and it would be nice if there was space for a dining area, as well. Separate bedrooms, of course, that went without saying, and Zillah should have the nicest room for herself. There would be a deep soft double bed in her room . . . The familiar surge of longing seized him, but with it was the familiar panic, because he had never actually managed to completely . . . It would be all right with Zillah, though. Those girls in the past had been wrong for him – too eager, grabbing and writhing. Zillah would not grab or writhe. She would be loving and natural. Quentin smiled at the prospect, and images of Zillah in a wide soft bed, her hair dishevelled against silken cushions, accompanied him into sleep.

'What did you think of her?' said Arabella to Phin. 'Is she just a standard adventuress sinking her claws into Toby, or is she something else?'

Phin was sorting through the contents of his case. 'I think there's a bit more to her than the average gold-digger,' he said. 'I think she might be capable of being very ruthless.'

'Aren't gold-diggers usually ruthless anyway?'

'I expect so, but Zillah struck me as being a level up from that. Maybe that should be a level down. Did you hear Toby tapping at her door a little while ago?'

'Yes, but I don't think she opened the door.'

'I don't think she did, either,' said Phin.

'I wonder what she'd have done if she thought it was you knocking on the door,' said Arabella, thoughtfully, and Phin looked at her, in surprise.

'That's one of the wildest things you've said for a long time,' he said. 'Of course she wouldn't have opened the door to me. I don't think she even liked me very much.'

'Don't you?' Arabella smiled. 'I think she liked you very much indeed. I think she'd have opened her door like a shot if you'd knocked on it.'

'Rubbish. In any case, I certainly wouldn't tangle with her,' he said. 'I don't want to tangle with anyone except you. In fact, if all the women in all the world paraded themselves in front of me, and performed every dance from the Seven Veils to collections from the Kama Sutra . . . D'you know, I'm sure I packed my pyjamas, but I can't seem to find them.'

Arabella, who was already in bed, said, 'I can't see the least need for you to wear pyjamas.'

'You're wearing a nightdress,' pointed out Phin.

'Yes, but that's so you can have the fun of taking it off.'

FOURTEEN

'I think,' said Arabella, as they drove out of Reivers towards Norwich and the library the following morning, 'that we should divide the task, don't you? So that we don't find we've both been working on the same things and duplicating the search.'

'Divide and multiply,' said Phin. 'Good idea.' He frowned at the road unwinding ahead of them, then said, 'How about if you take the 1600s onwards? It's possible that some of the really early stuff might be in Latin, and you're the linguist of the party.'

'You have such touching faith,' said Arabella, grinning.

'Also, you've already made a bit of a start – that book you unearthed in the antique shop sounded useful.'

'It's got some quite good stuff,' said Arabella. 'It was written in the mid-eighteen hundreds so it's not contemporary, but the author gives some primary sources that we might follow up.'

'Who's the author?'

'Somebody called H.J. Marplot, which sounds like a character from a Restoration comedy or a Sheridan play, doesn't it? There's a string of letters after H.J.'s name, and he – I should think it's a he – sounds alarmingly scholarly. There was quite a bit about The Tabor, and there's an author's note to say his own family came from Reivers somewhere in the distant past, so I should think he'd have a few inherited stories.'

'It sounds like a good source,' said Phin. 'In fact . . . Hell's teeth, I think that was the turning for Norwich and I've gone past it. We'll have to go on to the next one.'

'I've been distracting you, haven't I?' said Arabella. 'Shall I shut up?'

'No, don't do that. I like listening to you.'

'Even when I make you lose the way and stray on to the wrong path?'

'Especially when you make me lose the way and stray on to the wrong path,' said Phin, not taking his eyes off the road, but smiling.

'You had a *very* wicked glint in your eye when you said that.'

'You generate a wicked glint. And it looks as if we're back on the straight and narrow now – we should be able to take that slip-road and get into Norwich that way. See if you can call up directions to a car park, will you? As near to the library as possible.

'I suppose you're going after those suspicious-sounding almshouses, aren't you?' said Arabella, leaning forward to the sat-nav. 'If you take the second exit off this roundabout, I think there's a multistorey car park ahead.'

'I'll probably end up wading through years of church bequests and workhouse trusts and following up foundations and worthy benefactors,' said Phin, pulling the car over. 'I'm not very hopeful of finding anything, though. I think you'll have a much livelier time.'

But the search turned out to be more interesting than he had expected. He was allotted a desk with a monitor and keyboard and, after one or two false starts, began to plough doggedly through reports and minutes of parish council meetings and church commissions, and ponderous directives from prebendaries, from the late nineteenth and early twentieth century. There did not seem to be any mention of Walter Rivers, though, and after an hour Phin was just thinking he would collect two cups of coffee from the machine in the lobby and find out how Arabella was getting on, when he turned up a set of records titled 'Parish Records, 1920 to 1925: Almshouses and Chantry Houses'. Probably it would be another set of turgid, self-important reports and treacly memorials, but he would go through it anyway.

It was not parish records at all. It was a newspaper article, which had got itself into a file for parish records. The print was smudgy and the date at the head was so blurred it was difficult to make it out, but Phin thought it was March, or possibly May, and the year could have been either 1921 or 1922.

A name in the first line leapt out at him and sent all thoughts of coffee from his head. Walter Rivers.

> Members of the Parish Council received a shock when Mr Walter Rivers, of The Tabor, Reivers Village, entered unannounced into their meeting on Friday afternoon, for the purpose of objecting to the Planning Committee's proposal to exercise a Compulsory Purchase Order across a strip of his land, [see sketch map on adjacent page].
>
> Mr Rivers had brought with him a Charter dating to 1300, granting the land to the Rivers family 'in perpetuity'. A Council member, who has asked not to be named, told your reporter that Mr Rivers brandished the Charter at the assembled meeting, and informed them that he would have no truck with what he referred to as their outrageous plan to snatch his land from under his very feet.
>
> 'None of us knew quite what to do for a few moments,' said the Council member, 'so it was fortunate that a member of Mr Rivers' household – Mr Nicolas Trigg, who had driven him to the meeting – then entered the room, and was able to persuade Mr Rivers that he had made out a good case for his objection, and they could now return home.'
>
> The proceedings were recorded in the Council minutes.

Phin rather liked the possibility of Walter Rivers having been a rebel, and he scrolled down to see if he appeared in any more articles. He did appear again, although this next article was even more blurred, so that it was impossible to make out the date at all.

Mr Walter Rivers, of The Tabor, Reivers Village, was yesterday charged in Norwich Magistrates' Court with having committed a breach of the peace.

This newspaper has it on very good authority (and from several sources) that the breach consisted of Mr Rivers making a speech in the centre of Reivers itself. He spoke for some ten minutes, during which time he allegedly denounced all Councils – Parish, Borough, and County – of being tainted with what he referred to as the legacy of the Norman invaders who had tyrannized the land and appropriated whole swathes of it for their robber barons. He was, he said, extremely sorrowful to discover that this practice was still rife in Norfolk, and he would not kowtow to jumped-up, land-pilfering jack-in-offices, never mind they had increased their offer for his land fourfold in the last three months. They might increase it tenfold and a hundredfold, he said. Three witnesses report that at this point Mr Rivers shook his fist at the crowd that had gathered to listen.

Miss Matilda Savory, of Savory's Antique Emporium, told your reporter that Mr Rivers then produced a sheaf of notes, from which he quoted several laws. However, these laws were, said the good lady, so ancient that nobody had ever heard of them. Her sister, Miss Dorothea Savory, believed that the laws were in Medieval Latin and that Mr Rivers – who had been considered something of a scholar in his youth – read them in this archaic language. It was therefore hardly surprising that nobody had understood them, said Miss Dorothea, not even the Reverend Bream, who was always so learned. You only had to listen to his sermons.

The Court heard evidence from several witnesses who had been present on the morning, all of whom stated roundly that Mr Rivers had a right to his own land, and nobody should be allowed to take it from him. Why otherwise had their ancestors fought in Wat Tyler's Rebellion against Richard II and Henry le Despenser, and for why had Evelyn Rivers gone to that grisly death in The Tabor's own courtyard?

They were told by the magistrate on the bench that the Peasants' Revolt had nothing whatsoever to do with today's case, and that if they could not keep to the matter in hand and give plain straightforward evidence about the events of Thursday afternoon, they were please to leave the courtroom forthwith.

Other witnesses included Reverend Bream, the Misses Savory, Mr Giff Grindall, the local builder and handyman, and his daughter, Belinda Grindall, currently housemaid at The Tabor.

Reverend Bream deposed that Mr Rivers was a most law-abiding person, who had done a great deal of good work for the community. The brief burst of anger in the village square was, he was sure, due to a mere mental aberration – possibly to frustration because some plan he had was going awry. Doubtless he had been engrossed in a study of old land laws earlier in the day and that had informed his speech. Reverend Bream could certainly bear witness to the fact that Mr Rivers had referred to *feu* and *scutage*, which were not terms he himself had heard mentioned for a very long time indeed.

[Editor's note: *Feu* refers to rights granted by an overlord to a vassal who held it in fealty – "in fee" – in return for a form of feudal allegiance and service. *Scutage* was often a tax paid in lieu of military service. Source: *Magna Carta*.]

Miss Savory said that Mr Rivers had told no more than was God's truth about his family owning the land for several centuries, in which she was supported by Miss Dorothea Savory.

Mr Grindall said it was a sad day if a man could not be sure of keeping his own bit of land, never mind the Council saying they only wanted a four-feet-wide strip at the bottom of the garden for a bit of road-widening. You could not, said Mr Grindall, trust Councils from here to that door, and he did not mind who heard him say so.

Belinda Grindall deposed as having heard Mr Rivers

speaking in the village square while collecting provisions. She had missed the last part of the speech, however, on account of her father sending her running into The Daunsen to get a measure of whisky from the Jug & Bottle, since folks protesting their rights shouldn't ought to be left standing in the cold raw wind while bovine-faced constables argued about whether to arrest them.

(There was a brief delay at this point, while it was explained to the magistrates the exact meaning of a Jug & Bottle, it not being a term which Their Worships had encountered.)

Mr Rivers was bound over to keep the peace for a twelve-month, and ordered to pay for some trifling damage caused to the War Memorial in the square (erected in 1919 and dedicated to the Fallen of the Great War, see illustration on Page 5), which damage had occurred when Mr Rivers had accidentally chipped a corner of the stone plinth with the toe of his boot. Mr Rivers said that since he had commissioned and paid for the memorial's creation in the first place, he supposed he was entitled to gouge a bit of its stone out if he happened to take a mis-step. He would, however, foot any bills presented to him for the repair, and he dared say Grindall would not fleece him when it came to the work.

At this point Mr Grindall stood up in the public gallery, whence most of the witnesses had retired in order to hear the verdict, and was understood to say he had never fleeced a customer in his life, being a most moderate man when it came to charges. He added that since Mr Rivers had put a fair amount of work his company's way over the years, he, Gilbert Grindall, was not likely to bite the hand that fed him by presenting greedily inflated bills.

Mr Rivers was also fined the sum of one guinea, to which he retorted that he did not give a fig for guineas or pettifogging bindings-over, and the Court could have the money that very afternoon, and he would deliver it in farthings in a garden sack.

Footnote: This newspaper understands that Mr Nicolas

Trigg, who is part of Mr Rivers' household, presently
attended the clerk's office of the courts to deliver a garden
sack filled with farthings to the Court premises, labelled,
'One guinea, which represents a ten-feet strip of land
and a pound of flesh'.

The farthings were counted by two clerks, found to
total the requisite sum of one guinea, and a receipt was
issued.

Phin enjoyed these accounts so much he read them both twice,
and then sent a request for printing them. Arabella would enjoy
them, too, and there were several facts that might be useful
– including the name of Nicolas Trigg.

He typed in a search request for Mr Trigg, not especially
hopefully, but two results came up. Both were in an obscure
set of parish records for Reivers. The first was in a set of
minutes of a meeting, in which Mr Trigg was referred to as
'devoting a portion of his time to assisting the church authorities with administering Poor Relief funds', and to a discussion
of 'suitable remuneration'.

The second was a letter which Mr Trigg had written in
March 1921.

In a firm, clear hand, that managed to triumph over the
faded ink and slightly blurred scanned image, Nicolas Trigg
had written:

Sir,
I have the honour to respond to your letter of the 9th ult,
which you sent in response to the offer made by Walter
Rivers, Esq., to place at your disposal a portion of his
residence – The Tabor, in the village of Reivers, in the
County of Norfolk.

Your earlier letter drew to Mr Rivers' attention the
fact that the buildings he is prepared to make available
are what you term limited. By this, he assumes you mean
they will only house a very small number of people. Mr
Rivers would bring to your attention the fact that there
are only likely to be a small number of people in Reivers
eligible for this particular kind of charity.

Attached to his offer are the following stipulations, which he asks me to say are absolute and not open for discussion or amendment of any kind:

1. The Tabor is to be officially and formally registered by the Parish as an almshouse within the area of Reivers Village, and its environs, stretching to four miles on all boundaries. As such, it is to be given the legal safeguards accorded to all such premises.

2. The specific designation for the buildings is to be The Courtyard Rooms. Mr Rivers will not entertain your request that they be called by any other name; he has no mind to have any part of his house called a Chantry House or a Bede House, which, he asks me to remind you, are medieval terms, and as such hardly relevant in the twentieth century. He further adds that he did not endure the Great War or the rigours of the Boer War to be told what to call his own property by Church Commission underlings.

3. Mr Rivers will be entirely responsible for maintenance pertaining to The Courtyard Rooms, to include heating and general repair. Any incumbents will be provided with one main meal each day, available at noon. In this he will be assisted by the Misses Savory, who have undertaken to be partly responsible for such arrangements.

4. Mr Rivers will make all decisions regarding occupants of the rooms, and will not accept submissions or recommendations from anyone. This, too, is an absolute decision which is not open for discussion or argument. He asks me to point out to you that his family have lived in Reivers for several centuries, that he is perfectly familiar with its residents, and entirely able to judge for himself who is eligible for this help, and who is malingering.

I remain, sir, yours very respectfully,
Nicolas Trigg

'What comes across very clearly,' said Phin over a sandwich lunch with Arabella in a nearby coffee shop, 'is that although Walter designated those courtyard rooms as almshouses, he was fiercely determined to preserve the privacy of The Tabor. And the two things don't go together.'

He helped himself to two of the very substantial toasted sandwiches which Arabella had ordered and which were served with a large tub of French fries.

'And there's his fight with the planners,' he said. 'The planning application was on record – I found it, and they wanted the narrowest sliver of land imaginable. It was on the southern boundary, and it was only wanted as a kind of windbreak for something to do with a drainage system – underground pipes or something like that.'

'Which all suggests Walter had something to hide,' said Arabella, reaching for more chips. 'In the courtyard rooms themselves?'

'He certainly fenced them around with all kinds of restrictions,' said Phin. 'And Nicolas Trigg seems to have been part of it – oh, and a couple of Savory ladies. They keep cropping up every so often, don't they? They spoke for him in the magistrates' court when he was hauled up for a breach of the peace.'

'I like the way the local people did that,' said Arabella, rereading the print-out. 'Even the vicar. Would he have spoken out if Walter was up to anything dubious?'

'The Church isn't exactly a stranger to cover-ups,' said Phin, dryly, and then, 'Arabella, am I seeing mysteries where there aren't any?'

'No, you're playing devil's advocate,' said Arabella. 'As researchers should.'

Phin frowned at the print-outs again, then said, 'Let's forget Walter for the moment. What did you find? You had a definite sparkle in your eyes when we came out of the library.'

'I did find something,' she said, 'It isn't much, because there was far more archive stuff than I expected and I had to plough through acres of material. But I got print-outs, and they're all in my bag – wait a minute while I . . . Oh, don't say I left them . . . No, here they are.' She produced several sheets of paper. 'It doesn't look much of a result for the time spent, but when you read it you'll see why I might have looked quite sparkly. These are prints of the originals – they're very smudgy

and faint in places. The writer strayed into Latin here and
there and a good deal of that was beyond me. And these other
pages are my transcript, although a fair amount of it is
guesswork.'

As Phin began to read, he was struck, as he often was with
Arabella's work, by the marked contrast between her generally
chaotic life, and the organized neatness of her work. The print-
out was, as she had said, extremely faded and blurred, but her
own notes were clear and orderly.

'It's an inventory,' she said, leaning over to read it with
him. 'It was attached to a will dating from 1675 – it was a
fairly general practice to list the deceased's goods and chattels
like that when making a will. Infuriatingly the will itself didn't
seem to be in the archives, and it was the purest good luck
that I found this. By rights it should list the entire contents of
the house, but I doubt it does. People used to smuggle things
out if they thought they were going to miss out. But look at
the name on the inventory. And the address.'

'Jasper Rivers,' said Phin. 'The Tabor in the village of
Reivers, in the County of Norfolk. We haven't heard about a
Jasper before, have we?'

'No, and I don't know who we can attach him to. There's
no way of knowing exactly when he was born or when he
died, but this is dated 1675, so if he was in his late sixties or
early seventies he must have been born in the first few years
of the sixteen hundreds.'

'Will Kempe's time,' said Phin, thoughtfully.

'Well, yes. You don't need to plod through the entire list
– there are dozens of things – jugs and pots and salt cellars
and casks – oh, and a powthering tub.'

'What on earth—?'

'It's a tub for salting or pickling meat. I looked it up so I
could impress you with my knowledge. But if ever we needed
proof that The Tabor had been a tavern—' She broke off.
'You've seen it, haven't you?' she said. 'The item halfway
down page two.'

Phin said, '"Framed tapestry, believed to have been worked
by Jasper Rivers' mother. Showing the villagers gathered to
watch the Reivers Dance, which enacts the tragicke fate of

the rebel, Evelyn Rivers, executed by the King's men in 1381, which tragedie shadowed and tainted the Rivers family for generations. Embroidered date 1603, initial *R*". The next bit is faded, but I can just make it out. "In width one ell and a half, in height one ell". How long is an ell?'

'Roughly the length from the elbow to the tip of the fingers,' said Arabella, stretching out an arm to demonstrate and narrowly missing sweeping the coffee cups from the table.

'A bit over a foot,' said Phin. 'So this would have been – eighteen inches by twelve?'

'About that, I should think. Be glad they didn't calculate it in barleycorns or poppy seeds, or refer to puncheons of wine or kilderkins. I looked those up, too. To impress you even more.'

'You always impress me,' said Phin, rather absently, then said, 'In 1603 Jasper Rivers' mother made a tapestry showing the Reivers Dance – the Murder Dance. And it showed the villagers gathered to watch it.'

'That doesn't mean the Dance was performed that year, of course. But it's certainly what it sounds like.'

'Let's say for the moment that someone around Jasper Rivers' time either revived the Dance, or even actually composed it,' said Phin.

'Telling the story of the "tragicke fate of the rebel, Evelyn Rivers"? Would anyone have used that as a theme for a dance?'

'They might,' said Phin. 'Morris dancers often did act out real events – and some of them were quite dark. The Black Death, for instance – that's depicted in one of them.'

'Some of the dances were about cheerful things, though, weren't they?' said Arabella, hopefully. 'Robin Hood, and folk stories like Saint George and the Dragon.'

'Oh, yes. Let's assume the Reivers Dance was performed around 1602. How much of a leap is it to suggest that immediately afterwards a prison was created in those courtyard rooms?'

'Why? I mean why do you think that and why would a prison be created? It might have been there for years already. It might have been made to throw Evelyn the rebel in there . . . I wish I hadn't thought of that one,' said Arabella.

'Why? Because it gives that prisoner in the sketch an identity? And because Evelyn's cause was probably a good one?'

'Yes. Have you finished eating? We're going back to the library, aren't we?'

'Would you mind? It's open until five.'

'Of course we're going back,' said Arabella. 'For one thing I want to see if there's any more on Jasper and the tapestry.'

'I suppose it's long since vanished,' said Phin, as they left the coffee shop. 'We probably wouldn't ever have found it anyway. But I'd like to have compared it with that sketch.'

'The tapestry might still be somewhere in The Tabor. It looked as if there was a huge amount of stuff. I wonder if the tapestry and the sketch were done by the same person.'

'Jasper's mother? They might. But if you bring all this together,' said Phin, 'you've got the probable performance of the Dance around 1602, Will Kempe never dancing again after it and, according to The Daunsen sketch, a prison with barred windows in the courtyard rooms. Do those things add up to something, or are they just a series of unrelated incidents?'

'I don't know,' said Arabella. 'But I'd like to know who that prisoner was, who was staring through the bars of the window.'

FIFTEEN

Rosalind Rivers' journal, circa 1600

After Ralph brought the axe down on Greenberry's hands that night, through the screaming and the panic I have the memory of Master Kempe and his two gentlemen, who reached Greenberry first.

Greenberry's face was the colour of tallow, and blood was spurting like fountains from the jagged stumps that had been his hands – oh, dear God, *his hands* – and it was running across the ground, exactly as Evelyn's would have done two hundred years ago . . . Through the screams I could hear my own voice crying out for someone to help him, to do something—

And then there was Master Kempe's voice rapping out orders for strips of cloth – 'Quickly, we can't lose any time' – and twisting the cloth around Greenberry's wrists. Not, as I had expected, over the dreadful wounds with the glint of bone, but higher up, tying them so tightly, pulling on knots with all his might.

At my side, incredibly, were the Savory sisters, holding on to me, their voices kind and calming, explaining that what Master Kempe was doing might save him.

'It could staunch the blood, d'you see, Rosalind?' said Mistress Jael.

'It could save his life,' said Mistress Lydia.

I did not care what they did if it saved his life. I clutched gratefully at them, scarcely able to stand up any longer.

'Rosalind, let us take you back to the house,' said Mistress Lydia.

'No! I must stay with him. If he lives I must be here to help. If he dies . . .' The frantic chaotic courtyard spun in a sick whirl around me, but I fought it back, because I could not swoon, not here, not now. I must be with Greenberry. Even if he died, I must be with him . . .

But Greenberry did not die. He was maimed – so damaged that for a while I feared not just for his life, but also for his sanity.

Master Kempe, together with Bee and Slye, were finally able to carry him into the house, into the bedchamber next to my own. He was barely conscious, but he roused slightly, and his eyes went straight to me.

'I'm here,' I said, at once.

'Don't go away, Rosalind—'

'I'm not leaving you,' I said, and his eyes flickered as if in gratitude.

The Savory sisters were sending people scurrying off to their house to fetch ointments and salves. They bound up the terrible mutilated wrists, doing so with extreme care and gentleness. Shortly afterwards Jeremiah Grindall appeared, bearing a small flagon of some liquid.

'Best not ask what it is or where I got it,' he said. 'But it will soothe the poor man and take away some of the pain.' When he unstoppered the bottle there was a strong scent of something that made me think of poppy fields and drowsy twilights.

As I held a tiny cup to his lips, Master Kempe said, 'Ah – "And I drank of poppy and cold mandrake juice" . . .?'

'Aye, that's what it is,' said Jeremiah Grindall. 'Tried and trusted remedy.'

In a thread of a voice, from the bed Greenberry said, 'Mandragora . . . "And drinking it, I fell into a sleep of delicious sweetness".' He sipped the liquid, then in a slightly stronger voice said, 'Kempe, only you would quote Christopher Marlowe at such a time.'

'And only you would recognize it and respond with a line from . . . Where was it from?'

'Thomas Aquinas.'

'You never cease to amaze me,' said Will Kempe, as Greenberry took several more sips, then lay back on the pillows as if the small effort had exhausted him. 'And, my good friend, I believe you are going to be all right.'

'Am I?' Again Greenberry looked up at me, and I nodded.

'Indeed you are,' said Master Kempe at once, and that was when I stopped caring who was watching, and leaned right over the bed, putting my cheek next to his, so that my hair fell across his cheek and with it my tears, hot and painful, but tinged with hope.

I said, 'I will make you all right. I won't let you go.'

His eyes were already blurring from the poppy-scented syrup, but incredibly the trace of a smile touched his lips. He said, 'I don't want you to let me go, Rosalind. Not ever.'

Master Kempe, together with Parson Marplot, Jeremiah Grindall, and also Bee and Slye, held what I suppose I must call a meeting in the room that overlooked the gardens.

'There is a decision to be made, Rosalind,' said Reverend Marplot. 'And only you can make it.'

I had seated myself in the window recess. It was a favourite place of mine since I was a child, and over the last days it had even flickered on my mind that this was somewhere Greenberry and I could sit in the future. We would have a future, of course, I could not let myself think anything else. We would sit here with the sun warm on the bricks of the wall outside, its rays falling across the gardens in a soft glow of colour.

'Ralph,' I said, in answer to Parson Marplot, and felt a stir of relief go through them, almost as if they had expected me not to understand.

'Yes, Ralph. We must decide what will be done about him. My dear girl, if I could spare you this, I would, but it can't be ignored.'

'Where is he?' They hesitated, so I said, quickly, 'I know that you, Master Grindall, took him away after – after it all died down. But I don't know where . . .' I stopped, because I could not put into words the dreadful fear that my brother had been thrown into some miserable gaol, and was lying forgotten – or awaiting a judge's pronouncement over him of execution.

'He's still here,' said Master Grindall, and relief swept in. 'He's in one of the scullery rooms at the back of The Tabor. There's a lock on the door, and my boy is keeping watch.'

It was truly terrible to think of Ralph – my brother who had been that bright, good-looking boy – locked in a dark, dank scullery, with a guard at the door. But it was immeasurably better than those other images.

'Do you intend to turn him over to the authorities?' I said.

'If we do that, it would be the noose,' said Master Kempe.

'But he didn't actually kill—'

'Even so, it would still be the noose,' he said, and although he said it gently and kindly, he said it with authority, and I was aware that this was a man who had travelled widely and met a great many people, and that he would have an understanding of the law.

'Or possibly he would be adjudged a lunatic,' said Reverend Marplot, a bit hesitantly. 'And that could mean—'

'Yes?'

'The likeliest outcome for that would be the Priory of St Mary of Bethlehem,' he said.

'Bethleham . . . Bedlam?' The words fell on the air like a stone.

'Yes. Or perhaps The Bridewell.'

Master Kempe said, softly, as if quoting, 'The places they say are "for those raving and furious . . . for those who are likely to do mischief to themselves or others".' He broke off, then said, in a more down-to-earth voice, 'I have visited those places, and I've seen the life the poor souls in there are condemned to.'

I looked at them for a long moment. Then, taking a deep breath, I said, 'I can't let him be hanged. And I can't let him be thrown into one of those places – the Bridewell or Bethlehem. But I don't know what the alternative is. We can't keep him locked up in a scullery indefinitely.'

'Before you came in, we talked,' said Will Kempe. 'Your good Parson and Master Grindall and I. Bee and Slye too – I have no secrets from those two, you should know.'

Bee said, 'But we don't gossip, Mistress. We're quite safe to be told things. Slye's a bit chatty at times, of course.'

Slye, whom I had never actually heard utter a single syllable, made a gesture expressive of agreement.

'And we think there might be a way,' said Master Kempe. 'But for our plan to work, people would have to lie. People in this house – and perhaps people in the village as well. They would have to lie for a great many years.'

'A weighty thing to place on a man's conscience,' put in Reverend Marplot.

'My conscience would be clear enough,' said Jeremiah Grindall. 'Aye, and my son's, too. I can speak for him. We'll do and say whatever's needed. We'd always look after Mistress Rosalind, as I hope she knows.'

'Thank you,' I said, a bit awkwardly.

'People – that is, most people in Reivers – would have to be told that your brother was taken away and that he was to stand trial,' said Master Kempe. 'They all saw what happened, you see – they'd assume it was what would be done. But we would need to trust a small handful of them with the truth. Those of us here now. Master Grindall's son.'

'And perhaps the Savory ladies,' put in Master Grindall. 'I never thought to hear myself say it, but I believe we should bring them in on our plan. I believe we could trust them.'

'The truth would be that your brother would remain here,' said Will Kempe. 'But it would have to be – I'm sorry to say this, but it would have to be imprisonment inside The Tabor. Under lock and key, and guarded.'

'For how long?'

'I don't know that. We might find some way of – of restoring him to live normally again. We might let it be known that he was freed – pronounced innocent.' But his eyes slid away, and I understood that whatever story was told, he did not think Ralph could ever be allowed to be free.

'You said imprisonment. Where?'

'We think we could make a private set of rooms for him in the courtyard rooms,' said Master Grindall.

'Where I and my people slept,' said Master Kempe. 'And very comfortably too, I may say.'

'I could make those rooms secure,' said Grindall, eagerly. 'There'd need to be locks on the doors, and perhaps bars on the windows as well. They'd take bars, those windows – good strong frames they are. It could be done easy as blink your eye, and no one any the wiser. And he'd be perfectly comfortable, I promise you that.'

'An arrangement for taking meals over to him and suchlike,' nodded Bee. 'But there'd have to be a watch to be kept on him.'

'That would be a considerable task, though,' I said, trying to absorb all this. 'There would have to be several people involved in the – the watching. I couldn't do it by myself—'

Bee said, 'You wouldn't have to. I'd do it, Mistress. Slye, too. We've talked about it.'

Slye nodded.

'But your own work – your work with Master Kempe—'

'Master Kempe knows that our days of tramping the roads and finding a living in the theatres are over,' said Bee. 'We've been telling him so this many a month. We've always had a fancy to have a little tavern somewhere. Our own place. Slye's a good hand with the cookpots, and I enjoy a bit of lively company over a drop of good ale. But for the time being . . . Well, if you found it acceptable, Mistress Rosalind, we'd stay here as part of your household. We'd lend a hand wherever

was needed. But mostly we'd see to the care of your brother.
I won't say we'd be glad to do it, for it's not a thing anyone'd
be glad to do. But there it is, mistress. A fair and honest offer.'

'It's breaking all manner of laws, Mistress Rosalind,' said
Master Grindall. 'Laws of man and very likely of God, as well—'

'Indeed it is,' said Parson Marplot, rather sternly.

'But to my mind we're doing the best for everyone,' said
Grindall. 'It's for you to make the decision, though.'

I looked at them, my mind tumbling with confusion, because
this was wrong, we could not possibly do this – we could not
cheat the people of Reivers, and we could not cheat justice.

And yet . . .

And yet dreadful images were there again – of Greenberry,
lying on the ground, ragged bleeding stumps where his hands
had been. I thought: Ralph did that to him, and the memory
of how that terrible glaring *hating* madness had been in my
brother's eyes was with me again.

But there were other images – of Ralph being led to the
gallows, bound and shackled, bowing his head submissively
and obediently as they put the rope around his neck . . . Or
of him shut away in some dingy, rat-infested room in Bethlehem
or the Bridewell, half-starved, raving, confused and lonely
beyond imagining . . . I could not bear it.

I looked at the four men and I heard myself say, 'Yes. We'll
do what you said.'

Master Grindall and his son have worked hard on the courtyard
rooms, and Bee and Slye have helped them.

'And very useful they'll have been,' said Master Kempe.
'For they've been carpentering in any number of theatres for
most of their lives, not to mention constructing platforms and
the like for outdoor performances.'

As I write this I am in my sitting room, with the shutters
closed, because this morning they are to take Ralph across the
courtyard and lead him into the captivity of those rooms. I
can't bear to watch.

But the shutters are not blotting out the sounds, and I am
hearing the ringing footsteps on the iron stairs – and now
there's the clang of the main outer door closing. As the sound

reverberates, I've realized that tears are streaming down my face. That sound was as if a huge iron hand – or a massive cage – has clamped down on my brother. This is the moment when I know I have lost him for ever.

We've waited a little while to tell Greenberry what has been done. Master Kempe and Parson Marplot thought – and I agreed – that it was better to let him slowly recover and not think of anything else. His wrists are gradually healing – the Savory ladies' salves and ointments are being what they call 'sovereign' for that. I would not have expected to find such support in that quarter, but they are at The Tabor most days, and I am grateful to them beyond words.

But there have been many days when Greenberry gives way to despair, railing against the pain, and also the ugliness of his mutilations. One thing I will never forget, though, is that Kempe and the other men go to his room on most evenings, and somehow nearly always manage to pull him out of those bleak, dark moods. They swap stories – Master Kempe tells the most wonderful tales – and sometimes Grindall and Bee start a song, in which they all join. I suspect some of the songs are bawdy, because often they find a polite reason to send me out of the room, and minutes later I hear roars of laughter.

As I set this down, I am trying to remember the bright patches. The way Greenberry is mastering the art of manipulating spoons and mugs so that he can eat and drink unaided. Each time he masters some new skill he looks up at me, his eyes alight with such triumph – *see what I can do, Rosalind!* At those times I want to cry with gratitude and love.

This morning Master Grindall brought out an iron gate which he and his son fashioned on their anvil, and which they have fastened to the archway that leads into the courtyard.

'And a strong lock on it,' he said to me, as he finished the work. 'Even if you don't open up the tavern room again, we can't risk anyone wandering around and finding out the truth.'

I said, 'Let me go in there and talk to him. Let me make him think this is only a temporary arrangement.'

Master Grindall and his son exchanged looks, and then glanced to where Will Kempe was standing in the window recess, listening.

'Best not, mistress,' said Grindall, at last.

'Your brother believes he only needs to remain in hiding until things have died down,' said Master Kempe, coming into the room. 'Until people begin to forget what happened that night.'

'It isn't just until people forget though, is it?' I said. 'That's a lie.'

'Yes, it is,' he said. 'But it's kinder for him to believe it.'

But increasingly I feel a compulsion to enter those rooms and to see and talk to Ralph for myself.

Recently I discovered the tapestry that Mother began all those years ago. It was folded away in a Spanish chest with inlay on the lid, and I opened it without thinking very much about what might be inside it.

As I sat on my heels, staring at it, memory went looping back over the years, and I was seeing my mother stretching this canvas out on the floor, and crawling around it as she sketched out a design.

'The Reivers Dance,' she had said. 'That's what I shall show in my tapestry.'

At first I thought I could not bear to even touch the tapestry and that I would burn it. But after a while I began to think I might finish what Mother had begun – that I would make a picture that would show not just the Dance, but would tell Evelyn's story for people who would come to live at The Tabor after me.

I began work hesitantly and nervously at first, but then with more assurance, because incredibly there was a solace in this – perhaps because this was a piece of my family's history that I was setting down for others. And now I can say with truth that I'm finding a kind of companionship in the work.

Companionship . . . There's another companionship as well, of course. Greenberry is so far recovered that he's begun to move around the house, and he often comes to sit with me in the room where I work. Sometimes he reads aloud and we share the stories and the sonnets and the poems.

Last night he said, 'I'm recovering, aren't I, Rosalind?'

'Oh, yes.'

'I shall never be the man I was, though.' He said it almost pleadingly, his eyes hopeful.

I said, 'I like the man you are,' and I saw the light in his eyes – a light I had not seen since that first night.

He came to stand over my chair, and leaned close to me. Very softly and tentatively, he said, 'My hands may be beyond recall, Rosalind, but I believe the rest of me is in perfectly good order.'

I turned my head to look up at him, then I said, in the same soft voice he had used, 'I am extremely glad to know that.' The silence stretched out between us, and I understood that this time the move must come from me. He was so damaged, my poor dear love, that he had no longer the confidence to believe he would be welcome in my bed. So I put up my hand to lay it against his cheek, and he turned his head to press a kiss into my palm. I said, 'You won't have forgotten that my bedchamber is next to yours?'

'I haven't forgotten it.'

'The bed is as deep and as warm as it was that other night.'

'And,' said Greenberry, as if he hardly dared say the words, 'as welcoming?'

'Oh, yes,' I said. 'It always will be.'

He came to my room later that night. Of course he did. And in the privacy of these pages, with the morning sunlight spilling across this desk, I can write, with deep delight, that he had been quite right to say that although his hands were spoiled beyond recall, the rest of him was in perfectly good – and very loving – order.

The compulsion to see and talk to Ralph for myself has become almost overwhelming. I think that tonight, when the house is quiet, I shall take the keys that Master Grindall fashioned and which hang in the scullery, and steal across the courtyard.

SIXTEEN

Rosalind Rivers' journal, circa 1600

I write this with a cold grey dawn-light trickling through the windows. I think these pages will be stained with tears, for I am crying as I write them. Even so, I am determined to set everything down, because I believe it will be of help – perhaps it will be a kind of purging. Greenberry would understand that, for he wrote about everything that happened to him, and I know he found great solace in doing so. Until that night when Ralph . . .

It is only a few hours since it all happened, but it feels as if I have travelled from one world to another.

It began because I could not sleep; the thought of Ralph was filling my mind and, as the hours slid by, I finally acknowledged that I would not be able to rest until I knew he was all right. I needed to know – to see him, to talk to him, even to reassure him if I could.

And there was something else. I did trust Master Kempe and the others, I truly did, but there was a tiny sly voice deep in my mind whispering that what if they had deceived me? Supposing that, despite their careful explanations and the show of work on the courtyard rooms, what if they had really taken Ralph away and handed him over to answer for what he had done? I had to know.

The house around me was not completely silent, because houses are never entirely silent. But I knew the night sounds of The Tabor, and I knew no one was abroad. Earlier, I had heard a soft footfall on the landing, but that, too, was a sound I have come to recognize; it was Bee going quietly along the landing and down to the sculleries to brew up a drink. He is what he likes to call a martyr to his stomach, although Mistress Jael Savory has given him an infusion of ground ivy, which she says is a very good remedy for griping pains and choleric humours of the stomach.

I waited until he returned, and I heard the creak of his door as it closed. At last I slid stealthily from the bed, wrapped a thick shawl around my shoulders and stole down the stairs and across the hall.

The keys to the courtyard rooms are on a nail near to the garden door. Master Grindall has hung them on to a large brass ring, and there are two sets, for, as he said, keys have the way of getting mislaid, Mistress Rosalind, and a spare set never hurt anyone.

I took one of the sets, and went out very quietly. As I walked towards the courtyard there was no sound anywhere, except for the occasional rustle of some small creature in the undergrowth scuttling away from me, and a flurry of wings in a nearby tree where the owl makes its home every year.

Going under the stone arch was a curious experience. I had not been through it since the night of the Dance, and I suddenly had the feeling that Evelyn Rivers walked with me. It was somehow a reassuring feeling, as if Evelyn wanted to help.

The stairs swayed slightly as I went up them, and the shadows lay in clotted masses in the corners everywhere, so that I began to wish I had brought with me some kind of light – a horn lantern, perhaps. But that would have meant I might be seen from the house, and I did not want that.

A watery moon slid a little way out from behind a cloud as I went along the balcony, so that when I reached the door I could see the lock. There were two keys on the brass ring – did that mean there were two doors to unlock? But the first one I tried slid home and when I turned it there was a grating click, and the handle turned. The door swung outwards, which took me slightly by surprise, because I remembered it as opening inwards. But I pulled it back and paused, looking in at the shadowy inside of the rooms, remembering for a moment that this was where Greenberry and the others had lodged when they first came to Reivers.

I did not think Master Grindall would have altered the rooms so very much for Ralph's use, and I thought he and Kempe would have designated the room on the left of the hall as a bedroom. Would Ralph be in bed now? I had been imagining him seated by the light of a glowing candle, perhaps with a fire in one of the deep hearths, reading something, but there were no lights showing. The knowledge came reluctantly that perhaps Kempe and the others had thought it would be dangerous for him to have the means of making a fire, even for candlelight.

The room on the left of the hall was silent, and when I looked in, although I could see the outline of a bed, no figure lay on it. I came back into the hall and stood for a moment, then I said, very cautiously, 'Ralph? Where are you? It's me – it's Rosalind.'

Had something moved in response to my voice? Or had it only been a soft echo? Sounds are different in the dark. I called out again, and my voice bounced off the walls and came back at me. Still nothing stirred, and that small, vicious suspicion that Ralph was not here – that he had never been here – tightened its hold.

I went into each of the rooms in turn, walking stealthily now, which was absurd because if he was here I wanted him to hear me. I moved on, through the shadows, until I reached the room with the deep fireplace, and the desk where Greenberry had written his description of arriving in Reivers, and his reactions to The Tabor. I reached out to touch the desk's surface, liking the feeling it gave me of being close to him and to what he had been before the Murder Dance was performed, before his hands—

Hands. The hands came out of the darkness with no warning, and clamped around my throat. He had been here all along – he had been standing silent and still in a corner of this room, watching me, waiting for me to move closer to him.

'*Rosalind . . .*'

It came in a dreadful hoarse whisper, reaching me through the sick blurring of my vision, and it was dreadfully and macabrely my brother's.

'Rosalind – don't let them hang me . . . Promise you won't let them hang me.'

The grip tightened even more, but I managed a kind of half-nod, indicating that I promised.

The stranglehold relaxed then, and I half fell back, gasping, clutching the edges of the furniture to save myself from falling. In another minute I would have regained sufficient balance to get to the door and be out and down the steps to the ground. But I was terrified that before I could manage it, he would be on me again. I sought frantically for something I could say that would quieten him – that would quench the madness in his face, and the terror. The terror he had of being hanged . . .

As that last thought formed, I heard myself say, 'Ralph, you won't be hanged.'

He looked at me, and I said, 'He didn't die. Greenberry didn't die, Ralph. He survived. You didn't commit murder.'

I saw comprehension flare in his face, but it was replaced almost immediately with another emotion. Raging hatred. He had intended to kill Greenberry, but Greenberry still lived.

That was when I managed to get to the door and across the hall, and out on to the balcony. I pushed the door into place, and sagged against the outer wall, grateful to feel the cool night air clearing my senses. At last I managed to go shakily down the iron steps, clinging to the railing with each step, terrified I would fall.

It was only when I was finally on the ground that I dared to look up at the barred windows. The moon was still showering an uncertain light over the courtyard, and by its light I saw him. He was looking down at me, and his hands were gripping the bars. Even from the ground I could see the madness raging in his face. I knew in that moment that the madness was directed at Greenberry. I knew that if he could find a way to do it, he would kill Greenberry.

Once in my bedroom, I tried to feel safe. I tried to think nothing could happen – that Ralph was securely shut away.

But the image of him standing at the barred window and looking down with that insane hatred felt as if it had burned itself on to my mind. Presently I got out of bed, made a light, and sat at the little table in the window with paper and charcoal sticks. I sketched that image of Ralph. It was not a very skilful drawing, but I think I had the idea that it might remove from my mind the terrible picture that had painted itself there. As

I created that sketch, I tried to think what might lie ahead. I could hardly bear to think that he would live the rest of his life as a prisoner in those courtyard rooms – and that he would eventually die there.

If only it could have been so. If only I could have lived with the hope that one day the madness might lift and that a way could be found for him to return to the world.

I finally got into bed and tried to sleep, but now it was certainly impossible. In my room is what my mother used to call a turret clock – it had been a wedding present, and it's one of the few things I have that was hers. It strikes the hour, very softly and politely, and it's normally a rather companionable sound. Tonight it was not companionable at all; it was marking the hours until it would be full light – an hour when I could get up and the house would be awake and life would feel normal again. Except that life would never really feel normal again. I sought and found the thought of Greenberry, though, and it was as if a hand had closed comfortingly around mine. I remember I half-smiled, and thought: at least I have Greenberry. I was even wondering whether I would go quietly along to his room, and slip into bed with him, when there was the creak of a floorboard outside my door. It was a creak that only sounded when someone walked across that part of the floor, and it brought me sitting bolt upright in bed at once, because this certainly was not Bee going in search of a remedy for his ailing innards.

There was a further sound, and this time I knew it for Greenberry's bedroom door being opened – had I not opened that door in the soft quiet hours of the night myself over these last days?

I was across the landing and at his door before I realized it, and there, bending over the bed, was a figure whose hands were already around Greenberry's throat. The figure turned its head at my entrance, and there's a bitter shame in knowing that I did not immediately recognize it as Ralph. I can only say that the madness seemed to have consumed him so that he was almost unrecognizable.

Greenberry, pulled abruptly from sleep, was struggling,

hitting out, trying to land blows to defend himself, then instinct-ively reaching to the side of the bed to seize a weapon, but unable to do so, because his hand, *his hands* . . .

Somebody was screaming – terrible shrill screams that filled up the room and bounced off the walls. It took a moment for me to realize they were my own screams. Then I was across the room, and reaching for the heavy candle-stick on the mantel, knowing it would inflict a grievous blow on Ralph, and then hesitating, because I knew I could not do it – even with the madness and the murderous glare in his eyes, this was my brother – it was the boy I had grown up with, whose life I had shared, who had wept with me when our parents died . . . I could not do it, not even to save Greenberry.

But there was one who could do it. There was a rush of movement on the landing, then Master Kempe, with Bee and Slye behind him, came running into the room. Will Kempe launched himself at the bed, and tore – there is no other word to describe it – Ralph from the bed and from Greenberry.

Ralph fought. Oh, God, he fought like the mad wild thing he had become, trying to gouge Master Kempe's eyes, raking at his face with his fingernails, punching and battering him. Bee rushed to his master's aid, but Master Kempe had already managed to grasp the candlestick I had not been able to use, and he brought it down on Ralph's head. Ralph let out a yelp of pain, and then fell back. His eyes rolled up, and his whole body sagged.

It did not need Bee's terse question, or Master Kempe's brusque nod to tell me my brother was dead.

We sat around the scrubbed-top table in the scullery, Will Kempe and Greenberry and me. Bee and Slye were with us as well; Bee had taken a jug of milk from the cold slab and had heated it over the fire, and added a dash of brandy-wine and a spoonful of honey to it.

I had been sitting in a huddle in a corner of the kitchen, my hands cupped around the mug of warm milk, but after a while I managed to say to Master Kempe, 'I didn't lock the door properly, did I? It's my fault that this happened.'

He said at once, 'He would have found another way. It could

have been any one of us, Mistress Rosalind.'

'You knew this would happen, didn't you? Sooner or later. It's why you remained here.'

'I didn't know exactly,' he said. 'But I could tell your brother was – that there was great hatred in him.'

'For me,' said Greenberry. 'I'm at the heart of all this, aren't I?'

'The madness was already there,' said Kempe. 'It would always have come out sooner or later. Something would have kindled the spark.' He sat back, and for the first time I saw that for all his liveliness and his energy, he was not a young man. He said, 'And now, Mistress Rosalind, you may want to let the law take its course.'

'I don't—'

'Tonight I killed a man,' he said, and he sat back and waited.

I stared at him for a moment. 'Master Kempe,' I said, 'I would no more hand you over to the law for what you did tonight than I would hand over Greenberry. Or,' I said, 'than I would have handed over my brother after that night of the Dance.'

'Greenberry?' said Kempe, looking at him.

'Of course you aren't going to be handed over to justice,' he said, impatiently. 'Rosalind's quite right.'

Kempe smiled. 'Thank you,' he said. 'Both of you. But you know, I think I should leave Reivers. I think after this I need to – to keep out of public gaze.' He made a gesture with his hands, indicating a kind of philosophical acceptance of the situation. 'If what happened tonight were ever to come out – if it were ever discovered that I helped conceal your brother and then that I . . . that I committed a murder, the consequences would be severe and they would be far-reaching,' he said. 'Not just to me, but to you as well, mistress. To Greenberry, too.'

'And there's your connection to the London playhouses – to Master Shakespeare and Richard Burbage,' said Greenberry, a bit hesitantly.

'I dare say they can look after themselves, but it's a point to bear in mind.'

'But what will you do?'

'Well, do you know, mistress, I have a mind to head for Norwich,' said Kempe. 'I had begun to think I was getting past the days of ramshackling around theatres, in any case. And I have a friend in Norwich—'

'A widow woman,' said Bee, without expression.

'Yes, a widow woman she is, and no call for you to make your saucy suggestions, Harry Bee, and especially not with a lady present.'

Even with my heart in pieces and my mind still reeling from what had happened, I had the brief thought that this was an unexpected comment coming from a man who, by all Greenberry had told me, had romped around London stages, portraying for audiences a number of ale-quaffing characters, most of them with a lively taste for the ladies. I had found those tales rather endearing. I found it endearing now – and somehow comforting – to hear this sudden remark.

'The Norwich widow in question,' said Kempe, 'was kind enough to suggest there could be a lodging in her house if ever I cared to take up the offer. It's a comfortable enough place for a man, and there'd be good company to be had, and a good table of an evening.' He looked rather severely at Bee when he said this, and Bee looked back at him without speaking. 'And I have a fancy to write an account of some of my exploits,' he said. 'Those nine days of dancing from town to town. That will fill up a good deal of my time.'

Then he looked at me very directly. 'Mistress Rosalind, I noted down the steps of that Dance,' he said. 'Before . . . Well, before the tragedy.' A gesture indicating apology. 'I'm a performer,' he said. 'Dancing has been a large part of my life, and I was curious. I took some of the patterns of the steps from Parson Marplot's document, and some I noted down myself from what I saw. Now I should like to keep those notes as a reminder that a dance can sometimes stray into a very dark place. But if you would prefer not—'

I said, slowly, 'A reminder of that kind is good. Yes, keep your notes, Master Kempe.'

'Thank you. And,' he said, 'living in Norwich, I shan't be so very far away from Reivers. I'd like to think I could take the road back here from time to time. A few times in the year,

we could say. So I might feel I was part of a family now and
again.'

He looked at me, his eyebrows raised, and I said, 'There'll
always be a bed and a welcome for you.'

'And,' said Bee, 'if Slye and I manage to find our tavern
and open it up, we'll expect to see you there, as well. There's
a house in Reivers' centre that we've got our eye on at the
moment, in fact—'

'I daresay it's a tumbledown place, for you've no eye for a
property, Harry Bee,' said Kempe. He frowned, and for a brief
instant I had the impression of a man making calculations.
Then he said, 'How would it be if I took a look at it for you?
And then it wouldn't hurt for us to have a talk about the idea.'

We buried Ralph at the far end of the gardens, near to the old
wall. Reverend Marplot was with us. He has been a good
friend. Greenberry says the man has stretched his vows to
snapping point for this family more than once, and of course
he is right. But it meant Ralph has had a proper burial service
pronounced over him, and although I daresay this would not
matter to a great many people – that some would say he
deserved to be sent to his Maker without the blessing of the
Church – it matters to me, and it has given me a degree of
peace.

I think I shall close this journal now, although there may be
a day in the future when I may want to look at these pages
again – perhaps with Greenberry. He is at my side so often,
and it's a joy and a solace.

Earlier today, a package arrived, carefully wrapped and with
my name written on it in a generous, sprawling hand.

Inside was a small slim book, with a title on the cover
saying, 'Kempe's Nine Days' Wonder: Performed in a daunce
from London to Norwich'.

There's a dedication inside, 'To my dear good friends, RR
and G. Many things merry, nothing hurtful.'

It's a good way to remember him. Many things merry,
nothing hurtful.

It's a good motto to adopt for what lies ahead in my life.

SEVENTEEN

'Are you going after Walter again?' asked Arabella as they went back into the library after their lunch.

'Yes. Walter intrigues me,' said Phin. 'Those battles with planners and parish councils to stop them buying any land . . . But then he created almshouses which would surely have opened up the place to all-comers. Only he surrounded them with so many restrictions it doesn't sound as if anyone would ever have got a place in them. He's becoming a bit of an enigma.'

'Would there be more details about the almshouses in parish records?' asked Arabella.

'There might. We'll track down the local vicar tomorrow and see if we can get access,' said Phin. 'But any secret Walter might have had can't be connected to anything that might have happened in 1602. If anything actually did happen in 1602.'

'Unless,' said Arabella, 'we want to get into Glamis monster territory – the secret room with the centuries-old creature born into the noble family. Or the undead Count lying in the dungeons of the castle, creeping out after dark to ravage the population . . . Would Walter have got money for the almshouse thing?'

'He might,' said Phin, considering. 'But if he needed money, surely he'd have sold that strip of land to the council. I can't fathom Walter at all. But I'll start with newspapers in 1921 and see if there are any more reports about his activities.'

'I'll go back to Jasper Rivers,' said Arabella. 'I'm getting quite fond of him. I'd like to find that he had a gorgeous wife and twelve lively children. Good luck with Walter.'

'I think I'll need it. Always assuming I can find him in the first place, because there's no knowing how far back the archives go.'

But the newspapers did, in fact, go farther back than 1921.

Phin skimmed reports about the Great War and the heart-breaking lists of casualties of the young men who had died while fighting, but his attention was caught by a series of articles called *Theatre Notes and News* which a local newspaper appeared to have run for several years, apparently with the idea of rallying Norfolk's spirits during the conflict by reporting on various theatre shows and concert parties, with a conscientiously patriotic sprinkling of recruitment shows along the way.

It was not very likely that Walter or, indeed, the Reivers Dance, would feature in these particular columns, but it was an interesting sideline. Phin called up as many of these articles as he could, and then saw that the newspaper in question was called *Norwich Tidings*. He reached at once for the print-outs he had made in London about Will Kempe. Hadn't the newssheet that had published an obituary been called something like that? Yes, it was here. *Tydings*. It might not be the same set-up at all, but there was the Norfolk connection, so it was not impossible.

He worked his way through accounts of Theatres Royal, Pavilions, Piers, Corn Exchanges, and an assortment of play-houses dedicated to various members of royalty. It began to seem that *Norwich Tidings'* theatre section had reported on just about every player who had stepped into a beam of lime-light within a twenty-mile radius of Norwich. Phin was inclined to think the editor – or, more likely, the paper's owner – had been severely stagestruck.

It was a pity that printing techniques in the early years of the twentieth century had not allowed for actual photographs. Phin thought most illustrations of that time had been some sort of woodblock process – but that it had been such a lengthy process that newspapers had been quite sparing about using it.

The *Norwich Tidings* had ventured on a few illustrations, although they did not contribute anything to the search for Walter. Or did they . . .? Because halfway down one of the *Theatre Notes and News* reports – in an edition dated 1918 – was a grainy illustration of a gentleman striking a grand-iloquent pose, one hand placed gracefully on a chair back, the other appearing to caress a luxuriant moustache. He was gazing into the middle distance, and he looked like a cross between Svengali and photographs of the old Victorian actor-managers.

Nineteen eighteen might be a bit early for Walter's era, but it was only a few years before his almshouse exploit. With a jolt, Phin saw that the caption beneath the photo said: 'Sir Peregrine Pond, following his recent appearance at The Victoriana, interviewed by this newspaper while he was staying in a well-known manor house in the village of Reivers.'

Reivers, thought Phin. And a well-known manor house. He zoomed up the article and began to read. It was admiring to the point of sycophancy, but the content was very interesting indeed.

'It was a pleasure and a privilege to visit the beautiful old manor house of The Tabor,' it began, and even though Phin had been prepared for The Tabor after the caption's line about a well-known manor house in Reivers, it was still startling to see it set down in print.

Sir Peregrine Pond talked openly and entertainingly about his career – which has included key roles in *Richard III* and in the acclaimed dramatization of Alexandre Dumas' book, *The Three Musketeers.*

However, it was while appearing at The Thespis – sadly no longer standing – that Sir Peregrine's remarkable encounter with the past occurred. Several Shakespearean extracts were being performed – the praiseworthy aim had been the raising of funds to provide comfort for the troops in France, and Sir Peregrine had been part of the staging arrangements.

He described how he had been recovering from that evening's performance – 'Enjoying a dram or two of whisky at the local hostelry,' was how he put it – when shouts of 'Fire!' had gone up, and cries that the theatre was ablaze.

He had raced back to the theatre at once and had set about helping to douse the blaze.

'The fire brigade were already out in force,' he told

me. 'A splendid body of men they are, too, but I was able to help with organizing a chain of buckets to pass water back and forth. A small service, but one I was glad to perform.'

It was as Sir Peregrine and other members of The Thespis company were thus engaged that a request was made for help with rescuing any items of value from inside the theatre. The fire was doused, and a way had been cleared into part of the building.

Sir Peregrine had stepped up at once.

'It was not without risk,' he said, solemnly. 'But there was no knowing what might have been in there. The Thespis had a fine history, and there was a small library in the Green Room, which might have held all manner of memorabilia. First folios – handwritten director's notes from Garrick to Ellen Terry, for instance—'

Phin read this last sentence twice, and wondered how Sir Peregrine had thought that David Garrick, who had died around 1780, could have written stage directions to Ellen Terry, who he did not think had not taken to the stage until the mid-1850s. He began to enjoy Peregrine Pond – had that really been his name?

'It was no longer a raging inferno in The Thespis, but here and there were little tongues of flame licking at floorboards, and there was smouldering rubble in corners – and, of course, smoke everywhere.

'I made for the Green Room behind the stage, and for the alcove that housed the playscripts and old programmes and playbills, and I began sweeping things into a stage sheet which I knotted at the corners. I had gathered as much as I could, and I was on my way back outside, when a small tragedy struck – a tragedy for which I shall never cease to blame myself.'

He sighed, and you may be sure, readers, that I waited with bated breath for what came next.

'On the stage we had what in theatre parlance is called a cauldron trap,' said Sir Peregrine. 'There are many such structures that can be employed on a stage – usually with a platform beneath that can be lowered and raised as needed. In *Hamlet* there will be a grave trap, which is rectangular. And there are star traps in pantomime, so that demon kings and genii can be catapulted on to a stage. Although I have not,' he explained, carefully, 'ever been associated with pantomime myself, being a player of the classical mould. However, I have heard of such things. But in The Thespis there was a cauldron trap – a square opening towards the back of the stage, used for the witches' scene in the play we superstitious men and women of the theatre prefer to refer to only as *the Scottish play.*'

I suggested, tentatively, that the play was believed to bring bad luck, at which Sir Peregrine said, sombrely, that this was very true indeed.

'But we had performed several scenes from it as part of our Shakespearean season,' he said, 'and we had included the witches' scene.'

Here, he broke off his narrative to me, and launched forthwith into the famous witches' chant, about 'Double double, toil and trouble,' and very inspiring it was, and perfectly excusable that his memory should trouble him over the lines calling for eye of newt and toe of frog. It's a very long speech. He brushed the stumble aside magnificently, and went on with his story.

'The smoke was clouding my vision, but through it I heard someone calling for help, so of course I ran towards the cries. Well, I almost tumbled straight down into the open cauldron trap, which was gaping wide, some careless fool having neglected to shut it after curtain fall.

'And there – yelling to be got out – was a young man, lying on the ground, one of his legs clearly badly injured. I set about helping him at once – a coil of rope was to hand, used, I believe, for lifting some of the scenery, and eventually, with many a cry of pain from the young man, but with encouragement and determination from myself, he was brought out.

'As for the artefacts I had scooped up so hastily and almost randomly – ah, that was when I found the playbill.'

Sir Peregrine here paused impressively, then said, 'I have cherished it ever since, that playbill, for it has come down from one of William Shakespeare's men who was in Norfolk at the end of his life.'

He pulled out a thick envelope, wrapped in linen and silk, and displayed the playbill. And it is with his permission and approval that the *Tidings* is proud to reproduce it for its readers on Page 4.

Phin stared at the screen. This was the moment all researchers worked towards – and all too rarely reached. This unexpected but hoped-for discovery of some nugget of information that smacked into every one of your senses, and that was the vital piece of the jigsaw you were trying to assemble about the past. This was why he had spent most of his adult life chasing chimerae and phantoms and pinning down fragments and cobwebs of the past.

He stared at the screen for so long it flickered into sleep mode, which pulled him out of his abstraction, and he reached for his phone to text Arabella.

'Please come and hold my hand while I see if I can open a document that might have been left by Will Kempe.'

'Something rescued from a burning building,' said Arabella, having pulled a chair into place, and reading the notes Phin had made.

'Yes.'

'I hate to say this, and I know you want to go haring off in pursuit, but do remember—'

'That crumbling documents brought out of burning buildings usually turn out to be elaborate fakes?' said Phin. 'I know. It's the starting block for any number of tales about priceless objects being discovered – lost family wills and scandalous letters—'

'First folio Shakespearean manuscripts and never-published Beethoven symphonies at the bottom of old tea chests,' said

Arabella, promptly. 'This could be an early twentieth-century scam. It's a well-hidden one if so, though, I will say that. And also—'

'And also we do know, reasonably surely, that Will Kempe was in Reivers,' said Phin. 'This playbill might link everything up. Walter Rivers and The Tabor and Will Kempe and the Murder Dance. All brought together.'

'By an actor who couldn't remember the Macbeth witches' speech,' said Arabella, thoughtfully. 'How far can he be believed, d'you think, this Peregrine Pond? And what about this theatre – The Thespis? How far does that go back?'

'No idea. We'll google it when we get back. For the moment there's this playbill. If I can bring myself to see if it's reachable.' He stared back at the computer monitor. 'Because whoever scanned all this in could have missed Page 4. Or not bothered with it because it was lunchtime or five p.m. on a Friday. Or found it was too tattered to scan anyway.'

'Ever the optimist.' Arabella reached determinedly for the keyboard.

'It won't be there,' said Phin. 'It might once have been, but it's probably vanished into the netherworld of error messages and sites "no longer available"—'

'No, it hasn't,' said Arabella. 'Look there.'

The playbill was incomplete, but the title of the piece was readable.

'*A Knack to Know a Knave*,' said Phin, frowning and narrowing his eyes to read it. '"A Most Pleasant and Merrie Comedie".'

'Is that Will Kempe's name at the foot – it looks as if it's been torn away, but it could be.'

'It could, but I wouldn't bet the ranch on it,' said Phin. 'And infuriatingly there's no date anywhere. But we'll look up that play title as well, to see if Kempe was ever linked to it—'

'What is it?' said Arabella, leaning forward to see the small newsprint better.

'There's a caption. It's very small print indeed, but if I can zoom it up . . . Damn, it's blurred it too much. No, that's better. It says – "A facsimile of a playbill found by the distinguished actor, Sir Peregrine Pond, and his cherished possession". And on the last line—'

'Oh!' said Arabella, with a half-gasp. And then, 'I'll get a print-out before the library closes – it's almost six o'clock already.'

The last line of the caption said, 'The playbill bears hand-written notes on its reverse, which have been interpreted by Sir Peregrine as dance notation'.

'What now?' said Phin, as they stood on the pavement outside the library.

'Back to Reivers? Dinner at The Daunsen?'

Phin said, carefully, 'The trouble is that Quentin and Zillah would want to know how we've got on today – what we've found out, and—'

'And you don't want to share this yet.'

'It probably wasn't anything to do with Kempe or the Murder Dance,' said Phin, slowly. 'And I shouldn't think there's any way we can get our hands on the original playbill and see those handwritten notes.' He looked at her. 'How would you feel about getting something to eat here in Norwich, and not going back to The Daunsen until it's too late to talk to those two?'

'Let's do that,' said Arabella. 'I'll phone Toby – or text him, saying we won't be back until late. He'll be imagining us smashed up on a motorway otherwise.'

'True. And tomorrow morning we can have an early break-fast and head off to find the vicar.'

Arabella looked at him in surprise, then said, 'Oh, parish records. Walter and the almshouses.'

'You make it sound like a punk rock group. But yes, parish records.' He smiled at her and put an arm round her waist. 'For now let's find somewhere nice to eat.'

Over bowls of pasta and warm Italian bread, Arabella said, 'It isn't a definite link to Will Kempe, is it? That playbill?'

'No, but there's the title, which might tell us something—' Phin reached into a pocket for his phone, and tapped in a search request.

'Anything?' said Arabella, after a moment.

Phin said, 'Listen to this.

'*A Knack to Know a Knave* is a comic piece dating from the late 1500s, and is associated with the celebrated clown actor William Kempe. Kempe's applauded "merrimentes of the mad men of Goteham (in some sources, Gotham)" was considered a highlight of the play.'

He frowned at the screen, then said, 'There's a fair bit more which doesn't look especially relevant – dates of performances, and how the author is unknown, but how there was speculation as to whether Shakespeare might have dabbled in the writing.' He passed the phone over for Arabella to see, and after a moment, he said, softly, 'I think this is the proof – the confirmation that Kempe was here. The fact that dance notation was written on the reverse alone— And I don't think the playbill was a scam of any kind. Peregrine Pond doesn't sound as if he could have worked out the details. Someone who didn't know there was a good sixty or seventy years between David Garrick and Ellen Terry isn't likely to have fudged up a fake playbill for a three-hundred-year-old comedy.'

Arabella said, 'But if it was a fraud of some kind, it mightn't have been Peregrine.' As Phin looked at her, she said, 'I'm thinking about that young man who he rescued from under the stage.'

'You think he might have been part of it? But it was 1918,' said Phin. 'A theatrical scam about an Elizabethan comic was probably the last thing on that boy's mind.' He looked back at his own notes. 'Pond didn't say in that interview how old the boy was, but the implication is that he was quite young. I should think he was either on leave from France and the trenches, or he was expecting to go out to fight.'

'You're right, of course, but—'

'"But"?'

'I can't help wondering who he was, that boy,' she said. She sat up straighter, as if she was pushing an unpleasant thought away, and said, 'Are we having pudding? The menu says they do zabaglione with fresh raspberries.'

EIGHTEEN

'I thought I'd wear my red hat for the vicar,' said Arabella, the next morning, after an early breakfast. 'You don't think a red hat's too jazzy for a vicar, do you?'

'Vicars are quite jazzy themselves, these days,' said Phin. 'But the hat looks good. Are you wearing those glasses with it?'

'I thought they made me look suitably earnest and learned,' said Arabella, hopefully.

'I shouldn't think anything could do that.' Phin smiled. 'But I like the look. It turns you into a sexy academic. If the vicar doesn't like it, I do.'

'We've got to find the vicar first, though. Oh, wait, wasn't there a rectory or a parsonage or something along from the church? Or am I getting into Brontë country or Parson Woodforde again?'

'Probably. And probably the rectory will have been turned into a rehab centre or a food bank, and the vicar will live in a modern semi in the next town. But we'll start there.'

However, the four-square house along from the church had a neat sign outside, proclaiming it to be the home of the Very Reverend Pilbeam.

They were accorded a beaming welcome, although the Reverend Pilbeam explained that they had caught him between a community meeting with police representatives and the finance committee of the rural council. He was, however, charmed to meet Mr Fox and Miss Tallis, and very willing to provide access to parish records for such a distinguished gentleman.

'I read your book on that nineteenth-century Russian violinist a couple of years ago,' he said, studying the business card Phin handed to him.[3] 'A remarkable story you uncovered,

---

[3] See *Death Notes*

I thought. It was very enjoyable and also very illuminating. So it's quite an honour to meet you.'

'Thank you.'

'Now,' said the Reverend Pilbeam, 'will you be all right if I put you in my office, and leave you to get on with your searching while I go off to these meetings? I can put out whichever of the registers you want. Everything's kept here, you know – we don't leave anything in the church these days. It's very sad that people can't be trusted any longer, but there it is.'

'That will be fine,' said Phin. 'We're very grateful.'

'And we'll be careful with the old records,' put in Arabella.

'I'm sure you will. Now then, these are the registers – the traditional births, marriages and deaths – and these are notes of parish meetings. Not the actual minutes, but dates and attendees and a note of the main topic on the agenda. My predecessors were very orderly. It's all a bit dusty, I'm afraid.'

Phin said, half to himself, 'The dust on antique time lying unswept.'

'My word yes, that's very apposite, Mr Fox. I'll make a note of that for next Sunday's sermon. It'll make a good springboard for something or other.'

'*Coriolanus*,' said Phin, obligingly, as the vicar searched his pockets for a pen.

'Is it? Thank you. You're welcome to stay as long as you want. I'll be in and out for most of the day, but here's my phone number if you need to contact me. Oh, and my cleaner comes in today and she'll be here any minute, so she'll be around. I'll leave a note for her to bring in some coffee for you.'

'That would be very welcome.'

'I'll be very interested to hear if you turn up anything about The Tabor and the Rivers family,' he said.

'Of course we'll let you know.'

'You always go into a kind of self-conscious awkwardness if anyone ever praises your work like that,' said Arabella, after the door closed. 'I've noticed it before.'

'I'm always worried about sounding smug,' said Phin. 'But then if I'm too off-hand I think it might seem as if I'm not pleased at having something recognized or praised. Let's see if we can disinter Walter.'

'Straight into the antique dust,' said Arabella, taking off the red hat and adorning a plaster bust of a former incumbent of the church, which, according to the plaque, had been made by the Reivers Pottery Society. 'Are we going to divide and multiply again?'

'I think so.' Phin put his notebook on the desk and drew up two chairs. 'It looks as if each year is covered by two registers,' he said, studying the covers. 'The first of January to thirtieth of June in one, and then first of July to the end of the year for the other. Let's take half a year each, shall we, and work on the same year simultaneously?'

'Beginning with 1918 and working forwards.'

Almost an hour later, Arabella leaned back from the desk, stretching her neck muscles, and said, 'At least he is here.'

'He's on almost on every page,' agreed Phin, with a touch of exasperation. 'I hadn't expected him to be quite so – quite so overwhelmingly present. If he wasn't on just about every church committee going, he was heading enquiries into schooling and welfare – was it called welfare in those days? – and drumming up support for every local event that took place.'

'He found time for a wife, though,' said Arabella. 'I've found mentions of her in 1918. Maria Rivers, and she was on all kinds of committees and guilds and whatnot. The church had a service to mark the end of the Great War, and the Church Lads' Brigade held a march. Oh, and Maria Rivers distributed red silk poppies, and the church ladies decorated the village hall for a victory supper. I'm seeing her as one of those S-shaped Edwardian ladies, all bosom and floral hats and gracious benevolence.' She sat back as Phin leaned over the desk to see.

'And a minor royalty toured the country as part of the celebrations and was given afternoon tea at The Tabor,' he said, reading one of the entries.

'Yes, and I bet Maria Rivers dined out on that for years.'

'Were there any children?'

'I haven't found any yet. We could look back in the births register if you think it's relevant.'

'It probably isn't.' Phin sat back, his neck muscles aching, somewhat dispirited at the lack of any real discovery.

'D'you want some more coffee?' asked Arabella. 'There's still half a potful of it.'

'Thanks.' He drank the coffee gratefully, then returned to the registers. After another silence, he said, 'I've found the almshouses. And they look perfectly genuine.' He pushed the open register across to her. 'It's a record of a parish council meeting in June 1921. It's only a couple of lines – Rev Pilbeam did say the entries were just a kind of summary. Date, note of main topic, and who chaired things.'

'The meeting on 21 June 1921 was chaired by the Reverend Bream,' said Phin.

'So it was.' Arabella pushed her glasses more firmly on her nose, reading. 'In attendance were the Misses Savory – that's the antique shop dynasty. Oh, and Mr Gilbert Grindall. That'll be the grandfather – or even great-grandfather – of the present Grindall the builder. The topic of the meeting was the creation of almshouses at The Tabor.' She looked up at him. 'So they were real, after all.'

'Yes. It even says an administrator was appointed as well. That sounds fairly official, doesn't it?'

'It does, rather. Would an administrator be paid for that job?' said Arabella. 'I should think he would, though, don't you? Like Mr Bumble in *Oliver Twist.* Don't look so surprised – I remember Bumble the Beadle very well, because we did a stage version of *Oliver Twist* in the sixth form, and I played Mrs Bumble – with suitable padding. And I remember the scene where Bumble says, very sadly, that he sold himself for six teaspoons and a pair of sugar tongs and some secondhand furniture or something, and having been dirt cheap, because I had the retort about, "You were dear at any price, Bumble!" I used to belt it out really scornfully, and it got a laugh every night.' She looked back at the page. 'Oh – did you see who Reivers' Bumble the Beadle was?'

'Nicolas Trigg,' said Phin.

'Yes. Wasn't he—?'

'The one who wrote those letters to the Parish Council on Walter's behalf.' Phin was reaching for his notes from the library session. 'Hold on . . . Yes, here it is. Nicolas Trigg. He paid the fine after Walter accused the planners of pilfering his land. And,' said Phin, 'he was the one who sent that letter with all the restrictions Walter was imposing on the alms-houses. He said he was writing on Walter's behalf, but then—'

'But then he was made administrator for the almshouses themselves.' Arabella looked at him. 'So he was making sure those restrictions were put in place and accepting the manage-ment of the whole shooting match. That begs a few questions, doesn't it?'

'It does, rather. There was probably some perfectly good reason for it, of course.' But he frowned at the slanting graceful writing on the old register. 'I don't suppose we'll be able to trace anything about him,' he said. 'But I'd very much like to find out a bit more about Nicolas Trigg.'

*   *   *

Nicolas Trigg's journal, 1919/1920
I have a peculiar feeling that in writing all this down I'm echoing something someone did in this house a long time ago.

It's the house itself that's having this effect on me, of course. The Tabor. It plays tricks on you. It bounces the past into your face, so you find yourself thinking that if you walk along a particular corridor, or open a specific door, you could find you've stepped into a lingering fragment of a different century. There are pockets – echoes. You get the feeling of how someone might have sat at a particular table, or in one of the deep old window seats, and that if you look closely you might see a faint outline. Ridiculous, of course, but there it is.

And probably it's simply that the house has so many traces of its past. There's even a framed tapestry in one of the rooms dated 1603. It's a bit faded from where the sun slants in and catches it, but it's still beautiful, depicting an old Dance that was apparently performed here to mark the Rivers' involve-ment in the Peasants' Revolt. The year 1381 that was – I've looked it up.

And even writing this now, I'm thinking that once upon a time – and there's a good line to start a journal – someone might have sat at this very desk and looked out of this window and had this exact same view of the old courtyard and the stone arch.

I've no idea how old that stone arch is – it looks as if it could even be a remnant of a much older property. Whatever its age, it's looking very worn and battered, although I doubt it will be repaired or restored, because it's already clear that Walter Rivers has very little money. I suppose that's partly because of the war, which has virtually bankrupted a great many people, but also because of the demands of Maria Rivers. She is one of those acquisitive, social-climbing wives, who believes the money is there for whatever she wants, and all she has to do is keep nagging to get it. I foresee trouble ahead. I would like to think I shall no longer be at this house when that trouble turns up, but I like it here.

I will admit that I did not want to come to The Tabor at all, but there was not much choice. After Peregrine Pond sent me tumbling down below the stage of the old Thespis theatre, resulting in the permanent crippling of one of my legs, the options open to me have been quite limited.

I was barely seventeen when my leg was so badly damaged that I will limp and have some pain for the rest of my life. It was last summer when it happened – 1918, and the war was almost at an end, although we didn't know that at the time, of course – and I was waiting to go to France. I think I wanted to go to France – you don't admit to being afraid of fighting in a war for your country. So I'll say I was eager to go.

While I was waiting to actually leave, a temporary job came along, which I thought I might as well take, and which even sounded as if it might be interesting. It was a backstage job, helping with scenery-shifting and carpentering in a Norwich theatre. They were staging concerts and recitals for the soldiers, and raising funds for the troops along the way. I liked it. I enjoyed the work – sketching out how something could be constructed or how a piece of scenery could be made to look better – and the company was lively and friendly.

Within the company was Peregrine Pond. He liked to think he was in sole charge, and he certainly dominated everything – including the females, all of whom gazed at him with wide-eyed admiration. The men were slightly more wary, but he swapped bluff stories with them, and insisted that, Ah, if only his health permitted, he would not be here, he would be out there in France giving the Boche hell. I should think most of the men knew perfectly well that the truth was he was too old for active service; in fact I should think everyone knew. He carries his years well, and I don't know his exact age, but he can remember things like Queen Victoria's Diamond Jubilee – probably her Golden Jubilee as well.

But for all that he was an amiable person to work for – until, that is, the night when he had been rehearsing a couple of scenes from *Macbeth*, with which he was going to astound the Norwich audiences the following week. They had gone through the famous witches' scene around the cauldron, and then they all left rather noisily for the Pig and Whistle on the corner. I was about to follow when I saw that Pond had left the cauldron trap open, so I went in search of one of the stage-hands who knew how to operate it. That was when I smelt smoke. There was a fire – the smallest fire imaginable, but word of it went across to the Pig and Whistle, and Pond came puffing back, and went plunging across the stage, shouting that he would save the theatre's treasures. He ran smack into me in the process, and sent me tumbling headlong into the open cauldron trap. Through the dizzy pain I saw that a bone was sticking out of my leg at a sickening angle. I attempted to get up, and the pain took over, and spun me into a black whirling pit.

I woke up in a hospital bed to find that the Armistice had been signed, the country was rejoicing, church bells had rung the length and breadth of the country – and Peregrine Pond was seated at my bedside. It's not exactly the first sight you want when you're coming round from a hefty dose of ether and the ministrations of a surgeon's knife (although it was good news that the war was over), but there Pond was and, to his credit, he was genuinely appalled at what had happened. He explained that he had managed to call for help, and had clambered down to help extricate me from under the stage. He was filled with remorse at having ruined a young life, and had vowed to devote his remaining days to caring for me, a poor maimed soul, and making up for what had happened.

The reality of this was that I ended up becoming his assistant – his dresser and his secretary, which he called, very grandly, his amanuensis, although he never quite managed to pronounce that correctly, especially not after the second bottle.

I don't know that I particularly wanted the job, but I hadn't a brass farthing to my name, so it seemed the best option – well, it seemed the only option. After a time, Pond embroidered the story of the fire quite lavishly, making it out to have been an all-consuming conflagration, whereas the reality was that it was a bit of a smoulder in the theatre's Green Room, caused by someone having thrown a lit cigarette end into a pile of papers.

At intervals, when my lameness makes me feel more glum than usual, he attempts to cheer me up by reminding me that Sarah Bernhardt – 'the Divine Sarah' is how he always refers to her – recently had to have an entire leg amputated due to gangrene. 'All the way up to the hip they hacked it off,' he says, solemnly. 'But she still goes on acting, charming her audiences.'

I have never found this is a particularly helpful anecdote.

Since we came to stay at The Tabor – at the invitation of Maria Rivers, who was a Friend of Norwich Theatres or a Member of the Guild for Impoverished Actresses, or something – Pond has imported a 'Sir' onto his name. He sprinkles his conversation with airy references to such theatrical luminaries as Henry Irving and Beerbohm Tree, implying that he has acted alongside them numerous times, and that they are lifelong friends. The truth is that he was once in the crowd scene when Irving played Richard III, and he was a sword-bearer for Tree's portrayal of D'Artagnan in a stage version of *The Three Musketeers*.

Maria Rivers, however, is enthralled, clearly seeing Pond as a route to entering all manner of glittering circles. If it were not for her, Walter Rivers would probably have politely got rid of us long since, because the initial invitation was for a long weekend and we've been here for two weeks already.

Pond must be eating and drinking the man out of house and home, and he's dominating the conversation at dinner every night. I suspect Walter Rivers is finding him an increasing nuisance on a number of counts.

One of those counts is Walter's daughter, Juliette.

Juliette Rivers. Sixteen years old, innocent as a child, naïve as a nun, and as beautiful as a wood sprite flitting through a sunlit forest. Having reread that last sentence, I think I will add that I am not usually given to such poetic flights of fancy, but I feel it is warranted in this case, because she really is a very beautiful girl. From my point of view she has never stirred a heartbeat, however.

But since I've worked for Pond, I've observed some of his exploits with ladies, and they never end well. I have a feeling that this one won't, either, and it concerns me to see Juliette Rivers skipping around like a moon-struck gazelle, clasping her hands soulfully whenever Pond appears.

Tonight, over dinner, he told her the story of the burning theatre, and how he had braved the raging inferno to rescue me.

'And,' he said, drawing about him his mantle of romantic mystery which he assiduously practises before his mirror, 'I went back afterwards.'

'You went back? Into the burning building?' said Maria.

'I did, dear lady.'

I will add a note here that until I had met Pond, I hadn't realized gentlemen still called ladies 'dear lady'.

'There were,' said Pond, nonchalantly, 'treasures in that building. They had to be rescued.'

'Treasures?' said Juliette, gazing at him, wide-eyed.

'Theatrical treasures. Old manuscripts that might have been penned by – well, by anyone. Famous people have been to The Thespis in their time – it has an honourable history, that theatre. Also, old playbills and posters advertising the appearance of all manner of famous players. Who knew what might have been in there,' he said, musingly. 'And so there was

treasure, for amidst the smoke and the flames . . .' He studiedly
did not look at me when he said this, 'in the midst of it all,
I managed to gain entry to the old Green Room, where I swept
from the shelves miscellaneous ephemera, including . . .'

Here he paused. He has the actor's instinct for a pause, you
have to allow him that. Maria and Juliette leaned forward
eagerly, and even Walter paused in eating to listen.

'I could fetch it to show you this very minute,' said Pond.

'Could you? I think we should be interested to see it,' said
Maria.

'And,' said Juliette, 'you tell a story so beautifully, Mr Pond
– I'm sorry, I should say Sir Peregrine—'

'You should say Peregrine,' he said, in a voice that was very
nearly a purr, 'but only if you can be Juliet to me.'

At least he did not throw in one of Romeo's lines to Juliet,
although very likely he's forgotten most of them, and it must
be years since he played Romeo anyway. If, of course, he has
ever played it at all.

He got up from the table with one of his abrupt movements.
'I shall fetch it for you,' he declared. 'Without further ado, I
shall fetch it.'

'Then I'll tell them to serve coffee in the drawing room,'
said Maria Rivers. 'Bring – whatever it is – in there, will you.'

It was the dog-eared, chewed-end poster billing the old play,
A Knack to Know a Knave that Pond brought from his room.
Only the gods know whether he did rescue it from The Thespis
that night, or whether he's had it for years and brings it out
when it might impress a possible conquest. I've never even
been able to decide whether the thing is genuine at all, or
whether Pond had it created specifically for this kind of occasion – to impress a lady.

He treated it as if it was a cobweb that might dissolve
between his hands, and spread it lovingly on a low table. Then
he explained that although there was no date, there was a play
with this title that hailed from the seventeenth century, or even
the sixteenth, and there was no knowing when it might have
been staged at The Thespis or who might have appeared in it.
He managed to make it sound as if William Shakespeare,
Richard Burbage and the entire company of The Globe might

have travelled to Norwich to cavort across the stage in the piece.

During the conversation he managed to take Juliette's hand twice, and rather absent-mindedly keep hold of it. Except there was nothing absent-minded about any of it.

There was certainly nothing absent-minded in the way he sought out some local newspaper, and gave an interview, in which he sprinkled his discourse with various well-known names, spoke of his illustrious career, managed to imply the knighthood had been for services to the English theatre, and waved the playbill at a camera.

Nor was there anything absent-minded in the way he left The Tabor, going so quietly and stealthily that no one knew about it until the following morning, when it was discovered that his bed had not been slept in, his clothes had gone from his room, and no one had the smallest clue as to where he was.

It's now one week since Pond left The Tabor. This morning a letter arrived from him, explaining that his abrupt departure was due to his having received an urgent call from a distinguished theatrical colleague who required help in a famous London theatre. Goodness knows when he actually went, or by what means, because nobody heard him go.

His letter said, 'Modesty forbids me from naming either my colleague or the theatre, but be assured I shall let you know as soon as I can do so. In the meantime, I leave my kindest warm thanks for your splendid hospitality.'

The letter was addressed to Walter and Maria. There was no mention in it of Juliette.

There was no mention of me, either. He did not even leave me his kindest warm thanks, and he certainly did not leave me any money.

Nor did he include an address on his letter, to tell us from where it had been sent.

So for the second time in my life I seem to have been suddenly cast adrift, with not a farthing to my name, the prospect of having no roof over my head, and a very bleak outlook for the future indeed.

*   *   *

This morning, Walter Rivers called me into the untidy room usually referred to as his study – although I doubt anyone has studied anything in there for years.

'I've formed a very good opinion of your intelligence, Trigg,' he said, seating himself at the wide kneehole desk and looking out of place there. 'And I can tell you're one to be trusted.' He frowned, then said, 'Now look here, you've been as badly treated by that charlatan as the rest of us. But I've seen that you've the way with writing of letters, and to be frank with you I'm no hand at that kind of thing. Too hot-tempered to think before I write.' He smiled, unexpectedly. 'You'd be a real help to me with the estate work,' he said. 'And dealing with pettifogging clerks in offices and councils and parish jacks-in-office who pussyfoot around a matter until a plain man can't tell what they're saying. I've no patience with any of them. So how about staying with us and helping me with all that nonsense. I can't pay you anything worth mentioning, but there'll be bed and board for you. My wife will see to it that you have a decent room – you'd have your meals with us in the dining room, of course.' He hesitated, then said, 'And perhaps you wouldn't mind occasionally helping her with her various guilds and societies and charities and all the rest of it.' An impatient gesture with one hand. 'She likes to do all those things,' he said. 'They do a lot of good in the parish, of course.' He looked at me from under his bushy brows, and although he did not say, *and it keeps her out of the way*, I think we both had the same thought.

He was looking uncertain, as if he was not sure how I would react to the offer.

I accepted. Of course I did. I can't see what else there is to do. It's true that I know nothing about administering a country estate – or about guilds and societies and charities – but I can learn. I can work with Walter Rivers and I think I can cope with his lady, and I believe I can reach some understanding of what's wanted of me.

And in the privacy of these pages I can admit that I love this house. I love its echoes and the pieces of furniture that might have been polished by long-ago mistresses of the house, and the smooth-as-silk banisters, glossy and satiny because so many hands have slid along them on the way up or down the stairs. And the old tapestry, showing the strange Dance, of course.

The prospect of being part of its management – of finding out about its past and stepping unexpectedly into those pockets of other centuries – fills me with real delight.

NINETEEN

Nicolas Trigg's journal, 1920

I knew it! I knew Pond would end in getting that poor wretched moonstruck child into trouble, and I was right. He has.

The house is filled with hysterical sobbing from Maria Rivers' bedchamber, and on most mornings there are unpleasant retching sounds from Juliette's room. Over all of that is the sound of Walter Rivers, who is for ever stamping furiously around the house, slamming doors, and threatening to scour every theatre in the land until he has hunted down that blackguard who trifled with his daughter's affections and stole her innocence. There are mentions of horsewhips and shotguns at altar steps.

Juliette has not come out of her room at all, although several of the maidservants, looking scared or excited, depending on their outlook on life, go in and out.

Maria Rivers emerges from her sobbing sessions at intervals, and tells Walter – also me if I am in earshot, although I do try not to be – that Juliette has plunged the family into shame and scandal that will most likely echo down the generations. She objects to the shotgun and the altar steps, though, because she cannot bring herself to allow this philandering roué into the family, since it will certainly bring ruination and tribulation to them all.

A couple of times she has contemplated whether a hasty marriage elsewhere might somehow be arranged, but the likelihood of snaring some unsuspecting local young man is not promising.

I was thankful that she did not seem to be seeing me in this role, because I would not want to take on Juliette Rivers in any way whatsoever. But I think the family regard me as having one foot in the servants' hall, so I'm probably safe.

And at dinner this evening she declared that a scrambled marriage was not the solution to the problem. Apart from anything else, it would mean a series of soirées and entertainments beforehand, as well as risking unsavoury gossip and spending money they do not have.

'You know our financial situation by now, Mr Trigg, what with you helping so well with my husband's business matters. So I do feel I can speak freely on the matter, although of course I was brought up never to discuss money.'

'The sordid subject of coinage,' I murmured.

'Exactly. And you know, it's impossible to entertain people without spending a fair sum.'

'I'm sure it is.'

'Not but what a few modest events might take Juliette's mind from the loss of that philandering roué, and also allay any gossip that might be brewing in the village,' she said, and she sounded so mournful that I said,

'Mrs Rivers, I think we needn't trouble ourselves about people gossiping, and we should certainly try to put the philandering roué from our minds, and instead think how we can deal with the immediate problem.'

This, however, brought about a fresh access of tears. Between handkerchiefs pressed on her by me, and brandy poured for her by Walter, Maria sobbed that she had no idea what to do, and she would never have expected to have to face such humiliation, and she did not know what would happen next.

What happened next is that we all woke up this morning to the most appalling cries of pain from Juliette's bedroom.

I scrambled into my clothes, because there was no knowing what might be happening or what might be needed, and went out on to the landing. Walter was there, surprisingly authoritative in his nightshirt and cap, shouting that the sawbones must be sent for, there was clearly something dreadfully wrong with the child, and they must send the trap down to the village for Evershutt.

He was about to march back to his room, clearly with the intention of getting dressed, when Maria, wrapped in a dressing gown, came out to tell him that they must not have Doctor Evershutt here at any price.

'Do you want the whole village to know your daughter's condition?' she cried.

'I should think most of them know it already,' retorted Walter, 'for those servants are the worst gossip-mongers I ever knew, and I'd wager a hundred guineas that that Belinda Grindall has told most of Reivers already.'

Maria turned helplessly to where I was standing, a bit uncertainly, in the doorway of my room. 'Trigg,' she said, wringing her hands. I had never realized people actually did that, but there it was. 'Trigg, what do we do? We daren't call in Dr Evershutt, for everyone will get to know . . . But she's in agony, and she's already . . . Well, there are certain symptoms that . . .'

Her voice trailed away, and I understood that the habit of a lifetime held good, and that reticence had to be preserved, even when your only daughter is very likely bleeding like a stuck pig in her bed, which fairly obviously was what Maria meant.

I said, carefully, 'If not Doctor Evershutt, might the Savory sisters . . . I've heard they're very knowledgeable about remedies and herbal potions—'

Her face broke into almost a smile, and she put out a hand to me. 'Oh, Trigg,' she said. 'Nicolas. What a *good* person you are to have in our house. The Misses Savory would be the very people. And Miss Dorothea always so fond of Walter; in fact I was once told that before he met me people even wondered . . . But it's a family tradition, herbs and healing, all handed down from generation to generation. In fact it's said that their ancestors – Jael and Lydia that was, the Savorys have always been very biblical – it's said they helped a young man in this house in the past, and I don't know his name, but a terrible attack was made on him, and—'

'Shall I get one of the boys to take the trap down to their

house?' I said, before she could become involved in recounting
the history of Jael and Lydia and the unknown young man. 'I
can send a message to say there's illness in the house and we
would be glad if they could come straight out. It would sound
perfectly natural and ordinary.'

'And discreet,' she said. 'Do that at once, will you?'

The Misses Savory arrived within the hour, a bit breathless
and slightly dishevelled from having been bounced in the trap,
but very willing to give whatever help might be needed. They're
a pair of rather twittery ladies, of uncertain age and eager-to-
please disposition. They had clearly put on their best bonnets,
and Miss Matilda, the elder of the pair, was wearing a fur
tippet. With them was a kind of portmanteau of the sort I
remembered my grandmother using.

They were whisked up to Juliette's bedroom, with Maria
talking to them in frantic whispers. When the door of Juliette's
room was opened, the screams reverberated again, so I've beat
a retreat into the room that was Walter's study, but that has
more or less become mine now. There's a view over the gardens
which I like, and I've been able to import a few books and
knock up a few shelves – the local builder, Giff Grindall,
delivered some lengths of oak: 'Offcuts, Mr Trigg, but perfectly
sound.'

Grindall's daughter, Belinda, who's one of the housemaids, had come in while I was fastening the shelves, and
had offered her help. It was difficult sometimes to hold
things level, wasn't it? I said I was managing, thank you all
the same. She's a lively eyed girl, with a certain reputation
in the village, and I'm certainly not averse to the occasional
dalliance, but there's the old saying about not on your own
doorstep. If I'm going to dally with anyone in Reivers, it
won't be Belinda.

It's probably a touch heartless of me to be writing all this
down while mayhem and drama is being played out upstairs,
but it's calming and anyone looking into the room will think
I'm busy with estate matters and probably be relieved that I'm
keeping a polite distance. Which I certainly intend to do unless
called on otherwise.

It sounds as if the Savory ladies and Maria and Walter are coming back downstairs, and I can't hear Juliette any longer . . . I expect the Savorys will leave at once, though, and I'm not likely to see them. That being so, I shall finish this entry.

I was wrong about the Savorys leaving. It's several hours later, but they're still here; in fact they're in this room now.

I'm sitting quietly at the desk. I shouldn't be here at all – this is a private interview – dammit, I don't *want* to be here! But I've come up with every excuse I can think of, and they have insisted on my presence. Walter says I'm part of the whole thing anyway, what with knowing the treacherous seducer, Pond (his lip curls whenever he can bring himself to pronounce the name), and Maria has said there may be certain things that should be noted down, because her mind is so bewildered that she will not be able to take in above a quarter of what is said.

'And notes are always taken at Guild Meetings and Women's Institute Meetings.'

On a practical note she has added that Walter is apt to become dangerously angry, and that I seem to be the only person who can calm him down.

'And the last thing we want is for him to fall into an apoplexy.'

The Misses Savory are agreeable to anyone whom dear Mrs Rivers wants remaining, although Miss Dorothea has sent one or two slightly nervous looks in my direction. But I am trying my best to be unobtrusive, because I have not the heart to refuse Maria Rivers, and Walter has already sent an appealing glance in my direction and silently formed the words, *Please stay*.

The curious thing is that as I sit here at the desk, notebook and inkstand to hand, I'm experiencing another of those, 'This has happened before' moments. I know, with complete certainty, that there have been other times of crisis in this house, and that during those times someone with an eye for detail and an interest in people has sat quietly recording it all. In this room? In this window bay? I want to know that person – man? woman? – so strongly that for a moment the room has blurred slightly, and I have the sense that I might almost be able to put out a hand and draw aside a thin veil and see those other events and that person sitting here writing them down . . .

I've managed to push it away, that feeling, and I'm making these careful notes of what's being said – at least, I'm noting the salient comments, because it's a complicated conversation. Maria dissolves into tears all the time, Walter blows out his moustaches with rage and paces the room, and the Savory ladies are clearly caught between embarrassment and a determination to present the truth that they frequently speak over one another.

But the explanation they are giving is dreadfully clear.

'Miss Juliette has been given a potion to – well, to . . .' Miss Dorothea broke off and looked at her sister.

'A potion that, if I can quote Master Thomas Culpeper, the famous seventeenth-century herbalist, is intended to procure a woman's courses,' said Miss Matilda, firmly.

'Courses? Ah, yes, damn it, yes, I see.' Walter Rivers was scarlet with embarrassment. I bent over my writing, not meeting anyone's eyes.

'If I can use the word with no bark on it, Mr Rivers . . .' This is Miss Matilda again, firm and determined, 'She has been given an abortifacient.'

'An—?'

'Probably it was one of the flower-de-luce family,' put in Miss Dorothea, clearly relieved to be able to address more practical facts. 'Stinking Gladwin, it's called – a very unpleasant name, and in fact it has a great many useful properties.'

'But,' said Miss Matilda, jabbing the air with a finger, the better to make her point, 'if the root is boiled in wine and drunk, it – well, it brings about the expelling of an unborn child.' She sat back. 'It can be administered in other ways, of course, but we do not need to—'

'Indeed we do not,' said Walter. He looked across at me. 'Trigg, I don't know how much of this we actually need noting down—'

'I've just written down the name of that herb, Mr Rivers. That's all.'

'Ah. Yes. Good.'

'We think we have put matters to rights, though,' said Miss Dorothea. 'Since coming here we have given Miss Juliette an infusion of Bistorta. Snakeweed, it's sometimes called. It . . .' She hesitated, and her sister said,

'It has a binding property, if you take my meaning. It can halt the—'

'Yes, I see.' Walter's complexion was turning puce by this time.

'And it seems to have stopped the – ah – the progress of what was attempting to take place.'

'She's still with child?' To her credit, Maria managed to say this without any expression.

'Oh yes. There is no evidence of . . . And she is no longer in pain.'

'There's no danger to her?'

'We believe not.'

Walter said, 'But, look here, how did that child know what to take? She didn't come to you two ladies, I suppose?'

'Indeed she did not.'

'And if she had, we would never have given such a thing to her.' They were indignant at the suggestion.

Miss Dorothea said, rather timidly, 'But you have a young housemaid here, who might be somewhat knowledgeable—'

Walter thumped the table with a clenched fist. 'Belinda Grindall!' he said. 'By God, that little baggage! She was the one, I'll take a Bible oath on it.'

'We hope it won't be necessary for you to do that, Mr Rivers—'

'She's out of this house by nightfall, or I'll know the reason why,' shouted Walter. 'Maria, you'll see to that.'

'Walter, I can't.'

'What? *What?*'

'Because,' said Maria, who was as white as her husband was scarlet, 'I'm the one who asked Belinda to procure the – the draught.'

'Oh, dear God,' said Walter, and buried his head in his hands.

There was an awkward silence, then Matilda Savory said,

firmly, 'It's a very natural reaction, Mrs Rivers. You meant it for the best.'

'I wanted to get her out of the dreadful situation . . .' Maria was crying again, and Miss Dorothea silently handed her a handkerchief. 'And I thought Belinda would know what to get – who to ask. I can't dismiss her for that, Walter.'

'And,' put in Matilda, thoughtfully, 'it might mean that Belinda will now be feeling she owes you considerable loyalty. She's bound to be extremely contrite.'

'And therefore likely to give the family considerable loyalty,' nodded Miss Dorothea. 'Walter – I'm sorry, I should say, Mr Rivers . . .'

I had the feeling that something passed between them – some backward glance to something that might have been but never actually was, and I was aware of a stab of pity, because she must once have been very pretty, Dorothea Savory.

Walter looked at me, and rather unwillingly, I said, 'They're right, you know, sir. This is a time when you – the family – will need people close by who can be trusted. Because . . .'

I hesitated, and Matilda Savory said, 'Because there's still the question of what is to happen to Miss Juliette.'

'And,' said Miss Dorothea, 'to her child when it is born.'

Beyond these windows, the early winter night is already stealing across the gardens – a stealthy, secret kind of night, that makes me remember the strange hidden corners of The Tabor, and the shadowy pockets that probably hold all kinds of secrets – and that may be about to hold more.

Because there are parts of this old house where someone could be hidden without anyone being the wiser . . . Even where a child could be born without people knowing . . .

It hasn't been quite as straightforward as that, of course. It's taken planning, subterfuge, and practicality. What it's also taken is the help of Giff Grindall, who is so mortified to think his daughter participated in a near-tragedy that he will do anything asked of him, and has vowed to Maria and Walter that he will keep this secret under torture of the most extreme kind. To tell him that the entire village probably knows all about it anyway, and that Pond himself will doubtless brag about his conquest for the foreseeable future, would be grossly unkind.

'I blame myself to a great extent, Mr Trigg,' he said to me as we inspected the courtyard rooms with the aim of making them habitable and comfortable for Juliette over the coming months.

'Grindall, you shouldn't feel like that,' I said, as he tapped walls to see if there was the possibility of bringing in a water supply for what he delicately refers to as fittings for a necessary room.

'But it was my own daughter who was involved,' he said. 'My own kin, and that she should have brought about Miss Juliette's . . . Well, it hardly bears thinking what she might have brought about. She meant well, though,' he said, anxiously. 'There was no malice.'

'No, of course there wasn't. She was only doing what Mrs Rivers asked. And Mrs Rivers was doing what she thought best.'

'Well,' he said, moving along to examine a door, 'my Belinda'll behave herself now, I'll answer for that. If not, she'll be packed off to her aunt in Norwich – and a very strict lady she is, Mr Trigg.' He reached for a hammer. 'No mother, that's been the trouble with Belinda, what with my Hannah dying when Belinda was only a mite.'

I said, 'The Misses Savory think Belinda is likely to be very useful in what's likely to be ahead.'

'Good women, those two,' he said. 'And everyone knew Miss Dorothea was sweet on Mr Rivers. Not that there was ever anything between them; in fact I shouldn't think he ever knew. But still.'

'Yes. And it's very clear that Belinda wants to make amends for what happened – what nearly happened, that is.'

In fact, I felt rather sorry for Belinda, who had been genuinely horrified at the results of her attempts to help Juliette, and who had made extravagant promises about how she would help the family in this trouble, and how not a word of it should ever escape her lips – 'Not if I was held down and tortured, mum.'

'Miss Juliette she'll be snug as a bug in a rug here,' Giff said, after we had worked on the courtyard rooms for several days. 'I still don't care for those windows, but I daresay there was once a good reason for someone to fit the bars. I suppose we could remove them, but—'

'It'd probably mean quite a lot of work,' I said, a bit too quickly. 'We might as well leave them as they are.'

We looked at one another. Although it would be too much to say we shared a thought that barred windows might be a good thing to have, the feeling hovered on the air for a moment.

Then Grindall said, in a down-to-earth voice, 'You've been a powerful help, Mr Trigg. That lock – I'd never have thought of fashioning a lock that opened in such a way.'

'It opens from the outside by twisting the handle anti-clockwise,' I said. 'And it locks when the door's shut from the inside.'

'And only opens from inside with the key,' he said, nodding. 'A very good design, that. And you've had a bit of carpentering experience as well, I'd say.'

'Just a bit.' I thought, but did not say, that I had not expected those months of hammering stage trapdoors into place and fashioning scenery in provincial theatres to be useful in creating what's virtually a prison. But Juliette would not need to be here for long – five months would it be? About that.

But then there would be the child. I cannot, for the moment, think how we shall cope with the appearance of the child.

Or can I . . .?

This afternoon we took Juliette Rivers across the courtyard to the rooms we had made for her. In Maria Rivers' favour, I will say that she has done her utmost to make them comfortable and attractive. She had directed myself and Grindall to carry across Juliette's books – Juliette's not much of a reader, but there were some – and some needlework she had been doing. None of us has commented on the fact that since Pond left The Tabor, Juliette has not done very much of anything; she spends most of her time seated in the window recess in the hall, staring along the drive. I'm trying not to think that she's watching for him to return, because that's not a thought

I can contemplate without feeling extremely uneasy. I'm trying even harder not to think about the look on her face when she stares through the windows, but I know it's this look that prompted that curious moment between Grindall and myself – the moment in the courtyard rooms when we agreed that we might as well leave the bars in place at the windows.

Maria has found curtains in the attics of the main house, which are a bit old and slightly faded, but made of thick, soft brocade. We have managed to fit them to the windows. It softens the bars a bit. Also, there are several very good pieces of furniture that have been designated as surplus to requirements in the main rooms, and which we have taken across, struggling a bit to get them up the rather rickety stairs, but managing it in the end. There's a lovely old chest with a carved lid – Maria says it's what's known as a Spanish chest, and that it belonged to a long-ago Rivers lady.

'Her name was Rosalind, and she's supposed to have been so beautiful that men used to fall in love with her at first sight, and her own brother loved her so much he never wanted her to marry and leave him. I don't actually think she did, although I don't really know.'

I like the story of Rosalind. I'd like to think she might be the one whose presence I sometimes sense when I'm writing at the desk in the study. I'd also like to think that even if she didn't marry, she had a lover. And – this is descending into outright romanticism – but I sometimes pretend she was the one who created that curious tapestry. I like to imagine her being fascinated by The Tabor's past, and by the darkness surrounding the legend of that strange Dance. While all the furniture was being carried hither and yon, I quietly took down the tapestry from its hanging, and put it in my study. Nobody noticed or, if they did, they did not comment.

The rest of the furniture for the courtyard rooms is all in place. There's a small table with two matching chairs – the plan is that Juliette will eat at this table, and that one of us will carry her meals across to her. It might be possible to prepare her meals in the courtyard rooms themselves, because Grindall managed to pipe in water and also gas, and create what's almost a small scullery. And in the largest of the rooms is a beautiful old rocking chair, comfortable and relaxing, the beechwood frame polished to a satiny finish. It should be all right. I keep telling myself that it will be all right. But every time I walk away from those rooms, across the courtyard towards the old stone arch, I look back up at the rooms. And always – *always* – Juliette is standing at the window, her hands curled around the bars, staring out. And that look is on her face, and it's a look that strikes a chill into my heart.

TWENTY

Quentin thought he could regard his morning as profitable. Immediately after breakfast he had gone up to his room, and had set about compiling a list of people to whom he could pitch The Tabor project. With Grindall working out plans and estimates, and with the beginnings of a marketing campaign which Quentin himself was overseeing, he thought he was ready to invite investments.

He would probably be quite good at this part of the project, because of his market research work – you had to use tact and even a dash of imagination, and he had developed a very good strategy over the years. He drafted a possible letter to send to suitable companies, and after several attempts he was pleased with it. He might show it to Codling later on when he went to sign his will. It would be a good opportunity to let the man know about the progress Quentin was making, and it would save making a second trip. Very likely Codling made a separate charge for each appointment. You had to be alert to these things.

The appointment was at twelve o'clock, and although he called on Zillah to see if she wanted to come with him, she was involved in washing her hair. She would hear all about it later, she said. Phin and Arabella had gone off to search parish records, and of Toby there was no sign, which was good, because the greater the distance between Toby Tallis and Zillah, the better pleased Quentin would be.

Before setting out for Codling's offices, he went into the village, and introduced himself to some of the shopkeepers. They were all very pleased to meet him, and flattered that the new owner of The Tabor – you might even say – had sought them out.

They were all very interested in hearing Quentin's plans for the house. It was a pity that hardly any of them could spare time to talk for long, what with customers and clients, and phone calls that had to be answered and stock inventories that had to be checked. Quentin entirely understood, of course.

However, the two Savory sisters who ran the little antique shop in the square did not have to break off to deal with customers or check stock, because they did not seem to actually have any customers and their stock was all set out in the two big rooms that overlooked the square. They listened with absorption to the details of all Quentin's plans, and said it was very nice indeed to think The Tabor would become part of the community again. They could remember their grandmother and also a great-aunt talking about it.

'Great-Aunt Matilda, that was. She was the one who had the idea of starting up this shop. She was a very progressive lady for her day, although antiques were a perfectly respectable profession, of course. She and her sister – Great-Aunt Dorothea that was – knew Mr Walter Rivers and his wife quite well. They would be your ancestors.'

'They would. I'm not sure of the exact relationship, though.'

The sisters promised to do all they could to help with Quentin's plans, although the elder one said it was doubtful whether they would be able to invest any actual money.

'I'm sure you'll understand, Mr Rivers. The antique trade isn't what it used to be, and my sister and I . . . well, we're beginning to look towards retirement. We could display posters in the shop, though. And recommend the restaurant to our customers.'

'Oh, yes, we could do that,' chimed in the younger Savory.

*   *   *

The appointment with Codling was not quite so smooth, although Quentin signed the will which had been drawn up. He insisted on having each clause explained, because he was not going to sign anything he did not understand. Codling would respect that, even though it took a fair amount of time.

It was a surprisingly good feeling to have put his signature to the document; Quentin had a feeling of having put his life into proper order. This dealt with, he produced his draft letter and notes of his plans.

Codling was a bit impatient at the interview going on for even longer, but he read the draft letter. Annoyingly, he was quite fussy over one or two very minor details, pointing out what he said were inconsistencies in three places, and saying he hoped that Mr Rivers had prepared suitable projections and business plans to follow up this initial approach, because investment banks and city financiers were inclined to want a good deal of detail before handing out large sums of money.

It was very annoying of Codling, stupid old bumbler, to raise all these trifling objections. Quentin was polite, but he thought to himself that he might very well transfer his business to another firm of solicitors, because he was not going to be lectured to by some no-account country lawyer. There were no inconsistencies in his letter; he would provide financial details when he was asked to do so, and it was not a large sum of money he was requesting anyway, not compared to the returns that would accrue. As for all the gloomy prophecies about unscrupulous persons who fleeced trusting souls of their money, Quentin would not pay any attention. He was not going to be fleeced, and he was not so naively trusting that he could not spot an unscrupulous organization.

Driving back to Reivers, he thought again about the court-yard rooms, and how comfortable he and Zillah would be in them. They might have a sign on the wall, telling people what this part of The Tabor was called. It could say, *The Courtyard Rooms – Q and Z Rivers*. He liked the prospect of their names being linked in that way. He would make sure the sign also said *Private*, because they did not want people wandering in to that part of the grounds by mistake. Could there be a gate across the archway? He had a half-memory of seeing bits of

hinges attached to the walls, as if a gate had been fitted across
the archway at some time in the past.

It was very nice to find Zillah waiting for him when he got
back to The Daunsen. She wanted to know all about his
meeting, so Quentin described it, making quite an amusing
story of it, and telling her how he had signed the will with a
tremendous flourish, with Mr Codling's clerk or secretary or
somebody coming in to witness it.

'It's really signed and sorted out?' said Zillah, her eyes
huge. 'It's all legal?'

'It is.' It was lovely to see her wide-eyed fascination. Quentin
said, indulgently, 'So if I fall under a bus tomorrow, you'll be
quite a rich young lady.'

'Goodness.' She seemed to withdraw for a moment, then
she said, 'D'you know, Quen, I've been thinking about those
courtyard rooms. The ones you said we could turn into our
own living quarters. I think it could be brilliant.'

'I think it could.'

She clasped her hands together, and said in a kind of breathless rush, 'Let's go out there now. Can we? Just the two of
us. To look inside those rooms. It's only three o'clock – even
if there isn't any electricity in there, it won't start getting dark
for ages and we'll be able to have a good look round.'

Quentin thought how wonderful it was that their thoughts
had been running along the same lines. He said that certainly
they could go out there right away.

'I'll just get the keys from my room – I won't be a minute.
I'd better take this jacket off and put on a sweater. I don't
want to get it covered in cobwebs.'

'Oh, just get the keys – don't bother about the jacket,' said
Zillah, glancing around the bar. In a quieter voice, she
said, 'Arabella and Phin are searching church records – it
sounded as if they were going to spend the whole day on
it. And Toby said something about trying to find some old
theatre that Phin had found a mention of – some old actor he
thought might be linked to The Tabor. He suggested I went
with him, but I said I had to help you. But any one of them
might come back at any minute and we don't want to find
we've got to take them with us. I'll wait for you outside.'

As Quentin ran up the stairs to his room and scooped up the keys, his mind was alight with pleasure because Zillah had made these plans for the two of them to go out to the courtyard rooms together.

As Quentin turned into Drum Lane, Zillah was aware of the most tremendous sense of excitement. This was how she had felt all those years ago – on that afternoon when she had understood that someone called Evelyn stood in the way of The Tabor being hers, and that if only Evelyn could be got rid of, this marvellous house would one day belong to Zillah. And incredibly, within about an hour of that, there Evelyn had been. It had been so easy – laughably so – to give Evelyn that push, and see the flailing figure fall down on to the courtyard. It had been even easier to appear terrified and bewildered. She had thought they had believed in her fear – Osbert and her grandmother. But then Osbert had written that spiteful letter with those vicious accusations, and he had reneged on his promise to Zillah's grandmother, and The Tabor had gone to Quentin. The letter could not be helped, but it was so long ago that there would not be anyone still alive who would know about it. Zillah was perfectly safe on that score. As for Quentin owning The Tabor – she smiled inwardly. Not for much longer, Quentin.

He parked near to the stone arch and Zillah hopped out, and waited patiently for him to lock the car, which he always did, even inside his own garage. Her heart was pounding, and for a really bad moment she thought she was not going to be able to do this. But then she glanced back at the house, which, even in this desolate state, was beautiful, and remembered that Quentin had no right to a single brick of it.

As they neared the arch, she suddenly stopped and said, 'Damn, I've left my bag in the car – my phone and keys and wallet, and you never know who's around. I'll just nip back for it – let me have the keys, will you? And actually, now I think about it, you ought to take that jacket off before we go up there after all. It'll probably be pretty dusty. I'll put it on the back seat for you.'

He hesitated, then nodded, and slipped the jacket off. 'Make sure you lock the car.'

Zillah put Quentin's jacket on the seat, sliding a hand into
the pockets as she did so. If his phone was still on him the
plan might have to be abandoned, because he could not be
left with the phone in his possession . . . But it was all right.
The phone was in the inside pocket. She picked up her handbag,
so carefully left on the floor, then locked the car, making sure
Quentin saw her do it. She dropped the keys off-handedly into
the pocket of her coat. Her beautifully simple plan was working
out beautifully. She slung the bag over one shoulder, caught
him up and slipped a hand through his arm, feeling his start
of surprise, because she hardly ever made any kind of physical
move.

As they went towards the stairway, she gazed up at the
windows, and said, 'It would be really great if we could convert
this for ourselves, wouldn't it?'

'Yes, very.'

'I like knowing that this is our family home,' said Zillah,
with a sigh of happiness. 'And when it's all done, you'll
be working in the restaurant, and I'll be in our rooms out
here. Well, not all of the time, I don't suppose, because I
can help with some of the management stuff, can't I? Maybe
taking bookings. Or helping with table design – flower arrangements and things. I think I might be quite good at that.'

She almost gave a little skip, but it might be over the top
to do that, and she did not want to make him suspicious.

But he was not suspicious, of course. He had no reason to
be, and all she had to do for the moment was to be enthusiastic. And to put from her mind the memory of that sinister
figure unfolding from the rocking chair and coming towards
her, and reaching out with those hands . . .

Quentin was saying something about the stairway being a
bit wobbly. 'It doesn't look at all safe; in fact we should maybe
wait for Grindall to take a look before we go up there—'

'Oh, no,' said Zillah, at once. 'Now we're here, let's see
what the place is like. I think the stairway's safer than it seems.
We'll go up one at a time. You go ahead and once you're up
there, I'll follow.'

'All right. I've got the keys,' he said.

Zillah thought: you won't need the keys, because the lock

on that door is a special one – it twists around from the outside and the door clicks open. She did not say this, of course; she stood at the bottom of the stairway and watched. He was going quite cautiously, and halfway up he called back.

'They are safer than they look. But the railings aren't so good. Be careful not to hold on to them too much.'

'I won't.'

'And parts of the floor have fallen away altogether. So watch for those.'

'I am watching,' said Zillah, going slowly up the stairs. 'Goodness, it's higher up than it looks from below, isn't it? But this balcony's probably been here for centuries – it'll last for another half-hour. Is this the main door – yes, of course it is. Let's go in. It's exciting, isn't it?'

Quentin hesitated again, but reached for the keys, then frowned.

'There's no keyhole in the door,' he said.

'Isn't there? How peculiar.' Zillah pretended to peer at the door. 'I suppose it won't open without a key, will it? But I can't see how a key could be used—'

'Of course it won't open without a key,' he said, a bit impatiently. 'But there's nowhere I can see for a key to be used.'

'Try the handle anyway,' said Zillah, and by this time her heart was racing with excitement. Quentin shrugged, then, as if humouring a slightly stupid child, reached out to the handle. Zillah watched, willing him to twist it backwards, like putting a car into reverse. Easy. Just use common sense, Quentin.

He said, 'Ah – got it,' and the door swung open, clearly surprising him when it swung outwards. But he stood for a moment peering in, then he said, 'It's quite dark in there – where's my phone? Damn, it was in my jacket, wasn't it? I wanted the torch, but . . . I think I can see . . . No, it's too dark. Let me have yours, will you?'

Zillah pretended to rummage in her bag, then said, 'Oh, but there's daylight coming in from that door – on the right, d'you see? Open that. Much better if we can see everything by natural light.'

'Yes, all right.'

He went forward, and Zillah stepped back on to the balcony, grasped the edge of the door, and slammed it shut. As it clanged into place, she gave a cry.

'Quentin? Quen – are you all right? The door slipped – or maybe the wind blew it back—'

'Of course I'm all right,' he said, from inside the rooms. 'Open the door, though.'

'Yes – yes, of course . . .' Zillah rattled the handle, deliberately and carefully turning it the wrong way so he would hear and think she was trying to get the door open. 'I can't – Quen, it won't open.'

'It opened a minute ago,' he said. 'Turn the handle backwards like I did.'

'I am turning it backwards, but it won't move. It's jammed or something's snapped.' She managed to get a note of panic into her voice. 'Are you sure there's nothing on your side to use?'

'Yes, I am sure. Hold on, though, I'll open that door and see if any light comes in . . . God, it's dark in here . . .'

His voice was slightly distant, and Zillah imagined him feeling his way along the passage to the door that opened on to the big room with the hearth. And the rocking chair, where Evelyn had been sitting that day . . .

'Any good?' she said after a moment.

'A bit. There's quite a big room, and – oh, it's the window on to the balcony.' There was a movement at the window, and Quentin's face came into view. His hands came up as if to beat angrily on the glass. 'Zillah, for heaven's sake get the door open – it's dark in here and cold and disgustingly dirty.'

'I'm trying,' said Zillah, forcing a sob into her voice. She was gripping the door handle with both hands, making sure he could see. 'It won't budge though . . . Quin, what do we do? Are you sure you can't free the door from that side?'

He disappeared from the window and she heard him on the other side of the door again. 'I can't,' he said, after a moment. 'You'll have to get help – a locksmith.'

'But—'

'George Grindall,' said Quentin. 'He'll be able to free the door. Phone him now.'

'Yes. Yes, I will. Have you got the number?'

'On my phone,' he said, and the angry impatience was strong in his tone. 'In my jacket in the car.'

'All right. I'll be as quick as I can.'

She went down the stairs, being careful not to touch the railings, and across the courtyard again. Quentin would not be able to see her from the courtyard rooms, but Zillah got into the car anyway. She would give it ten minutes, then she would go back. She glanced at the sky, and then at her watch. Four o'clock. Not starting to get dark yet, but not far off. Good.

'Well?' said Quentin, when she climbed back up the stairs fifteen minutes later.

'I can't get him.' Zillah was pleased at how anxious she sounded. 'It's just voicemail. I left a message, but it's anyone's guess when he'll pick it up. Don't builders and plumbers and people usually have a mobile with them? He didn't, though. But there'll be someone at the yard, surely?'

Quen said, 'There'd have to be. Listen, can you drive out and find him? Bring him back?'

'Well—'

'Zill, it's the only thing I can think of! Unless we can get this door open, I'm trapped.'

'Yes, of course it's the best thing.' Zillah was extremely glad the suggestion had come from Quentin. She said, 'Good thing I've got the car keys, isn't it? I'll go out there now. I'll be as quick as I can.'

As she set off, she thought it was a pity it was not yet dark enough to put into action the next piece of the plan, but whatever she did on the balcony in this light would be seen through the barred window by Quentin.

TWENTY-ONE

At half past one, Phin and Arabella took a brief break from the church records, and ate rolls and fruit sitting on Walter's bench outside the church.

'I wonder how Toby's getting on,' said Arabella. 'He was very keen to dash off to find out about old theatres in Norwich, wasn't he, although I have a feeling he planned it with the aim of taking Zillah with him and spending the day with her. Pity she wasn't interested. But he went anyway. He's got some idea of trying to locate the theatres where that flamboyant old actor appeared. Peregrine Pond.'

'*Sir* Peregrine Pond,' said Phin, grinning. 'And The Victoriana, wasn't it? And that other one that was burned – The Thespis. Where Pond reckoned he found that old playbill he said had belonged to one of Shakespeare's men.'

'Could it have been Kempe?' said Arabella.

'I'd like to think so, but I wouldn't put money on it. I wouldn't put money on Pond's story about rescuing a priceless bit of theatre history from a burning building, either.'

'Nor would I. But never say die. And we've still got plenty of avenues to explore. Have you had enough to eat? Shall we renew the assault on the church records?'

As they walked back to the rectory, Arabella said, 'Rev Pilbeam's being very generous and open-house, isn't he? Letting us have a free hand with all the records and things. Actually, I think he's quite intrigued. We'll have to make sure we tell him what we find.'

'Depending on what we do find,' said Phin. 'All kinds of scandals might come to light.'

'I shouldn't think he'd mind a bit of scandal, providing it's far enough in the past.'

Even after a few hours, there was a pleasant sense of familiarity in returning to the study and to the sight of the church records on the table, and Arabella's red hat adorning the pottery head of the vicar on the mantelpiece.

They sat down, and the silence that had fallen on to the room earlier that morning came back. Phin, working his way through columns of names – of past Savorys and Grindalls and other names of people who all seemed to have played their part in the running of the village – thought it was extraordinary restful to be working like this, with Arabella nearby. Once she got up to take down another of the registers, and twice she frowned and turned a page back as if to check something, but when Phin looked up questioningly, she shook her head as if to say, Nothing, or, False Alarm.

The slanting graceful writing – writing in several different hands over the months and years – was starting to blur slightly. Then Arabella suddenly said,

'This probably isn't relevant, but it's interesting.'

'What?'

'At the end of 1920 – December, in fact – Walter registered the birth of a child. Evelyn.'

'That might be someone else to trace. If she was married from this church, it would be recorded—'

'It wasn't a she,' said Arabella. 'It was a son.'

'Unusual for a boy to be called Evelyn,' began Phin. 'What are you looking for?' he said, as Arabella delved into the large shoulder bag she had brought.

'That book I found in the Savorys' shop – the one on local history, written by someone called H.J. Marplot. Because,' said Arabella, 'it gives a description about a member of the Rivers family being executed during the Peasants' Revolt. Thirteen hundred and something, and I'm sure the name of the ringleader of the local rebels was Evelyn . . . Yes, here it is.' She pushed her glasses more firmly on to her nose. 'It describes how several local people signed up for the Peasants' Revolt because Evelyn Rivers did so.'

'Evelyn,' said Phin. 'So it was a family name, and Walter and his wife revived it.'

'Yes. Evelyn and his gang went stomping off to London to help with sacking the Tower of London and storming bishops' palaces and things,' said Arabella. 'It says they were called "Belligerents" by some people, and they rampaged through the streets, shouting warlike cries.' She glanced up from the pages. 'What would they have shouted? "Death to the greedy land-owners", maybe?'

'You can hear very similar shouts on a protest march today,' remarked Phin.

'They killed the Lord Chancellor,' said Arabella, returning to the book. 'Which I should think was a hugely serious crime all by itself.'

'What happened to Evelyn?'

'Wait a minute . . . Yes, this looks like it. Evelyn was hunted down by the King's men after the rebellion had been more or less squashed.' She turned a page. 'They marched out to The Tabor, stormed in through the gardens, and carried out the execution there and then. According to the author, there was no trial, no warning, nothing. Evelyn was put to death in front of the whole family.' She turned to the book's title page. 'H.J. lists a few primary sources, but he says the account of Evelyn's execution is credited to a Rivers lady from the early 1600s, which was handed down to him from an ancestor of his own.' She frowned, then said, 'Phin – the inventory! That reference to a tapestry depicting the execution and showing the Murder Dance. Where are my notes – I typed them on to the tablet, and it's in here somewhere . . . Yes, here.' She flipped on the tablet, and scanned the documents. 'This is it. The inventory was attached to Jasper Rivers' will: "1675. Framed tapestry, believed to have been worked by Jasper Rivers' mother. Showing the villagers gathered to watch the Reivers Dance, which enacts the tragicke fate of the rebel, Evelyn Rivers, executed by the King's men in 1381, which tragedie shadowed and tainted the Rivers family for generations. Embroidered date 1603, initial *R*". I don't know that finding a modern-day Evelyn gets us any further, though,' said Arabella, sitting back and frowning at the small screen.

'Other than that the first Evelyn was still remembered in the early twentieth century,' said Phin, thoughtfully. 'They certainly kept that legend alive, didn't they?'

'I wonder what happened to Walter's Evelyn,' said Arabella, and looked at the bookshelves with the registers stacked on it, all neatly labelled. 'Would it be all right to take down a couple more of those, do you think?'

'I should think so. Rev Pilbeam gave us a free hand. What are you after?'

'I'd like to see if Evelyn got married, and if there were any children. See how he links up with the old boy who lived in The Tabor later on and left it to Quentin. I'll try from 1940 onwards. He might have got involved in parish activities.'

'By that time it's more likely he was called up for World

War II,' said Phin, returning to parish records for 1921. 'He was probably killed, and that's why the house went to Osbert.'

'I expect so.' But she took two registers from the shelf, and set them down on the table. The silence came down again, and this time lasted quite a long time – so much so that when Arabella spoke, Phin jumped.

'We more or less decided that the Reivers Dance wouldn't have been performed for centuries, didn't we?' she said.

'Yes.'

'We were wrong. Listen to this. It's in the parish stuff about meetings, and again it's only the heading for the meeting's topic. But in December 1941 . . .' She pushed her glasses more firmly on her nose, then read, '"Parish sub-committee meeting to discuss performance of Reivers Dance as part of celebrations to mark twenty-first birthday of Mr Evelyn Rivers. Meeting chaired by Evelyn Rivers".'

She looked at him. 'So it has been performed since 1602. And it was performed as recently as 1941. Phin, there could be people still alive here who saw it – or, at least, whose parents saw it. Does it feel as if we've reached out and taken a hand from the past, and as if the hand might belong to Will Kempe?'

'It'd be nice to think so,' said Phin, leaning over to read the brief entry. 'I suppose it's not so odd that no one's mentioned it. Or is it?'

'Quentin and Zillah wouldn't know about it, because they've never been here before,' said Arabella. 'I think they're quite distant members of the family, and I don't think Quentin expected to inherit The Tabor. It's interesting that Evelyn doesn't seem to have been away fighting the war, doesn't it? I suppose he might have been on leave, though.'

'He might not have fought in the war at all,' said Phin.

'Why wouldn't he?'

'The estate to run – overseeing the growing of food, maybe. Farming was a reserved occupation, wasn't it? Or he might have been a conscientious objector, or—'

'Yes?'

'Or there was some other reason,' said Phin, slowly. 'Physical or mental . . .' He made an impatient gesture. 'I'm seeing mysteries again, where mysteries probably don't exist.'

'But you're thinking about the almshouses that don't seem to have existed,' said Arabella, looking back at the entry for parish meetings. 'And that sketch in The Daunsen of the barred windows and a prisoner behind them.'

'Yes.' Phin thought for a moment, then said, 'There's two things we should do. We ought to go out to The Tabor. I haven't seen it yet, and I'd like to. I'd like to see those courtyard rooms, and see if there's anything to say they were almshouses. You were going to take some photos anyway, weren't you?'

'Yes. Good idea. What's the other thing?'

'I'd like to find out if anyone in the village has any memory of those birthday celebrations when the Reivers Dance was performed – it'd probably be a memory from parents or grand-parents, and it'll have to be someone whose family's been here for a long time—'

'George Grindall,' said Arabella. And then, 'Or even better – the Savorys.'

'Let's make it the Savorys first. What time is it? Half past three. The shop will be open, won't it?'

'I should think so,' said Arabella, as he began stacking up the registers, and carrying them back to their shelves.

'We'll leave a note for the Rev,' said Phin, reaching for a pen. 'We'll phone him later as well, but for the moment, we're heading for the 1940s via the Savorys.'

Alice and Flora Savory were delighted to meet Miss Tallis again, and charmed to be introduced to Mr Fox.

They told him all about Arabella's previous visit to their shop, and described how she had upset a tray of Victorian jewellery – 'Entirely accidentally, of course, and there was absolutely no harm done to anything—'

'But she insisted on getting some green felt stuff from the stationer's and laying it all out, and it looked absolutely beau-tiful, Mr Fox, much nicer than we had displayed it.'

'Miss Rivers bought a necklace on the strength of it – we owe that to you, Miss Tallis,' said Alice, happily.

'The jewellery's gorgeous,' said Arabella, glancing at the display, 'And I see you've still got that topaz ring. Beautiful. Can we talk to you about the history of this village?'

'The word is that your ancestors lived here for centuries,' said Phin, hoping this was the right moment to step into the conversation. 'If we could persuade you to tell us a bit about the past—'

Alice and Flora were delighted to be asked such a question, and by such a distinguished gentleman as Mr Fox. Alice had always had something of an eye for a good-looking young man, and Flora had had two quite close relationships when she was younger. It was a pity that neither had ended in marriage, but you could not have everything, and they enjoyed their life and the antiques, and were very companionable with one another and with people in the village.

They invited Arabella and Phin into the small back room which they used as an office and which had comfortable chairs, and Flora put on the kettle for a cup of tea.

Phin, accepting the tea, which was served in exquisite, thin china cups, and which he tried not to think he might drop and break, said, 'It's the Rivers family we're trying to find out about—'

He glanced at Arabella, who said, 'In fact, it's the Reivers Dance.'

The Reivers Dance. The words dropped into the comfortable old-fashioned room like stones.

After a moment, Flora said, 'We do know about it, of course. But it hasn't been performed for a very long time indeed, that Dance, you know.'

'Three hundred years, wasn't it, Flo?'

'Nearer four, I think.'

They looked hopefully at Phin, and he said, 'The odd thing is that we found a mention that suggested it might have been part of birthday celebrations for Evelyn Rivers in 1941. But perhaps it was just an idea somebody had and nothing came of it.'

Again the silence, then Alice Savory said with decision, 'There is a story— It was before we were born, of course, but we had two aunts – Matilda and Dorothea they were – and they were very much part of what went on at The Tabor.'

'They used to talk about the family sometimes,' put in Flora. 'You remember, Alice? We'd visit them when they got older, and Matilda always baked gingerbread and scones, and we used to have afternoon tea in the school holidays.' She sent an apologetic glance at Phin. 'People don't do that kind of thing now, of course.'

'Some people do,' said Phin. 'And it's a pity more of them don't.'

'Especially when there's home-made gingerbread,' put in Arabella. 'Can you tell us some of the stories? It isn't for anything anyone would mind – Quentin Rivers would like to know about the family's past in case he can use it for publicity.'

'For his restaurant, I suppose.' This was Alice. 'I don't know much about restaurants, but I do know they cost a lot of money, so unless he's richer than he seems—'

'And The Tabor needs a great deal of work doing to it,' put in Flora. 'Osbert Rivers let things go, so I believe. Of course, once that secretary died—'

'Secretary?'

'Mr Trigg. Nicolas Trigg. He'd been with Osbert for a great many years. He'd been with Walter, too, I think.'

'The aunts used to talk about him,' nodded Alice. 'They liked him. I think everyone liked him.'

'He loved that house,' said Flora. 'It was almost as if it was part of him. He knew about the Reivers Dance. And he knew quite a lot about The Tabor's past.'

'How did he know?' said Phin, leaning forward, and putting his teacup on the low table. 'Did he find papers – diaries, maybe?'

Arabella said, 'You notice how his eyes light up when there's a possibility of old diaries? The researcher's treasure-house, diaries.'

'Not diaries,' said Alice. 'Not exactly. But . . .' She looked at her sister, who nodded.

'I don't see why they can't be shown it,' she said. 'I'll get it. We keep a few things locked away, you know. Things that aren't really for sale, but that make for a link to the past for us.'

It was a small book, clearly very old, but nicely bound, with gilt-tipped deckled edges to the pages, and an attractive cover. Across the front, in an elaborate slanting typeface, were the words, '*A Savory Herbal: Compiled by Miss Matilda Savory*

*and Miss Dorothea Savory from the receipts, cures and simples
of the ladies of their family.'*

'Those were the great-aunts we mentioned,' said Alice, proudly.
'They put together all of the cures and potions that had been
handed down in the family for – well, several centuries, I'd have
to say. The ladies of our family were very well known for that
kind of thing. We've been too busy with our antique business,
but we kept this. Sentiment, really, but we like to do so.'

'Matilda had it privately printed, mostly for local circula-
tion,' said Flora. 'I think it was in 1925. It'll say on the
endpapers, though.'

Phin had already opened the book and was delightedly
reading the opening notes. 'Yes, 1925 it is,' he said.

'And they've listed some of their ancestors' names,' said
Arabella, reading it with him. 'Mistress Jael Savory – that's
a really old biblical name, isn't it? And Lydia.'

Phin, who wanted nothing more than to sit down with the
book and shut out the entire world so that he could absorb its
contents, said, 'This is a terrific find. Thank you.'

'It gives a surprising amount of information about The Tabor
and the Rivers family,' said Alice.

'I can see that already.'

'And the Reivers Dance is certainly referred to.'

'The aunts once told us how they took a very long time
deciding whether to mention that or not.'

'It wasn't regarded with any . . . People associated it with
tragedy, you see,' said Alice.

'Will it be helpful, to you, Mr Fox?' said Flora hopefully.

'Helpful?' said Phin. 'You have no idea . . . This is like
finding gold. Better than finding gold.' He looked up at them.
'Could I borrow it for a few hours? I'd take the greatest care
of it. And bring it back – say tomorrow?'

'We don't usually let it go out at all,' said Flora. 'Because
it's the only copy that's left. But I think, on this occasion, we
could make an exception. Alice?'

'Yes, certainly we could. Clearly this is important.'

'I'll tell you the full story when I've pieced it all together,'
said Phin. 'We'll even bring some gingerbread in memory of
your great-aunts.'

Alice and Flora liked this. They wrapped the book in cello-
phane and bubble-wrap, and handed it to him.

'Either Arabella or I will bring it back tomorrow,' said Phin.

As they went out into the little square, he suddenly said,
'Damn – Arabella, I've left my notebook in there. You go on
and I'll catch you up.'

He went back inside the little shop, and Alice and Flora
looked up.

Keeping one eye on the window, Phin said, 'That ring that
Arabella liked – the topaz one – can you put it very quickly
into a bag and process the payment for me before she realizes
what I'm doing. Here's my card—'

'Don't you want to know how much—?'

'If it hits four figures, you'd better tell me, but
otherwise—'

'Oh, it's nothing like that.' They were shocked at such a
possibility, and Flora turned over the tiny price tag for him to
see.

Phin smiled. 'Very acceptable,' he said.

He had expected them to flutter and take a long time over
the transaction, and for Arabella to come back in, but Flora
reached into a drawer for a small leather jewel box, while
Alice slid Phin's card into a machine, and spun it round for
him to enter his PIN. The whole thing took barely five minutes.

Phin said, 'Thank you – so much.'

'She'll love it,' said Alice, beaming with delight.

'It's almost the exact colour of her eyes,' said Flora.

'I know,' said Phin, smiling at them. 'That's why I had to
buy it for her.'

TWENTY-TWO

It was only just on four o'clock when they got back to The
Daunsen, and they went straight up to the bedroom, although
Arabella went into the bar to ask if they could have a pot
of tea sent up to the room.

Phin threw off his jacket and sat down on the bed to unwrap the Savory Herbal, and Arabella perched on the dressing-table stool. After a moment she said, 'Would it work if you read out the relevant sections and I typed it straight on to the laptop? That way we could make sure of returning the book to the Savorys tomorrow.'

'Yes,' said Phin, who had already been stepping into a world of hitherto-unknown herbs and plants, with names such as Yellow Bedstraw, Bishop's Weed, and Brank Ursine, but who managed to bring his mind back sufficiently to remember about laptops and note-taking. 'Yes, that's a good idea. And it'd mean we'd be more or less reading it together.'

'I promise not to chime in with inane comments,' she said, opening the laptop.

'Your comments are never inane. And they're very often helpful.' He looked across at her. 'We make a good team, don't we?'

'I'm beginning to think so.'

'I've thought so for a while. In fact . . . Oh, that sounds like our tea.'

Phin did not quite swear at the interruption, because of being more than half into the world of the herbal and its possible revelations, but he was aware of a stab of annoyance. But by the time the tea was poured and Arabella had opened the laptop, he had been pulled back into the past.

Handing him a cup, Arabella said, 'Is there an index of any kind? Is it arranged alphabetically or in date order, or what?'

'There's no index,' said Phin. 'And it looks as if it's alphabetical, which is a bit of a nuisance, because it would have been much easier if I could work through it chronologically. Oh, but there's a kind of chatty comment at the head of each one, which might help. Things like how this was found efficacious for Albert Pocket's ague or the Reverend Marplot's gout—'

'Marplot,' said Arabella, looking up from typing in a heading for the notes. 'That's the man who wrote that local history.'

'So it is. Another link. And then,' said Phin, turning pages carefully, 'there's one explaining how ground ivy eases gripes and choleric humours of the stomach, and how an infusion of

it was given with great success to a gentleman called Bee. No
idea if that's an actual surname or meant as an initial.'

'Names changed to protect the innocent, perhaps,' nodded
Arabella. 'Or in this case, abbreviated.'

'Yes. Oh, and it was found to help the itch, scabs, and
wheals. What on earth is a wheal – no, I'd rather not know.
There's nothing about the Reivers Dance yet, though.'

He went on turning the pages, then suddenly said, 'This
looks interesting.' He glanced at Arabella, then read aloud.

'It's headed, "A draught prepared to help the travail of
childbirth". There's a list of ingredients, but it says,
"Administered at The Tabor in November 1920, and successful
in easing pain and the fearful state of mind of the mother".
The date,' said Phin, thoughtfully, 'is November 1920.'

'Evelyn? His birth was registered in December 1920. It
would fit.'

'The date could be a coincidence. And yet – why were the
Savorys in attendance and administering draughts and things?
Why wouldn't there be a doctor?'

'It'd be pre-NHS, of course,' said Arabella, frowning at the
laptop's screen. 'But there'd be a doctor – or a local midwife
of some kind, wouldn't there? Village people might not be
able to afford a doctor's fees, but you'd expect the owners of
The Tabor to.'

'Unless,' said Phin, 'it was a secret birth?'

'An illegitimate one? And the details of the treatment written
down long afterwards? But why would Evelyn have to be born
in secrecy?'

Phin was still reading the entry, and after a moment he
said, 'There's a note at the very end after the list of ingredients, and how to infuse things and steep leaves in vinegar.
And it says . . .' He broke off, staring at the page, then said,
slowly, 'Isn't it remarkable how something from the past
can still slam into your emotions. Arabella, the footnote says
that the baby – a boy – was "not completely whole and
sound", and that,"the poor mother blamed herself most griev-
ously and had to be restrained, necessitating a soothing
draught". An emulsion of poppy seeds was given to her,
which "stupefies the senses and therefore should not be taken

inwardly". But that "applied outwardly to the temples, it provides sleep".'

As Arabella typed all this, Phin laid the book down. Then he said, 'Are you getting the same picture that I am?'

'That whoever gave birth that day was sent into a mad frenzy by the sight of a child "not completely whole and sound".' Arabella finished typing and sat back. 'And that whoever it was had to be restrained. I see what you mean about the past still having the power to affect you. It's dreadfully sad. Was it Evelyn who was born that night, d'you think? If there was a – a deformity, it could explain why he didn't seem to have been in the army or anything in 1941.'

'And the mother who was sent into the mad frenzy could have been kept in the courtyard rooms,' said Phin. 'In 1920 – that was still an era when any kind of mental illness was shameful.'

'And when mental institutions were dreadful places,' said Arabella. 'They'd have kept her with them, that girl who was Evelyn's mother. They'd have seen it as the humane thing to do. I hate the idea of the barred windows—'

'Which could date much farther back anyway,' said Phin. 'Remember the *Cwellan Daunsen* sketch?'

'Oh yes, I was forgetting. Thanks. I can take the barred windows for Evelyn's mother, I think.'

Phin turned the page, and said, 'There's a bit more in the entry – a link referring the reader to an earlier recipe, and . . . Oh God.'

'What? Phin, *what*?'

But Phin was already reading it out. '"Here we give the receipt handed down by Lydia Savory, which was used to soothe and heal the wounds inflicted on Master Greenberry during the performance of the Reivers Dance many centuries ago. As a remedy it was proved to be sovereign for severe wounds, including—"'

'Including?'

'Including the severing of a hand,' said Phin.

For a long time neither of them spoke, then finally Phin said, 'Arabella, could you bear to have a break from cures and simples and grisly fragments of people's past? And look at a different bit of it?'

'The Tabor?'

'Yes. Is it too late to go out there now?'

'It's a quarter to five,' said Arabella, glancing at her watch. 'No, it isn't too late. It'll start to get dark quite soon, but we could see it fairly well.'

Phin said, 'I think the lawyers call it seeing the *locus in quo*.'

'Ah. The place where the action happened. In fact,' said Arabella, 'the place where some of those cures were given. Evelyn's mother, who probably had to be locked away in those courtyard rooms. And Master Greenberry, who was attacked during the Reivers Dance.'

Phin looked at her gratefully. 'I am glad about you,' he said. 'And yes, it's exactly that. We needn't be away long – we'd be back in plenty of time for dinner.'

Arabella closed the laptop, and as she reached for the scarlet hat, she said, 'I'm glad about you, as well.'

Phin was silent as they drove out of Reivers, Arabella directing him. He was experiencing the feeling he sometimes had with his work – the conviction that the past was almost close enough to touch. But which past is it? he thought, as Arabella indicated the turning into Drum Lane. Is it Will Kempe and his era, or is it nearer than that? Walter Rivers and Nicolas Trigg? Evelyn Rivers, born "not completely whole and sound"? Evelyn's mother, sent into a mad frenzy at the sight of the child?

But it was not until they were out of the car and walking towards the stone arch that he had the sense of touching the past properly. Because this was where the strange sinister Murder Dance would have taken place – the Dance that had been worked into a tapestry by the mother of a long-ago Rivers man called Jasper, and that had depicted villagers watching a performance – 'showing the tragicke fate of the rebel, Evelyn Rivers, executed by the King's men in 1381, which tragedie shadowed and tainted the Rivers family for generations'.

And this was where a famous clown-actor, Shakespeare's

inspiration for Falstaff, might have performed. Will Kempe, thought Phin, standing very still and staring up at the dark old manor house. Had Kempe really been here?

As they neared the arch, he remembered, as well, that this was where a prison with barred windows had been created – causing some long-ago artist to sketch that harrowing image that still hung in The Daunsen.

The past swirled and eddied all around him for a moment, and then he frowned, forced his mind back to the present, and followed Arabella towards the stone arch.

*   *   *

Nicolas Trigg's journal, 1920
The solution to the problem of Juliette has been glaringly obvious to me almost from the beginning – almost since it was known she's to have a child. I thought the solution would be glaringly obvious to Walter and Maria, but the weeks have gone along and it's clear that it isn't. That means I'm facing the prospect of explaining to them what I think we will have to do.

I have no idea why I care so very much about the lives of this family, but since I was stranded here (that wretched Pond altered the course of several people's lives!), they've been good to me. Which does beg a question – are they seeing me as the son they always wanted? Or is it being conceited to think that way? Whatever the truth is, I would like to do what I can for them. Also, of course, I'm in love with the house itself.

It's turning out to be easy enough to keep Juliette in the courtyard rooms. A kind of docility has descended on her, and Maria is inclined to give thanks to a merciful God for bestowing on her this serenity. Don't I agree with her? she keeps asking me.

I don't agree, but I haven't yet had the courage to say so. Because there are times when Juliette turns her head slowly, and when something that's neither docile nor submissive glares out of her eyes. It's a cliché to say it chills my very marrow, and I daresay Pond would talk about his soul being harrowed, but whatever description you give it at those times, I'm extremely grateful for the bars at the windows in the courtyard rooms, and I'm even more glad to know that the door-lock fashioned by Grindall – the lock he and I designed between us – means that the outer door slams in place and the lock drops instantly and very securely indeed. And that, in doing so, Juliette is shut inside with no means of opening the door and getting out.

This morning I summoned up as much courage as I could, and talked to Walter and Maria about my plan.

'You would have to pretend to everyone,' I said, looking very directly at Maria. 'You would have to live in seclusion for – well, from now until the birth. But afterwards life could return to normality.'

'But with the addition of a child,' said Walter.

'Yes.'

'Which we would have to bring up as our own son or daughter.'

'Would you find that difficult?'

I saw the memory of Peregrine Pond graze his mind and understood he was thinking that the child would be Pond's son or daughter. But he's a sensible man, Walter, and after a moment he said, firmly, 'No. I don't believe I would. Maria?'

Maria said, slowly, as if testing each word, 'I would have to pretend to – to have given birth.'

'Yes.' I'm rather pleased that I managed to meet her eyes squarely at that point, because it isn't an easy task for a young man of barely twenty to look straight at a lady almost twice his age and tell her she must act out the part of an expectant mother, and then pretend to actually give birth. But I managed it with – I think I can say – a degree of equanimity.

Walter said, 'But look here, there'll have to be help with the birth itself, to – hum – to assist. Anyone who does that will know the truth.'

'Yes, but there are two ladies in the village who already know the truth. They've proved themselves trustworthy throughout, and they're knowledgeable about these things. I think we could ask Matilda and Dorothea Savory to be present when it comes to it.'

*   *   *

They're going to do it. Of course they are – I think I knew
they would weeks ago. I do wish the idea had come from
them, though, because they could so easily blame me if
anything goes wrong. Not that anything will go wrong.
Everything is arranged – we have worked out all the details,
and the Savorys are already planning what potions and infu-
sions they will use, explaining that the leaves of columbine
steeped in wine are what they call sovereign for the birth of
a child. They have attended at births before, they assure us.
And if Mr Trigg will be so kind as to drive the trap into the
village to their house immediately they are wanted . . .

'Immediately, you understand, and never mind if it's the
middle of the night.'

'I understand,' I said. 'And I'll come for you if I have to
drive to the ends of the earth to find you.'

They liked that. Miss Matilda approved of determination,
and Miss Dorothea said she had always admired a young man
who had a colourful turn of phrase.

I find I'm reassured by all this. It's a good plan that we've
made, and nothing will go wrong.

The plan has gone dreadfully wrong. I'm writing this in the
study that's now virtually my own, seated at the desk, with
the courtyard rooms in direct line. I've had virtually no sleep
for the last twenty-four hours – I don't think anyone in The
Tabor has.

It began quite early in the morning. Belinda had gone
across the courtyard to Juliette's rooms – we have worked
out a rota for this; Walter says it's how it was done when he
was a young subaltern in the Boer War. I think he rather
enjoyed displaying his organizational skills. And whoever
goes over there always takes the special key from its hook
just inside the scullery door. We're careful about that. As
Grindall said, the door opens very easily from the outside
– by twisting the handle backwards – and it locks from inside
purely by slamming the door shut.

I was just drinking a cup of coffee and contemplating a
plate of scrambled eggs and kidneys – Walter and Maria may
plead poverty, but they keep a very good table – when Belinda

came running into the dining room, helter-skelter, panic in her face, and her apron awry.

'Madam – Mr Trigg – oh, madam, it's started, and Miss Juliette lying on the bed screaming like a trapped hare.'

I gulped down the remains of the coffee, and I'd like to say I leapt up from the chair, but that wretched damaged leg prevents me from leaping anywhere. But I moved fast enough, telling Belinda to run to the stables and have the trap harnessed. As I went through the hall to the main door, Maria followed me, wringing her hands, and I paused for just a moment to reassure her that everything was in hand.

The Savorys were very efficient. They had been seated at their own breakfast table, but as soon as I entered they got up, and while Miss Dorothea carried the tray of plates and cups to their scullery, Miss Matilda fetched the portmanteau that had been placed in readiness for the summons. Everything was in there, they assured me. They put on their bonnets, and slid their little feet into their shoes, and we were away, rattling back through the village, and along Drum Lane.

As soon as we were at the top of the stairway and on the long balcony, we heard the screaming. It reverberated all around that semi-enclosed space, and it was a dreadful thing to hear. They opened the door – they had visited Juliette several times recently and they understood about the mechanism, and I followed them inside, carrying the portmanteau. I was about to go back out and find Walter so that we could wait things out in the main house, when one of the Savory sisters – I have no idea which one – screamed to me for help.

It's not a situation where any man would want to intrude, but nor could any man ignore it. I went forward. Into Juliette's bedroom.

There was a thick coppery stench on the air that after a moment I identified as blood, and I thought: then she's dead. Or the child's dead.

But Juliette was not dead, and nor was the child. It lay squirming on the bed, emitting small cries, and Juliette was crouching over it. Her hair hung half over her face, in lank strings, and her face was streaked with tears and sweat.

She was still screaming, and Matilda Savory was trying to restrain her, while Dorothea was reaching for the child.

For a dreadful moment I thought Juliette was trying to get at the child – that she was going to harm it, and something painful closed around my heart, because it was so small and helpless . . .

But it was not the child Juliette was struggling to reach; it was Maria. Maria had been standing at the side of the bed, but as Juliette fought to get free of Matilda's grip, Maria shrank against the wall, her expression one of terror. I went forward at once – although I have no idea, even now, whether I was intending to help Matilda restrain Juliette or whether I was reaching for Maria to pull her out of Juliette's reach. Whichever it was, I failed.

Juliette had already fought free of Matilda's hands – I had time to think that for a woman just emerging from childbirth, she seemed to have extraordinary strength, but then I saw the wild glare in her eyes and I understood, with a feeling of dread, that this was the strength of insanity. That was the moment when, may God forgive me, I froze – I will always remember it as the moment I could have saved Maria Rivers but failed.

In that moment Juliette pulled her mother down on the bed, screaming in a harsh ugly voice that was barely recognizable as Juliette's own normally gentle tones.

'Your fault!' she was crying. 'This is your fault, you bitch! You made me drink that filthy stuff – you said it was the only way to avoid ruin and shame! You made me try to murder my own child! But he's the one who's ruined! You see it? Do you? Look at him! He's all I've got left of the man I loved, but he's maimed—'

I think there was a moment when the three of us were so stunned we had no idea what to do. Then Juliette scrabbled at the sheets and dragged herself across the bed, holding out her hands as if reaching out to her mother. Maria took the reaching hands at once – instinctively, I imagine – but at once Juliette pulled Maria down on to the bed, and her hands closed around her mother's throat.

For a dreadful moment the three of us froze, unable to

believe what we were seeing, unable to think what to do. Then the child wailed, and Dorothea went forward and managed to lift him clear of the bed. She backed away slightly, holding him against her, trying to quiet his cries, and Matilda and I reached frantically for Juliette, grabbing her upper arms and her shoulders, trying to pull her away from Maria. She fought like a wildcat, and at first I thought we had succeeded in breaking her hold on her mother, but Maria was already flailing weakly at the air and her face was becoming suffused with crimson. Juliette was holding on to her throat for all she was worth – her knuckles had turned white with the force of her grip. I grabbed at her fingers, trying to prise them free – and that's another of the memories that stays with me – the feel of those fingers that were like steel.

I have no idea how long it takes to strangle someone. All I know is that it was almost as if time ceased to exist while we fought to get Juliette away from Maria. You would think that two people – a young man and a not-so-young but certainly healthy and determined woman – would have managed it, but Juliette was in the grip of such madness that we could not do it. I think we knew, long before we stopped, that it was a useless struggle, but we used every ounce of our combined strengths.

At last Maria gave a dreadful bubbling gasp and her head fell back. Her eyes rolled up, showing only the whites, and Juliette gave a cry of triumph before falling back on the bed.

TWENTY-THREE

Nicolas Trigg's journal, December 1920

I am writing this by the drawing-room fire – it's dark outside, but this room is brightly lit and warm. I'm feeling icily cold, though, and I'm not sure if I shall ever really be warm again. I certainly don't think I shall ever be free of the sight of Juliette

Rivers, mad beyond all help, strangling her mother. Nor shall I ever be free of the guilt, because I did not manage to stop Juliette – she committed murder tonight, and I should have been able to prevent it. But I didn't.

After Maria fell back and Matilda went forward to see if she could be revived, Juliette collapsed on the bed. If I were to be fanciful, I might say it was as if the madness had suddenly drained from her.

Dorothea set the child down in the crib that had been brought here weeks earlier, and although she was herself shaking violently, she somehow got Juliette back into bed and covered her up.

Matilda straightened up from Maria and looked at us.

'Is she—?' But of course I knew the answer.

Even so, Matilda said, brusquely, 'I'm afraid so. Nothing to be done.' As Dorothea let out a gasp, Matilda went to the half-open bag, and took from it a small flagon and a jar.

'We have to look to the living now,' she said, pouring a thick liquid into a small cup. And, glancing at me, 'Laudanum, Mr Trigg – not something to be given lightly, but on this occasion necessary, if Miss Juliette is to be made calm.'

But Juliette had already fallen into a kind of stupor, although she drank what was held to her lips obediently, then lay back, staring at nothing. The jar contained an ointment which Matilda rubbed into Juliette's temples. 'An emulsion of poppy seeds,' she said. 'Very soothing.'

This done, we carried Maria's body into the smallest of the rooms, and draped it with a sheet.

'We'll arrange for a proper laying-out presently – no one will need to ask any difficult questions,' said Maria.

'Death in childbirth,' nodded her sister. 'Dr Evershutt will accept that from us. It will all be perfectly seemly and straightforward.'

'But the immediate task,' said Matilda, rather grimly, 'is to tell Mr Rivers.' She looked at me. 'Will you come with me?'

It was the very last thing I wanted, but I had already realized I would have to do it, so I said, 'Yes.'

We left Dorothea to sit in an outer room to watch Juliette.

She was within sight and sound of her, but she was also within reach of the main door. She could run out to call for help if she had to.

'Don't forget to slam the door shut if you need to get out,' said Matilda, as they wrapped an extra blanket around the child. 'But the laudanum will keep her like this for several hours.'

I said, tentatively, 'Even then, I don't think you will have to come out to call for help, Miss Savory. I think the madness is over.' I remember very clearly saying that, because it was the first time I had used the word *madness* about any of this. Writing this now, I'm trying not to wonder how much we're likely to use it in the future.

It was a curious scene that was played out inside the main house, but I'd like to set it down as clearly as I can. Telling Walter Rivers what had happened is already a blur in my mind – it was what came afterwards that stands out so clearly.

We were in the long drawing room, and Belinda Grindall had made up the fire and had fed the child with warm milk from a stoppered bottle. Then she went across to the courtyard rooms, taking the place of Miss Dorothea, who came back over to the house.

'She's still deeply asleep,' she said, glancing worriedly at Walter, who was slumped in a chair, his face haggard and drawn, and then accepting the small measure of brandy I poured for her. 'Although I don't normally drink brandy, Mr Trigg, but perhaps just this once—'

'I think you need it,' I said. Personally, I would happily have downed an entire bottle of brandy if I thought it would have blotted out the memory of what I had seen earlier, and if it might have come up with a solution to what we were to do next. I supposed a doctor would have to be called to see to Maria's body, and the vicar would need to be told.

The fire had burned considerably lower when Walter finally roused himself from his silent misery, and looked across at the child swathed in its shawls and blankets. Almost to himself, he said, 'When the people in the village see that child, they'll say he has the Rivers taint. That's what they'll say.'

The Rivers taint. The words dropped into the room like stones, and I was aware of a sudden chill.

Matilda said, 'No one will say that. No one will even think it.'

'In any case, no one remembers any of those tales after all this time,' said Dorothea.

Walter glanced at me, and for a moment his expression lifted. 'We're intriguing Trigg,' he said, 'But he's much too polite to ask what we're talking about.'

I said, 'Then I'll be impolite and ask. What do you mean by the Rivers taint?'

For a moment I thought I had overstepped a mark, but then Walter said, 'A very long time ago, an ancestor, Evelyn Rivers, joined a rebellion against the King – against the government and the establishment. But he was taken by the King's men, and executed in a very brutal way – here, in these grounds.'

'In the courtyard,' said Dorothea in quiet voice.

'Yes, they did it in the courtyard,' said Walter. 'It was vicious and cruel, and the villagers kept the memory of it for a very long time. A long time later – two or three hundred years later, it was – a man who came to this house was butchered in exactly the same way by a jealous Rivers man who remembered what had been done to his ancestor.'

'What exactly—'

'At that long-ago execution, everyone thought Evelyn was to be beheaded. But the King's men said the offence against the King had been committed with Evelyn's hands, and therefore his hands must be struck from his wrists.' A pause. 'And so they were,' said Walter, and again there was the glance towards the courtyard. 'They did it to him out there, in full view of half the village,' he said, softly.

'And the – other man?' I said, after a moment. 'The later one?'

'A lover of Rosalind Rivers, so the story goes,' said Walter, and despite the grimness of the situation, I was aware of a tiny stab of pleasure to know Rosalind had had a lover.

Walter said, 'He, too, was mutilated in the same way, although I believe he lived – the story is that two earlier Savory ladies saved him.' He glanced at Matilda and Dorothea, who nodded.

I looked at the tiny creature in the crib by the fire. A fold of the shawl had fallen aside, and the small arms were showing. But at the ends of those arms—

'Incomplete,' said Matilda Savory, following my gaze. 'Such things happen from time to time.'

'They'll say it's the Rivers taint,' said Walter again. His tone was so dispirited, and he looked so dreadful, that I started to say something, and then stopped, because I could not think of anything to say.

It was Dorothea who spoke up. 'It's a small deformity compared to many,' she said. 'It's tragic and terrible, but with kindness and understanding the little one will adapt.'

'It's possible this was an early birth, Mr Rivers,' put in Matilda. 'If so, his hands – should be regarded simply as – as God's work not having time to be finished.'

'Unfinished,' said Walter, half to himself, and bizarrely I heard Pond's voice in my mind, and the bitter cry of Richard Plantagenet. *Deformed, unfinished, sent before my time into this breathing world, scarce half made up . . .*

And now, in the room on my own and finishing writing this, I have to record that I have no idea what is ahead. I have no idea what is to be done with Juliette, or how this household is to be managed. Nor have I any idea of how that tiny boy is going to live his life with the deformity. Unfinished. It's a kind way of describing it.

March 1921
Of all the roles I ever imagined for myself, I never in my wildest dreams imagined this one. But here it is. I've been appointed – officially and with church and rural and parish blessing – as an administrator of almshouses within The Tabor's environs.

Almshouses, for goodness' sake. I've looked up the meaning, and almshouses date back a very long way indeed – as far back as the tenth century. They were sometimes called bede-houses, *bede* being an Angle-Saxon word for prayer. It seems philanthropic ladies and gentlemen down the years had often tried to provide what's termed as succour, sustenance and shelter, to the unfortunates of the county. A good many seem also to have left orders for prayers or Masses to be said for their souls.

I daresay most of these good people were genuine and well-meaning, but there's also the sense of a *quid pro quo* here and there. As in: I'll build a couple of almshouses for the village if you'll promise to organize regular petitions to the Almighty on my behalf after I'm dead. But I suppose that's a cynical outlook, and it has to be said that I'm certainly learning a great deal about things I never thought I'd encounter.

The whole situation is bizarre, but it's Walter's solution to keeping the courtyard rooms safe from casual prying eyes. And, incredibly, it seems to be working. We've put a gate across the stone arch – Grindall said there were already hinges there, would you believe that, Mr Trigg, and very likely better not to wonder about the reason for them.

Whatever the reason for them, it means no one can wander in there by accident, and Walter has told the local councils, very vehemently indeed, that he retains the right to choose, and that he alone will make the selection of who can benefit from the rooms. I know how vehement it was, because he dictated a letter that I had to write out in a fair hand and deliver to the various local councils.

No incumbents ever will be given a place in The Tabor almshouses, of course – no homeless person or vagrant or beggar or widow with her mites will be offered a room across the courtyard.

It all means that Juliette is safe and secure in those rooms. None of us knows how long the situation will continue. None of us dares look that far ahead. Belinda Grindall, I have to say, is keeping to her word and is looking after Juliette, and we have drafted in a kind of nurse-warden as well. An older woman who comes from somewhere near Norwich, and who hasn't the local connections that might pose problems.

Life is going on, although I'm hating that I have to be devious over the almshouses. I'm constantly fearful that there will have to be some kind of official inspection or that someone will find out by chance what really lives behind those walls. I console myself with the thought that it can't go on for ever.

As a footnote – and then I believe I shall close this journal

– one of the astonishing things about this family is the discovery that – despite owning this beautiful old manor house – they are practically flat broke. When it was realized that the almshouses brought a fee from the parish – I believe there's a rather arcane law that allows regular payments – Walter almost tripped over himself to accept it. It comes from the parish accounts straight into his own bank. In fairness, I should say he insists on giving me a modest salary each month. I take it a bit reluctantly, but I do take it. I manage to salt most of it away. It isn't a huge amount, but it's a kind of insurance against what might be ahead – against a time when I might have to leave The Tabor. Not that I think I could bear ever to do so. It would break my heart far more thoroughly than any woman ever could.

Walter is fiercely determined not to allow any officials of any kind into the grounds. He has taken to reading up on ancient land laws, and he goes around the house muttering about incomprehensible things such as infangentheof and the statute of mortmain, and about assumpsit and gavelkind. I haven't yet fathomed the meaning of assumpsit, but gavelkind is apparently a Saxon form of limited land ownership. This morning over breakfast he quoted sections of Magna Carta.

Sometimes I wonder what I'm doing here in this remote old house, with a poor deranged creature locked up in the courtyard rooms like the first Mrs Rochester in her attic, and an employer who talks about Magna Carta while I'm eating kedgeree and drinking coffee. This afternoon he told me that Goethe's *Dr Faust* stated that, 'All rights and laws are transmitted like an eternal sickness'. I daresay Goethe was right.

*   *   *

Quentin was trying not to notice how dark it was becoming outside the courtyard room windows. He was able to see the time on his watch, though, and he saw that it was only a little after four o'clock. It was annoying that his phone had been in his jacket in the car. But when he had said to Zillah to try to get it to him, she had not been able to see how that could be done, and Quentin had to admit he could not see it, either. There was no slot in the door – it was not like a conventional door with a letterbox, of course – and the bars at the windows meant that even if the glass were to be smashed, there was no way of getting in or out. He had already made several attempts to loosen the bars, but they were absolutely firm. He did not speculate as to why the bars had been put there in the first place.

It would very likely take Zillah some time to track down Grindall, and to get him to come out here. Probably the lock would have to be broken, which was a pity, because it had seemed to be a sturdy arrangement and it would be expensive to replace. Quentin had tried several times to find a way of opening it from this side, but it was impossible.

He sat down in the large room with the brick hearth to wait. There was an old rocking chair, which creaked a lot and whose cushions and padding were worn, but which was surprisingly comfortable. From here he could see the window, and it was now dark enough for Zillah to need the car's lights when she drove, and he would see them sweep across the gardens beyond the stone arch.

As he sat rocking in the old chair, for the first time he was aware of the extreme age of this place. If you were inclined to be fanciful – which Quentin was not, of course – you might almost start to think you could hear soft footsteps, as if someone was creeping along the balcony outside. Quentin went to the window and peered through the bars, but he could not see anyone. Imagination, that was all. He sat down again, and tried not to think the footsteps seemed to be going back.

The minutes ticked along. Five o'clock was it now? He peered at his watch. Yes, just on five. Surely she would not be much longer – surely she would have found Grindall by now?

And then, with considerable relief, he heard unmistakable footsteps coming up the rickety stairs, and Zillah calling to him.

Quentin went to the large barred window at once, and Zillah came into view, hurrying along the balcony, her hair untidy, and, even in this half-light, a faint flush on her face.

'Grindall's on his way,' she said. 'He had to finish something off somewhere – I didn't get the details – but he says it sounds as if the lock has jammed and he's given me something – I don't know what it's called, some kind of key that should override the mechanism.'

'How—?'

'I don't know,' she said, a bit impatiently. 'But I'll try it. Oh, but Grindall says you need to push against the door from your side – really push hard at the same time. All right?'

'Yes.' Quentin went thankfully out to the door, and waited.

After a moment there was a scrabbling, scratching sound from outside, then Zillah's voice said, 'Ready? I think something's starting to give way . . . Yes, I'm sure it is. OK – throw all your weight against the door. As soon as it gives, I'll stand to one side so you don't knock me over.'

The scrabbling came again, and then the unmistakable sound of something – some small mechanism – giving way. Quentin placed both hands on the door's surface, and threw his whole weight against pushing it.

It gave way at once – with a speed and a smoothness that astonished him. And it was too sudden – the force of his pushing propelled him straight through the door, and on to the balcony. He fell against the railings, and sick panic swept over him, because the railings were giving way – he was about to fall down to the courtyard below—

He heard himself cry out Zillah's name, and he tried to reach out for her, because she would grab his hands and help him to right his balance, of course she would . . .

His hand brushed her coat sleeve and he clutched it wildly. The dimness of the balcony seemed to be whirling around him – he thought he was still half lying against the railing, but the fall had sent his senses spinning. But there was a moment when he felt, quite distinctly, that Zillah's hand came out to him, and he was aware of sudden thankfulness.

And then the hand pushed him.

Quentin cried out, and grabbed at Zillah's arm, instinctively trying to save himself. The blurred surroundings spun again, and he heard Zillah give an appalling scream. Seconds later there was the most dreadful sound he had ever heard, and even like this – dizzy and disorientated from falling – Quentin knew what it was.

It was the sound of a human body falling to the courtyard below.

As he clawed his way to his feet, he saw the crumpled shape

lying beneath him, with Zillah's crimson scarf still around its neck.

And then he saw that standing in the stone archway were Phineas Fox and Arabella.

Phin and Arabella sat over a late dinner in The Daunsen, with Toby a silent, white-faced third.

'She isn't going to die,' he said, after a while. 'They've said so – I talked to the medics – there're times when it helps to be in the profession. Well, not quite in, but very nearly. And she'll survive, although—'

'Although?'

'They wouldn't tell me anything major, of course, not being a relative, but they told Quentin and he told me . . . There's a strong likelihood of paraplegia – as a permanency,' said Toby.

Phin said carefully, 'Paralysis? Paralysis below the waist?'

'Yes. With spinal injuries it depends on whether it's above a particular level. She's got some broken bones as well, but that's relatively straightforward. It's the spine damage.'

'Might it mean a wheelchair?' said Arabella.

'It might. Yes, it might. So Quentin's planning to find a bungalow for them to live.'

Phin and Arabella looked at one another, then Phin said, 'Not The Tabor?'

'He says he can't bear to even see it. He'll probably let the National Trust or somewhere like that have it.'

'So no restaurant,' said Arabella, half to herself. 'No unrolling of the house's past.'

'The National Trust might do that for their own publicity.' Toby got up. 'If you don't mind, I'll go back to the hospital,' he said. 'I can't do anything, but poor old Quentin – well, I haven't got much in common with him, but there doesn't seem to be any family, and he's there on his own.'

'We'll come out later if it would help,' said Arabella.

'Thanks. I'll let you know what's happening.'

As he got up to leave, Phin said, 'Toby – what do you think you'll do?'

'They won't want me around,' he said, and made an impatient gesture with his hand. 'Even if I could take on the . . .'

For a moment his expression was more serious and more sombre than Phin had ever seen it, and he was deeply grateful to Arabella for getting up and putting her arms around Toby.

'You'll do something that's right for you,' she said. 'Whatever it is, I'll be pleased about it. So will Phin.'

A glimmer of the old Toby showed then. He said, 'You never know – if I qualify at the end of this year, I might throw convention to the winds and set off into the sunset to provide medical aid in some far-flung corner of the world. Mean giving up the flat, of course, but it might be time to do that anyway.'

He glanced at Arabella, then nodded to Phin and went out.

Phin looked at Arabella. 'Zillah was trying to push Quentin over, wasn't she?' he said.

'That's how it looked. But I don't know if I'm sure enough about it to say anything. To the police, I mean.'

'Same here. And,' said Phin, thoughtfully, 'if she's going to be confined to a wheelchair for the rest of her life—'

'It's punishment enough?'

'I think so.'

'Why would she do it, though?'

Phin said, 'I can only think it was because she wanted The Tabor for herself.'

'But Quentin was going to share it with her, wasn't he?'

'Was he? He would have been very much in the driving seat. And Zillah . . .' Phin spread his hands. 'Greedy,' he said. 'She wanted the whole package.' He leaned back in his chair. 'I wonder what the National Trust will do with the place if Quentin does let them have it,' he said. 'I wonder if they'll find any more about its past than we did.' He looked at Arabella. 'Whether they'll trace Will Kempe and Jasper Rivers.'

'And,' said Arabella, softly, 'Nicolas Trigg.'

'Yes. I'd like to know what happened to Trigg,' said Phin. He stood up and reached for her hand. 'Let's go back to the Savory herbal,' he said. 'There's still more than half of it to read. We might find out the truth about the Murder Dance.'

TWENTY-FOUR

Nicolas Trigg's journal, 1941

I 've returned to these pages after a long absence – and I know that I've done so because I'm increasingly worried about what's going to happen here tomorrow night. It's said to be cleansing to the mind to write about your fears, and that's what I'm doing now.

Tomorrow is Evelyn's twenty-first birthday, and to mark it he's arranged for a performance of the ancient Reivers Dance. This ought not to alarm me – I ought to be seeing it as interesting and unusual, the revival of a very old local tradition, and entirely suitable to celebrate the coming-of-age of the Rivers heir. The trouble is that I haven't lived here for twenty years without learning a bit about this family and this house – and the fragments I've learned about the Reivers Dance suggest it's best left alone.

But Evelyn is adamant. He says it's his heritage, and he intends to bring all the villagers out here to witness the performance. I've tried to talk him out of it, but I can't outright argue against him, and I certainly can't override his arrangements – it would involve most of the village, or, at least, those of the village who aren't away at the war. And to all intents and purposes, Evelyn is my boss. Dear Walter is so frail now, so endearingly anxious that Evelyn should lead as normal a life as possible – so grateful when Evelyn joins in with village activities – that he will let him do almost anything he wants.

There's been so much to do in the years since I opened these pages. There's been the estate to deal with – especially in the face of Walter's increasing years – and making sure Juliette is properly guarded and looked after. And, of course, administering the almshouses – which is to say keeping up the pretence that there really are almshouses there. At times I think Walter has come close to losing this house, but somehow each time we've scraped through and the income from the church's almshouse funds has been the saving of The Tabor several times. I feel bad about that, because the entire thing is a blatant deception, but somehow I was drawn in, and now there's no going back.

And now there's the war to contend with – although curiously that's helped with the financial difficulties, because there've been government grants for the growing of food. Even so, you don't expect to live through two wars in your lifetime, and although people say this is a continuation of the Great War – 'Unfinished business', insists Giff Grindall – it feels to me as if this is a separate conflict from the Great War of my youth.

I couldn't fight in that war all those years ago, and I certainly can't fight in this one. Too old for one thing, and too lame for another. But there are other ways to contribute. Food to be grown, local organizations to help with. Local Defence Volunteers, firefighters. Coastal defences.

And The Tabor to be run.

Two days ago, Walter called me into his room to witness Evelyn's and his signature to some documents.

'Ahead of the birthday,' he said, smiling fondly at Evelyn.

Evelyn smiled back, and, as God is my witness, it was the greediest smile imaginable.

'All this is to be put into your name, my boy,' said Walter, happily, spreading out the documents adorned with red seals and green tape. He had put a fountain pen nearby and blotting paper. 'The Trust Fund and these investments.'

Evelyn sat down and read the documents, his face absorbed. Then he nodded, and took the fountain pen between the stumps of his hands, and made the cross which is all he can do in the way of a signature. I saw Walter wince – he hates seeing Evelyn's fumbling awkwardness with such things – but Evelyn didn't seem to notice.

'And now, Trigg?' said Walter, handing me the fountain pen. 'If you'll be so good . . .'

I added my signature as witness to the documents, and

turned to leave the room. But before I could do so, Evelyn said, 'What about the other one?'

'What other one? No, Trigg, don't go, you'll probably understand things better than I do these days.'

Evelyn said, 'The Deeds for this house.' He stared at Walter. 'You are handing The Tabor to me for my birthday, aren't you?' he said.

There was a rather dreadful silence. Then Walter said, 'No, I'm not. In fact legally I can't.'

'But I always believed . . . And if there's any old-fashioned nonsense about entails—'

'It isn't an entail,' said Walter, slowly. 'The house isn't mine. It belonged to – to my wife. She was the Rivers who inherited. She was in direct line.'

'So what? My mother died when I was born. Now I'm next in line.'

The careless disinterest in his voice brought a look of pain to Walter's face – I knew it was as much at the memory of Maria, as at the deception that's been practised on Evelyn all these years.

Walter said, 'Her will was very specific – it was made shortly before your birth, and the provisions were legally set out. They can't be altered – the law permits ladies to do whatever they wish with their property. It has for nearly eighty years now. This house is held in a kind of Trust, and when I die it must go to . . .' He paused, then said, 'To Maria's daughter and mine. Juliette. Mr Codling and Trigg will administer it and act as Trustees.'

Evelyn's face was white, but his eyes were blazing, and I flinched, because not since that night with Juliette had I seen such a look.

He said, 'That's ridiculous! Juliette! Just because she's older than me . . . I'm the son, I should have it. It's my right to have it.'

At his tone I felt as if something harsh and cold was scraping across my skin, and I think Walter felt something of the same. But I willed him to find some way round it – some lie that would satisfy Evelyn. There had been a clause in the will about funds always having to be available for Juliette's care – he could surely make use of that. But he did not. He sat up a little straighter, as if preparing to take on some great weight, and with a sharpness I had not heard in his voice for some years, he said, 'Evelyn, I hoped never to have to tell you this, but you aren't my son. Not mine or Maria's.'

'Who—?'

'You're Juliette's son,' said Walter. 'Born of a . . . a long-ago love affair. Your father was – he was a distinguished and vivid man.' I saw from the tightness around his mouth that it had cost him a good deal to say that, but I understood he was trying to give Evelyn some comfort. There was no reply, and Walter pressed on. 'In accordance with the terms of the will and Maria's wishes, you can't inherit this house until your mother – your real mother – dies.'

At last Evelyn spoke. In a voice filled with such hatred and such loathing I could almost see it take shape in the room, he said, 'That – that *creature* in the courtyard rooms is my mother?'

'She is.'

He recoiled as if he had been dealt a blow. Then, with a truly terrible gesture, he held out his hands. 'This is her fault, isn't it?' he said. 'She tried to get rid of me. She drank some filthy mixture or – or had something done in some squalid backstreet room. Only it didn't work. But damage was caused. These hands. Oh, God, that bitch – that vicious, selfish whore—'

'Stop!' shouted Walter. 'You will not speak like that about your mother. I won't allow it. All you need to know is that Juliette – your mother – was left heiress to this house. There's an end to the matter.' He got slowly and painfully out of his chair, and I put out a hand instinctively to help him. I thought: he really is old, and he's very fragile. And there's nothing more I can do to help him.

It's very unusual for anyone to stay at The Tabor (Walter is afraid of people finding out about Juliette, of course), but a young cousin called Elwen Rivers is to stay for a week to be part of Evelyn's birthday. Walter has asked her here because – I can hardly bear to write this – because he's seeing her as a possible wife for Evelyn. Is he trying to appease Evelyn in some way? I can't tell, and I can't ask.

I asked him if he would tell Elwen about Juliette, and he

said, fretfully, 'I shall see how things develop – whether she
and Evelyn take to one another. But that side of the family
has no money whatsoever, you know – they'd very likely be
glad of the match.'

I didn't remind him that this was practically the middle of the
twentieth century, and that marriages were no longer arranged.

'It's only for a week,' said Walter, 'and I've asked that boy
– Osbert – to come at the same time. He's only nine or so,
and Elwen can take charge of him.'

I can't tell him that Evelyn has never shown any interest in
girls, any more than I can tell him that there are times when
he looks at people in the way that his mother, Juliette, looked
at us all on the night he was born. Juliette doesn't look at
anyone like that now – Matilda and Dorothea Savory are
assiduous in bringing to The Tabor their mixtures and potions
which, they promise, will keep the poor soul calm and tranquil.
Juliette is very calm indeed. She sits and rocks in her chair,
and stares at nothing.

Evelyn's birthday. This morning I went into the village and
there's a buzz of excitement and expectancy everywhere.
They're all looking forward to seeing the Reivers Dance – and
in some cases to performing it. Most people are delighted,
saying isn't it just what the village needs in these dreary times,
how marvellous to think of such an ancient tradition being
revived, and all credit to poor Mr Evelyn, poor soul, battling
with his deformity, not that you'd notice it most of the time,
him being so deft with everything.

There was a bit of good-natured grumbling because the
Dance can't be in the evening, with torch flares, but it's agreed
that you can't trust Göring not to send his Luftwaffe screeching
spitefully across the skies halfway through. And the black-out
has to be obeyed, of course. We don't get many bombs in this
part of Norfolk, but we do get a few. However, the afternoon
it has to be, and everyone is saying that please God the rain
will hold off.

An early lunch has just been served, and the two housemaids
are carrying chairs and small tables out to the courtyard.

Belinda Grindall will make sure Juliette is in her room, with
all doors shut and curtains closed. Not that Juliette is likely
to peer out of any of the windows, but Belinda will make sure.

In case anyone in the future might read this, I'll explain
that the housemaids we're able to have are older ladies – all
the young ones are caught up in the war.

I wish I didn't feel this mounting apprehension about this
afternoon, and I also wish that Elwen hadn't sought me out
earlier, and confided that she and Osbert are going to watch
the Dance from a hiding place – one of the alcoves in the
courtyard.

'My cousin Evelyn told me to stay away and to keep Osbert
with me. He was quite stern. He said none of the village
children are being allowed here today. I don't know why.'

'I don't, either,' I said, in surprise. 'It's something most
children would enjoy. And it's part of your family history,
isn't it? Osbert's too.'

'It is. Perhaps the Dance is a bit saucy, though, so Evelyn's
said no children.' She smiled, and for a moment it was the
smile of a wood sprite about to go on the loose.

'You could be right,' I said.

'Are you going out there to watch?'

'I'm going to watch from in here,' I said.

'From this room? I like this room,' she said, unexpectedly.
'It's got little bits of the past in it, hasn't it?'

'Yes,' I said. 'And you're the only other person who's
realized that. But I'll probably go upstairs to watch – there's
a view straight across to the courtyard from one of the
bedrooms.'

As she went out, I had the oddest feeling that for those
few moments Elwen Rivers and I had met on some strange
mental level and had understood one another. It's quite a
good feeling.

And now I'm sitting in the window of a big bedroom – and
I've spared a thought for Elwen, who would probably sense
those fragments of the past up here, because this is another
of those slightly eerie times when I have the strong feeling that
this has happened before. That somewhere in this old house's

long history, someone else waited for this Dance to begin, and felt the same mounting apprehension I'm feeling now.

The dancers are coming towards the house – I can hear the music and the laughter and cheering . . . They're coming through the garden gate at the back of the grounds – I hadn't expected that, but they're scampering through the gardens now, manoeuvring around the big vegetable beds where we grow food for the troops and the local people.

And now they're going through the stone arch into the courtyard – I can see them quite clearly. Some of them are wearing the old costumes – heaven alone knows where those were found, but it adds another fragment of the past to the scene. Elwen will be thinking that, I expect.

It's all lively and colourful and cheerful, and I think it might be all right after all. I've just spotted two small figures darting around the edges of the courtyard and vanishing into a corner, and I'm smiling, because it will be Elwen and Osbert.

I've suddenly realized something though, and I don't know whether it's disquieting or reassuring. It's that Evelyn doesn't seem to be down there. But of course he must be – it's just that I'm not seeing him through the dancers. Or is he going to make some kind of dramatic entrance? With that thought comes the memory of Peregrine Pond, his father, who saw almost every situation as a setting for a dramatic entrance—

Oh, dear God, Evelyn *is* making a dramatic entrance. He's appeared at the head of the balcony stairs – he's come out of the courtyard rooms. And with him is Juliette. *Juliette.* And seeing the two of them is striking a chill into my body, because this is wrong, it's all wrong . . .

In a moment I shall have to go out there, because something is going to happen. He's coming down the stairway now – moving quite slowly, holding on to Juliette's arm. He does it awkwardly because he can't grip things in the same way as other people, because of his hands. But he's got a tight hold on her for all that.

They've all seen him now, and some of the people are cheering and singing, 'Happy Birthday to you'. I think it will be all right. I don't think I need to go out there . . .

The singing has faltered, though, and they're staring at the

figure Evelyn is leading down the steps. Most of them won't
know who she is, but a few will. Dear old Grindall will know,
of course, and Matilda and Dorothea Savory. They're here,
and seeing them makes me suddenly feel just a little bit better,
because they'll understand and they'll know what should be
done. Perhaps nothing will need to be done. But even as I
write that, it's as if a soft voice in the room is telling me that
of course it won't be all right, and of course something will
need to be done, because this is the Reivers Dance, it's the
Murder Dance . . . This is the Dance that ended in brutality
and death last time, and unless you stop it, Nicolas Trigg,
unless you seize your courage and go out there at once, the
same thing will happen again . . .

Evelyn and Juliette are at the centre of the dancers now,
and he's somehow forced her to a kneeling position, and I see
now that he's managed to wind a rope around her wrists . . .
Even from here I can hear that he's screaming, and people
have no idea what to do . . .

I have no idea what to do, either, but I'll have to go out
there . . .

Night has fallen on the courtyard and it's pressing down on
this house like a leaden cloak. I'm setting this down to try to
clear it out of my mind, but I'm shaking quite badly, so the
writing isn't very legible.

Earlier I went out to the courtyard – going as fast as I'm
able – and with every awkward uneven step I felt as if I was
running towards a dark, dreadful core. I remember I could
hear someone shouting to the dancers to go – to leave the
courtyard – there was a crisis, an emergency – and it was a
shock to realize it was my own voice.

'Go!' I shouted. 'Quickly – get back into the gardens –
through the door into the lane! As fast as you can!'

They obeyed straight away, and I thanked whatever powers
might be appropriate that in times of war people don't stop
to question an order. They assume there's a raid – or an attack
– or that the invasion has come. They crowded through the
arch, and I heard them running across the gardens, and then
came the sound of the old door into the lane creaking back

and forth. Tomorrow there would have to be some sort of explanation, but for the moment . . .

For the moment there was Evelyn and he was standing over Juliette, holding between his stunted, incomplete hands, an axe. The image of the old tapestry came rushing at me then – the execution scene, the brutal slaughtering of that long-ago Evelyn Rivers in this courtyard. If I could not reach the present-day Evelyn, the same thing was going to happen.

I went as close as I dared – but he heard me and half turned his head. And, oh God, the madness in his face – the sheer raging insanity and the hatred . . . But I said, 'Juliette – can you get free? Come over here to me. It's Trigg, Juliette – we know one another very well, don't we? I'll look after you.'

'She can't get free, you stupid creature!' said Evelyn. 'Don't you see I've got her tied up? She ruined me – she tried to kill me before I was born! That deserves punishment, doesn't it? *Doesn't it?*' For a moment I almost thought his eyes showed red, then he said, in a voice that was very nearly reasonable, 'The punishment has to fit the crime, of course. You remember the song? Of course you do, though. You have to let the punishment fit the crime.' He looked down at Juliette with such loathing that I felt sick.

I had no idea whether to try reasoning with him, or whether to take a chance and simply bound forward and trust to luck that I could wrench her from his grip. But a lame man doesn't bound – he can't – and there were twenty years between us, and Evelyn would be by far the stronger.

Even so I tensed my muscles ready to move, but it was already too late. Evelyn brought the axe down on Juliette – straight on to her wrists.

There was a second when something seemed to blur and for that second I thought I was seeing not Evelyn and Juliette, and the deserted courtyard – but a crowd of people with horrified faces, all of them dressed in unfamiliar garb, and at the centre of the courtyard a man standing on a platform of some kind, bringing an axe down in exactly the same way . . .

Then I blinked and the blurred image had gone, and there was only Evelyn and the body of Juliette, blood pouring from her wrists.

And then a movement in a corner of the courtyard, and with
fresh horror I saw Elwen and Osbert huddled against the wall,
their arms around one another as if for strength, their faces
drained of all colour. And more terror in their faces than I
have ever seen in any living soul's.

TWENTY-FIVE

Nicolas Trigg's journal, 1941

My study has seen some strange gatherings over the
years, but the one that took place a short while ago
must be the strangest of them all.

Walter sat hunched in a chair by the fire, occasionally putting
out his hands to the flames for warmth. Elwen was on the
other side of the hearth, Osbert was curled at her feet. I had
hesitated about Osbert, but I had concluded that it might be
better for him to know what was happening – and what was
going to happen – than to imagine things for himself. Walter
offered no opinion about Osbert – I think he's content to sit
back and let the reins pass to another now. I wish that the
'another' didn't have to be me, but there's no one else.

The Savory sisters were present, of course, handing round
soothing draughts of something or other. Miss Dorothea
smiled when Walter waved it aside and said he would be
better soothed by a stiff brandy and he dared say I would, too.

The group was completed by Grindall and Belinda.

I don't think I can set down the whole of the conversation
that took place – it was emotional and fragmented and
punctuated by brief sobbing from Elwen and Belinda,
and interjections from the Savorys.

But I remember I more or less took charge and that, curiously,
it did not feel in the least bit wrong to do so.

'There's no question but that we keep all this from the village,'
I said, firmly. 'They'll wonder and they'll speculate, but there's
so much going on in the wider world, they probably won't

speculate for long. Mr Grindall, if you hadn't come running
back to the courtyard, I am not sure what would have happened.'
'A feeling, that's what I had,' he said. 'A feeling telling me
something was wrong. I'm very glad I did so, Mr Trigg.'
'As for unseemly speculation,' said Matilda Savory, 'my sister
and I will quash that. You may trust us on that point, Mr Trigg.'
'Thank you. Now Juliette,' I said, 'will have to be buried
here in the grounds. Privately and secretly. No one knows
she's spent the last twenty years locked away. We can't risk
an enquiry or an inquest – not if we're to protect Evelyn.' I
looked at Walter. 'I assume we do want to protect him? You
don't want to hand him over to the authorities?'
That roused him. 'No,' he said. 'No – please, not that. It
would drag everything out – Maria – the birth. The almshouse
arrangement . . .'
I did not say the awkwardness of the almshouse arrangement
had occurred to me as well, or that it was something we did
not dare let be known about. But frankly I was glad he had
said it, for my own part in that deception would not bear too
close scrutiny.
So I said, 'We're agreed that Juliette will be quietly and respectfully given a place in the grounds here. As for Evelyn . . .' I
looked at them. 'Evelyn will take Juliette's place as the prisoner
in those rooms,' I said. 'There's no other solution.'

The solution was put into place right away. Evelyn was sullen,
furious, and threatening, but Grindall and I, with a bit of help
from Belinda, managed to get him in there in the end. Even
so, the slamming of that outer door, and the sound of the latch
dropping into place, was a terrible one.
When I went back to tell Walter, he was still slumped in
his chair, and his face had taken on a grey tinge. I do not think
he will last much longer.

Osbert left this morning. Before he got into the trap which
would take him to the railway station and, hopefully, on to
the one train that's still running out here, he came to my study.
'Mr Trigg,' he said, and looked at me from the corners of
his eyes.

'Osbert.'

'This is a big secret,' he said, confidingly, 'but my cousin
Walter has just told me that one day this house is going to be
mine.' His eyes shone. 'Isn't that wonderful?'

'Very wonderful.'

He traced a fingertip along the edge of my desk. 'I 'spect
you'll still be here if I come to live in it, won't you?'

He sounded hopeful, so I said, 'I'll be here if you want me
to be, Osbert.'

'Oh, good. I'd like that. I shan't know what to do, you see.
But you could tell me, couldn't you?'

I took his hand. 'Yes, Osbert,' I said. 'I'll be here, and I
could tell you everything you'd need to do.'

He smiled and went off, running lightly and happily across
the oak boards of the hall.

Elwen left this afternoon. She came to see me, as well. Her
eyes were bright, and she sat in my study, looking about her
in a pleased way. Then she said, 'My cousin Walter has promised to leave me The Tabor.'

For a moment I had no idea what to say, then I said, 'That's
very generous.'

She studied me solemnly. 'It's payment, isn't it?' she said,
suddenly. 'It's in return for my silence about what happened
in the courtyard. Evelyn and Juliette. He didn't say it, not
right out, but I know that's what it is.'

'Not necessarily, Elwen. I think he will want the house to
go to someone who will love it.'

'You love it,' she said. 'You'd be here if it happens, wouldn't
you? If I own The Tabor?'

I looked at her for a long moment. Then I said, 'Yes, Elwen.
I'd be here.'

After they had both gone, I sat lost in thought for a long
time. Those two will remember what happened here for the
rest of their lives. They'll remember Juliette and Evelyn, and
the whole dreadful tragedy of it all.

But neither of them will speak of it. Walter has made sure
of that.

*   *   *

Now that the house is settling into a degree of calm, I find myself wondering about Elwen – wondering if I want to try taking that acquaintance any further. But I know that I don't.

I'm not a libertine, although I don't pretend to be a saint, and there have been one or two very pleasant interludes with ladies over the years. I shan't record their names, though. Anything that happened between us is just that – between us. It's nice to remember them, though. But Elwen . . .

There must be twenty years between us. She wouldn't so much as look at a forty-year-old man with no real prospects – who lives in someone else's house, and who has a lame leg. But it's nice to think there could have been something – to remember those moments in this study, where she told me she could sense fragments of the past. I rather like the idea of a might-have-been. I think Elwen might like that, too. I hope she does inherit The Tabor, but somehow I don't think she will. I think Walter will cling to the old ways – to the belief that it's gentlemen who should inherit a property, and I think he'll bequeath it to young Osbert. Will he name me as some kind of guardian or trustee – official or unofficial? Someone who will make sure Evelyn is looked after?

I would accept such a charge, of course. I would accept anything that lets me live in The Tabor for the rest of my life. It's a good thought that whichever of those two gets the house – Elwen or Osbert – they want me to stay.

But I do wonder what will happen to it in the future.

*   *   *

Phin closed the Savory Herbal and looked at Arabella. For a long time neither of them spoke. At last, he said, 'I think we know most of it, don't we?'

'I think so. And I think we've got it into chronological order. But let's read it through again before we take it back to the Savorys. You read and I'll follow on my laptop notes. Double check.'

'Good idea,' said Phin, and, turning the pages back, he began to read.

'"Receipt handed down by Lydia Savory, which was used

to soothe and heal the wounds inflicted on Master Greenberry
during the performance of the Reivers Dance many centuries
ago".'

'His hands,' said Arabella, with a small shiver.

'Yes. But it sounds as if he survived.'

'He did, didn't he?' she said, eagerly.

'I think he did. And straight after that one,' said Phin, 'is
the indigestion mixture. "Ground ivy to ease choleric humours
of the stomach, found helpful for Master Bee".'

He was relieved to see that, as he had hoped, this struck a
lighter note. She smiled. 'That one's rather endearing,' she
said. 'Poor old Bee. I hope he really was cured.'

'Taking them in sequence, I think the next one is this,' said
Phin. 'Which isn't such a good one again.'

'Ralph.'

'Yes. "Mixture created for Master Ralph Rivers, to give his
poor deluded mind calm and to aid the prayers our good Parson
Marplot said with him and for him. We called it The Salve of
Captivity."'

'The courtyard rooms. And captivity . . . Ralph was the
original prisoner in those rooms, wasn't he? Don't look scep-
tical, Phin, it all fits. It's sad, but it fits.'

'I'm not arguing. Where have we got to?'

'The childbirth one,' said Arabella. 'We'll spare your male
sensitivity, but it's about feverfew cleansing the womb, and
sow-fennel for labour pains. But the Savorys write that
"Mistress Rosalind Rivers spoke well of it". Rosalind Rivers.
Jasper's mother?'

'It must be, because the next page says, "A linctus to help
the small Master Jasper Rivers' troublesome cough – very efficacious, and Master Greenberry and Mistress Rosalind grateful.'

Arabella smiled. 'I like reading that. And I like that Jasper
kept his mamma's tapestry showing the Reivers Dance.'

'Me too. But,' said Phin, 'the real jewel in the crown . . .'
He looked up and Arabella smiled.

'Read it out again,' she said.

'I will. There's a list of ingredients – most of which I've
never heard of, but at the head it says, "The ointment prepared
for Master Will Kempe's aching joints, which we put in a

stone jar, with written instructions for him on how to apply it". Master Kempe. He really was here,' said Phin. 'Proof positive. And all thanks to the Savorys.'

He closed the book, and Arabella said, 'Speaking of the Savorys, we'd better take this back to them, hadn't we?'

'All right. But I want to make a quick phone call to the Reverend Pilbeam first.'

'Why?'

Phin said, 'I want to ask how far back the parish registers go. And if they go as far back as I hope, I'd like to have a look.'

'This covers 1600 to 1605,' said Arabella, staring at the open page in the Reverend Pilbeam's study. 'Faded and dim and cobwebby, but still just about readable. What exactly are you looking for?'

'I'm not sure. Probably there won't be anything – I should think these records were kept quite haphazardly, but—'

He stopped, staring at the thick old parchment. 'I think this is what I wanted to find,' said Phin. 'It's in Latin and I can read the names, of course, but as for the rest . . .'

He looked at her and Arabella leaned over the pages. Her hand came out to enclose his, and she said, 'Marriage celebrated by the Reverend Humbert Marplot between Mistress Rosalind Rivers, Lady of The Tabor, and one Greenberry of London town.' She looked up at him. 'Rosalind's signed her name, but as you can see there's a cross next to it. Beneath that, it says, "Master Greenberry, his mark".'

Very quietly, Phin said, '"*The receipt used to soothe and heal the wounds inflicted on Master Greenberry . . . As a remedy it was proved to be sovereign for severe wounds, including the severing of a hand . . .*"'

Arabella looked back at the page. Then she said, 'Phin – this next line gives the names of the people who witnessed the marriage. They were two gentlemen called Bee and Slye, described as music-makers, and their address is given as The Daunsen Inn, Reivers. And the third witness—'

'Yes?'

'Was William Kempe.'

*   *   *

As they walked back to the square, Phin said, 'Bee and Slye. Of The Daunsen Inn.'

'And described as music-makers,' said Arabella, delightedly. 'Kempe's musicians,' she said. 'They came with him to Reivers, and—'

'And they stayed,' said Phin, looking across the square to where lights glowed in The Daunsen's windows. 'We didn't only find Kempe, we found his company. Bee, Slye – and Greenberry the chronicler.'

As they walked towards the antique shop, Arabella said, 'The only one we haven't found is Trigg.'

'I wonder if Trigg would want to be found,' said Phin. He glanced at her, then said, 'I have the feeling that all he wanted was to be part of The Tabor. I think he had found his place in the world, and that was enough for him.'

'A minor player in the story?'

'I don't know. He might not have been all that minor.'

Alice and Flora Savory were delighted that their great-aunts' book had been so useful. Alice had always thought – and Flora had often said – that you should never throw anything away; you never knew what might come in useful.

'And since you are here, Mr Fox, Miss Tallis, we've been thinking about something else.'

'Yes?'

'Probably it isn't relevant, and it's unlikely to have any connection to The Tabor or your research, but it once belonged to someone who stayed here for a short time. The great-aunts met him and it was when they were thinking about starting up this shop, so they were on the lookout for items they might collect.'

Phin said, very carefully, 'This would be – around when?'

'Towards the end of the Great War,' said Alice. 'In 1918, although I couldn't say exactly when in 1918—'

'They said he was such a distinguished gentleman,' put in Flora. 'And very well-known in theatrical circles, seemingly. In fact, a local paper wrote a very interesting article about his career, and we do know he stayed at The Tabor, so—'

Phin said, 'What was the item that belonged to this distinguished gentleman?' Don't expect anything, said his mind. It won't be anything – it's too much of a coincidence . . .

Alice had opened a large cupboard, and was taking out a cardboard portfolio – of the kind artists often used to store or transport unframed paintings.

'We've sometimes thought of having this framed,' said Flora, as if she had picked up this thought. 'But it's – well, frankly, it's a bit tattered, and we really only think of it as a keepsake from Matilda and Dorothea.'

'And,' put in Alice, 'someone has scrawled all over the back of it.'

She unfolded the portfolio and stood back.

Phin felt the room – with its antique furniture and jewellery and porcelain, and the scents of polish and old wood – whirl about him. He had to wait for it to right itself, and then he leaned forward to read what lay in the portfolio.

He had, of course, seen it previously, but that had been a blurred and very old newspaper reproduction. This was the original. It was clear and sharp. The black print at the head, said, '*A Knack to Know a Knave*'. Beneath, in smaller typeface, was the line, 'A Most Pleasant and Merrie Comedie'.

Phin heard Arabella's gasp, and he heard her say, 'Peregrine Pond's playbill. Rescued from a burning theatre.' He thought one of the sisters said something about the name – that it was the name their great-aunts had mentioned to them.

With a hand that was not quite steady, Phin picked up the fragile playbill, and turned it over. On the back, in great detail and with beautifully clear diagrams, was the layout for what could only be a dance.

Will Kempe's notation for the Reivers Dance.

Quentin thought that the bungalow he had found for himself and Zillah could hardly be bettered. Spacious rooms with wide doorways through which her wheelchair could easily be propelled – he was going to see about a motorized one for her soon. There was certainly sufficient money for that kind of thing; the National Trust was paying very well indeed for leasing The Tabor from Quentin. A five-year arrangement, to be reviewed at the end of that. Meanwhile, they would restore it and furnish it, and they would hold events and conferences there. There had been talk about an annual pageant, as well, with the Reivers Dance performed. Quentin had liked this, although when he went around the village to bid people goodbye, he had been surprised to encounter dissent. That was strange, because you would have thought people would want their historic old Dance to be revived. There was no accounting for tastes.

And really, it was for the best not to have that huge encumbrance to restore and a restaurant to run – most likely people had been right when they told him it would be a chancy venture, and better stay clear.

Best of all, he and Zillah were together. To be sure, it was a sad thing to see her in a wheelchair like this, but she was very grateful when he took her to places, manoeuvring the chair in and out of the new car. She attracted a good deal of attention, what with being so very pretty. She still dressed beautifully; Quentin did not in the least mind that she ordered expensive clothes from top designers. She deserved it. As for the physical side . . . That might be considered to be the absolute best part of it all. There would be no worries about any closeness – about embarrassing things such as an inability . . . No, not an inability exactly, and not really an inadequacy . . . He would just acknowledge that he would rather have Zillah as a perfect porcelain figure who must be guarded and cared for and not sullied. He would not let himself think it was rather a relief to know there was no possibility of any kind of physical relationship.

Zillah thought the bungalow Quentin was so delighted with was the ugliest place she had ever seen.

She did not let him know this, of course. She smiled and said it was beautiful, and she would be able to scoot around the rooms very easily, and if he thought they could manage one of those invalid cars for her that would be marvellous. All the while, the image of The Tabor with its soft rose-red bricks, and the glinting diamond-patterned windows and the sense that it lay in some long-ago century was in her mind.

But something else was in her mind, and she set it next to

The Tabor's image where she could unfold it whenever she wanted. It was the memory of the most recent appointment with the consultant who had been treating her injuries. Spinal injuries they were, caused by the fall that had gone so disastrously wrong. But everyone knew quite well that it had not been Zillah's fault – she had fallen against the rickety railings, and clutched at Quentin to save herself, but had fallen. Quentin had been distraught.

But the consultant was very pleased indeed with the newest batch of X-rays and CT scans. He had said there were definite signs of healing – that with patience and physiotherapy there was no reason why Miss Rivers could not eventually get back to a normal life. Perhaps not quite 100 per cent normal – she would not be able to run marathons or climb mountains, he said, and they had laughed together. But certainly there would come a day when the wheelchair could be thrown out.

Zillah had listened and smiled and thanked him, and arranged her next appointment. She asked him please not to tell her cousin, because it would be too upsetting if things did not quite go according to plan. She would rather present him with the whole picture, she said. A wonderful surprise for him. The consultant had quite understood. It would be their secret, he said.

What would also be a secret – one that Zillah would not be sharing with anyone at all – was the new plan she was already making. The Tabor was still rightfully hers, despite the National Trust's involvement. Five years, Quentin had said, and Zillah thought five years was not so very long a time. She would be strong and mobile by that time, and she would have worked out a plan to become The Tabor's owner. And this time the plan would not fail.

Arabella flopped down in the fireside chair in Phin's flat, and said, 'It's so good to be here again.'

'You like it here?'

'You know I do.' She sat up straighter. 'Phin, is Toby serious about this mad plan to go off to work in – where was it? Romania? Serbia?'

'The country changes from day to day,' said Phin, leaning

against the mantelpiece and looking down at her. 'I think he means it, though.'

'You'll have someone new in his flat.'

'Yes.'

'Always a bit worrying in a flat, isn't it? You never know if they're going to belt out heavy metal at three a.m. or import a trampoline.'

'Did you know these two flats – mine and Toby's – were once the whole of this first-floor front?' said Phin.

'I think I knew vaguely.'

'This is the dividing wall,' he said, indicating it. 'It wouldn't take much to knock it through.'

'Would the owners – freeholders or whatever they are – would they allow that?'

'Well,' said Phin, 'it seems that providing it's done properly, with surveys and approved builders, they would.'

'You've asked?'

'Yes.'

Arabella looked at him. 'It would make for a beautifully large flat, wouldn't it?'

'Yes. Two people could live in it and still have their own space. A study – or a separate sitting room each – a bedroom each if that was wanted—'

'And a really big sitting room in here for evenings together.'

They looked at one another. 'What do you think?' said Phin.

'I think,' said Arabella slowly, 'that it would be a very good idea.'

Phin smiled. 'I hoped you'd say that.' He held out his hand and she took it, but his other hand went into his jacket pocket, for the small leather box from Savory Antiques.

'What's that?'

'A ring. I don't know if it will fit, though. Not for certain.'

He held it out and saw her eyes light up. She said, 'The topaz ring from Savory's.'

'Yes.' Phin waited, and Arabella met his eyes.

She said, 'I think it will be a perfect fit.'

AUTHOR'S NOTE

I t's always a good moment when a little-known character
from history presents him- or herself as a possibility for a
plot. For the writing of *The Murder Dance*, the Elizabethan
comic actor, Will Kempe, presented himself unexpectedly,
but very amiably, and generously handed to me the basis of
the story.

Master Kempe doesn't figure particularly prominently in the
annals of the sixteenth and seventeenth centuries, nor is there
very much information about him. He was well known in
his day, though – he was a clown-actor, a fellow player of
William Shakespeare and Richard Burbage, and considered
the successor to the great comic-performer, Richard Tarlton.
He was also an early investor in The Globe Theatre, and he's
believed by many to have been the inspiration for Shakespeare's
Falstaff.

Despite his many stage appearances, Will is mostly remembered for having embarked on an astonishing marathon, in
which he danced from London to Norfolk in nine days – a
feat which one legend says he undertook for a bet. In writing
The Murder Dance, I was helped enormously by his own
account of this journey, which he published shortly afterwards
and which incredibly can still be found in later reprints. Even
after so many centuries, Kempe's enthusiasm and delight for
his dancing comes endearingly off the pages.

Fragments and the flavour of Kempe's music have come
down to the present – two of his jigs survive in English and
two in German. Scores titled 'Kempe's Jig' are held in the
Cambridge University Library, and a famous seventeenth-
century 'Kempe's Jig' was published in *The English Dancing
Master* by John Playford, around 1651. The man himself has
been portrayed in modern-day films and on TV: most notably
in the film, *Shakespeare in Love*, and remarkably in a *Doctor*

Who TV episode. He may have been sparsely documented, but his name and his legend have survived into the present.

And so, Master Kempe, thank you for accepting that extraordinary bet, and for chronicling your astonishing nine days of dancing from London to Norfolk. And thank you, especially, for capering into my imagination and providing me with the core of the plot for *The Murder Dance.*

Sarah Rayne